I0614248

Operation Stormwatcher

by

Gerard Poulin

This is a work of fiction. Names, characters, places, and incidents are either the product of the author's imagination or are used fictitiously, and any resemblance to actual persons living or dead, business establishments, events, or locales, is entirely coincidental.

Operation Stormwatcher

COPYRIGHT © 2022 by Gerard Michael Poulin

All rights reserved. No part of this book may be used or reproduced in any manner whatsoever without written permission of the author or The Wild Rose Press, Inc. except in the case of brief quotations embodied in critical articles or reviews.
Contact Information: info@thewildrosepress.com

Cover Art by *The Wild Rose Press, Inc.*

The Wild Rose Press, Inc.
PO Box 708
Adams Basin, NY 14410-0708
Visit us at www.thewildrosepress.com

Publishing History
First Edition, 2022
Trade Paperback ISBN 978-1-5092-3952-8
Digital ISBN 978-1-5092-3953-5

Published in the United States of America

Several things bothered Bak. The young woman insisted she locked her front door, double-checking before leaving. Yet, there were no signs of a forced entry. The victim had been dead for some time; with rigor mortis already setting in, and Ms. Guy had just returned from work. Assuming her alibi checked out, she was in the clear. *Someone had a key to her front door made*.

The victim had skin under his fingernails—whoever did this had deep scratches, and the young woman who called this in had none, and Bak made it a point to check. Whoever hanged the victim was strong; lifting Mr. Chang this high would be too much for one man alone, most men anyhow. She told Bak that Chang worked for her at Duffy Club. The pay stub in the victim's wallet confirmed it.

Ms. Guy made it clear that Chang wasn't a lover or roommate. *So why was this man hanged here, in this apartment? To send a message?*

Bak knew that Myung-Dae Tang owned Duffy Club. That Tang paid Anjeong-ri KNPA Commandant Choson to look the other way when Tang's name appeared in a police report was common knowledge.

The detective hadn't yet met Tang personally, although he'd occasionally seen the man and his thugs, always from a distance. *Strong thugs, able to do this kind of work*.

Bak knew he would meet Tang face-to-face for the first time sooner than he ever wanted.

Dedication

To my family and Elaine.

Dedication

To my Mum and Dad

Chapter One

Tuesday, January 9, 2018
Misawa Air Base, Japan

And to think I wanted to be an astronaut.

Mike Porter was a nine-year-old boy when that dream perished. The television images of AA flight 11 slamming into the North Tower on 9-11 were still hauntingly fresh in his mind. His father, a general practice attorney with an office on the 109th floor, jumped to his death that morning. Already in a state of disbelief, Porter and his little brother watched their mother collapse on the kitchen floor. At that moment, the boy became a man.

He thought about his father's choice more than he cared to admit. He couldn't imagine a more hideous, horrifying one. It prompted him to join the Marines after his high school graduation and the CIA after getting his degree. This marked his third year with the agency and his first assignment. He'd been on this northern Japan air base for sixteen months.

With the engine cut and car lights off, Porter considered Air Force Staff Sergeant Orson O'Hara while waiting in the recreation building's parking lot on this dark early morning. *Today's the day this penguin-lookin' motherfucker goes down.*

Porter's breath poured out in a cloud as he adjusted

the rearview mirror. His fingers batted the zipper of his U.S. Army camouflage jacket, and he once again glanced at his watch. The agent wore sergeant chevrons on his left sleeve. *Relax a little, huh? You're not the one buying bogus tech.*

The concealed wire he wore transmitted audio to the base MPs, who would make the arrest. "Can you hear me okay?" he asked the MP Officer-of-the-Day, a captain named Hightower.

"Copy that."

"Getting a signal on the GPS?"

"Affirmative."

A car's headlights reflected off Porter's rearview mirror. As the vehicle pulled up next to his, Porter recognized O'Hara's SUV.

Here we go.

O'Hara got out and walked to Porter's driver's side window, tapping it lightly. *He's empty-handed.* In his swollen white parka over civilian clothes, the pudgy O'Hara resembled a walking marshmallow. Porter rolled his window down a crack.

"We'll take my ride," O'Hara said.

"Just get in, O'Hara. I don't have all day."

"If we're doing this, we're taking my car. It's not up for debate."

Would he kill the deal if I insist on driving? No, I've invested too much time to take that chance. Porter rolled the window up, snatching and pocketing his car keys. After removing the leather briefcase from the passenger seat, he climbed out and remotely locked the sedan.

The briefcase contained agency-altered, cockpit navigation circuit-board schematics for Mustang III fighter jets, still in development at Groom Lake.

With Porter buckled up, O'Hara turned the vehicle around and exited the parking lot, taking a left toward the main gate. They passed the large mess hall and Enlisted Men's Club to the right and a sea of enlisted barracks to the left. The theater and commissary soon came into view before passing rows and columns of tidy houses that made up the enlisted family quarters.

"Where are we going?" Porter asked.

"Ever been to the beach?"

"Sure. Last summer. Why there?"

"Should be empty."

Porter didn't doubt it. Misawa was seasonal, with a harsh winter beginning in November and ending in April. Even now, snow spat against the windshield, prompting O'Hara to flip on the intermittent wipers.

The SUV continued to the main gate, with neither man saying much. Porter knew little about Orson O'Hara personally, even after their first meeting fourteen months ago. Unless meeting, they kept their distance. With Porter working for base logistics and O'Hara on the flight line, their paths didn't cross during a typical workday anyhow.

The agency had O'Hara in their crosshairs before sending Porter to make contact. Reeling this fish in hadn't been easy. The purchase or sale of top-secret technical information carried the potential of a life sentence in federal prison if convicted of treason. Porter didn't know how the agency caught on to O'Hara, but their suspicions were on the money. The man was a legitimate player.

The front gate lights came into view, and soon a sentry appeared. She glanced at the pair and waved them through, the SUV now in the heart of Misawa City. O'Hara took a right at the first stoplight, heading east. The beach was five miles away.

Though not yet 0600, the northern Japanese city's commercial center stirred. The city was compact, with most buildings three stories high and precious little space between them. Colorful neon signs appeared in windows or doors.

Double-parked trucks loaded goods to retailers and restaurants. A pachinko parlor did brisk business, with cigarette smoke billowing from a dimly lit room through a partially opened door. Farther down the sidewalk under a streetlamp, young boys gathered at a vending machine to purchase their choice of soda, cigarettes, beer, or soft-core porn DVDs.

The city soon gave way to residential sprawl. The car's headlights splashed off the windows of the modest cookie-cutter houses—so dense and bunched together they would pass as town houses in the United States. Some had lights on. Porter caught a whiff of sea air.

Without warning, the car veered off the paved street to the right. There were tire tracks in the shallow snow leading to the ocean. O'Hara parked the car behind an oversized dune, hiding them from the highway. He cut the lights and ignition.

"I need targeting schematics, Mike. Plus, we're looking to miniaturize." O'Hara referred to the hardware and process to arm warheads and torpedoes with nuclear weapons.

Porter took a breath as the knot in his stomach tightened. *So much for foreplay; he couldn't ask for anything scarier. Whoever he's with is going all-in.* "Your people have the enriched uranium?"

O'Hara scoffed. "That's not difficult in certain circles. The schematics and miniaturization hardware, are those something you're able to get your hands on?"

"That's a pretty big get. And carries a shitload more risk than what I'm used to." *Nobody told me to expect this.*

"We expect to pay. The only questions are who we buy from and at what price."

"You have other sellers?"

O'Hara grinned and shrugged.

I'm sick of this cat-and-mouse bullshit. C'mon, O'Hara, let's make the exchange so the MPs can take you into custody. "I'll sniff around. But I'm not stupid enough to guarantee anything."

"That's all I can ask. When will you have an idea?"

"Gimme a couple of weeks. Anyhow, let's wrap this up. I'm told locals surf this beach, even in the burr-ass cold."

O'Hara turned the headlights on. "Yeah. But before we start, I need to pat you down. Nothin' personal."

Stay calm. "You gotta be shittin' me. How many months have we been talking?"

"Only now money's changing hands. And you're not the only one with things to do today. So let's go outside, chop, chop."

Porter unbuckled his seat belt and exited the car, leaving the briefcase on the floor. He reached into his pocket, palming the small GPS device as he stepped out onto the snow-covered sand. Because the temperature in O'Hara's SUV was Africa-hot, it felt good to be outside. As sea air filled his lungs and cooled his cheeks, Porter asked himself what other surprises O'Hara had in store. That the man could be a

Gerard Poulin

disenfranchised NSA or sub-agency asset crossed Porter's mind from the beginning of this engagement.

O'Hara got out of the SUV, meeting Porter at the front of the car. "Hands on the hood, feet apart."

Porter followed O'Hara's instructions. The staff sergeant's hands moved quickly and smoothly over and under Porter's arms, torso, groin, and legs—narrowly missing the wire. Thus reminding Porter that O'Hara was no cop. Except O'Hara's hand brushed up against the polymer ankle holster Porter wore, carrying a nine-millimeter pistol. Porter tensed, his heart pounding, unsure how O'Hara would respond. The man had no history of violence. *Not yet, anyhow*.

"Find any polyps, and they're yours," Porter said.

"Very funny. Get back in the car."

Porter marched to the SUV's passenger door, discreetly returning the GPS to his jacket pocket. He climbed back in, wondering why O'Hara said nothing about the holster.

O'Hara cut the SUV's headlights and turned on the dome light. "You gonna let me see what I'm buying?"

Finally. Porter brought the briefcase up from the floor, handing it over. O'Hara placed it on his lap.

"What's the combination?"

"Not so fast, Orson. Where's the cash?"

O'Hara reached to the back seat. He handed Porter a blue nylon gym bag.

"Three zeros," Porter said.

Porter unzipped the gym bag while O'Hara set the combination. The briefcase latches released and popped open. While O'Hara examined the fake schematics, Porter gazed upon the gym bag's contents. Bundles of hundred-dollar bills stacked and wrapped in bank sleeves. Porter brought the first bundle up and slid the paper sleeve off, shuffling the bills with his thumb.

The currency felt crisp to the touch. Porter held one bill against the dome light, pretending he could identify counterfeit bills on sight. It didn't matter to Porter if the money was counterfeit—it would be one more crime to charge O'Hara with if it was.

Porter shuffled the bills in the stack once more. "Is this stuff real?"

O'Hara's eyes drifted from the schematic to Porter. "They came from a Tokyo bank yesterday."

Porter nodded, letting the stack drop back into the gym bag before re-zipping it. "Are we good?"

O'Hara rubbed his jaw and closed the briefcase, putting it on the back seat. "Put the gym bag in the back until we're back on base."

Except Porter knew the truth, he'd known the moment O'Hara insisted on taking his car. There was no going back on base. Leaving the base with the briefcase and gym bag carried more than enough risk. Trying to reenter with the goods was foolhardy. And foolhardy was the least applicable adjective when describing O'Hara.

Porter carried the GPS for this purpose. The word "zeros" was the safety word. The base MPS, working with the civilian Misawa police, would give them Porter's position and take both men into custody. Then the base MPs would collect them and arrest O'Hara.

Porter put the gym bag on top of the briefcase. He heard a gun's hammer lock. A .38 revolver gleamed in O'Hara's hand.

"Who do you work for, Mike? Where did those schematics come from?"

Porter remained calm. "Put that revolver down before I break your arm, O'Hara."

"You'd better tell me before I—"

In the blink of an eye, Porter reached down and grabbed O'Hara's hand, pushing it and the revolver back until he heard the wrist snap. The gun toppled harmlessly to the driver's side floor mat.

O'Hara's screams drowned the sirens as a pair of sedans came around the dune. Blue and red lights danced on the snowy sand. Porter recognized the civilian Misawa police cars immediately.

Four Japanese police officers quickly pulled both men out of the car, putting them in separate vehicles, leaving O'Hara's SUV on the beach. But not before the Misawa cops pulled the briefcase and gym bag out of the vehicle and put them in the car transporting Porter.

Porter and O'Hara's stay in the civilian Misawa police station would be brief. Within minutes, air base MPs took both men back on base, again in separate cars, with Porter carrying the briefcase and gym bag. The MPs brought O'Hara to the base hospital—where he was x-rayed, treated, and discharged before being thrown into a cell.

"I need to use a secure phone," Porter told Hightower in the station house.

The MP OOD led Porter to a back office down a corridor.

"Misawa PD doesn't fool around," Porter said as they walked. "For a second there, I thought O'Hara might accidentally pull that trigger."

Hightower shook his head. "I can't believe you broke the guy's wrist with a gun in his hand. You're lucky he didn't find the wire. If he had, I doubt we'd be here talking about it."

"Check that currency. No bullshit, the bills don't feel right to the touch. You're getting O'Hara's car?"

Hightower nodded. "Being towed as we speak."

Hightower opened the door to the last office on the left, giving Porter the tiny, cramped space. On the desk, a telephone. Porter checked the time; it would be early Monday afternoon in Los Angeles. Porter punched in the number and called his boss, CIA Special-Agent-in-Charge (SAIC) of the Los Angeles office, Walter Stillson.

"Mike," Stillson answered. "Is O'Hara in custody?"

"Affirmative."

"Any problems?" Stillson asked.

"He pulled on me, and I ended up breaking his wrist. MPs took him to the base hospital."

"Just so long as he finds a way into a cell."

"I'll stay with the MPs until he is. Something else, whoever he's with already has enriched uranium. They're looking to miniaturize. You'll read it in the transcript."

Stillson didn't respond right away, and Porter wondered what his boss was thinking.

Stillson sighed. "I've heard better news, O'Hara said nothing about who he's with?"

"Nothing. He seemed more interested in who I'm with."

"That's my problem now. Is your cover still intact?" Stillson asked.

"Yes."

"I'll debrief you here. That was a tough assignment. Don't bother reporting to work; just start packing. I'm sending you an itinerary; you'll fly out tomorrow morning. So take a few days and be in my office Monday morning, nine o'clock."

"I'll see you then, Walter."

Chapter Two

Myung-Dae Tang was late. The small, elderly Korean man lumbered ahead of the pair of hulking associates down this narrow street. With a head full of white hair and a white goatee, Myung-Dae's distinctive look made him easy to pick out in a crowd. Being so cold, he wore a thick brown parka and matching corduroy trousers.

The trio navigated the maze of back-alley streets liked they owned them, and in a manner of speaking, they did. This was Anjeong-ri, the South Korean village just outside of Camp Humphreys Garrison's front gate. Humphreys was host to thousands of soldiers and was the closest U.S. military installation to the Demilitarized Zone, the often-contentious border between North and South Korea.

Myung-Dae had a meeting with Sergeant Alexander Tomlinson in a cafe deemed off-limits by Army CID, the acronym for Army's Criminal Investigation Command. Undercover CID investigators posed as off-duty soldiers, wearing civilian clothes, on the lookout for GIs entering specific places outlawed by the Camp Humphreys Commander for various reasons. Other CID agents hid in plain sight as soldiers in a unit.

Tonight, Myung-Dae planned to purchase a blank U.S. Armed Forces identification card from Tomlinson. The card was necessary for getting onto the base to use

Humphreys' services or purchase goods from the commissary.

Spitting snow found the lenses of Myung-Dae's gold-rimmed bifocals. The cafe's small neon sign, all in Korean characters, came into view. This part of Anjeong-ri consisted of decrepit tenements and small houses. You won't find anything here on the cover of a real estate magazine. The trio reached their destination, coming to a halt.

"Wait out here," Myung-Dae told his men.

Both Gunn Lim and Kiwoo Jong were tough, trusted, and tenured. Gunn was trim and fit, with thick black hair and menacing eyes. Kiwoo was taller and heavier, with a shaved head. Both were hapkido first-degree black belts. They were bodyguards who occasionally served as bouncers in Myung-Dae's saloons—Jumpin' Jack Flask and Duffy Club. Both were popular entertainment venues off the base.

Along with the bars, Myung-Dae owned several of the more unsavory apartment houses in Anjeong-ri as well. Anything illegal in Anjeong-ri, Myung-Dae got a piece of. And nobody dared complain.

Myung-Dae entered the cafe. It was a small place, with a bar and six tables, each with two chairs. In one corner stood a kerosene heater, and the place reeked of it. Tomlinson sat at a table with his back to the door. Myung-Dae took the seat opposite the husky American and cleaned the lenses of his glasses. On the table stood an open bottle of beer.

"I see you ordered without me," Myung-Dae said with a wry smile. As a younger man, Myung-Dae had broken a lateral incisor tooth and had the dentist fit him with a gold-veneer replacement. When catching the light in the right way, the tooth winked before disappearing, as it did now.

In the company of Americans, Myung-Dae spoke English. He took pride in his ability to speak the language, having acquired it from watching American movies in his youth and refining it from listening well in his Anjeong-ri nightclubs.

"You're late, Mungdung."

Myung-Dae's grin turned upside down. "Unavoidable. And don't call me that. It's undignified and disrespectful." Myung-Dae pointed a bony finger at the chubby, curly-haired Tomlinson. "You were with Jeong last night."

Jeong Guy managed Myung-Dae's Duffy Club. She was a stunning woman, intelligent and beautiful, with long black hair, high cheekbones, and a dazzling smile. Myung-Dae's obsession with her now a long-standing village rumor, despite the age gap and Myung-Dae's marriage.

"Jeong's got nothin' to do with this. You have the money?"

"I told you to stay away from her." Myung-Dae held up the index and middle fingers of his right hand. "Twice."

Tomlinson's face reddened. "Let's get this straight. You don't get to order me around like one of your stooges, and Jeong's not part of this. So I ask again, *Mungdung*, do you have the money?"

"I told you not to call me that!" Myung-Dae's fist slammed against the table, getting the bartender's attention. Seeing Myung-Dae, he returned to the magazine in his hand. "Do you have the card?"

Tomlinson shrugged. "That depends. Do you have

the money?"

"Is close."

Tomlinson leaned back and sighed. "Is *close*? What the fuck is that supposed to mean?"

"Just what I say. Money is nearby. I don't like to travel with so much cash."

Tomlinson scoffed. "You've got your goons; who's going to rob you in Anjeong-ri?"

"One never knows in this village."

"Is that so? Let me show you something." Tomlinson removed a nine-millimeter pistol hiding in the right pocket of his parka, allowing Myung-Dae a glimpse before putting it back. "I know enough to carry this. If somebody tries to rob me after you pay for the card, they'll be wearing three slugs, minimum."

Myung-Dae shook his head. "Very dangerous, carrying a gun in this country. Maybe it's okay in America. Getting caught here is a ten-year prison sentence."

"I'll have to remember that the next time I'm on a game show. I don't want to hunt for another buyer. But unless you tell me something I wanna hear in the next ten seconds, I will."

Myung-Dae said nothing, and the pair sat in awkward silence for several seconds. Tomlinson then rose and started for the front door when Myung-Dae leaned forward and grabbed the sleeve of the American's parka.

"What's your hurry? You're not going anywhere with my men standing outside."

"Let go of my jacket. I didn't come here to play games."

"Alex, relax. You know I have the money. So sit

back down."

Tomlinson sat back down, a smirk on his face.

Myung-Dae stroked his goatee. "We need to have an understanding about Jeong. I'm told you were looking at engagement rings earlier today."

Tomlinson's eyes widened as all color drained from his face. "How the hell do you know that?"

"You underestimate me. Shame on you." The gold tooth winked.

"I'll say this; you don't miss much. Yeah, okay, I looked at rings. Not that it's any of your business."

"Why do you insist upon insulting me? When I tell you to back off Jeong, you shop for engagement rings. Why don't you listen?"

"Why do you keep dragging her into this? She has *nothing* to do with this transaction."

Myung-Dae dropped his head and sighed loudly. "We're not progressing as I'd hoped. You win. We meet in Duffy Club, thirty minutes." He stood as Tomlinson took a swig from the bottle. Myung-Dae couldn't help but notice the smug, self-congratulatory look on the soldier's face as he walked away.

Now back outside, Myung-Dae saw the snow fall faster.

"Where to?" Gunn asked.

"Duffy Club. Seems we have work to do."

****

Jeong entered Duffy Club from the back entrance, unlocking the metal door alongside the large fiberglass bay door by the loading dock.

On the schedule, she had the night off. Only Myung-Dae called her in, citing an emergency. Down the hall, past Myung-Dae's office and the stockroom—

she now stood behind the bar. Two bartenders worked feverishly as a trio of waitresses stood in line with empty trays.

Jeong saw Doyoon Chang first. The relatively new bartender had been here two weeks, and Jeong was glad she hired him. The young man wasn't only quick with orders but good with bad customers and not prone to idle chitchat.

"I thought you were off tonight, Jeong?"

"Myung-Dae called me in, told me there was some kind of emergency. So what is it?"

Doyoon shook his head as he flipped a bottle to impress the ladies. "If there is, it's news to me."

Jeong scanned the twenty barstools, fourteen tables, and hardwood dance floor. All things considered, it appeared to be a typical Thursday night. The tables were mostly full, many occupying the four chairs around them. There were no empty barstools.

Soldiers and working girls, the local euphemism for prostitutes, engaged in conversation or negotiation. Here, the distinction was often thin and fuzzy. A blue haze hung in the air from residual cigarette smoke that never seemed to leave. Two couples danced to a slow ballad.

Why am I here?

She thought about calling Myung-Dae to ask for clarification when Tomlinson strolled through the front doors. He wandered to an empty table and sat down, a strange look on his face. Jeong, knowing Myung-Dae's cameras were watching, went to him anyhow. He looked up as she approached.

"I thought you had the night off?" he asked.

"Myung-Dae called me in," she replied in English.

Like Myung-Dae, she was self-taught. "I don't know why."

Tomlinson glanced at the bar. "I'm meeting Myung-Dae; we're finishing up a deal. You'd better take off; he's having a meltdown about us spending time together."

Jeong sat down. "That's none of his business."

Tomlinson peeked at his wristwatch. "Text me when you get home tonight. We've got some celebrating to do."

"Really? Why?"

"My orders came in today. I'm going to Texas."

"I'm happy for you. It's what you wanted."

"That's not all of it." He reestablished eye contact and grinned.

"What's the rest?"

"It's a surprise. Do me a favor? Have someone bring a shot of tequila and a bottle of beer, any brand. Tell 'em to put it on Myung-Dae's tab."

"Don't you have to work tomorrow, Alex?"

His fingers strummed the table. "Don't worry about that. I see Myung-Dae talking to a bartender; you'd better take off."

Jeong rose and approached the bar. There, she saw Myung-Dae glaring in her direction. She knew what came next as she lifted the section of bar to access the area. Myung-Dae stood there to greet her.

"Didn't I tell you I don't want you consorting with that man?"

"Yes, Myung-Dae." She turned to one of the waitresses and conveyed Tomlinson's drink order before pivoting back to Myung-Dae. "What's the emergency?"

"I'll get to that. What did Alex want with you?"

"He told me he had orders for Texas."

Myung-Dae's eyebrows arched. "Oh? He said nothing about a ring?"

"A ring? What kind of ring?"

"Your answer tells me he didn't."

"Tell me what you meant by that."

Myung-Dae shook his head. "Not here, not now. It would spoil the surprise."

"Alex mentioned a surprise. Tell me."

Myung-Dae gestured for her to join him in the hallway. "Very well. An old friend owns the jewelry store in the village. He showed me a video of a man shopping for an engagement ring. I recognized Alex. I'm surprised he hasn't popped the question, as the Americans like to say."

Jeong tried to hide her disappointment. She liked Alex. But marrying the man never entered her mind. Sure, she would love to break free from Myung-Dae. But to live in a foreign country with a man she didn't love? Not for her. *Now I'm forced to let him down gently*. "He said nothing about a ring."

"Perhaps he lacked the courage, dear."

"Why am I here, Myung-Dae? Bar traffic is normal, and we're well-stocked. Both bartenders and four waitresses are here working their shifts. Did a toilet break?"

"I want Doyoon to learn how to close the bar. Print the checkout procedures and go through it with him."

That got Jeong's attention. Myung-Dae and his men closed Duffy Club before moving on to Jumpin' Jack Flask. She couldn't remember the last time she needed to close.

"I can close if you and your men won't be here. Doyoon hasn't been with us that long."

"His tenure isn't my concern. He seems bright and responsible enough to do this. I need you to show him how, step by step."

Where does Myung-Dae think I'll be?

"I'll print the checklist out now," Jeong said.

Myung-Dae grinned. "Explain everything thoroughly and make sure he has your cell phone number. Just in case."

Jeong went over the list with Doyoon when things slowed. Periodically, she glanced over to see if Tomlinson lingered. His presence bothered her, even if she didn't know why.

"All that's left is the safe, right?" Doyoon asked.

Jeong nodded. As she turned for the hallway from behind the bar, Tomlinson lurched up from the table, his arms pinned to his torso like something invisible held him. He staggered several feet before collapsing to the floor on his knees. After vomiting, he began convulsing.

Everything in Duffy Club stopped. Jeong shrieked and went to him, getting down on one knee, mindful of the puddle. "Alex, what's wrong?"

White, chalky bile formed at the corners of Tomlinson's mouth. He tried to talk, but nothing came out. Curious bar patrons gathered in a semi-circle. It wasn't unusual to see an intoxicated soldier in here. But nothing this extreme.

"Doyoon, go find an MP," Jeong hollered. She glanced at the two waitresses standing there. "Bring a glass of water."

"No MPs," Gunn's voice boomed from behind the

crowd.

Looking up, Jeong saw Myung-Dae and his men push through the crowd.

"We'll let him sober up out back, in private," Myung-Dae said. "You focus on teaching Doyoon how to close."

Kiwoo and Gunn got under each of Tomlinson's arms and carried him to the back of the bar. Jeong, worried about the man, tried to focus on Doyoon's questions after ordering a waitress to clean up the mess.

Myung-Dae returned to the bar ten minutes later. "Does Doyoon know what to do?"

"Yes. Did Alex go back on base by himself?"

Myung-Dae nodded. "The poor man just needed some air."

Then why didn't he come back here to tell me he was okay? How did he get sick? I still don't know why I'm here.

"Put on your jacket, Jeong; it's cold out there," Myung-Dae said. "I want you to see something."

"Can't you just tell me? I'm tired; this was to be my night off."

"Take Sunday night off instead."

Myung-Dae's not letting go. "Whatever," she mumbled under her breath. And retrieved her ski jacket from the coat tree in the office.

Myung-Dae's luxury sedan idled out back, parked by the dumpster. The four-wheel-drive pickup truck his men drove was no longer there. She could make out the tracks in the fresh snow. He unlocked the car via remote.

"Where are we going?" she asked.

Myung-Dae opened his car door. "The farm."

"Why there?"

Myung-Dae didn't answer as he slid in behind the wheel and buckled up. Jeong got into the passenger seat, the leather warm and comfortable.

"At least let me drive," she said. "The roads will be slick and your eyesight—"

"Is fine. I'm quite capable of driving short distances, Jeong."

He watched Jeong buckle up and promptly put the car in reverse.

While the farm was only five miles away, this short trip wasn't without peril, thanks to Myung-Dae's nearsightedness. His first order of business was to barrel through the village's only stoplight, which went from yellow to red quickly, the vehicle nearly clipping a taxi.

That Myung-Dae appeared to be in a hurry seemed odd, except for the look in his eyes. If not for her fear of the man, she would never agree to this. The car accidentally slid off the pavement on Jeong's side, mere inches from the guardrail. Myung-Dae cut the wheel violently as they swung back onto the asphalt.

"Please pull this thing over and let me drive, Myung-Dae. You'll kill us both."

"I drive fine. Please stay calm."

"What's so important?" she asked.

"I told you, there's something I want you to see."

"Why can't you just tell me?"

"Words won't make as much of an impression."

Jeong shivered. *Something's not right. He's not making sense.*

Myung-Dae soon turned off onto a road on the right that led to his farm. It was a long gravel driveway through S-turns among dense birch and spruce pine trees, giving way to a long, straight downhill descent with a view to the barn and farmhouse. The buildings were fifty feet apart, with the driveway separating them. There were lights on in the two-story farmhouse, but not the barn.

The car's lights caught the bed of the four-wheel-drive pickup truck and Myung-Dae's men sitting atop the wooden-framed barbed wire corral in front of the barn.

Myung-Dae parked the luxury car alongside the truck, facing the pen. He cut the engine, and they exited the vehicle.

"Must that pen have barbed wire, Myung-Dae? Wouldn't ordinary wood serve the same purpose?"

"Even the most obstinate of creatures learn barbs are painful, especially when you run an electrical current through them."

Myung-Dae and Jeong walked toward Gunn and Kiwoo, both goons wearing leather jackets, despite the temperature. "Go turn on the floodlights, Kiwoo."

Kiwoo jumped off the fence frame and turned his cell phone flashlight on before running into the barn.

The floodlights came up, illuminating the space between the house and barn. They lit the corral nicely. It took a few seconds for Jeong to spot Tomlinson. He appeared in the center of the pen, buried up to his armpits, his head drooping forward. Everyone but Jeong knew Tomlinson was on his knees in that position, the backhoe only able to take up so much of the frozen mud.

"I knew it was treachery! Myung-Dae, what have you done?" Jeong rushed toward the pen's gate when

Gunn grabbed the back of her jacket. He reeled her in, gripping her forearm.

"Is he still alive?" Myung-Dae asked Gunn.

"When we put him there, yes. But this is cruel even for you."

Myung-Dae shot Gunn a hard glance before walking toward the pen's gate.

With Jeong sobbing, Myung-Dae opened the gate and walked into the pen. Each step produced a crunching sound against the brittle, frozen tundra. Now close enough, Myung-Dae bent and grabbed Tomlinson by the soldier's curly hair, bringing his head up.

"Alex. Are you still with us?"

Tomlinson groaned and vomited. Myung-Dae quickly let go and sidestepped the purge before turning to his audience.

"He is alive. Just barely, but alive."

Myung-Dae returned to the still-sobbing and visibly shaken Jeong. "I told him to leave you alone. Does he listen? No. Does he stop? No. Instead, he insults me, disrespects me. You knew this had to happen."

Jeong's sobs subsided. "Don't you dare blame me. And the warnings—who are you to tell me who I can and cannot spend time with?"

"I want *you* to understand what happens when these men test my limits. Because they don't listen, you must do it for them."

"Please don't kill him, Myung-Dae. I beg you. You have my word; I won't see him again, I promise."

"I'm afraid it's far too late for that, dear. We are well past the point of no return."

"Take me home. I want no further part of this."

"Nonsense. You'll stay as my guest. Kiwoo, release the pigs."

Jeong twisted out of Gunn's grip, dropping to her knees. "The pigs? No, Myung-Dae! You have the power to stop this," she screamed.

"You've made your point, Myung-Dae," Gunn said. "The man has suffered enough. Let me end this with dignity, and I will take her home."

"One more word, and you'll take his place, Gunn. I didn't ask your permission."

Kiwoo entered the corral, walking past Tomlinson. Against the barn, low to the ground, was a door secured by a bolted latch. Kiwoo pulled back the latch, the door falling to the frozen mud. He then pounded against the barn's siding. It woke the animals inside. Then the large Korean came out of the corral and relocked the pen's gate.

"Here, you hold her, Kiwoo. I'm going inside," Gunn said. "There's no dignity in this."

Gunn walked Jeong to Kiwoo before heading toward the farmhouse.

"Please take me home," she said to anyone who'd listen.

"You don't want to watch?" Myung-Dae asked.

"I don't want to see it or hear it. I want to go home."

The angry, hungry pigs wasted little time finding their breakfast. Myung-Dae hadn't fed them since noon yesterday, in case this needed to happen. Having gained an appetite for human flesh, the swine knew the scent and taste. And enjoyed it.

Jeong closed her eyes and, after twisting from Kiwoo's grip, ran to the car. Only Myung-Dae relocked it via remote before she could open the door. With the first of the screams, she held her fingers to her ears.

But she could still hear it. And it went on forever.

"I wish to go home," she told Myung-Dae after the screaming stopped.

"Are you certain? We're having lobster."

"Take me home," she whispered.

"Very well. Kiwoo will drive you. I can only hope this message resonates."

"And the animals?" Kiwoo gestured to the pigs.

"When they get cold enough, they'll go back inside. Cut the floods. Then take her home."

Kiwoo jogged into the barn.

And as the lights went out, Jeong realized a simple truth. Her life would never be her own until Myung-Dae was no longer part of it.

Chapter Three

The small, bespectacled man got out of his car and jogged to the Company B barracks on Camp Humphreys—one of sixteen identical cinder block structures on the camp's eastern side. This one housed the 501st Intelligence Battalion.

He wore a leather bomber jacket over a camouflage uniform. The gold leaf clusters on his hat, announcing his rank, glinted in the light of the frigid midmorning sun.

Entering the building's east-side glass door, Major Arthur DiSilva, the company's commanding officer, was now officially on duty. He walked swiftly to the admin office door and opened it.

The first thing DiSilva saw was Master Sergeant Oliver Martz. The top sergeant served as the battalion's operations department head. He sat at the metal desk belonging to Tomlinson. A pair of desktop computer monitors, a keyboard, and telephone faced Martz, with bookcases stuffed with manuals and filing cabinets against the wall behind him.

Martz's starched camouflage uniform fit snugly, his shirt pressed and pleated with chevrons, displaying his rank. Well into his forties, Martz was an epitome of physical fitness, with a shaved head reminiscent of Mr. Clean. He could pass for a professional wrestler, albeit a short version, free of anabolic steroids. To see him anywhere near the pasty-faced, potbellied DiSilva was a study in contrasts.

On the other side of the office stood DiSilva's cherry-laminate desk. That too had a phone, a pair of computer monitors, and a keyboard. There were several photos in a cubed glass display, pictures of family back in America. On the credenza against the wall behind him, a large framed wedding photo taken last October with Chona, his Korean bride. A unit flag flanked the desk's left side, with an American flag to the right. It gave the area an official appearance. The cheap wooden bench facing the desk looked sadly out of place. DiSilva removed his jacket and hat before sitting down.

"I see Alex still isn't here," DiSilva said.

"No, sir. We looked everywhere. One of the houseboys checked Alex's barracks room, and I even sent Claude into Anjeong-ri to check Alex's hooch. The landlord let him in, but no sign of Alex. Didn't see him in the mess hall or the small PX, either. He's officially off-the-reservation unauthorized absent."

Houseboys were local subcontractors hired by the Army to oversee routine barracks maintenance and common-area cleanliness. They supplemented their income by caring for individual rooms and doing laundry.

DiSilva pushed back his short, thinning blond hair and adjusted his glasses. "Now I'm worried."

"And one other thing."

DiSilva's head dropped as he rubbed his temples. "Yup, here it comes. What?"

"An ID card is missing from the safe."

DiSilva shook his head. "Aw, shit. You don't think he boosted it to sell on the black market?"

"What else could he do with it? The log reconciled last month, and there's been no activity since."

The major leaned back in his synthetic leather chair. "What do you suppose a blank ID's worth out there? Why the hell would he do such a *stupid* thing?"

"I don't know, Major. But whatever his motivation, Alex decided the reward was worth the risk. I suppose it's only a coincidence his orders came in late yesterday afternoon."

"I knew he was short," DiSilva said. "Where to?"

"Fort Bliss in El Paso."

"This ever happened to you before, Top? Guy this short jumping the fence?"

Martz shook his head. "I've never even *heard* of anything like this before."

"How long do you figure he has to be missing before they'll send a replacement?"

"Good question for someone from legal. I'm sure it's longer than two hours, though. I'll call them at noon, assuming Alex doesn't show."

"You don't suppose this has anything to do with the woman he's sometimes with?" DiSilva asked.

Martz rubbed his jaw. "Could be. Nothing surprises me anymore."

"I'm of the opinion we shouldn't do anything rash. It's possible he'll come to his senses and return."

Martz's eyes met DiSilva's. "He's not coming back, Major. That blank ID is the smoking gun. Even if he came back, he's looking at losing a stripe and doing time in the stockade, and he can forget about reenlisting again."

DiSilva's fingers tapped nervously on the desk. "Is there anyone you can spare from the security building to pinch-hit?"

"I'll work the schedule and free Claude Dunbarton for a few days as a stopgap. Only he's never done this kind of work before, so we'll both have to be patient."

DiSilva nodded. "Did anything else turn up missing?"

"No, sir." Martz stood and grabbed his hat from off the desk. "I'll get on the schedule and talk to Claude, Major."

DiSilva nodded, not hearing a word. He picked up the phone to leave a message for his wife. Chona DiSilva worked at an Anjeong-ri private school teaching English. While the couple often went to her parents for Sunday dinner, this news gave the visit a rare sense of urgency.

There was a reason. Chona DiSilva was Myung-Dae Tang's daughter.

****

"Are you busy, Doyoon?" Jeong asked when her shift as Duffy Club's afternoon manager began.

"Not so busy we can't talk."

"Myung-Dae took cash out of the safe and wrote out a receipt with your name on it. What did you do for him?" As the club's general manager, she saw all of Duffy Club's financial transactions.

"Myung-Dae told me to keep my mouth shut. I'm afraid if I tell you, he'll find out and dismiss me. And some here have told me stories that make me afraid he could do worse."

She shook her head. "Myung-Dae won't find out. You have my solemn vow."

Doyoon took a breath. "He gave the money as a tip. Last night, Myung-Dae handed over a tiny plastic bag with a brown powder that he said was a laxative. So I mixed it with the American man's tequila. Myung-Dae said it was a practical joke. I wanted to tell you last night but couldn't. Please tell me the man is okay."

Doyoon will find out one way or another that Alex died. No point in lying. "The powder wasn't a joke, but that's not your fault. Myung-Dae lied to you."

"Yes, but what about the man?"

Jeong looked down, trying desperately not to cry. She wanted to tell Doyoon that Tomlinson returned to the base. She really did. Instead, tears welled up in the corner of her eyes.

"What is it, Jeong?"

She looked up, tears flowing freely.

"He's dead?" Color drained from Doyoon's face as he asked. The glass in his hand fell to the concrete floor, smashing into several large pieces.

"You had no way of knowing Myung-Dae's intent. You followed an order, nothing more."

Doyoon rubbed his forehead. "That makes me a murderer. I could spend the rest of my life in prison, and for what?"

"You will not go to jail. It is *not* your fault, Doyoon. And this conversation stays between us."

Doyoon's face reddened. "I should've known he was up to some kind of evil. Why didn't he put that stuff in the drink himself? Now I have to live with that."

She put her hand on his shoulder. "Shh…be careful what you say. Myung-Dae might be in his office or the stockroom."

"I'll be okay." He gently wriggled away before removing his apron and tossing it on the bar. "But I'm done with this place, Jeong. Done working for Myung-Dae Tang." Doyoon walked toward the time clock in the hallway to punch out.

What was I thinking, asking about that payout from Myung-Dae? You knew Doyoon acted strange after Alex got sick. And just as we're about to get slammed on a Friday night. I doubt my backup bartender will come in on such short notice.

"Please, Doyoon, don't quit now. Not on a Friday night. This place will be a madhouse in three hours."

"I'm sorry, Jeong. You're a sweet woman, and I hate doing this to you. But I'll not spend one more second working here. Please mail my paycheck; I'll never set foot in this place again." Doyoon punched out and grabbed his jacket from under the bar. "Don't forget your promise."

At that moment, she wanted to be Doyoon, despite the man's pangs of guilt. To walk away from Myung-Dae and this place, free to find work elsewhere. No, it wasn't slavery. Yet it was close enough.

"I won't forget," she replied. "You'll find a job in five minutes. Just be careful who you tell that story to."

Doyoon said nothing more as he walked to the front door. Leaving Jeong to wish she could do the same.

Chapter Four

Through the early morning darkness, a black van traveled north on I-89 headed for Swanton, Vermont. A national brand's office supply logo stickers adorned the vehicle's side panels, but it carried no such cargo.

The stretch of freeway in northern Vermont appeared barren. Cognizant of the speed limit, the vehicle only flirted with it. Luther Voline knew where Vermont State Troopers liked to hide.

In the light of day and with snow on the ground, it displayed a sea of dark green and white. Thick spruce pine stood at attention on both sides of the highway, as scenic and pastoral as one could want.

At night, however, this stretch of highway became a different animal, an occasional deadly one. Particularly in winter months. With weather often unpredictable, and without distractions to challenge the mind, eyelids sometimes got heavy. Luther looked at the clock on the dashboard. It was three fifteen in the morning.

He tasted adrenaline the closer he got to the U.S. Customs and Border Protection crossing. Sweat bubbled and trickled down both temples. With a bandana, the young man wiped away the sweaty buildup on his neck as he listened to music from his cell phone.

Take a breath. Looking spooked is a major red

flag.

The young man had been watching this Highgate Springs border crossing station for the last six weeks, using a small waterproof camera discreetly mounted on a nearby birch that his Canadian partner installed. The video fed into his laptop, and after securing the okay to transport the shipment to Sherbrooke, Quebec, Luther chose this morning to act on it.

On six consecutive early Saturday mornings, he watched the older man working at the first booth. That agent didn't send a single two-axel vehicle to the separate customs inspections bays between two and five o'clock in the morning. The van Luther drove carried a quarter-ton of pure Colombian cocaine, five hundred pounds in one night, for a very large payoff.

Still, homework or not, this carried an enormous risk. And Luther wouldn't think to do it if the money wasn't right. But Abbey's pancreatic cancer moved swiftly from stage two to three. She discovered a German treatment center whose success rate got her attention. Only the treatment wasn't cheap. And because it wasn't on American soil, the insurance carrier wouldn't touch it.

Luther estimated an eighty-six percent chance of getting through without a search as long as the elderly man worked the booth. Try getting those odds at a casino.

He tried not to think about the flip side of the coin. If sent to the customs bays, Luther had no magic substance to throw off the canines. Considering the mutts could detect deceased bodies submerged underwater for weeks after an accident or homicide, why bother trying? The only way to keep the dogs off was to avoid them altogether.

More sweat trickled down Luther's temples as the border-crossing lights came into view. He took up the bandana once more as he slowed the van. Three booths had green lights, and there were no other vehicles around. The booths were rectangle-shaped and tall enough to accommodate a tractor-trailer. There was a half-door where drivers and agents interact. In this weather, agents kept the half-door's sliding glass partition closed. Luther approached the first booth, the van creeping forward.

The border patrolman waited. He appeared close to retirement age, by Luther's reckoning. There sat a mammoth Styrofoam cup of coffee and a sports magazine on the countertop behind the bulletproof glass.

Luther stopped the van and rolled down the window. He kept his eyes on the border patrol agent; everything moved in slow motion. The man's head popped up, and he slid the partition open.

"Where you headed, young man?"

"Sherbrooke."

"You call this in already?"

"Yes, sir. Here's the ACE e-manifest." Luther handed over a clipboard, the manifest on top. Pinned under it was his passport and driver's license. Sweat rolled down Luther's neck, and he wiped it away with the bandana, hoping the border agent didn't notice.

Slowly and deliberately, the old man looked the documents over. He spent more time examining the manifest than Luther expected.

"Excuse me a minute; I need to make a phone call."

Phone call? All the time I watched him, he didn't pick up the phone, not once.

Luther pulled himself together as he watched the agent slide the glass partition back and pick up a handset. The conversation didn't last more than a few seconds, and Luther's anxiety zipped off the map. The agent put the handset back down and reopened the partition.

"You been through here before?"

"No, sir."

"Do you have a criminal record, Mr. Voline?"

"No." *Not yet.* "Why?"

"Routine question. I'll run your license through the database after the cargo check. How long do you expect to be in Sherbrooke?"

Cargo check? He only does cargo checks on ten-wheelers in this time slot.

"Just a turnaround."

Luther heard a car's brakes squeal, and he turned to see a Vermont State Police cruiser park just outside the three-bay inspection station twenty yards ahead to the right. Two troopers got out, one holding the leash of a beautiful German shepherd. Once inside the station, the troopers turned on the lights and opened the first bay door.

"Where are you coming from?" the agent asked.

Luther tried regrouping. This was so much more scrutiny than he'd seen on video.

"Burlington."

The border patrol agent's eyes stayed on his. "Uh-huh. Pull your van ahead to the first bay; the troopers will take it from here. You can have your documents back." The agent returned the clipboard to Luther before closing the partition once again.

It took every ounce of self-control not to vomit; Luther had never been so scared. Sure, he could try to outrun the state troopers—force them to give chase. They could post the video online, displaying Luther's stupidity to anyone who cared to watch. He doubted a federal prosecutor or judge would find the humor in it.

Luther had no choice but to drive the short distance to the inspection station bay. The taller of the two troopers gestured for the van to pull forward, guiding it onto a vehicle rack like an attendant at a franchise oil-change garage. After positioning the van properly, the trooper gestured for Luther to stop and get out.

"Do you need the stuff I showed the ICE agent?" Luther asked.

The taller trooper shook his head.

The shorter trooper came out of the office with the dog. When the animal started barking, Luther resigned himself to a lengthy prison sentence. He never wanted to believe this would actually happen. His future tarnished in the blink of an eye.

They opened the back of the van. It took them less than a minute to find the bricks of cocaine. The shorter trooper led the canine back into the office while the taller trooper handcuffed and read Luther the Miranda warning.

The troopers quickly stuffed Luther into the cruiser's back seat. Next stop, the Northwest State Correctional Facility in Saint Albans.

What Abbey would do now, Luther didn't know. He was too busy contemplating what was about to happen to him.

Chapter Five

At eleven o'clock Saturday morning, Myung-Dae Tang heard the doorbell ring at the front door of his two-story Georgian-style brick house in Anjeong-ri. His scheduled appointment had arrived.

With the four tall, white columns out front on a huge end lot, one would presume that Myung-Dae and his wife Moon-Kym were prosperous. Especially when seeing the small, unkempt houses that bordered it.

In reality, this was more Moon-Kym's house than Myung-Dae's. His wife of fifty-two years liked the convenience of living in the village. It was within walking distance of everything she needed. Myung-Dae, on the other hand, preferred the quiet of the farmhouse.

The elderly man sat at his desk in the first-floor study at the far end of the house, surrounded by hardcover ledgers. Except for checking his stock's performance or watching surveillance cameras as they roamed both nightclubs, Myung-Dae didn't trust computers. Instead, he preferred paper ledgers and an abacus.

"Moon-Kym, please answer the door," he bellowed.

Today's meeting was with soldiers from Camp Humphreys. They brought him black-market business, most of which he and his wife consumed. The rest he gave as gifts or rewards. He preferred doing business with men belonging to the 501st Intelligence Battalion, Company B. There was a reason for that.

The doorbell rang again, and Myung-Dae's already worn patience evaporated.

"Don't you know I'm busy Moon-Kym? Will you please answer that door?" Myung-Dae knew that Moon-Kym was in the upstairs kitchen. He could hear her clang-banging around. "Moon-Kym?"

"Stop your bellyaching, old man. I didn't realize you've become crippled."

He listened as she descended the stairs, muttering curses under her breath. Myung-Dae knew the door would open, and she would lead the men to his study. Soon the pair of American soldiers—Cameron Shanahan and Gilbert Trotter—stood in the doorway. Moon-Kym departed as Myung-Dae's eyes quickly pounced on the sagging gym bags both soldiers carried.

"Welcome, my friends," Myung-Dae said. "So, let's see what you brought for me."

The study contained interesting and expensive artifacts. Upscale and imported liquor bottles graced an entire wall's glass display, while the opposite wall featured figurines made of various metals and gemstones. In another glassed-in lighted display were four elaborate chess boards. In another corner, a knight's brass armor stood with a magnificent sword. To push away any thoughts these two may have about wandering off with anything valuable, Myung-Dae insisted they sit quietly until their business concluded.

As they sat unzipping the bags, Myung-Dae considered the pair. The huskier, shorter Cam opened his bag first. Myung-Dae liked him. He appeared to be more responsible than Gil and calmer. In his gym bag were two cartons of cigarettes, a bottle of vodka, three boxes of K-cup coffee, and a case of American beer in cans. Myung-Dae's eyes danced.

"Oh, this is good." Myung-Dae looked at the taller, thinner Gil. "What about you?"

Gil displayed a bottle of rum, a bottle of bourbon, and two cartons of cigarettes to go along with three boxes of coffee. Everything but the coffee was black-market merchandise. Myung-Dae clapped his hands.

"Very good. You have receipts?"

Both men expected the request and handed Myung-Dae envelopes. They understood it would take several minutes for him to record the transaction in his ledger. He paid double their cost from the Camp Humphreys PX. He paid them in Korean won and not U.S. dollars. But it mattered little. They spent the money freely in Myung-Dae's Duffy Club anyhow.

While the Americans understood that their black marketeering was illegal, they didn't know *why*. It came about during the Korean Conflict in 1950 when the U.S. Army rationed alcohol and tobacco products. It has been that way ever since.

A GI apprehended and convicted for black marketeering would lose a stripe and do time in the stockade. However, Myung-Dae paid a great deal to the local chapter of the Korean National Police Agency, or KNPA, for protection. Without intelligence from the KNPA, U.S. Army CID was toothless.

Cam and Gil watched, mesmerized as Myung-Dae's fingers whirred on the abacus like a classical pianist. After the abacus and journal entries, Korean won changed hands. Myung-Dae then placed an order for next week, and when he stood, the soldiers understood it was time to leave. They got to their feet and grabbed their empty gym bags.

"Just a moment, please. I have a proposition."

Both men stopped and turned to listen.

"I have a need," Myung-Dae said. "Mitchell no longer wishes to sell cocaine for me. Perhaps one of you could use the extra money."

Both soldiers knew Myung-Dae was talking about their friend, Mitch Carruthers, a base medic who worked in the Camp Humphreys hospital. Gil was one of Mitch's busier accounts, and Cam was no stranger either.

"Why does Mitch want out?" Gil asked.

Myung-Dae shrugged. "You'd have to ask him. Do either of you want it?"

Cam shook his head. "I'm short, Myung-Dae. Out of here at the end of February. I won't do it."

"You leave Korea in February? Out of the army?"

"Going home to Detroit."

"We need to talk."

"I'm in Duffy Club every night I'm working day shifts. You know where to find me."

Myung-Dae nodded, his eyes turning to Gil. "What about you?"

"How much can I make?"

Cam took Gil by the elbow. "Excuse me, Myung-Dae, do you mind if I have a word with my friend in private?"

"Yes, yes. Go outside and talk among yourselves."

Cam grabbed Gil by the elbow. "Outside," he whispered.

****

Together, the soldiers walked out of the front door. Cam waited to speak until he'd closed it shut.

"Are you out of your mind? Selling coke in Anjeong-ri for Myung-Dae? The Koreans don't have to turn you over to Camp Humphreys MPs if they nail you. They can take jurisdiction, and that means a Korean court and prison. And no offense, dude, you wouldn't last a week."

"Mitch has been selling since before we got here. Nobody's up his ass. You're startin' to sound like my grandmother."

"What's the upside in selling coke for Myung-Dae Tang? Mitch told me that old prick's with some kind of Korean mafia."

Gil scoffed. "You don't believe that shit any more than I do. He owns a couple of bars and apartment buildings in Anjeong-ri and cuts guys like Mitch in to sell blow. He's not the Korean Al Capone."

"Give me one good reason, and I'll shut up."

"It's Gayoon, okay? Her family wants a big wedding; it's a Korean thing, I guess. So I pick up a few bucks on the side to make that happen; it'll keep her *and* her mother off my ass." Gayoon was Gil's live-in girlfriend and fiancée—they'd been together ten months.

"That's a shitty way of goin' about financing it, brother. But you're a big boy, so do what you want."

They both went back inside.

"I'm leaving now, Myung-Dae. Catch you in Duffy Club," Cam said.

"Don't forget: we need to talk." Myung-Dae's eyes turned to Gil. "So…what do you say?"

"How much money can I make?"

"Does this mean you say yes?"

"I'm always interested in a buck, Myung-Dae. So tell me."

"You can do very well if you learn. Sit down, and I will show you how."

Gil sat as Myung-Dae instructed. His first lesson was about to begin.

Chapter Six

DiSilva returned home from the Camp Humphreys' PX at nine o'clock Sunday morning. He got out of his car and carried an expensive bottle of scotch and a bag of groceries into the Anjeong-ri condo he shared with Chona.

A neighbor, seeing the bottle while walking his dog, gave DiSilva a disapproving smirk as the American went inside.

How DiSilva met Chona was blind luck. He first saw her eighteen months ago, three weeks after she'd graduated from Seoul National University. She worked for Myung-Dae as a server in her father's Jumpin' Jack Flask nightclub, as he desperately needed extra help but didn't have enough time to vet new hires.

How Myung-Dae learned of DiSilva's rank and role on the base, DiSilva never inquired. It seemed odd that Chona rebuffed DiSilva's initial dinner invitation, only to change her mind an hour later.

After a lengthy courtship, they wed three months ago. Whether Chona loved him remained open to interpretation, and DiSilva contemplated it often. But he loved her. That was enough.

He put the groceries away and put on coffee before entering the bedroom. Chona sat upright in the queen-sized bed, watching the news.

"Why do young people riot in your American

cities? What do they believe will happen as a result?" Chona asked. The couple spoke Korean, as DiSilva was fluent.

"They just want to riot, mostly. I don't think they know what they want."

"I'm thankful you put in for an extension. Who would ever want to live in a place where that goes on?"

"Every generation has their rebels, I guess. Why are you still in bed?"

"I'm so tired, Arthur."

He walked over and kissed her forehead. "I bought those waffles you like from the commissary."

Chona glanced at her husband and grinned.

DiSilva grabbed his tablet device from atop the nightstand and brought it to the kitchen table. After he poured a cup of coffee, Chona walked in and took a cup from the cabinet.

"What do you think about going to your parents a little early today?" he asked.

"Oh? Since when are you so eager to visit my parents?"

"One of my men turned up missing. I want to ask your father if he knows anything about it."

"How would my father know anything about one of your men?"

"He may not. Can't hurt to ask."

Chona nodded. And while the couple never openly discussed it, DiSilva wondered just how much his wife really *knew* about her father's business operations and the methods used to get the desired result.

"Mother has been asking when she will have grandchildren."

"Tell her we're trying."

"She tells me to tell you to try harder." Chona giggled.

DiSilva closed the tablet's cover. "Then maybe we should start now."

****

The trip across Anjeong-ri took only minutes, and the couple soon arrived at the Tang house. Not everything about these visits was dull and obligatory. DiSilva appreciated the size of the house, so different from the cramped condo and the double-wide he grew up in with a single mother in Toledo, Ohio.

Myung-Dae appeared pleased to accept the bottle of scotch and, after the meal, brought DiSilva and the bottle down the stairs to his study.

The host poured them both a glass and offered his son-in-law a cigar. DiSilva took an animated whiff before lighting up. Myung-Dae sat at his desk while DiSilva occupied the chair Gil Trotter had only yesterday.

"Thank you for this generous gift, Arthur. So tell me what's on your mind."

"One of my men turned up missing that you do business with."

Myung-Dae took a sip of his scotch and nodded. "Alex Tomlinson."

"Yes. Alex."

"You will need to find a replacement."

"Excuse me?"

"You won't see Alex again, Arthur. I'm sorry."

"What's that supposed to mean?"

Myung-Dae grinned, his gold tooth winking. "You will need a replacement. I could draw you a picture if you'd like."

"Are you saying Alex Tomlinson is dead?"

Myung-Dae's eyes bored into DiSilva's. "Yes, Arthur. Alex Tomlinson is dead."

"Why would you *do* such a thing?"

Myung-Dae shifted his weight in the leather chair. "Unavoidable, I'm afraid. He compromised future objectives."

"What the hell are you talking about? What future objectives?"

Myung-Dae leaned forward, his eyes hard on DiSilva's. "I don't appreciate your tone. You forget yourself, Arthur."

"I can't believe you murdered one of my men. And the body?"

"I believe *corpus delicti* is the Latin phrase. You won't find a body. While the action regrettable, someone should have taught that arrogant jackass some manners. Had he displayed a modicum of humility and respect, we wouldn't be having this conversation."

"You have no idea what kind of shitstorm this will bring."

"And you'll weather such a storm, Arthur. Now, are you ready for some good news?"

DiSilva found a book of matches on the desk and lit the cigar. "After this, I can't imagine anything you say will be good."

"Stop your whining. As for Alex, a replacement will arrive, problem solved. Now for the good news. I've struck a deal with a Chinese Red Army official to transport ten thousand cadavers into Mokpo Port via a refrigerated Chinese freighter."

"What's so great about ten thousand Chinese stiffs coming into Mokpo?"

"Odd as it sounds, there is a market. I have a buyer, two million won per cadaver. My buyer sells to North American medical schools. But that's not the best part."

"And what is the best part?"

"Every cadaver is carrying a kilogram of heroin. I'll not see an opportunity like this again."

DiSilva shook his head. "The risk is enormous. You of all people should know that."

"I have a buyer for the heroin as well. After the Chinese freighter docks, we move the heroin to the buyer's van and transport the cadavers to a waiting Norwegian freighter that makes port in Seattle. This time of year, because of the temperature, we have a little more time to move the dead bodies. I stand to clear the equivalent of twenty-five million U.S. dollars in this one deal."

"You stand to spend the risk of your life in prison."

Myung-Dae scoffed. "I know who to pay and how much. I don't rush into a deal unless I know who I'm dealing with."

DiSilva took a sip of the scotch. "I hope it all works out for you, Myung-Dae."

Myung-Dae took a sip. "I'm willing to give you a significant cut."

"To do what, exactly? I've got one more tour before retirement. No way I'm getting involved in your narcotics trade."

"Are you sure? Serving as my point man is worth ten million dollars to me."

The cigar nearly dropped from DiSilva's mouth. "Ten million?"

"It's worth that much to me. You'll have Gunn and Kiwoo at your disposal, and they'll be in charge of ten forklift operators Gunn has already hired."

"Not Gunn, Myung-Dae. The man can't stand the sight of me."

"Gunn is my very best man. If there is trouble, you'll be happy he's there."

"Do you expect trouble?"

"No, I do not. But trouble often comes when you least expect it."

"Has money changed hands?"

Myung-Dae took a sip of his drink. "I've made a nonrefundable deposit, and both my heroin and cadaver buyers have done the same. The bulk of the transaction I'm financing conventionally; the loan should close later in the week. I expect the Chinese to deliver the first week of February, although I don't have a firm date yet."

"What happens if the Korean Navy boards the Chinese vessel?"

"They won't."

"And why is that?"

"They'll have no reason to. Everything comes at a price, Arthur."

DiSilva dreamed that one day he would be a man of wealth and influence. This kind of money was more than he could *ever* hope for. More than enough to bankroll a campaign if he decided to run for office after retirement. His heirs would live on trust funds.

"What would I have to do?"

"We'll need to weigh the heroin; we can't have someone walk away with inventory they think we'll overlook. Then you'll oversee the transfer of the cadavers. It's a great deal of work in a very narrow window of time; ten hours is the estimate."

This is trouble. There's something he's not telling me.

"How did the Red Army amass such a large quantity of dead bodies?" DiSilva asked.

"In China, who the hell knows? But I'm sure most weren't willing donors." Myung-Dae grinned, his gold tooth winking. "So are you in or out?"

"And the Dokgo brothers?"

Myung-Dae exhaled a puff of cigar smoke. "What about them?"

"They're going to want a piece."

"I'll offer tribute at the appropriate time. If I see fit."

DiSilva shook his head. "Now I understand why you want Gunn in on this. That's a dangerous game, and you know it. Throw them a bone; you don't need a war. And I don't want to get caught in the crossfire. You don't have to do it for me, but for Moon-Kym and Chona. You don't want them in the middle of something like that."

Ryung and his younger brother Jaewon Dokgo headed up the South Korea Syndicate, a network of local and provincial crime lords. Members paid tribute at ten percent on the honor system, the money going to sympathetic political parties, judges, and prosecutors. It kept every faction from waging war on another, thus keeping the peace.

The last member who refused to pay tribute went for a boat ride with Jaewon and two of Jaewon's men. Once aboard, Jaewon's men chained the malcontent's legs to cinder blocks before dumping him in the middle of Korea Strait, still breathing.

"Let me worry about the Dokgos. Can I count on

you?"

I'll never see this kind of money again if I live to be a thousand.

DiSilva raised his glass.

Myung-Dae grinned, and the gold tooth flashed. "You're making sense. What of Sean Miller's wife? Did her visa application go through your American ICE at the embassy? I paid the young man, and he married that whore. Now get them to America."

"Alex didn't finish the application. *Now* do you understand the importance of telling me *before* you do something rash?"

"But you're in control and can take care of it. Right?"

"Yes. But dealing with the embassy and immigration, it's gotten so much tougher now."

Myung-Dae brushed his hand as if swatting a fly. "Immigration policy changes with the political winds. Which of your men is next out of their Army obligation?"

"Cameron Shanahan. He does business with you, too."

"Yes. I've spoken briefly with Cameron. I will miss him."

"So you made the approach?" DiSilva asked.

Myung-Dae nodded. "He didn't jump on it as the others did, so I suspect he'll pass. A first since we began."

"Had to happen. Maybe it's just as well, what with your ship literally coming in."

Myung-Dae took a sip. "Where are my grandchildren, Arthur?"

"Chona and I were talking about that very thing at

breakfast this morning. We're working on it."

Myung-Dae raised his glass. "When will you learn of Alex's replacement?"

"As soon as the orders come in. I have no control over that."

"And what of you, Arthur? Have you heard anything more about staying here another year?"

DiSilva took a deep breath. This was a subject he wanted no part of today. "There's no confirmation yet, but my guy in Washington told me not to worry about it. So I'm not worried about it."

Except the detailer in Washington made no such representation. This marked the first time DiSilva blatantly lied to his father-in-law. DiSilva changed the topic to American politics, and both men had another drink.

And when Chona said it was time to go, DiSilva jumped to his feet.

"What did you and my father talk about all that time?" she asked from behind the wheel as they drove back to the condo.

"Mostly American politics."

"You spent two hours talking about American politics?"

"Not all of it. He said something about grandchildren, too."

Chapter Seven

With Myung-Dae and his men closing Duffy Club for the night, Jeong walked to her apartment alone. She lived several blocks down from her work, just off the thoroughfare. She still struggled with Tomlinson's death and the cruel manner in which he passed.

Jeong trotted up the stairs, mindful of her elderly neighbor, even if the sweet woman with the noisy Shih Tzu was going deaf. Jeong's was an airy four-room apartment, her taste in contemporary furnishings what you'd expect from someone with a keen eye. The building served as a steel foundry back in the day, the high ceilings giving it a roomier feel. Her lone complaint was the thin drywall, the contractor cutting corners, no doubt.

She often felt guilty about living here comfortably while her sister and father lived in a cramped apartment in the city of Daegu. Jeong knew that would soon change, with Sejun on pace to graduate from the technical college in that city in May. After Sejun found employment, she and their retired father could then find a more suitable place to live.

Jeong would bring Kwang here to live if not for Myung-Dae. Granted, Myung-Dae had a long reach if he wanted to harm them because of her. But why make things too convenient?

She put the key into the slot and realized her door

was unlocked. That sent an icy shiver down her back; she double-checked locking the apartment every time before leaving, without exception. Jeong removed the pepper spray she carried in her bag and opened the front door cautiously, nudging it open with her boot instead of entering. It was pitch black inside the apartment; Jeong reached in and flipped the light switch. Looking up, she stumbled back, nearly falling down the stairs, never frightened to this degree. Several seconds passed before her mind processed the image staring her in the face.

Hanging from a nylon rope fastened to a beam over the kitchen table was Doyoon. His tongue hung out, with dead, staring eyes gazing skyward, his face bloated. There was no blood; the man's wrists bound with duct tape. He wore a lightweight ski jacket and thick corduroy trousers. Between his lips, a single sheet of paper with Korean characters. She got up on a chair and took the note.

"I talk too much," it read.

In a fog, Jeong closed the front door and walked into her living room. She sat on the sofa as tears fell. Doyoon stood by the courage of his convictions to up and walk out...she admired that. He was honest and had no harsh words for anyone except Myung-Dae. The guy didn't do anything to deserve this.

When Jeong could cry no more, she removed the cell phone from her bag and called the KNPA.

****

Jungho Bak, the major crimes unit senior inspector with the KNPA's Anjeong-ri station house, arrived soon thereafter with a pair of forensics experts and a photographer. The tall and lanky detective with graying hair at the temples asked Jeong a series of questions. Satisfied the young woman held nothing back, he asked her to wait on the living room sofa while they cut Doyoon down and finished up.

Several things bothered Bak. The young woman insisted she locked her front door, double-checking before leaving. Yet, there were no signs of a forced entry. The victim had been dead for some time; with rigor mortis already setting in, and Ms. Guy had just returned from work. Assuming her alibi checked out, she was in the clear. *Someone had a key to her front door made.*

The victim had skin under his fingernails— whoever did this had deep scratches, and the young woman who called this in had none, and Bak made it a point to check. Whoever hanged the victim was strong; lifting Mr. Chang this high would be too much for one man alone, most men anyhow. She told Bak that Chang worked for her at Duffy Club. The pay stub in the victim's wallet confirmed it.

Ms. Guy made it clear that Chang wasn't a lover or roommate. *So why was this man hanged here, in this apartment? To send a message?*

Bak knew that Myung-Dae Tang owned Duffy Club. That Tang paid Anjeong-ri KNPA Commandant Choson to look the other way when Tang's name appeared in a police report was common knowledge.

The detective hadn't yet met Tang personally, although he'd occasionally seen the man and his thugs, always from a distance. *Strong thugs, able to do this kind of work.*

Bak decided he would meet Tang face-to-face for the first time sooner than he ever wanted.

Chapter Eight

Porter parked his SUV in a lot close to the downtown Los Angeles federal building. Why people chose to work in the city baffled him, and he felt glad he didn't have to be here often. The security guards—not recognizing him—checked the young agent's credentials before letting him pass.

The agent moved to the elevators and got on with several others; one passenger with perfume so thick Porter had difficulty breathing. On the fifth floor, he exited speedily and walked down a long, glistening hallway. He walked into Special-Agent-in-Charge Walter Stillson's corner office, where a pretty assistant looked up.

"Are you Mike Porter?"

"Yes."

"Go on in. He's expecting you."

Porter moved to the door and knocked.

"Come in."

Stillson had a roomy office with a gorgeous view of the city, or at least the smog it wallowed in. U.S. and CIA flags flanked the oak desk, and an array of framed diplomas and awards decorated the wall behind him. This was an accomplished man. There were photos of Stillson with President Trump and a vast array of leaders and dignitaries from around the globe. Against the far wall were nine TV screens, all on but mute. On his desk stood a pair of monitors and a telephone.

"Take a seat." Stillson gestured to a pair of cushy chairs facing the desk. The man looked more like a church deacon than someone in charge of the agency's Southeast Asia operations and compliance arm.

Porter sat down.

The meeting started well enough, with Stillson once again expressing his appreciation in the way Porter went about capturing Orson O'Hara. The SAIC then went about critiquing Porter's performance.

"Now you understand the danger in relinquishing control to the investigation subject," Stillson said. "You could've returned in a body bag."

"I thought O'Hara might bail if I made too big a deal out of who drove. Besides, the base MPs were on top of it. The risk seemed minimal."

Stillson nodded. "I read the transcript. You had to trust your instincts."

"Any idea where I'm going next?"

Stillson rubbed his jaw. "Some of that is up to you. Let me start with a question. Do you know the Vermont State Police arrested your brother over the weekend?"

Porter's face reddened. "You know about Luther?"

Stillson chuckled. "We're a spy agency. Did you think we wouldn't find out?"

Porter's head dropped. "Is this the part where I resign?"

Stillson leaned back in his oversized leather chair. "That depends. Do you want to resign?"

"Want to? No."

Stillson leaned back in. "Good. We have a situation. How much do you know about North and South Korea's history and current detente?"

"Just what I've seen in the news. The north's always been hostile. The North Korean president has a knack for killing family members when he's not making threats. But what's that got to do with me?"

"I'm getting to that. Let's talk about Luther trying to transport five hundred pounds of cocaine into Quebec from Vermont. The federal prosecutor will try to put him away for thirty years. Maybe even life."

Porter understood he needed to choose his words carefully. "I wish my brother had come to me first, but that ship sailed."

"I'm going to offer you the chance to rectify Luther's current…status."

Porter's eyebrows arched. "How?"

"We have a development in South Korea. I'm sure you know the PyeongChang Winter Olympics start in three weeks. While the games are in progress, Kim Jong-un and Moon Jae-in are meeting in Panmunjom as a precursor to their April peace summit. We don't have the exact time and date they're meeting yet. We've been tracking chatter the last couple of days; it's clear someone intends to assassinate Kim Jong-un before that meeting. From three hundred yards out from Peace House as he enters the building. That means sniper."

"And the shooter?"

Stillson's brow furrowed. "Unknown."

"Could be disinformation."

"There's that possibility, sure."

"We don't have a source?"

"Comms are brief and never from the same place twice. This just came in, so there hasn't been enough time to organize a countermeasure. This is where you come into play. How sharp are you?"

"Indoors with a pistol, I'm fine. I'd need a few reps working outside with a spotter to get my bearings with a rifle. Panmunjom is north of the Demilitarized Zone, isn't it?"

Stillson nodded. "Yup, North Korea. You're no stranger to this kind of work, and that's imperative. Agency could send an Olympic marksman up there, but if they've never pulled on a human and freeze, what's the point? And frankly, we don't have the time to recruit someone from outside this office. We can jam North Korean radar and set you down by helicopter early morning on the day of the summit. Getting back is the challenge."

"Let me understand. You've got a shooter and spotter going into North Korea to neutralize an assassination attempt in the dead of winter. You can set them down but aren't sure about the exfil?"

Stillson's right pinky started tapping on the desk. "At present, that is correct."

"This time of year, we can't dig in anywhere. Even if we get aerial images of a place to hunker down, who knows if we're walking into a minefield? Do we have drone video to look at?"

"Two drones went up from Osan Air Base last week," Stillson said. "Neither returned."

"North Korea has the tech to take out a drone?"

"Maybe, maybe not. But China sure does."

"Whole thing sounds like a shoot and scoot. If flight ops can't come in for the exfil, it's a sprint to the DMZ with the entire North Korean Army chasing us. That's a race we won't win."

Stillson's pinky tapped harder. "If we can set you down, we can sure as hell pick you back up. It's a work-in-progress. Until now, our focus has been on the prevention of the attempt. Don't worry about the exfil. We'll get you and your spotter out. I need a yes or no."

"If I decline?"

Stillson's pinky stopped as he leaned back. "Luther's conviction means revocation of your top-secret clearance. And let's be honest, Luther has no case; I read the report. You'd no longer be a field agent."

"Maybe I don't like Kim Jong-un so much."

"Maybe you don't. But the man's willing to come to the table. And whoever takes his place might not want to sit at the table. Or admit the table exists. Or instead maybe wants to launch an ICBM to Hawaii or downtown Los Angeles."

"You have a spotter lined up?"

Stillson nodded. "Out of this office, been on Camp Humphreys eight months. Humphreys is forty miles south of Seoul, the closest base we have to the DMZ."

Porter took a deep breath. "And if I agree to do it?"

Stillson leaned back in. "What if I told you I could get Luther a presidential pardon?"

"A good lawyer might find a technical glitch in discovery."

Stillson scoffed with a backhanded wave. "You should read the Border Patrol's report. What I'm offering in exchange is unconditional *and* irrevocable. Even if the op gets scrubbed, Luther walks in seven weeks, and you keep your clearance and your job."

"That's great for Luther. Only I'm the one wearing the bullseye."

Stillson nodded. "Here's a sweetener. How about a bump to GS9 without the master's degree? There's an opening on Kadena in Okinawa you'd be in play for. I'll personally pitch you to the regional director. That's as good a deal as I'm authorized to make."

This is a death sentence, and Stillson acts like he's doing me a favor. "When would I leave?"

"As soon as we can arrange a billet for you on Humphreys. Day or two tops."

"Why not send me as a civilian contractor?"

"We can hide you better in a uniform. If you decide to do this, you're on standby from your first step out of this office."

Porter's eyes locked onto Stillson. "What're the odds of making it back whole?"

"Somewhere between seventy-five and eighty percent. It's dangerous, sure. But not suicide."

"Why'd the spotter volunteer?"

"You should ask him, although I'd rather you didn't."

"And why's that?"

Stillson shook his head. "His reasons might not align with yours. And I don't need the two of you trying to psychoanalyze one another before the bird leaves the tarmac."

"Is everyone in on this ex-military?"

Stillson nodded. "That is correct."

"My spotter. How many KIAs did he register? If we're pinned down, I need to know he'll come out swinging."

"Three registered kills. He served in Afghanistan when you were in Iraq," Stillson said. "He'll hold up his end if it comes to that."

"Just so long as he doesn't panic in a tight spot."

"I need an answer, Mike. Yes or no?"

Porter thought about Luther and Abby and his mother. "I'll do it. But I need something else from the agency. I need Luther *out* of Vermont, like yesterday. And done quietly."

Stillson cocked his head. "Any particular reason?"

"I imagine whoever owned that cocaine will want it paid for."

Stillson nodded. "Done. I'll email everything we have on the base you won't find on the website. Read it."

"What do I tell my brother about the move and pardon?"

"You don't. The op's classified. He'll think President Trump did him a favor, and that's that. This is Operation Stormwatcher, and you're now part of it. You'll meet the rest of the team on an as-needed basis at Camp Humphreys. We're on the clock, so once a billet opens, you're in LAX. So have your gear ready. Someone will be at the airport with a briefcase—inside will be a GPS, government passport, your orders, records, itinerary, and tickets. Check your agency comms twice daily and turn the GPS on every time you leave Humphreys. Every time."

"Other than team members, are there other assets working this?"

"Need to know, Mike. Your spotter will expect you to make contact within a day of you reaching Humphreys. I want you both working together outside as often as you're able. There's also a training regimen I want you both following. Any calls to the agency you make from a secure landline. I know you know that, but it bears repeating."

"Yes, sir."

"For what it's worth, I think you made a wise decision," Stillson said. "I'll be sorry to lose you to Kadena."

Of course you think it's a good decision. You got what you wanted.

The meeting over, Porter left the building. He started packing again the moment he returned to the hotel.

****

KNPA Senior Inspector Bak walked past the throng of soldiers huddled in front of Duffy Club. Most were eating vile sausage sandwiches from the trio of cart vendors. *These young men have never experienced food poisoning.*

An inebriated soldier draped around a working girl exited the bar. *The only thing worse than the food is the prostitution.* He found it disgraceful that these poor young women surrendered to this and were not given other opportunities to make a decent living. But he wasn't a social worker. He was here on a mission.

Bak hated to acknowledge his nervousness. Like everyone else in Anjeong-ri, he'd heard the stories. And he believed them. That Tang had no criminal record was laughably tragic.

The pretty Jeong Guy recognized him immediately from behind the bar and offered a welcoming smile. Bak couldn't help but feel sympathy for her and anyone else in Tang's employ.

"Nice to see you again, Mr. Bak."

Bak nodded. "I'm hoping Mr. Tang is here and can spare a few minutes."

"I'll see if he's here. Can I get you something?"

"I'm good, thank you. I forgot to mention this last

night, what with everything else going on. You should hire a reputable locksmith from *outside* Anjeong-ri to install a new lock and deadbolt."

She nodded and departed from behind the bar, leaving Bak to take in the scenery of soldiers and prostitutes. He had been in enough places like this throughout his twenty-year career and disliked them on principle.

Jeong returned. "Myung-Dae will see you."

"Thank you, young lady."

She lifted the section of bar reserved for employees and led him down the hall. A door to the right looked partially open, and she knocked on it before stepping aside to let Bak take her place in the doorway. Myung-Dae looked up from the monitor he watched.

"Well? Who are you, and what do you want?"

"A minute of your time, Mr. Tang. I'm Jungho Bak, senior inspector with the Anjeong-ri KNPA." Bak held up a badge. "May I come in?"

Myung-Dae nodded and gestured toward one of the two cheap plastic chairs facing the desk. "Tell me what this is about; I'm a busy man."

Bak sat down and reached into the inside breast pocket of his topcoat and produced a trio of photographs taken at Jeong's apartment last night. "I'd like you to look at these." He slid the photos forward.

Myung-Dae reached over and gave the first photo a cursory glance. Bak followed the old man's gaze.

"What am I looking at?"

"Don't you know? I'm here to ask about a body we found last night. In the apartment of the pretty young woman who works for you."

Myung-Dae's eyes found Bak's. "Appears to me

this man hanged himself. Poor fellow committed suicide."

Bak chuckled. "Except he didn't leave a suicide note, and we found skin under his fingernails. He fought to stay alive. The men who work for you, I've seen them around. They look quite capable of helping this man commit *suicide*. Are they in the building?"

Myung-Dae leaned back. "Are you making an accusation? Because if you are, I will need to make a phone call. And you might be looking for another job."

"I'd like to get a look at their arms, faces, and necks."

"There are many things I'd like as well, Mr. Bak. But want doesn't necessarily get."

Bak nodded. "While I'm here, perhaps you'd be so kind as to permit me to take a peek at your arms and neck?"

"You believe I'm capable of such a thing, Inspector?"

Bak shrugged. "Probably not. Why not humor me?"

"I could say no and file a grievance with Commandant Choson."

"I'm sure you could. But doing so would only further arouse my suspicion."

"You're willing to challenge me about an obvious suicide?"

"There is no evidence of a suicide. Don't you recognize Doyoon Chang? He worked for you."

Myung-Dae glanced at the photo again. "Now that you mention it, he looks familiar. What was he doing in Jeong's apartment?"

"I was about to ask you that very thing. I have

several questions. It bothers me there was no forced entry. Someone had a key made to Ms. Guy's apartment that I suspect she knows nothing about."

"So why are you telling me this, Mr. Bak?"

"Where were you and your men last night?"

"So you *are* making a baseless accusation? This has been fun; I'm confident you'll find the guilty party or parties and bring them to swift justice. Now, if you don't mind, I have a business to run. So I can pay taxes, which in turn allows you to further annoy me."

"May I see your arms and neck?"

"If it means getting you out of here faster, very well." Myung-Dae rolled up his shirt sleeves, prompting Bak to stand and look.

"And your neck?"

Myung-Dae leaned forward, stretching out his collar so Bak could get a good look from every angle. Bak could feel the rage simmering from the old man. *He'll keep his thugs away until their wounds heal. Such a hateful little man.*

"Satisfied?" Myung-Dae inquired, rolling his sleeves back down.

"Yes, thank you." Bak reached down and grabbed his photos. "I'll leave you to your work. But this doesn't mean my investigation is over. I do believe our paths will cross again."

"I look forward to your visits at all hours of the night. Try not to slip and fall on your way out. My insurance premiums are expensive enough."

Tang grinned as Bak turned to leave. The KNPA inspector hoped coming back wouldn't be necessary.

Chapter Nine

Porter returned to his Manhattan Beach hotel room with a bag of fast food takeout when he felt his cell phone vibrate. He glanced at the caller ID and saw Stillson's name. He called from the hotel landline, and his boss picked up.

"And here I was, just getting ready to eat," Porter said.

"I'm sure the in-flight meal will be great. Billet opened up. You're on a plane to Seoul, departing in five hours."

"Unit?"

"The 501st Military Intelligence Brigade. Company B. I'm emailing a unit roster with CVs of everyone assigned. Your orders will read that you came from Camp Zama, Japan. You were an administrator with the 78th Signal Battalion. You came to Los Angeles because you had a death in the family."

"And if someone on Humphreys had friends on Zama?"

"We cross-checked everything, Mike. That's why we chose Camp Zama."

"So I'm the unit administrator?"

"Yeah. The guy you're replacing jumped the fence."

"What?"

"It gets stranger. Staff sergeant by the name of

Tomlinson took off, and he was short, just got orders to Fort Bliss in El Paso, Texas. *And* he reenlisted three months ago. So keep your wits about you; none of it adds up."

"Is Luther out of Vermont?"

"FCI, Allenwood, Pennsylvania."

"I appreciate it, Walter. Getting back to the op, any idea who we're looking for yet?"

"Not yet, but there's still plenty of time. We believe it's a lone shooter; the chatter's been clear about that."

"Confirmed time and date?" Porter asked.

"Not yet. Exfil's in development."

"Yeah, okay. How long has it been since anyone had eyes on Panmunjom?"

"There's some unclassified video on the internet, but that won't help much. There's another drone scheduled to launch out of Osan sometime next week, but don't get your hopes up. If it goes down, it's doubtful the Pentagon will send another. Your spotter knows you're on your way; he has everything ready in an armory locker. So call or text him when you get a minute once you're on Humphreys."

"I will. What else?"

"Someone at LAX will hand you a briefcase with everything you need like we discussed. I'll keep you in the loop as things develop. Have a safe trip."

The call ended. And Porter double-checked his bags before calling a cab.

****

Namil Seu walked briskly to the market in the residential area of Daejeon, South Korea. Today was his six-year-old daughter's birthday, and he needed to purchase a cake and presents. This marked the first time he could celebrate it with his little girl and her mother.

The convicted felon served five years in the Pohang Correctional Institution for felony larceny and breaking-and-entering. He and an accomplice broke into a precious metals warehouse and, not satisfied with the bullion gold and silver they'd snatched—opened the safe and robbed it. There was only one problem. The cash was counterfeit. The KNPA found both men in less than two weeks.

Without warning, a white minivan pulled to the curb several feet in front of him. A bald, burly man emerged from the vehicle's open side door and grabbed Namil, throwing the skinny young man into the back before sliding the panel shut. The bald man put a black hood over Namil's head, blinding him.

"Who the hell are you? What's this about?"

"Shut up."

The pain accompanying those words knocked him unconscious. And Namil fell into a deep and dreamless sleep.

****

"Hey, kid. Are you awake?"

The bald man repeatedly slapped Namil's face, the young man groggy and disoriented, the hood off. He sat on a cold concrete floor against the wall of a dimly lit room with his hands clasped in metal handcuffs behind him. Seeing the furnishings and smelling the stale beer and residual cigarette smoke, Namil believed he was in a bar. Several feet away, two impeccably dressed middle-aged men sat at a table, staring at him. The suits looked sharp, and the pair wore matching and expensive watches.

His bald head glistening with sweat, the big man placed his hands under Namil's armpits and hoisted him up—helping him to a chair at the table. Once seated, Namil couldn't help but breathe in the cologne. The bald man retreated behind the bar, where he watched and listened.

"Do you know who we are?" the man with graying temples queried. The men looked alike. Namil believed the man with the graying hair to be the older of the two. Then it came to him.

"You're the Dokgo brothers. I've seen your pictures in the papers."

It was common knowledge that the brothers owned a great deal of real estate in the area, both residential and commercial. Including several bars, just like this one. They also operated several underground casinos and moved large quantities of narcotics.

The older brother nodded. "Good. I'm Ryung Dokgo. This is my brother, Jaewon. And the man behind the bar is Whan Kym."

"What do you want from me? I told my probation officer I'm on the straight-and-narrow, and I promised my woman I'd stay out of trouble. I went out to buy my kid a birthday cake and presents when your man grabbed me."

Ryung glanced at the bald man. "Whan, take those handcuffs off Mr. Seu."

The bald man grunted as he climbed down off the barstool and removed the handcuffs from behind Namil. The young man rubbed his wrists, red from irritation.

"Better, yes?" Ryung inquired.

"Yes, sir. I still don't know why I'm here. My woman's going to worry where I went."

"This won't take long. We're interested in hiring you. I apologize for the unorthodox method we used in getting this interview, but we had no other way. You possess a particular skill set we find ourselves in need of."

Namil's brow furrowed. "Skill set? I think you have the wrong man."

"No, we have the right man. It's come to our attention that you're an accomplished safecracker who ran into a little bad luck. We were told you also work as a bartender."

"I tend bar in a social club across town; it's the only place that would hire me. But I don't touch safes anymore."

Ryung cocked his head. "Having such a talent, it seems a shame to let it go to waste. It makes me sad. Are you saddened, Jaewon?"

"I'm saddened, yes. Saddened for her." Jaewon took out his cell phone and placed it in front of Namil. On the cell phone was a photo of Namil's daughter and girlfriend, taken outside of her mother's apartment building recently.

Namil's eyes widened. "How do you know about them?"

"What an adorable child," Jaewon replied. "Wow, your girlfriend is pretty too."

"You wouldn't."

"Jaewon and I wouldn't touch your child or woman," Ryung said. "However, the same isn't true for Whan over there."

Namil glanced over. Whan held a large Bowie knife with a hideous grin.

"What would you have me do?"

"Before I answer, let me say we'll pay for the work you do on our behalf. I doubt you're running a charity, and we're not communists," Ryung said.

"Paid well," Jaewon added. "Making it a win-win for everyone. Well, maybe not everyone. Let's say everyone in this room."

Ryung rubbed his chin. "Your father has a cousin, Kiwoo Jong. Am I right?"

Namil nodded. The depth of the intelligence these two gathered was impressive.

"Kiwoo's current employer owns bars in Anjeong-ri. His name is Myung-Dae Tang. Have you ever heard of him?"

"I've heard stories. People say he's old and psychotic. I'm sure they're only half right."

Jaewon chucked. "You disbelieve the stories?"

"Maybe there's *some* truth. But I think they're exaggerated."

"As luck would have it, Mr. Tang is looking for a bartender," Jaewon said. "We believe Kiwoo's influence will help you get that job."

Namil shrugged. "If I asked Kiwoo, sure. But I still don't understand."

"Here's what we want you to do," Ryung said. He and Jaewon disclosed the rest of their plan.

Chapter Ten

A large man wearing a regulation U.S. Army camouflage jacket and uniform waited outside a security checkpoint at Seoul's Gimpo Airport. He held up a crudely written cardboard sign bearing Porter's name.

Porter wore civilian clothes—decked out in a leather jacket, denim jeans, hiking boots, and sweater. The cart Porter rented carried the duffle and garment bags, along with the briefcase Stillson arranged for. Porter approached the large man.

"Are you from Camp Humphreys?"

The big man nodded. "Corporal Claude Dunbarton." Dunbarton held out his hand, and Porter shook it. "You're gonna freeze to death wearing that leather coat, Sarge."

"I came here from LAX, so I'll have to buy a ski jacket."

They continued toward the door marked for ground transportation. Soon the pair sat in a Camp Humphreys motor pool sedan, creeping their way through city gridlock. Porter found Dunbarton to be engaging and unafraid to render an opinion. They discussed Tomlinson's sudden disappearance and Anjeong-ri nightlife.

Then Dunbarton said something Porter didn't expect. "A lot of guys get married here, especially those getting out of the suck and goin' home. That's gotta be a happy day, getting your separation orders. Anjeong-ri is just down this hill."

Porter remembered his last day as a genuine soldier. Getting separation orders was one of his better days. He had no intention of ever wearing a uniform again, yet here he was. And the last thing he wanted to do back then was to get married.

"Did I hear that right? They get married *after* they get their separation orders?"

"It happens here, and it happens *a lot*. Some guys have been with their women a while, others not so much. My buddies in other units don't see it, either. Did that happen in Japan?"

Porter shook his head. "No."

Anjeong-ri came into view. And beyond the village's commercial district sat Camp Humphreys, complete with twenty-foot high white walls and crowned with razor wire. The wide gatehouse stood dead center, and Porter could make out an MP sentry waving a car through. Even from this distance, Porter could make out the letters: Camp Humphreys Garrison. The place had all the charm of a maximum-security prison.

This road became the Anjeong-ri thoroughfare, the village's Main Street. There was one stoplight, and the thoroughfare effectively cut Anjeong-ri in half. Cramped two-story commercial buildings ran along both sides of the street. An elaborate temple on the left side of the thoroughfare appeared majestic, but only because everything surrounding it was cookie-cutter bland.

Entering village traffic, Dunbarton slowed down.

Locals and GIs alike walked the streets, window-shopping. Several of the young women either carried an infant in a baby wrap or pushed a stroller.

Dunbarton stopped the sedan at the front gate barricade, and a tall, beefy MP emerged from the gatehouse. Dunbarton and Porter flashed their identification.

"New man checking in," Dunbarton said.

"Pull the car over there, Corporal," the MP told Dunbarton, pointing to a pair of parking spaces reserved for the occasion. "You got bags, Sarge?"

"Two in the trunk plus this briefcase."

"Bring everything inside."

Dunbarton cut the engine and walked to the back of the car, opening the trunk.

Porter lugged the duffle bag and briefcase while Dunbarton snagged the garment bag. The canines in cages didn't blink as they passed.

"Copy of your orders," the MP said to Porter, who opened the briefcase to comply.

A shorter MP put both bags on an x-ray conveyor belt like those in an airport. He examined the contents over the monitor. "Bags are clean."

Dunbarton started hauling the duffle and garment bags back to the car.

The taller MP gestured to the briefcase. "What else is in there?"

"Copies of orders. Medical and dental records," Porter replied.

The tall MP looked in the back compartment and pointed to the GPS device. "What's that?"

"Run-of-the-mill GPS. I like to hike; it sets a starting point in case I can't get my bearings."

The MP looked it over and nodded. "Welcome to Camp Humphreys Garrison."

Dunbarton restarted the car as Porter climbed back in, carrying the briefcase.

"Any trouble, Sarge?"

"Nah. Call me Mike. And thanks for taking the bags."

"No biggie. You want the tour?"

"I checked out the website, Claude. Most of the base services are to the west, and we're to the east. They keep all the spook units to the east."

Dunbarton nodded and took a right at the gate. "That about sums it up."

Of all the military installations he'd ever been on, and there had been several, this place had a vibe all its own. *It's just different, that's all. It's the op spooking you.*

On the snow-covered recreation fields below, companies of soldiers marched in formation. A series of faded-white cinder block structures were in a row on a road off to the right. Dunbarton stopped the car in the second building's U-shaped courtyard. The sign in front read "501st Intelligence Battalion, Company B."

The pair exited the car, and Porter took a good look around while Dunbarton opened the trunk.

Across the paved road sat a large commercial building with a sign that read "Enlisted Men's Club." Fifty yards up the hill from that was a large Quonset hut with a roof vent emitting the smell of fried food.

Just up the knoll from the barracks on this side of the road were two long double-wide faded white trailers, joined end-to-end. Across the road next to the EM Club stood a bus stop.

"What the hell is that supposed to be?" Porter gestured to the long cigar-shaped double-wide.

"Small PX. Big one is across camp."

Porter gestured to the Quonset hut. "That the mess hall?"

"On this side of camp, yeah."

Porter turned to the paved road that disappeared beyond the incline across the road from the PX. "Where does that road lead?"

"Security building is down there. Intel workspaces."

"Is that where I'll be?"

"Nope," Dunbarton chuckled. "Admin office is in the barracks."

There were glass doors at the front and sides of the building. Porter took the duffle bag and briefcase, while Dunbarton grabbed the garment bag.

"So in theory I could roll out of bed, toss on a uniform, and be in the office?"

"In theory, sure. But I wouldn't recommend it."

"We'll stow your gear, and then I'll take you to the admin office," Dunbarton said. "The major and master sergeant are anxious to meet you."

"Meet me? My orders are to report tomorrow at 0800."

"My orders are to bring you to the admin office after you stow your gear."

While Porter outranked Dunbarton, it made more sense to simply comply. Why wage war your first day over something so petty, especially on a temporary assignment? And burning the bridge he'd built with Dunbarton, who'd proven to be an ally so far, made no sense either. "Sure, Claude. I'm just a little tired."

They entered the building through the front doors. Inside the barracks, the pair took a left and walked down a burgundy-carpeted corridor until Dunbarton stopped in front of room number eight. He fished a key from a front pocket and unlocked the door, letting Porter and his duffle bag in first.

It was a standard enough barracks room, not unlike the one he left in Misawa. Even the tall, double-door wardrobe and lock keypad seemed similar. Against the far wall Porter noticed a writing desk with a pair of books stashed neatly in a compartment. They were *The Holy Bible KJV* and a *U.S. Army Sergeant Advancement Exam Study Guide.*

Porter untied the mattress, laying it flat over the springs. He then put the briefcase, duffle and garment bags on it.

"Here's the wardrobe combination. Don't lose it." Dunbarton handed Porter a small sticky label with a five-digit combination. Porter punched in the numbers, and the lock released. After opening it, Porter hung the garment bag inside.

"Ralph Simpson's got the bunk on the other side of the room," Dunbarton said, gesturing. "He's on a day shift. Bed linen should be in the locker. See it?"

"Got it. Damn, I had my own room back on Zama."

"This side of camp, space is at a premium. That's why a lot of guys have off-base apartments they pay for out-of-pocket." Dunbarton handed keys over, one for the building, the other for the room. "Got your service record and a copy of your orders?"

"In the briefcase."

"You'll need 'em. Might as well get this over with."

With Dunbarton watching, Porter grabbed the briefcase and locked the room. The big man led him down the hall. On the way, a scrawny Korean man scurried by as they passed the bathrooms and showers.

"That's Song-He," Dunbarton said. "His crew has this barracks." Dunbarton then explained the houseboy's roles and the cost associated.

The pair continued down the hall, Dunbarton stopping at the door marked Administration Office. It had been the last two rooms on the right side of the barracks at one time. He knocked.

"Enter," someone from inside shouted.

Dunbarton opened the door for Porter, letting him go in first. The CIA agent apprehensively took center stage.

Porter's eyes met Martz's. The master sergeant sat at an antiquated metal desk that presumably had been Tomlinson's. With the bald head and fit frame, Martz appeared vastly different from what Porter expected. Fitness was generally the first thing senior NCOs discarded on their way up the food chain.

On the other side of the room sat DiSilva, trying his best to appear in command. His pasty face, skinny arms, and potbelly belied Porter's expectations.

"As ordered," Dunbarton said, still standing in the doorway.

"Yes, thank you, Claude," DiSilva said. "Why don't you bring the car back to the motor pool?"

"Yes, sir."

Porter heard the door close from behind.

"I'm Commanding Officer Major DiSilva, and this is head of operations, Master Sergeant Martz. Welcome aboard."

"Sergeant Michael Porter."

"Do you prefer Michael or Mike?" DiSilva asked.

"Mike is fine, sir. Thank you."

Martz eyed him. "Why aren't you in uniform?"

"I came in on a commercial flight from LAX, Top. My orders were to be here at 0800 *tomorrow*. I didn't know you wanted to meet today until Claude told me." Standing there, Porter felt their eyes examining him, looking for fault. And while he expected their scrutiny, all he could do was wait until they'd had enough.

DiSilva asked Porter for his service record. After walking it to him, Martz moved to the bench, relinquishing Tomlinson's desk to Porter. DiSilva and Martz took turns looking at performance reviews and prior duty stations.

"So you came to us from Camp Zama," DiSilva said. "Were you told anything about this duty station when you received your orders?"

"Nothing beyond a heads-up that I'm replacing a guy that went AWOL."

Martz closed the service record, and his head came up slowly as he turned to Porter. "You climbed up the ladder faster than most. Then again, you're older than most. Is there something I'm not understanding?"

"I'm a four-year vet who dropped out of college and decided to give the Army another shot. It's not supernatural, Top." Porter guessed from the look on Martz's face that his reply didn't go over well.

Service record in hand, Martz stood and slowly walked toward Porter, stopping directly in front of him. Martz's eyes met Porter's and stayed there.

"Here's a concept you'll need to understand quickly. I'll be writing your performance evaluations when they come due. So if you're thinking of getting promoted again anytime soon, my input *will* affect the outcome. Got me?"

"Loud and clear."

DiSilva cleared his throat from across the room. "That'll be enough drama, gentlemen."

The master sergeant placed the service record on the desk before pivoting back to the bench.

"We wanted to have this chat before you bolted into Anjeong-ri and did something…ill-advised," DiSilva said. He stood, grabbing his hat off the desk. "This place is different from most, and we thought a quick orientation might be in order. I'll let Master Sergeant Martz explain further." His eyes moved to Martz. "I'll be in the security building if you need me."

"Yes, sir," Martz said.

Remembering protocol, Porter got to his feet as DiSilva left the room.

Martz waited until DiSilva closed the door before commandeering the major's desk. Porter sat back down, and Martz flashed a gap-toothed grin before putting his feet up on the desk.

"We're gonna be working closely together, and it's important you and I communicate. I'm sure you're excited about going into the village tonight. Every swinging dick comes off the plane thinking this is one big wild world of pussy. What you need to understand is there *are* rules, some more subtle than others."

Porter was sure from Martz's smooth delivery and diction this speech was well-rehearsed.

"Did Claude give you the rundown of places out-of-bounds?"

"Pharmacies, barber shops, and massage parlors.

Are there more?"

"I'll keep it simple. If there's not another soldier inside or an English letter on the sign, stay the fuck *out*. CID is everywhere, and it's for your own safety they are. Do yourself a favor, run with guys that've been in-country, and don't run alone. Ralph Simpson will help you acclimate. That's why I put you together."

Porter nodded. "Okay."

"Did Claude tell you about the houseboys and how it works?"

"He did."

"Good." Martz nodded. "It saves on barracks inspections. But I insist that personal grooming and appearance be in accordance with Army standards. I'm also a stickler for discipline. Showing up late for a shift or being impaired on duty *will* get my attention in the worst of all possible ways."

Martz paused, looking like he expected a response.

"I understand."

"Hope you do. We're too close to North Korea to be unprepared or sloppy. I have to bear down because we need to maintain a state of suspicious alertness despite the allure of Anjeong-ri. You don't have to like it. But you do need to comply. We're sixty miles away from a country that won't think twice about killing everyone here and launching ICBMs to Hawaii and the west coast. One other thing—I don't give a shit how they did things on Camp Zama. Here, we do things my way."

Wish I had a nickel for every time I've ever heard that.

"I left some things on the desk we need to talk about. That plastic credit card with your name is a rations card. You'll need it for PX purchases and the mess hall. Lose it, and I'll have your ass."

"Rations card?"

"Along with prostitution, the village has a very active black market. And because of it, the Army rations alcohol and tobacco products. The card resets every thirty days, and what you don't use, you lose, which I personally believe only encourages black marketeering."

Martz then itemized each allotment and explained the keys.

Porter waited until Martz finished. "I'm not a heavy drinker, and I don't smoke."

"Funny thing about this place. Everyone seems to learn pretty fast. I want this office and all of its contents locked whenever you leave, and this room is empty. There's a safe tucked away in that bookshelf behind you. That's where we keep our blank IDs."

"And where's the combination if someone needs a replacement?"

"Then you pick up the phone and find me, Major DiSilva, or Captain Lambert; he's the unit executive officer."

"And if I'm alone and none of you are available?"

"Then the moron who lost his card will have to wait. Your computer's password is spook501. All lowercase. Got that?"

"Very original," Porter said.

Martz smiled a gap-toothed grin. "Another wiseass zinger. You'd better start getting on my good side, and I mean fast. Questions?"

"What's the best way of getting a cab out here?"

"You just got here. What the hell do you need a

cab for?"

"I've got a buddy from Zama that works the flight line. I want to say hello."

"Call ahead or catch one over at the EM Club. Taxis rarely sit around waiting for business on this side of camp. There's a list of phone numbers to your right under the desk protector."

Porter found the list. He pulled out his cell phone and quickly punched in the cab company's phone number while Martz got to his feet and put his jacket on.

"I've gotta go to the intel building. Why don't you go back to your room and settle in? Ralph will take you into Anjeong-ri tonight if you're not too tired. I'll expect you here at 0800 tomorrow morning. Not 0801 or whenever you think to get around to it, this ain't no country club. Anything else?"

"I think I'm good," Porter said.

"We'll find out soon enough. The MPs here don't put up with a lot of shit, either. Crack wise with them at the gate or on the street, and they'll throw your ass in the stockade."

Porter waited until Martz closed the door before powering on the desktop computer and punching in the password. He logged on to his agency email account and found what he needed. As Stillson promised, the email had his spotter's name and contact number. Porter punched the info into his cell phone and shut the computer down before locking the office. He returned to the room down the hall.

He called Brock Ferguson from his cell phone. Calling the spotter from a cell phone without identifying the op or disclosing classified information violated nothing.

"Ferguson," a man's voice answered.

"Hey. Mike Porter. How you doing?"

"I'm good. Glad you got here safely."

"Any chance we could meet in the armory in an hour?"

"Sure. Meet me out front. And bring a copy of your orders."

"Copy that. See you then."

Porter checked the time and called for a cab to meet him in front of the EM Club in forty-five minutes. Then he started unpacking. He thought about calling his mother back in Vermont, but after checking the time difference, decided it could wait until tomorrow.

Forty minutes later, Porter was still unpacking when he peeked out of his room's window and saw a cab in the EM Club parking lot. He grabbed what he needed and jogged outside.

Chapter Eleven

The armory was one of the bigger buildings on Camp Humphreys. Surrounded by a razor-wire fence and sentries posted on each side, it was also one of the more secure. Surveillance cameras faced every angle from under the metal roof eaves. Porter approached it on foot, having ditched the cab when he turned his medical and dental records over to the camp hospital. He checked in with the MPs after meeting Ferguson.

Aside from housing munitions, the Camp Humphreys armory allowed for base MPs to train with small arms. There were two locker rooms, one for men and another for women. The lockers housed their weapons and body armor.

Porter saw a tall, thin man pacing by the armory's front glass double doors.

"Are you Brock Ferguson?" Porter asked.

"Finally, we meet." Ferguson extended his hand, and Porter shook it. "You like Michael or Mike?"

"Mike's fine."

"You remembered to bring a copy of your orders?"

"Yeah."

"I put your gear in locker twenty-one—right next to mine. They'll give you an inventory list and locker combination," Ferguson said.

By the front door, Porter noticed an electric eye and doorbell. Ferguson swiped an armory ID through a card-reader and faced the security camera. The door buzzed, and Ferguson pulled it open, letting Porter enter first. Ferguson showed the young corporal sitting behind the access cage with the same ID he used to get in the building. The corporal's name tag read McFarland.

"You're new here?" McFarland asked Porter.

"Yeah. I need an armory ID." Porter gave the young man a copy of his orders and held up his military ID.

McFarland looked at the computer monitor as he examined the orders and pecked away on the keyboard. The printer on the shelf behind the man whirred to life, spitting out terms and conditions and the locker's contents and combination, just as Ferguson said.

"Make sure you turn in your armory ID and the contents of your locker before transferring off of Camp Humphreys permanently. Step on the tape, and I'll fix you up with a picture ID."

Porter stood at the X. The computer's camera took the photo. McFarland laminated the card and gave it to Porter, still warm.

"Swipe the card's bar through the reader and face the front door security camera to get buzzed in," McFarland said. "We're open and staffed twenty-four seven."

"Thanks."

Porter followed Ferguson to the empty locker room down the hall. It was the first room on the right and filled with tall orange metal-mesh, double-door lockers stationed around the room's walls and in aisles. Black metal-mesh benches faced the lockers. And right now, they were the room's only occupants.

"Does this building have showers?" Porter asked.

"No. But the rec building across the street does. That's open twenty-four hours a day too."

Ferguson sat on the bench in front of his own locker; Porter's locker was to its left. He secretly observed Ferguson punch in his combination before looking at the printout to open his own.

Porter first examined the white body armor, helmet, boots, cowl, and gloves. He and Ferguson would resemble skinny astronauts. Farther back, he found the sniper rifle and five-cylinder riot gun. On the top shelf lay a nine-millimeter pistol, along with polymer ankle and shoulder holsters. On the locker floor stood boxes of ammo and tear gas canisters.

Porter showed Ferguson the riot gun. "It's Christmas morning in here."

"Hippie control, Mike?"

Porter removed a canister of tear gas, showing it to his spotter. "This'll slow 'em down if we get pinned in on foot. What about you?"

"M-4 and twenty-gauge shotgun."

"You didn't want a twelve-gauge?"

"I wanted something light. I figure we'll be on the move. How much does that riot gun weigh?"

"Feel for yourself." Porter handed it over.

Ferguson slung it over a shoulder. "Not bad."

"You tried on the body armor, Brock?"

"Call me Fergie. Yeah. It's lighter than you might think."

Porter removed the armor's chest plate. "What's this made of, do you know?"

"Kevlar bi-weave, I think," Ferguson said. "I'm sure McFarland can pull the specs."

Porter put the chest plate back and removed the helmet. "These things have respirators and night-vision built in?"

"State-of-the-art," Ferguson replied. As Porter's spotter, Ferguson was not only responsible for identifying the target but also disclosing distance and identifying other variables that affected aim and confirming a hit or miss.

With Ferguson watching, Porter put on the hard-plastic ankle holster and slapped a mag into the pistol before putting it in the holster.

"You're taking that now?" Ferguson asked.

"Either that or I buy one on the black market."

"The gun laws here are archaic…this ain't back home."

"I know that."

"Did Stillson authorize it?"

Porter shook his head. "No. You gonna tell him?"

"Of course not. But get caught with it off the base, and Camp Humphreys will report it as stolen. Then it's a State Department issue that turns into an agency issue."

"The dude I'm replacing went AWOL. Nobody knows where he went or why. I appreciate the concern, but I'm still carrying."

"Suit yourself. But if Stillson straight-up asks, I'll tell him the truth."

Porter nodded. "That's cool. Anyplace in town better than the others for R and R?"

"Depends on the music you like." Ferguson went down the list of watering holes.

"If we see each other off base, we're strangers; Stillson made that clear. He also wants us running, full gear, four miles every other day. He wants us shooting outdoors too. You've been training on your own?"

"I've been doing three miles a night since I got here."

Porter looked at him and chuckled. "Well, I haven't. We'll start tomorrow. Meet me here at five-thirty," Porter said. "Buy some hand weights, ten-pounders, first chance you get."

Ferguson nodded. "There's a gravel pit at the northeast quadrant of the camp where we can shoot outside. They halted construction of some project until the spring, and I got permission from the MPs. You check in with them yet?"

"I did. What kind of distance?"

"Two hundred yards, give or take."

"It'll do. Can you free up on weekends? With such short days, it's the only practical time I can get out without drawing attention," Porter said.

"Weekends are good for me too. Do you know who?"

Porter shook his head. "Don't know who. Don't know when."

"I hope they'll give us a little heads-up."

"I'm sure they will. Can I ask you a question, Fergie?"

"Sure. What?"

"Why'd you volunteer for this?"

Ferguson's expression was one of mock horror. "Are you kiddin'? You'll never get this close to something with so much on the line the rest of your life." He took a breath. "How could I say no? What about you?"

"I heard that." Porter doubted that he sold it, but

Ferguson didn't call him out. Besides, Ferguson's reason sounded better than anything he could conjure up.

Porter stowed his gear, and they split up outside the armory. After that, Porter walked into the big PX to buy a ski jacket, gym bag, warm gloves, running shoes, and ten-pound hand weights. Then he took a cab back to the barracks and unlocked room eight.

"You must be Sergeant Porter."

Porter hadn't closed the barrack's room door when the chubby-cheeked, curly-haired Ralph Simpson appeared, hand extended. Wearing dress slacks and a collared, button-down shirt, Simpson looked more like a Jehovah's Witness than a soldier. Porter forced a grin and shook Simpson's hand.

"Call me Mike. That makes you Ralph Simpson."

"I wondered what happened to you. Looks like you found the PX," Simpson said, eyeing the trio of bulging plastic PX bags.

"I dropped off my medical and dental records and then looked up a friend who works the flight line. Yeah, I needed a few things."

"I'll bet you're eager to go into the village tonight. Most nugs are."

Porter squinted and scratched his head. "Nug?"

"New guy. You're the nug until a new nug takes your place."

Porter nodded. "I wouldn't say eager. Curious is more like it."

"Top wants me to show you around."

"Martz told me the same thing, but I don't want to put you out, Ralph. I'm sure I can manage."

"I gave Top my word. But only for tonight. I'm not

as big a fan of Anjeong-ri as others around here are."

"It's okay to sit this one out. If Martz asks, I'll tell him you showed me around."

"That would be a lie."

"Consider it a noble lie. Ever read Plato's *Republic*, Ralph?"

"The Bible is the only book I need."

"I'd say that, and the *Army Sergeant Advancement Exam Study Guide*." Porter gestured toward the desk.

"Okay. Then two books."

"Really, Ralph, if I can handle Baghdad, I sure as hell can handle Anjeong-ri."

Simpson huffed and retreated to his side of the room. Porter took the reprieve as an opportunity to finish unpacking.

A knock came on the door. Porter recognized Song-He. The chief houseboy reinforced what Dunbarton told him earlier about their services and fees. Money changed hands, instructions given, and Porter felt good knowing he wouldn't have to deal with Martz about an unmade bed or wrinkled blouse for the duration of his stay.

Simpson reappeared, sitting at the desk with the reading lamp on, perusing his study guide. That he was quiet was good enough, and Porter readied his uniform for his first day.

Porter hoped a shower would help shake the cobwebs. Fourteen hours in the air for a guy that didn't enjoy flying felt like a lifetime. He stripped, removed the ankle holster with his eyes on Simpson's back, and put the loaded weapon, his wallet, and GPS on the locker's top shelf. Porter then put a towel around his waist before grabbing his toiletry bag and closing the locker door, leaving everything else on the bed.

"You gonna be around for the next fifteen minutes, Ralph? I'm gonna grab a shower."

"Knock yourself out."

Porter walked down to the showers. He introduced himself to a couple of the men from the unit while he shaved. Then Porter returned to the room, where Simpson still sat at the desk, absorbed in study. Porter dressed.

"So, what'd you decide about going into Anjeong-ri, Ralph? Forget about what you think you owe Martz. What do *you* want to do?"

Simpson turned his head, but not enough to make eye contact.

"I hate Anjeong-ri. Only I gave my word."

Porter opened the locker and slipped on the ankle holster with a cautious eye on his roommate, sliding the pistol in next, gently snapping it shut. He grabbed the GPS from the top shelf and opened the briefcase on his bed, snagged the map of Anjeong-ri, and spread it out.

"Do me a favor and point out a couple of places worth going to on this map, Ralph."

Simpson got out of the chair and stood alongside Porter, examining the map.

"Duffy Club is popular." He pointed to it. "Some guys like Rasputin's and Memories."

"Now you can look Martz in the eye and tell him you showed me around Anjeong-ri with a clear conscience."

"I'll tell him you didn't want me going with you. That's the truth of it. You got a key to the building, right?"

Porter fished through his pockets. Everyone gave

him a key today. "I'm pretty sure."

"You'll need it to get back in. Houseboys lock the barracks after dark."

Simpson went back to his study guide. Porter snipped the tags on the ski jacket before slipping a full ammo magazine in a pocket. *Just in case.*

"You want me to lock the door, Ralph?"

"I'm good."

Porter walked into the hallway and exited the east-side glass door, the frigid night air giving a jolt. He was glad to have a heavier jacket; even without the wind chill, it was brutally cold. And he was glad not to have to drag an apprehensive Simpson along. This wasn't a church social.

The agent looked to the camp's front gate and turned his GPS on. Under the street lamps, lines of men from both sides of Camp Humphreys formed to exit the base. He walked down and got in line. He felt conspicuous and vulnerable. Most of these soldiers traveled in packs of threes or fours.

With the sentries focused on incoming vehicles and pedestrians, leaving Camp Humphreys on foot was as simple as walking out the gate. But with so many soldiers squeezing through one long, narrow exit, the bottleneck was predictable. Patiently, Porter inched his way off the camp until he set foot in Anjeong-ri.

Chapter Twelve

Soldiers, cabs, villagers, and pairs of MPs wearing white hats and gloves swarmed the streets. Fast-food vendors lined both sides of the thoroughfare; the pace and scents reminded Porter of Lansdowne Street outside Fenway Park, both before and after a Red Sox game.

Porter randomly followed a cluster of soldiers as they took the first street to the left off the thoroughfare. One hundred yards down, past a variety of well-lit shops, he took in the yellow glow from neon lights ahead and heard the din of rock music. From the map he memorized, this alleyway led to Duffy Club.

Trash and debris clung to the sides of the buildings, and a pungent odor of urine hung in the air. Men walked up and down the street in various degrees of inebriation, some holding hands with relatively unattractive women.

The closer he got, the clearer the music. Up ahead, a pair of MPs approached, and Porter felt a knot form. Coming face-to-face with the MPs was certain—he only hoped they wouldn't notice the ankle holster.

"You must be new here. A word of advice, friend," the taller MP said. "Keep your wallet in your front pocket. Pros work these streets."

Porter quickly moved the wallet. "Thanks."

The MPs continued on their way, and Porter felt

relieved and moved on. Rock music blasted louder still, and Porter saw Duffy Club's lemon-yellow neon sign.

Out front, food vendors worked a growing crowd of GIs, and Porter got in line to enter the bar. If there was an occupancy limit, this place had to be in violation. A pair of men leaving had women, their arms around each other as they walked. The line progressed at a pace that suited Porter, and soon he was inside.

GIs and the women they were with filled the tables. To the right was a long bar with thirty barstools, every one occupied. GIs stood and mingled between the bar and tables. A blue haze of cigarette smoke hung in the air. To the left, a hardwood dance floor with several couples dancing so poorly that Porter thought he crashed a wedding reception.

He fought through the crowd, creeping toward the bar, finding a spot between a drunken soldier and a working girl intent on belittling him. Two bartenders worked feverishly amid a pyramid of liquor bottles. A beautiful woman from behind the bar suddenly appeared, catching his eye. Dressed in a stylish blouse and slacks, she differentiated herself from the uniformed bartenders and waitresses. She looked at him and grinned before saying something to one of the bartenders. Then she disappeared.

The inebriated soldier on the barstool to his left suddenly stood, his hand over his mouth. With traces of vomit slipping between his fingers, he ran into the crowd, pushing his way through to what Porter assumed was a restroom. Because Porter stood off the soldier's shoulder, he slid onto the barstool.

"What you want?" the bartender hollered.

"One of those," Porter replied, pointing to a bottle

of Korean beer on the bar two seats over.

Soon the bottle came. "One thousand won," the bartender said. "Or one U.S. dollar."

Porter handed the man a five-dollar bill. "Don't forget about me."

The bartender snatched the bill, grinned, and nodded.

Porter took a hit off the beer, surprised it tasted so good. From his vantage point at the bar, he couldn't see much. There were too many bodies on all sides.

One beer led to two and two to three as Porter waited to see the beautiful woman again. If not for her, he would've returned to the barracks. All things considered, the experience disappointed. The frenzy soon thinned, and barstools and tables opened up.

Clack! Porter heard a cue ball strike against another.

"You have a pool table here?" he asked the bartender, who had bottle number four for Porter in his hands, popping the top before serving.

"Four tables around the corner over there." The bartender gestured. "Past the restrooms."

"What time do you close?"

"Two in the morning."

Porter slid off the barstool and grabbed the bottle before heading for the lavatory.

He glanced in the game room along the way. Players occupied all four pool tables. But the last table down got Porter's attention. An animated, husky soldier held court with two others and a trio of women as he handled the pool cue as if playing a guitar. There were several empty drink glasses on a nearby counter.

For no reason, the animated man looked over and

made eye contact with Porter. No smile, no gesture, just a stare that lasted all of five seconds. Then the man picked up where he left off, and Porter walked on.

Once properly relieved, Porter didn't bother looking back into the game room. To stare again risked confrontation, and getting into a bar fight his first night here wouldn't impress anyone he answered to.

As Porter turned the corner from the game room, the gorgeous woman from behind the bar he'd been waiting for appeared out of nowhere. She toppled into him, grabbing his hands as both regained their balance.

"I'm sorry," Porter said. "I didn't see you."

He looked at her closely. Long black hair came down to her hips, her high cheekbones giving way to coal-black, almond-shaped eyes. She even wore a scent that he liked.

"It's my fault. I didn't look where I was going," she said, her English better than he expected. She smiled, and he felt weak in the knees.

"Do you manage this place?"

"Yes. You're new on Camp Humphreys."

That it wasn't a question bothered Porter. "I am. But how do you know?"

"Your hair is too long. And I've not seen you before."

"I suppose that's true."

"Are you with the 501st?"

"How the hell did you guess that?"

"Are you a friend of Cam or Gil?"

Porter shook his head. "Who are they?"

"The guys at the last pool table down you were looking at."

She's been watching me. "I got here this afternoon

and don't know anyone. You're very observant."

"Can we talk for a minute?"

Porter grinned. "Has anyone ever said no to you?"

"Come," she said, gesturing for him to follow.

He watched her glance at an overhead speaker along the way. *She's looking for cameras. Gotta be a Chinese or North Korean asset.*

She led him to the last table against the far wall, now empty. Porter took the seat opposite her and put the beer bottle on the table. Her eyes met his.

"What do you do?" she asked.

"You mean what is my job?" *Yup. She's an operative. Damn.*

"Yes."

"I'm only a clerk. What's your name?"

"My name is Jeong Guy. And yours is what?"

Porter fought off her eyes; he was getting lost in them. "Mike Porter. I'm pleased to meet you, Jeong."

Porter held out his hand for her to shake. Jeong's palm was moist, her fingers soft and delicate. He didn't want to let go.

"Did you take over for Alex Tomlinson?"

Porter sat back, this innocent flirtation having vectored into deeper waters.

"Out of everyone stationed here, you guessed that?"

Jeong grinned. "You're with the 501st and brand-new."

"That's twice you've surprised me. Yes, but how do you *know* that?"

"Your hands. I can sometimes…see."

Oh, c'mon. You don't expect me to believe that, do you? "Did you know Alex Tomlinson?"

Her head dropped as she glanced at the floor. "Yes."

"Do you remember the last time you saw him?"

She looked up and reestablished eye contact. "I remember. But we can't talk here. Would you be willing to meet somewhere outside of Anjeong-ri?"

"Sure. But why can't we talk in Anjeong-ri?"

"Is dangerous for me; I'll explain later. There are cameras in here."

"Who's watching and why?"

Jeong shook her head. "So we will meet outside Anjeong-ri?"

Porter nodded. "Okay. But where?"

One bartender shouted in Korean, telling Jeong they were low on ginger ale and gin. She got to her feet.

"We'll talk again soon, Mike Porter." Just as quickly as she appeared, Jeong vanished.

Porter stood, feeling mildly buzzed. That the beautiful woman knew something about Tomlinson was exciting and unsettling in equal parts. *But why the cameras in here? She didn't ask about my security clearance. Maybe she doesn't work for the Chinese or North Koreans.*

He walked back to Camp Humphreys before 2300 and turned the GPS off after passing the sentries at the gate. The air didn't feel as cold as it had earlier. *Better start enjoying these nights, buddy boy. Soon you'll be flying north.*

Porter entered the barracks, relieved that his key actually worked. He saw light bleed from under his room's door before he unlocked and opened it. Simpson had the reading lamp on at the desk.

Simpson's head turned. "Well, well, well. I can

smell you from here. So what'd you think?"

"Overrated."

Simpson nodded and chuckled and turned back to his book. "So now you know."

Porter set the alarm clock, opened his locker, and began undressing. He again paid particular attention to Simpson as the holster and pistol came off. Porter closed the wardrobe door and fell asleep two minutes after the second sock hit the carpet.

****

As Duffy Club prepared to close, Myung-Dae played the video back on his monitor several times. Employees thought they knew the location of the cameras, but Myung-Dae had Gunn and Kiwoo move them from time to time to keep everyone honest.

Okay, so who is this guy? Myung-Dae called Gunn's cell phone from his office telephone.

Soon Gunn knocked on the door. "You need something?"

"Come over here and have a look at my computer screen."

Gunn walked to Myung-Dae's desk as the old man repositioned the monitor and played back the video of Jeong and Porter.

"Who's the soldier?" Gunn asked.

"That's why I called. I'm not sure. I want you to watch her until further notice."

"Seriously? With everything else we've got going on, you want me wasting time watching her?"

"I want to know if this warrants further action. I'd so hoped she learned something."

"Let's face it, Myung-Dae. Some learn slower than others."

"If you see them together, I want to know when, where, and for how long. Find out who the man is, who his friends are, which unit."

"I'll do my best, Myung-Dae."

Gunn exited the office.

Kiwoo stuck his head in the open doorway. "You have a guy here asking for you about that bartender's job. He's been here for some time; I told him to wait."

"What's his name?"

"Namil Seu. I know him. He tended bar at a social club in Daejeon I know."

"He is no longer employed at the social club?"

"No. He told me he quit," Kiwoo said.

"You think I should hire him?"

"You're looking for a bartender, and he tends bar. If you don't want to talk to him, I'll send him away."

"I'll talk to him. Let's hope he can work under pressure. This isn't a social club."

"He's a good kid. You'll like him."

"Does he have a criminal record?"

Kiwoo recoiled. "How would I know?"

"But is he trustworthy, Kiwoo?"

Kiwoo considered the question.

"A simple yes or no will do."

"Yes."

"Then send him in."

Based on Kiwoo's recommendation, Myung-Dae hired the man. Tomorrow night he would introduce Namil Seu to Jeong. Myung-Dae understood she appreciated interviewing the people working for her, but ultimately it was his decision and money. And tomorrow night's crowd would be as good a barometer as any.

Chapter Thirteen

The alarm clock on the floor rang, jolting Porter awake. His mind quickly turned to the beautiful woman he met last night. *Why is it dangerous for her to talk in the village about Tomlinson?*

"Hey, Ralph, you there?"

Hearing nothing, Porter crept to the desk to take a peek. The bed was empty and unmade. Somehow Simpson had dressed and slipped past him. Jetlagged or not, Porter found that unnerving.

He opened his locker to begin his day. Once again, he met others from the unit as they readied for a day shift. The introductions were brief, everyone in a hurry.

When Porter felt ready, he examined himself in the mirror one last time. He checked the time on his cell phone, 0753. Except for the mildly bloodshot eyes, he hadn't appeared this regulation since his second boot camp. After locking the room, he headed down the hall, office key in hand. The aspirin he took earlier started kicking in.

Finding the office door already unlocked, he entered. Across the room, Martz sat at DiSilva's desk with his feet up, reading *Stars and Stripes*, the U.S. Armed Forces newspaper. Closing the door, he heard Martz fold the newspaper.

"Two more minutes would've cost you a night of R and R."

"I'm not late."

"No. But you were definitely flirting with it. I should've mentioned this yesterday, but I hoped you would've taken the initiative after our meeting. When did you last get a haircut?"

"The day before I left Zama."

Martz chuckled. "Then you should ask for a refund because you got cheated. When you and Claude break for lunch, I want him to show you where the barbershop is across camp. I'll expect that mop cut."

"Whatever," Porter mumbled under his breath as he unlocked the master-key lockbox.

"I'm sorry—what was that? I didn't catch all of it. You got something to say?"

"I didn't say anything."

"That's what I thought. So what did you think of Anjeong-ri? Did Ralph show you all the local hot spots?"

"Ralph sat this one out, at my request. He didn't want to go, not really. I thought it best to respect that."

"Yeah, okay. Well? What'd you think?"

"I think you people should get out more. Borderline depressing."

"I'm surprised to hear you say that. Just be careful who you associate with."

"Are we talking about guys in the unit or village bogeymen lurking behind sausage carts?"

"Both, actually."

"You have a list? It'd make things easier."

Martz shook his head and chuckled as he put the newspaper back on the desk before getting to his feet. He grabbed his hat and jacket. "I'll be at my office in the security building. Call only if you can't figure it out

103

for yourself."

"Okay."

"Claude should be here any minute. He'll show you what he was working on." Martz put his jacket on and left the room.

Porter texted Stillson, telling his agent-in-charge he'd arrived safely and would call soon. Then he began sifting through unit incoming message traffic. Someone knocked on the door, and Porter yelled for whoever it was to enter.

Dunbarton walked in, quickly eyeing DiSilva's side of the office. Satisfied Porter was alone, he grinned. "What the hell did you do to Martz?"

"Nothing. The guy belongs in a dinosaur exhibit in the nearest museum."

"Be careful, dude. He's got the juice to make your time here pure hell."

Porter didn't reply, and the two started working.

****

Ralph Simpson knocked on Martz's office door in the intel/security building and waited until the master sergeant invited him in.

The space was dark and cramped, without windows, which described the entire building. A bank of computer monitors overlooking various workstations occupied one corner. Next to them stood a small metal desk with a single computer monitor, keyboard, reading lamp, and telephone. A large whiteboard was against the wall behind the desk chair, and on it was a two-week schedule, the writing scribbled on by black magic marker. Why Martz preferred the whiteboard to a computer spreadsheet, Simpson had no way of knowing without asking, which he wouldn't think to do.

Martz, wearing reading glasses, glanced up from behind the desk.

"Ralphie, my boy. Whatcha got for me?" Martz removed the glasses. He didn't ask Simpson to sit down because there were no chairs.

"Porter went into town on his own. He gave me the option of begging off, so I did."

"Yeah, he already told me. That's okay; Anjeong-ri nightlife isn't everyone's cup of tea. Is there anything else?"

"Did you see the email I sent you earlier this morning?"

"No." Martz sat up and began pecking away at the keyboard. After finding the email, he opened the attached pictures Simpson sent of Porter's locker contents. "You got these shots before he left for Anjeong-ri last night, Ralph?"

Simpson nodded. "Affirmative."

Martz looked at the second of four photos. "Last I checked, they don't sell handguns or ammo in the camp PX."

"No, they don't, Top."

Martz rubbed his eyes. "Any idea how he appropriated a pistol in such a short space of time?"

"He was on the other side of camp when I got back to the room. Said he dropped off medical and dental records and something about a friend working the flight line before hitting the PX. I honestly don't know how or where he could've pulled it off."

"I doubt he's a magician. So I need another favor, Ralph. I want you to follow him for the next couple of days. Keep a log. What I'd like to know is who he's with and where he went. I'll put you on days for the next week. Hit me up daily by email."

"I'll do the best I can, Top."

"Did he talk about anything or anyone in particular?"

Simpson shook his head. "Nothing you'd think twice about."

Martz ran a hand over his bald head. "What time did he get back?"

"Just after eleven. Question. What if he catches on that I'm tailing him?"

"I'll be curious to learn how he handles it. Don't worry about him over the weekend. There's no need to be too obvious."

"Sure, Top."

"If *anything* doesn't pass the sniff test, you'll email right away, yes?"

"Sure."

"Carry on, Ralph."

Simpson pivoted for the door, happy to be on day shifts for the next week. He studied better at night.

****

Porter and Dunbarton returned from the other side of Camp Humphreys before noon. Porter ran his hand down the back of what had been a healthy head of hair, now reduced to stubble.

They entered the small mess hall on their side of camp. Inside the oversized metal Quonset hut were columns and rows of long metal picnic tables. There were pockets of American and Korean soldiers.

Dunbarton reached for his wallet and produced his rations card. "Got your card? You'll need it."

They passed through the chow line. With a full tray and looking for a place to sit, Porter recognized two of the men from last night. The husky, animated man and his buddy from the Duffy Club game room. Porter spotted vacant seats across from the pair and led Dunbarton to them.

Dunbarton sat down alongside Porter. "You met Cam Shanahan and Gil Trotter yet, Mike?"

Both men had corporal stripes on their camouflage uniforms.

"Mike Porter." Porter shook Shanahan's hand first, then Trotter's.

"Weren't you in Duffy's last night, Sarge?" Shanahan inquired.

"Call me Mike. You were both in the game room. There was another guy with you."

"Mitch Carruthers. He's a medic at the hospital," Trotter said. "I'm Gil."

"So you're Alex's replacement, huh? I go by Cam or Cameron."

Porter nodded as he examined the hamburger on the tray. "Yeah, I'm Tomlinson's replacement."

"What do you think of the place?" Cam asked.

"Martz is a bit of a douchebag. Otherwise, it's fine."

Porter caught Shanahan and Trotter exchange glances.

Shanahan looked at Dunbarton. "Hey, Claude, did my orders come in yet?"

Dunbarton's head rose from his tray. "Nope. Not yet."

"Seems like I've been waiting forever. I wanna start shipping stuff home."

"And I wanna win the Tennessee lottery," Dunbarton shot back.

Porter took a bite of the hamburger. "So where are you going?"

"Home, brother. Michigan. I'm out. Thirty-five days and a wake-up."

"I remember when I got my separation orders," Porter said, nodding. "It's pretty surreal."

Cam leaned in. "You were out and came back in? What the hell were you thinkin'?"

Had it really happened that way, Porter would've asked the same question.

"I struggled in college. I missed it."

"Missed what? The weird work schedules? Guys like Martz riding your ass? This fine four-star cuisine? Not me, man. I've been dreaming about this day since I got off the bus at boot camp."

"I'll let you know when the orders come in. If you trust me with a cell phone number, I can text you."

"Thanks, man. I appreciate it," Cam said. "It'll be nice dealing with someone who gives a shit. I'm not talking about you, Claude."

Claude grunted with a nod.

Porter took a slug from the small milk carton on his tray before asking. "How do you mean?"

"Alex could be an asshole when he wanted to be." Cam then read his cell phone number off to Porter, who dutifully punched it into his phone.

"Who'd you get stuck bunking with?" Gil inquired.

"Ralph Simpson."

Cal and Gil started laughing, with Dunbarton joining in.

"Oh, man," Gil said. "You're in Martz *and* DiSilva's wheelhouse every day, *and* they put you in with Simpson? That ain't fair."

"Just be careful about what you say in front of Ralph," Gil said. "It goes directly to Martz."

"Can't say that comes as a surprise."

"What're you doing tonight?" Cam asked Porter.

"I hadn't thought about it." Porter misrepresented himself; he wanted to see Jeong again.

"We're on day shifts, so we'll be in Duffy Club. What's your room number?" Cam asked.

"Eight. Only I've got a buddy from Zama. We've been working out together for a long time. Earliest I can make it off-camp would be eight o'clock, give or take. I can catch up with you later."

"Fitness freak, huh? I'll start when I leave here," Cam said. "We'll be in Duffy's until eleven or so."

"Did I see you talking to Jeong last night?" Gil asked.

"Yeah. Attractive lady."

"You're gonna wanna be real careful. She belongs to the old guy who owns Duffy Club," Cam said.

"Belongs to how? I didn't see a ring."

"Not married. The rumor is he keeps her. The job, apartment, paying the bills. More like friends with benefits. Only *friend* isn't the right word either."

"We talked casually for a couple of minutes. Nothing more."

"Doesn't much matter to Myung-Dae," Cam said. "You're better off avoiding her."

Porter recoiled. He didn't know why what he just heard troubled him. But it did. "Myung what?"

"Myung-Dae Tang. That's the one guy in Anjeong-ri you don't play with."

Gil looked at his watch. "Damn, Cam, it's getting late. We better get back."

Both Cam and Gil stood, putting on their hats and jackets, picking up their trays.

"See you tonight if you can make it," Cam said.

"I'll be there."

Dunbarton waited until Cam and Gil were well out of earshot. "Hanging out with them is trouble."

"Why's that? They seem okay."

"They're good guys, don't get me wrong. But Martz can't stand them, and around here, you're the company you keep. And they're right about Myung-Dae Tang and Jeong."

"You gotta be kidding—you too? She almost ran me over, coming around a corner, and apologized. End of story."

"My woman told me Myung-Dae Tang is some kind of Korean gangster, and he's protective of her." Dunbarton peeked at his watch. "Yeah, we better get back, too."

They finished up and returned to the empty admin office. Even working, Jeong didn't stray too far from Porter's mind.

****

Major DiSilva strolled into the admin office unexpectedly at 1500 hours, and Porter got to his feet.

"As you were, Mike," he said, taking off his hat as he walked briskly to his desk. "Listen, when it's just the two of us, I think we can dispense with the formalities, okay?"

"Thank you, sir."

"Well, I see that you're still in one piece." DiSilva chuckled, removing his jacket and putting his hat on the desk. "So…what were your impressions of Anjeong-ri nightlife?"

"Disappointing."

DiSilva nodded. "I hear you. Just between us, I never cared for it myself. And wait until payday night. It's sharks to chum."

Porter chuckled. "Yes, sir."

"And the office? What's your assessment of the overall condition?"

"Claude did okay, considering this isn't his MOS. He told me we're going into Seoul to drop off a visa application on Monday?"

"I enjoy knowing the embassy got them. Do you have anything I need to sign off on?"

"No, Major."

DiSilva imitated Martz, putting his feet up on the desk and opening the newspaper. He spent the next thirty minutes flipping pages and left shortly thereafter without turning on his desktop computer or saying anything more.

Neither Martz nor DiSilva returned that afternoon. At 1705 hours, Porter shut everything down and locked the office. Thinking about Jeong bled over to Myung-Dae Tang. She didn't impress Porter as a docile houseplant wanting to be kept. Then again, how much could he know about her after one brief encounter?

He looked forward to going back to Duffy Club.

****

After his session with Ferguson, Porter had no trouble leaving camp and strolled into Duffy Club shortly after eight o'clock. True to their word, Cam and Gil were in the game room with their women.

Gil's woman Gayoon was short and pretty with a warm smile and a gentle way about her. It was difficult to picture her as a working girl, swimming with the piranhas. Cam's woman Nari was a different story. She wasn't as pretty or as passive.

Besides Jeong, Porter had another reason for being here. He didn't want to be alone, especially after working alone for a large chunk of the day. Porter did what he could to avoid thinking about how he came to be here, despite Stillson's self-serving assessment of coming out of it whole.

Hearing laughter and revelry among this group proved a welcome diversion. Yet, he didn't let himself get carried away.

In the end, Porter didn't see Jeong. At eleven p.m., Porter left the others to go back on base. Both of his new friends had off-base dwellings. He didn't know if Cam or Gil had daily contact with Martz, but he did. And that seemed a good enough reason to exit Duffy Club with a clear head.

Chapter Fourteen

Mid-afternoon the following day, Jeong showered and dressed. She had several errands to run before her shift started at five o'clock that afternoon.

Heavy steps sounded on the stairs to her second-story Anjeong-ri apartment. Two sets of steps. Men's steps. Jeong doubted it was anyone visiting her neighbor with the Shih Tzu. As if on cue, the dog started barking.

Jeong heard the old woman slap the animal and the whimper that followed. The barking stopped. The knock on her door sounded loud and aggressive, and Jeong became still, hoping that whoever it was would assume she wasn't home and leave. Instead, the knocking intensified, and the dog started barking again.

"Jeong?" She recognized Myung-Dae's voice. "I know you're in there."

She tiptoed to the door. The knocking recommenced and then paused. Jeong heard a key slide into the doorknob, but it didn't budge. The Pyeongtaek locksmith she hired had been here earlier today. *So you did have a key made, Myung-Dae.*

"Jeong?" Myung-Dae called out again.

Deciding he wouldn't leave, she slowly opened the door as far as her new lock's chain would allow.

"What do you want, Myung-Dae?"

"I see you installed a new lock. No doubt the

KNPA idiot scared you into it."

"I'm glad he did. Now, what do you want?"

"May Kiwoo and I come in? I'd like to talk to you."

"Whatever this is can't wait another three hours?"

Myung-Dae didn't reply. *He has no intention of walking away.* Reluctantly, she disconnected the chain and opened the door.

Kiwoo pushed the door open and marched in first, moving Jeong aside as if clearing a path. Myung-Dae smiled as he entered, his gold tooth winking. He walked to the kitchen table, and Kiwoo held a chair for him to sit.

She knew Kiwoo was there for a reason. And it had nothing to do with knocking on doors or holding chairs for Myung-Dae.

The dog in the adjacent apartment started barking again. Once again, the old woman slapped the dog, and the barking ceased.

Myung-Dae glanced at Kiwoo and grinned. "Perhaps I should hire the neighbor. Seems she has a way with obstinate animals."

Kiwoo nodded.

Jeong eyed the old man as one would an unleashed dog. Maybe it was safe. Maybe it wasn't. "You still haven't told me why you're here."

"Come and join me at the table."

Reluctantly, Jeong walked into the kitchen and slumped down opposite Myung-Dae.

Myung-Dae leaned back. From where he sat, his gaze connected with the sword mounted on the adjacent living room wall. "That sword. Is it real or decorative?"

"It belonged to my father; he served as a Republic

of Korea Army captain as a young man. You were just about to tell me why this visit was so urgent."

Myung-Dae looked down, fingering the tablecloth. "I understand you spoke with a man the other night. The waitresses tell me he's quite handsome and nobody has seen him before. Who is he?"

I should've known he'd be watching.

"When I came around a corner in a hurry, I nearly ran that guy over. I apologized. Is that what you're talking about? I'm surprised everyone has so much time to gossip."

Myung-Dae eyed Kiwoo. The thug reached down and grabbed Jeong by the throat, lifting her up and out of the chair, slamming her against the kitchen wall. She gasped for air as her arms flailed and her bare feet repeatedly kicked at his shins. Yet nothing loosened his grip.

With oxygen now at a premium, she felt light-headed, and her bladder released. She never saw Myung-Dae's gesture for Kiwoo to release her. When he did, she crumpled to the floor in the puddle of urine. Jeong took giant gulps of air as color returned to her face.

"Why do you lie and disrespect me so?" Myung-Dae asked. "Alex made the same mistake. I had so hoped that you learned something."

Jeong couldn't answer, instead taking in as much air as her lungs would allow.

"Why?" Myung-Dae slammed his fist on her table, making Kiwoo jump.

"The conversation…lasted a minute."

Myung-Dae gestured once more to Kiwoo. She felt the goon's backhand across her face, catching her eye.

"Yet another lie. No, you spoke for *several* minutes," Myung-Dae said. "A simple apology wouldn't take so long. Who is the man?"

"Something Porter."

"Something Porter she says." Myung-Dae's eyes glanced at Kiwoo without gesturing. "And the topic?"

"He asked for directions to Rasputin's. That's all."

Myung-Dae shook his head. "I don't believe that for a minute. I don't want to see you talking to him again. Should that man suffer the same fate as Alex?"

Jeong didn't answer right away.

Kiwoo nudged her with the toe of his boot. "Myung-Dae asked you a question." He raised his hand to strike her again, but the Myung-Dae shook his head.

"I heard you, Myung-Dae." Jeong got to her feet, tonguing the cut lip. "And you know the answer."

Her cheek and eye stung. They would soon swell, and the eye would blacken. She walked to the utility closet just off the kitchen to retrieve a bucket and mop. She put the bucket in the sink and mixed hot water with a floor cleaning liquid.

"What would you have me do when someone asks a question, Myung-Dae? You tell everyone you're a reasonable man, but that isn't a reasonable expectation."

"I don't want to see you alone with that man again, period. Do we have an understanding?"

She glanced at him from over her shoulder. "Yes."

"Good." Myung-Dae's eyes moved from her to Kiwoo. "Go to Jumpin' Jack's office, Kiwoo. I'll call for you to pick me up after I've finished my chat with Jeong."

"You got it, Myung-Dae."

Kiwoo wasted no time leaving Jeong's apartment. She listened as his heavy boots pounded down the stairs. Then Jeong cleaned the kitchen floor while Myung-Dae watched. She knew why he lingered and what he wanted. He had that look in his eye from the moment he entered.

"After you clean the floor, I want you to shower," he said.

"Myung-Dae, I don't want—"

"Why else do you think I'm here?"

"I am bleeding."

Myung-Dae appeared crushed. This ruse had worked before; she could barely believe it worked yet again.

"Aww. That is a shame."

"I told you it's wrong. What people think matters to me. And what of your wife and daughter? Don't you care? Rumors in Anjeong-ri don't easily diminish."

"Who are you to lecture me? Maybe I should call Gunn. Kiwoo is gentle by comparison."

Jeong wanted to scream. But even if she did, and the KNPA showed up, they would take one look at Myung-Dae and leave. Or maybe throw her in jail. After that, Myung-Dae would call in Gunn. The only way out of this vicious circle was to find a safe haven in another country with her family. *But where? And with what? And with who?*

Myung-Dae rose from the chair, picked up the telephone, and called for Kiwoo to return. The thug returned to her apartment five minutes later, collecting Myung-Dae.

She put the mop and bucket away before showering again. And while she showered, Jeong wondered if the man who replaced Alex would be in a position to help her.

****

By eight o'clock, Duffy Club was in full swing. That it was almost a week before next payday served as a testament to the club's popularity, the vast majority of enlisted men running on financial fumes.

It had been ages since Mina Chung had been inside Duffy Club. She'd tried modeling in Seoul for a short time several years ago but found the profession harder work than she wanted or was used to. So she became a working girl.

But not just any working girl. Mina learned what men desired and mastered the art of stroking their ego before touching anything else. She became the consummate professional.

As she entered, things quieted to a hush. One man, fortified by liquid courage, approached her. She casually rebuffed him before taking a seat at the bar.

Soldiers crowded around her barstool, hoping to catch her eye or start a conversation. It was unicorn-rare to see Mina in a bar; her select clientele didn't include enlisted men of any rank. Men came to her, not the other way around.

Jeong soon appeared behind the bar. The women had no use for each other. It seemed odd considering both came to Anjeong-ri from Daegu and grew up together. But when Jeong lost her first love, a high school crush, to Mina as a teenager—a feud developed.

Mina had an amazing figure and pretty face, a testament to her diet and fitness regimen five times a week to keep it all tight and looking good. Her dyed blonde hair was shoulder length.

"Ugh. What are you doing here?" Jeong asked her.

Mina glanced at Jeong's black eye and scoffed. "Looks like you were in a fight and lost. How do I look?"

"Like the common trollop you are. But why are you here?"

"Still bitter after all this time? Face it. I can have or steal any man here, including any desperado chasing the likes of you. If you must know, I have a meeting with Myung-Dae."

"He said nothing to me about an appointment with you."

Mina chuckled. "Why would he? Word on the street is you're fucking the old goat every time he refills his Viagra prescription." She gestured to Myung-Dae's back office. "You're lucky he's so cheap. But in the plus column, you do get laid twice a year. Would you be a love and tell him I'm here? He's expecting me."

"I'm sure he knows you're here. He has cameras everywhere."

"Whatever. Just tell him I'm here."

"Go down to his office and tell him yourself." Jeong opened the pop-up bar section and let Mina through, leading her down the corridor to Myung-Dae's office. Then Jeong knocked on the door and strolled away.

"Come in," Myung-Dae hollered from behind his desk.

Mina opened the door and entered.

"Oh hello, Mina dear," Myung-Dae said in a singsong voice. "Aren't you looking well? Come closer. Let's have a look at you."

Mina walked toward Myung-Dae, trying to

disguise her fear. As much as she loathed Jeong, she couldn't help but admire her. Not everyone had the constitution to work for such a man. Mina forced a grin and presented herself. Tonight she wore a gray parka, yellow sweater, and denim jeans so tight they appeared painted on.

Myung-Dae gestured with his finger for her to twirl, wanting to leer at her from every angle. "Lovely. You are taking care of yourself, I see. Won't you sit down?"

Mina chose a chair and sat down.

"You're probably wondering why I asked for you. I'm interested in hiring you."

"Hiring me to do what? You know I won't wait on tables."

"No, no, no. To utilize your gifts. A job that pays you one-and-a-half-million won every week for perhaps a year."

The mention of so much money made Mina lean forward. "Every week? What do I have to do?"

"It's simple enough. I want you to keep a man company. Are you currently in a relationship that you can end without complication?"

"I have my regulars, but nothing steady. Is he a GI?"

Myung-Dae nodded. "An American GI who's here now, in the game room. I need you to seduce and keep this man. Only he can know nothing of our arrangement. Let him believe you want him."

"Who knows, but maybe I will. Will he pay me, too?"

"I'm sure he'll offer, although not as much as me. This man isn't an officer, so I hope your ego doesn't get in the way."

"You're paying me well enough. That isn't an issue."

"But you are not to ask him for money, you understand. You do not pressure him. Look at you! He may fall in love and want to take you to America."

"An American wife! With the right man, I could do that."

"So what do you say? Do we have a deal?"

"I need to see him first, Myung-Dae. If I'm not physically attracted to him, it will be difficult. The act needs to be convincing."

Myung-Dae pecked at keys on the keyboard. "Come see for yourself." He gestured for her to stand behind him.

Mina stood just off of Myung-Dae's shoulder. From the game room camera feeding video to the monitor, they saw three young American men standing at the last table down. On the bench facing the table, two working girls sat and watched.

Myung-Dae pointed to Porter as the camera zoomed in. "There's your man. Dark sweater."

Mina took him in, watching for several seconds. "No problem. We have a deal."

"Every Friday at noon until our arrangement ends, we will meet in my Jumpin' Jack's office, and I will pay you for the upcoming week. That is acceptable?"

Mina nodded. "Very much so."

"One last thing. You will stay *only* with him. That means no other business. If I discover that you're conducting other business, our arrangement ends."

"I understand."

Mina moved away from Myung-Dae, going around

the desk to reclaim the chair.

Myung-Dae opened the top desk drawer and held up an envelope. "This is your first week's pay." When he stood to hand her the envelope, Mina did likewise, snatching it from Myung-Dae's hand. With the desk so cluttered with hardcover ledgers, receipts, and invoices—he couldn't slide the envelope over.

"I appreciate you paying me upfront, Myung-Dae."

"I'll only say this once. Do not cheat me."

Mina nodded, opening the envelope.

"Don't sit there counting. Strike while the iron is hot."

She put the envelope in her purse and shot up out of the chair, hurrying out of the office, her hands and knees shaking. She took a moment in the hallway to regroup. Then she went back out to the bar, opening the bar section and letting herself out.

From the game room door, Mina saw him. Her mark was attractive, a delightful bonus. She glanced at the other women sitting on a bench at the last table. Mina had no use for either Gayoon or Nari, considering them everyday, disposable whores.

She strutted into the game room. Every man who saw her stopped to stare.

"Hi," a soldier from table two clumsily muttered as she passed.

Laser-focused, Mina didn't answer. She didn't need to. Her mark had his back to her as he lined up a shot. She loved the way a man looked at her for the first time.

"Who are you?" she asked Porter, tapping him on the shoulder.

He turned around, and Mina got the look she

coveted. It was a combination of lust and fascination.

"My name is Mike. And you are?"

"I'm Mina. Buy me a drink?"

Porter eyed her cautiously and looked around the room. "Who sent you in here?"

"Why would you ask me that?" she asked, hands on her hips.

"Let's call it a hunch."

"Does that mean no drink for poor Mina?" She moved in close, letting him smell her imported perfume.

Porter backed away. "I suspect poor Mina has *never* paid for her own drinks. Somebody sent you here."

Offended, she glared. "What's your problem? You like little boys or something?"

Porter turned his back to her to shoot. No man had ever done that before, not ever. "No. I like women. But you're a ringer. Someone sent you here."

Mina moved closer and pressed up against him. "Come with me," she whispered.

Porter turned back around and grinned, shaking his head. "Sorry. Not a chance."

Mina looked at Porter with genuine disbelief, trying to hide the hurt. Rejection had never before reared its ugly head. She doubled-down. "Just a drink? I think you will like me."

"I'm flattered, but unless I know who you're working for, this conversation is over."

Humiliated, Mina stormed out of the game room, avoiding eye contact with everyone on her way out. Seconds later, she knocked on Myung-Dae's office door.

"Come in," Myung-Dae called out.

Mina walked in, the envelope in her hand. "I need to return this."

"Come in, dear Mina, sit," Myung-Dae called out. "Don't feel so bad; there's a first time for everything."

She walked the money to Myung-Dae, who put the envelope back in a desk drawer. She returned to the chair and sat.

"You were watching?"

Myung-Dae leaned back. "Did you think I wouldn't be?"

"I've never been so embarrassed in all my life. He asked who sent me."

"And what did you tell him, dear Mina?"

She recoiled. "Nothing. I didn't want to make you angry."

"Yet, you accomplished just that. I ask you to do one thing for me. One thing." Myung-Dae got up and walked to her. Mina saw a look in his eyes that gave away his rage. As he moved in close, and with no warning, he slapped her face. "You were to engage that man, entice him. Pay a compliment or two and capture his interest. Instead, you came off like a cheap, vulgar strumpet. It's no wonder he refused you."

Mina started crying.

Myung-Dae grabbed a box of tissue from atop the file cabinet and handed it to her. "Please compose yourself. It's not the end of the world. Would you like to leave the back way?"

"Yes, I would."

Mina stood, and Myung-Dae led her down the hall to the door out back. Whatever Myung-Dae's intentions, she realized this had backfired. Mina knew the next time she set foot in Duffy Club again would be when Jeong no longer worked there, and Myung-Dae no longer owned it.

****

Jeong watched Porter dust Mina from the shadows beyond the game room entrance. If anyone had ever refused Mina before, Jeong had no way of knowing. She liked this new man from the beginning. And knocking Mina down a peg put Porter in a special place in her heart, although she couldn't tell anyone. Not even Porter.

Yes, this man could help her. She could *feel* it.

She scribbled the note in the stockroom and kept tabs on the game room. As Porter departed Duffy Club shortly after eleven, Jeong slipped the note in his hand.

If he showed in Pyeongtaek on Saturday, his stock would rise even more. Maybe it wasn't fair putting this man in danger because of her. Yet, she sensed he could handle it.

And hoped she was right.

Chapter Fifteen

Porter got to his feet after the second snooze alarm rang. Between the traveling, anxiety, training, and nights in Anjeong-ri, he looked forward to sleeping in this weekend. Plus, the idea of avoiding Martz until Monday appealed to him.

The dream before the first alarm was in color and very lucid. Felicity looked like she had on their wedding day—holding the baby as he and Ferguson got ready for the flight line in the armory locker room.

Felicity brushed the hair from her eyes. "Where are you going, baby?"

Porter reached over and smiled at his infant daughter. Baby Sara wrapped her tiny, thin digits around his index finger and cooed. He couldn't ask for a prettier child.

"I can't tell you."

"When are you coming home?"

"Soon."

"We'll be waiting." And just like that, Felicity and Sara vanished.

Porter remembered the night the Virginia state trooper told him Felicity and Sara perished in a car accident three months before taking the Misawa assignment. Even now, the pain and bitterness lingered. God, how he missed them. He reminded himself it was only a dream as he checked on his roommate. But

Simpson had once again slipped by unnoticed.

Porter's thoughts then turned to Jeong and the note she slid into his hand last night. He knew little about Pyeongtaek other than it bordered Camp Humphreys to the north. Her black eye bothered him. Why anyone would strike her was unthinkable. *Maybe it was some kind of accident*. He couldn't dwell on it further, and Porter opened his wardrobe to get ready for the day.

****

Porter was still eating breakfast in the mess hall when Cam and Gil sat down with full trays.

"You are a rock star, bro. I still can't believe you blew Mina off like that," Cam said.

"Gayoon told me every woman in Duffy Club wanted to clap," Gil added.

"No, Gil. She said every woman in there *had* the clap."

Porter laughed. It felt like forever since the last time he had. "I thought she was some kind of ringer."

"That sounds right. Gayoon told me Mina only does officers."

"The whole thing felt staged. Would this Myung-Dae character send her in to…what, test me?"

Cam shrugged as he looked at his eggs. "I suppose he *could*. But why would he? Doesn't matter now; you tossed her."

Porter nodded and checked his watch. He wanted to get in before Martz to read his agency email.

"You going to DC tonight?" Cam asked.

"DC?"

"Duffy Club."

Porter shrugged. "It's either that or watch Simpson study."

"Friday night is the best of the week," Cam offered.

"I won't get out much before seven."

"That's cool. We wait for the lines to die down on Friday nights anyhow."

"Wait doing what?"

"We go to the EM Club, grab a bite, and hang out there. You should stop by."

"Sure. But why the EM Club?"

"With everyone clawing to leave camp, the EM Club's quiet. Unless there's a function going on, anyhow. It's cheap, and the food's decent, too."

Porter glanced at his wristwatch again. "I'm gonna bug out. It's easier to check email without Martz hanging around busting balls. I'll see you at seven."

Porter left the mess hall. When he entered the office, Martz sat behind DiSilva's desk, his face hidden behind the newspaper.

"You're in early. I like that," Martz said.

A sudden thought came to Porter as he powered on the desktop computer. "Do I man the office over the weekend, Top?"

The paper came down. "That's right. We didn't discuss it. You have a cell phone?"

Porter cocked his head. "Yes."

"Give me the number. If I need you, I'll text. Unless you hear otherwise, you're back here Monday at 0800."

"Why would you need me over the weekend? It's an honest question."

Martz's eyebrows arched. "Cutting emergency leave orders, or we're being overrun by the enemy. Were you sick the day they covered emergency leave orders in tech school?"

"Fair enough." Porter read his phone number aloud, and Martz pecked it into his phone's contacts. The master sergeant didn't hang around for long. And after he left, Porter checked his agency email before researching the manual and section covering the preparation of leave orders, emergency or otherwise. So far, he'd been able to pull this off, although Martz's expression just now seemed troubling. He needed to continue this charade until the time came to hit the flight line.

Porter didn't see Martz or DiSilva the rest of the day. He emailed Stillson, telling his boss all was well and that he'd call next week. He didn't ask about the drone, the target, or the exfil strategy. That would wait until next week too.

****

It was 1730 hours when Porter met Ferguson at the armory. Tired, they cut the routine short after two miles and thirty minutes in the weight room.

Porter returned to the barracks after the workout, relieved that Simpson wasn't around. He grabbed a quick shower and crossed the street to the EM Club.

This EM Club was nicer than most. It'd gone through a recent refurbishment, the furnishings new, and the spacious rooms had a fresh-paint smell. The long bar featured six large, flat-screen televisions showing tape-delayed college and professional basketball games.

Cam and Gil were there, beer in hand. The trio ordered a pizza and ate at the bar. Porter listened to Cam and Gil talk about previous duty stations and their women.

If any one thing in particular thing stood out, it was Gil's genuine affection for Gayoon. That they were marrying in April came as a surprise. Cam's relationship with Nari sounded purely physical.

"You came at a good time," Cam said. "Payday and the five days that follow are brutal. But it slows down a lot after that."

Porter discreetly observed the pair, both men in their early twenties. They were easy enough to distinguish physically. Gil reenlisted only last month while Cam couldn't wait to get out. What Porter found distinctive were their speech and mannerisms; Cam the faster talker and thinker. Another difference was Gil's propensity to see things through rose-colored glasses while Cam remained grounded and the more cerebral of the two.

Just before eight o'clock, they left the EM Club.

"The herd will have thinned out," Gil said.

"So fast?"

"Those looking for women will have found them. The others won't have the cash to hang long," Cam opined.

Leaving camp proved a straight shot, with more soldiers returning than leaving. Porter reached into his jacket pocket and activated the GPS device.

When they passed the street off the thoroughfare leading to Duffy Club, Porter thought for a minute they intended to introduce him to another bar.

"Don't look now, but Simpson's tailing us," Gil said as they crossed the street.

"What the fuck?" Porter stopped and pivoted. He glimpsed Simpson trotting back for the gate and shook his head in disbelief. "Why would he care where we're going? By the way, where are we going?"

"I need to stop by my place for a second; then we'll go to Cam's. We'll hit DC after a couple of beers," Gil said.

Porter and Cam stood on the street outside a tailor's shop while Gil scampered to the building he lived in with Nari. He returned five minutes later, and the three resumed their journey.

The apartment Cam sometimes shared with Nari was farther down a maze of several alleys. While they walked, Cam explained that the hooch had belonged to him and Gil. After Gil moved in with Gayoon, Nari stayed over when Cam worked day shifts.

It was a first-floor corner unit in a dilapidated brick tenement. Even inside, Porter saw his breath as he exhaled. The apartment's interior was void of any charm, a poorly appointed man-cave. Frayed towels with holes adorned the windows, pulled tightly together and held in place by clothespins. In the kitchen sat a small, round table with two chairs while an ancient refrigerator whirred, a rusty stove next to it. The L-shaped laminate countertop was barren.

The kitchen opened to the living room. In the middle sat a hideous green-fabric sofa and a cheap wood-laminate coffee table in front of it. Instead of end tables, oversized brown bean-bag chairs flanked both sides of the sofa.

A pair of fiberglass guitar cases leaned against a wall while a kerosene heater rested in a corner. Against the back wall, a series of plastic boxes served as a makeshift entertainment center. And on top of the boxes stood a modest sound system and metal tower of bootleg compact disks. A pair of discount speakers adorned both sides of the plastic boxes.

Cam gestured to a closed door. "Bathroom's over there." Opposite it another door appeared, presumably leading to the bedroom.

After firing up the kerosene heater, Cam turned on the stereo and put a compact disk in the player. He retreated to the kitchen, opened the small fridge, and brought back cans of beer. Gil reached into his parka and pulled out a large cellophane bag with a leafy substance that Porter recognized as marijuana. A packet of rolling papers soon followed, and Gil began laying everything out on the coffee table to roll a joint.

Cam watched and then looked up at Porter. "You smoke pot, Mike?"

You're asking me that now? For all you know, I could be CID. So much for these guys being smart. While not a court-martial offense, Cam could kiss that honorable discharge goodbye while Gil would be looking at a demotion and any plans of reenlisting again.

"Not since college. But I'll pass; the stuff doesn't agree with me."

This time Gil looked up. "You're okay with us smoking a blunt?"

"Do you guys ever worry about the dogs?"

Gil looked at Cam. "No. But then again, we don't go right back to camp afterward."

"I hate to ask, but would you guys mind firing up outside? I'm leery of those dogs."

Cam looked at Gil, who nodded. "That's cool."

"What if I was CID?"

Cam scoffed. "I can smell an agent a mile away. Most CIDs are lifers that talk and act the part. Take

Ralph Simpson, for example. He's a lifer and looks like a choirboy. I've always suspected him of being CID. Any idea why he tailed us, Mike?"

"No idea. He wanted to show me around my first night, but I told him I'd go it alone."

Cam glanced at Gil. "That's gotta be Martz. He's maybe afraid you'll follow Alex's footsteps, whatever they were."

"Just out of curiosity, do you guys know anything about what happened to Tomlinson?" Porter asked.

Cam took a sip of beer and shrugged. "We didn't know the dude all that well; he stayed pretty much to himself. I know he sold black-market crap to Myung-Dae, but if he got into anything heavier, it flew under the radar."

Gil nodded. "Has that been bothering you, Mike?"

Don't say a word about seeing Jeong tomorrow. I'm seeing why Martz has such a hard-on for these two.

"Not really. I figure he was on the wrong side of something."

Cam nodded. "Listen, you can crash here tonight and avoid Humphreys until morning. I'll fix the sofa up."

"Thanks. Maybe I'll take you up on that. Those dogs spook me, no bullshit."

"So you went to college, Mike? Where?" Cam inquired.

"U-Mass, Boston."

"I just got accepted to Michigan State," Cam said proudly. "Starting in September."

"Congratulations. That's a good school."

Gil rolled a pair of joints, putting them in an empty breath mint canister. Soon, the mood softened, with one beer leading to two. Gil reached into another parka pocket, removing a single slick bathroom tile, a capped razor blade, and a small plastic bag with white powder.

Gil once again peered at Porter. "You do coke, Mike?"

"I'll pass on that too. Don't you guys ever worry about random drug tests?"

"Haven't had a drug test since me and Cam were in Italy," Gil said. "I don't carry dope on camp. That's why we made the pit stop."

For Porter, the fear of having someone like DiSilva, Martz, or even Stillson ask for a random blood or urine sample was always a possibility. If they found narcotics in his system, Porter's fledgling CIA career would effectively be over. It was an unacceptable risk with no payoff, even if done undercover to fit in. That tactic may fly with other government agencies. But not the CIA.

Gil opened the bag and separated six lines of the powder using a razor blade. He rolled a dollar bill, and he and Cam took turns snorting the lines. After finishing, Cam brought out three fresh beers, and the topic turned to the Duffy Club.

"I'm surprised Jeong talked to you," Gil said. "She rarely talks with customers."

Porter nodded. "She's sharp. She figured out that I'm Tomlinson's replacement in less than a minute."

"Just be careful. If you're looking to hit that, be smart and do it far, far away from Anjeong-ri," Gil said.

"I thought about what you told me. If that old man is keeping her, why the hell is she managing his bar?"

Gil shrugged. "Maybe it's easier for him to keep tabs on her. We know the guy a little and heard some of the horror stories about him. Things like hacking off a thumb if you rip him off, things like that. But he hasn't done or said anything you'd think twice about, at least not in front of us. The locals like to exaggerate."

"Then why hit it far, far away?"

Gil chuckled. "Just in case we're wrong."

"Sometimes you'll see his goons hanging around," Cam interrupted. "Whether or not the stories are true, Anjeong-ri is like any small village. Rumors start and stick, true or not."

When the cans were empty, they were ready to go to Duffy Club. Outside, snow fell, giving the place a cozy look and feel. Away from the nearest street light, Gil removed one joint from the canister, and he and Cam smoked it as they walked. Porter stayed well downwind. Soon the three were in downtown Anjeong-ri.

The line into Duffy Club ran only ten deep, and Porter got in it. Cam grabbed Porter by the sleeve and, along with Gil, led him out back to a metal door by a loading dock. They climbed the short set of wooden stairs, and Cam rang the doorbell. One minute led to two, and Cam hit the plunger again. This time, the door opened. It was Jeong. She glanced at Cam and Gil and nodded. Porter went last, and for him, she smiled.

Jeong led them behind the bar, lifting the pop-up section. She stayed behind the bar as Gil took the point and led the group to the game room. They returned to the last table down—the only table that offered a bit of conversational privacy.

A pair of soldiers currently occupied the table. Gil put four quarters above the coin slot to challenge, and Nari and Gayoon walked in. Porter wondered privately what happened to these women after their men transferred out. It seemed logical they would re-circulate and work the bars again. But what happened when men no longer sought them out as they aged?

A waitress came by, and they ordered. Gil, easily the best of the pool players, quickly won the table. They would stay at that end of the game room for the rest of the night.

Porter picked up on a couple of things. The first, Cam and Gil had plenty of cash. That all the other GIs were on a tight budget seemed only too obvious. The second was more troubling and concerned only Gil. Every so often, a soldier approached Gil, who would then grab his parka. The pair huddled in a corner while keeping their backs to everyone else. After the quick exchange, the acquiring soldier vanished while Gil returned with his jacket.

The CID could have eyes on all three of us. Wouldn't Martz love that? And Porter wondered how often and how much coke these two consumed, Gil in particular. He clearly sold for a third party. And Porter assumed the third party was Myung-Dae Tang.

By ten o'clock, you could move about Duffy Club easily. Cam and Gil bought rounds freely, flush with cash. How Gil supplemented his income seemed only too apparent. Cam was another matter. And because Porter worried about Martz, who should appear?

The CIA agent's heart stopped to see the master sergeant's glistening bald head wander into the game room, red and wet from the cold and spitting snow. He had on a lightweight parka and jeans; it seemed strange to see him in civilian clothes. Martz lumbered toward them as if invited, holding a popular brand of American beer.

"Well, well, well…isn't this a sight? And then there were three." Martz glanced at the women. "My apologies, ladies. Hope I'm not intruding."

Nari and Gayoon, picking up on the men's consternation and the sudden change in atmosphere, turned quiet. Porter took a step toward the senior enlisted man.

"Slumming it tonight, Top? What'd you do, leave Ralph outside?"

Cam chuckled. And because he did, Martz rolled away from Porter to zero in on him first, getting far too close, looking into Cam's eyes, and taking an animated whiff of his shirt.

"I'm glad to see everybody having fun. Good *clean* fun, right, boys?"

Martz turned back toward Porter, getting in his face so close that Porter could smell the Salisbury steak still clinging to the man's breath. Martz teetered and pivoted, turning at last to Gil.

"I understand you're the resident pool shark, Trotter."

"I'm better than most."

"Better than me, you think?"

Martz moved in closer still to Gil, taking yet another unwanted, animated whiff.

"Way better than you, Top."

Martz flashed a gap-toothed grin and nodded. "Eight ball?"

"This just for fun or you wanna make it interesting?"

Martz glanced at the empty glasses stacked up on table four's counter. "Sure doesn't look like you need

137

my money. Which is kinda strange, what with everyone else sucking hind tit. But what the hell, let's do it."

Gil reached for his wallet and pulled out a twenty-dollar bill, putting it on the table's bumper. Martz nodded and did likewise before feeding the table's slot with quarters.

"Nice to see you guys still have money," Martz said. "My only question is where it came from."

Gil pulled a quarter from his jeans pocket. "Flip for the break, call it in the air." He flipped the coin.

Martz waited until the quarter reached its zenith. "Tails."

The coin landed on the table's felt. It was tails. Gil racked the balls.

The pair played as everyone at the table went quiet. It didn't last long as Gil went on a run and ended it quickly. The contest over, Martz took a deep breath as he put the stick back and his jacket back on. Gil snatched the money from the table, unable to conceal the smile. They waited until Martz left before speaking.

"I think I just shit myself," Gil said. "What the fuck was that about?"

"Know what's scary?" Cam asked. "This is the first time I've seen him off base. Who would've expected that?"

Cam pivoted toward Gil. "Dude, do us all a favor. Sell out of your apartment, where you can control who sees what. You didn't see Mitch sell out in public."

"I'm not psychic, Cam. Martz just showed up; it had nothing to do with me."

"Doesn't matter. How many times have I told you that Myung-Dae has no control over someone from camp ratting you out to the CID?"

Gil looked down. "Yeah, all right."

The mood soon picked back up, and they continued to shoot pool and drink, although the pace slowed considerably. At twelve thirty, the group put on their jackets and departed Duffy Club. Porter saw Jeong again for the briefest of moments and winked at her. She smiled at him.

"Your offer still open?" Porter asked Cam once they were back outside.

"Anytime I'm on a day shift."

Soon the group of five whittled down to three as Gil and Gayoon split off.

And in Cam's hooch, sleeping on the sofa, Porter had no choice but to listen to the sounds of the lovers in the bedroom. It amused and distracted in equal parts. Porter wouldn't fall asleep until after Cam and Nari finished.

Porter considered the strangeness of the evening. The reckless nature of Cam and Gil's drug use troubled him. Martz showing up unexpectedly troubled him even more. Porter wondered how many more nights in Anjeong-ri he had left.

His thoughts soon turned to Jeong. It became increasingly difficult to set her aside and focus on Panmunjom. But she'd been on his mind most of the day. He wondered if she felt the same. Or anything at all, for that matter. He couldn't deny that he wanted her. Lust and love. He remembered thinking about how blurry that line got before marrying Felicity.

Jeong's ability to see things unrevealed gnawed at him too. *Does she know I'm CIA? She figured out I was Tomlinson's replacement easy enough. Is she playing me? Why would she? But if she asks what I'm cleared for tomorrow, the game is up. She'll have broken my heart.*

That was Porter's final thought before falling asleep.

Chapter Sixteen

Porter woke in darkness Saturday morning. Neither Cam nor Nari stirred as he dressed and departed.

Alone on the vacant street, Porter took advantage of his first opportunity to enjoy the village without company or the typical chaos. He casually strolled back to camp, watching the snow fall under the streetlamp lights as his mind turned to Jeong. He so looked forward to be with her later today.

Close to the thoroughfare, thirty yards down, a local bar's lit neon sign caught his eye. The turquoise Hangul characters displayed the name Blue Turtle Bar. It was the only place in the entire village with a colorful neon sign still lit.

He saw the door open as a tall figure stepped out, a dark scarf across their face. The person pivoted toward the thoroughfare and jogged toward it. But by the time Porter reached the main street, the figure disappeared. Porter looked up the street toward the gate and saw no one. Neither did he see anyone walking in the opposite direction. Sure, he could track their whereabouts in the snow. Only he wanted to get a few hours of sleep before meeting Ferguson and then Jeong later today.

Porter continued toward the front gate. The sentries didn't bother looking up from their cell phones as he passed, ID in hand. With fingers crossed, he strolled by the caged canines. One of the three German shepherds raised its head but didn't bark, and Porter strolled back inside Humphreys. After turning the GPS unit off, the young agent made a mental note to buy reserve batteries for the device.

Reaching the barracks, he crept into the room. He listened as Simpson lightly snored.

Porter undressed, hurriedly taking off the handgun and holster and closing the wardrobe door.

When his head reached the pillow, Porter thought again of Jeong and considered Myung-Dae's fixation. And understood it only too well.

****

Gayoon looked out the bedroom window of the Anjeong-ri apartment she shared with Gil, who was currently in the bathroom. The snow accumulated fast, an inch or more already on the windowsill.

"Turn the heat up on the way back, Gil." Gayoon would get up and make coffee after it got just a little warmer. She loved that her man had the weekend off, a rare treat.

Of all the men she'd been with, Gil was the only one who treated her like a lady. When he brought her little gifts, like a fresh red rose or box of chocolates, she melted. Best of all, Gil never laid a finger on her in anger.

He promised to take her to America. This tactic nothing new; so many men here did. But Gil's eyes and tone reflected a sincerity, and she believed him, especially now that he'd asked her to marry him and bought a ring. It was a cheap ring, to be sure, but a ring nonetheless. Gayoon couldn't remember being happier.

Soon Gil hopped back into bed and cuddled up beside her. "Brrr, baby. It's ca-ca-ca-cold out there."

Gayoon giggled and turned away, aware Gil liked to cuddle side-by-side, with her back to his chest. "My mother asked if we picked out a caterer yet," she said.

"I left the planning to you. Just stay within the budget, please."

Gayoon thought about the burgundy gym bag hiding in the closet. Its contents troubled her deeply. She understood the inherent danger of being in business with Myung-Dae Tang and gently voiced her concerns. Yet Gil refused to listen. Making matters worse, he consumed too much of the powder personally. She likened it to a child owning a candy store.

"Gil, please stop working for Myung-Dae. We don't need such a big wedding."

"You said you wanted a big wedding. Everything costs money, my love. So I have to do extra."

"I'd rather have a simple wedding, and you quit Myung-Dae. That powder will kill you one day."

She could feel him breathing as his hands moved from her belly to her breasts. Gayoon giggled. "No, Gil...this is serious."

The cheap, hollow, wooden door to their apartment burst open violently, shattering to splinters. Gil and Gayoon jumped from the bed, Gayoon covering up with a blanket. With the bedroom door open, they both saw Gunn Lim. Gayoon had seen this in a nightmare. In a black tracksuit and hiking boots, Myung-Dae's number one enforcer appeared more than a little irate.

"You," Gunn said, pointing at Gil. "Had appointment with Myung-Dae."

Gil stood naked, staring at the open door. "Not until ten this morning." He glanced at the clock on the kitchen wall. It was eleven thirty. "Relax, dude, okay?

143

Where's Myung-Dae now?"

"Waiting for you. We will go. Now."

"Lemme put some clothes on first, huh?"

Frantically, Gil dressed while Gunn and Gayoon watched.

"Hurry up," Gunn said as the soldier finished tying his boots.

"This won't take long," Gil said, blowing Gayoon a kiss after opening the closet and grabbing the gym bag. "And tell the super we need a new door thanks to this asshole."

Gayoon realized the irony. The building superintendent would notify the owner of this firetrap. Who happened to be Myung-Dae Tang.

****

"Unacceptable." Myung-Dae's open palm slammed against the desktop when Gil entered the old man's study alone. Gunn waited by the front door. "Can you not tell time?"

"I forgot the time. But your goon didn't need to bust the door down and drag me here like a three-year-old."

"I am here, waiting. I remembered the time, and you wasted it." Myung-Dae got to his feet; his eyes fixed on the gym bag. "Well? Are you going to bring me the bag? Or shall I take you by the hand?"

Gil approached the desk, gently placing the bag on top of it. He mockingly bowed before sitting down.

Myung-Dae scowled and unzipped the bag. He removed the scale and the large cellophane bag holding smaller cellophane bags. Myung-Dae then took the cash bag and notebook and started taking his counts. Gil understood this would take time. All he could do was

144

sit and wait. Fifteen minutes passed before Myung-Dae took a deep breath.

"You are short, Gilbert. Five grams short."

"Yeah, I'm sorry about that. Just deduct it from my cut."

"This is *not* the way I taught you. It seems you don't listen either. Perhaps you have a learning disability? Cash to equal amount of grams sold. This is not complex; others who've worked for me had no such problems. If you consume personally, you must pay personally. We discussed this very thing in this room only last week."

Myung-Dae reached into a desk drawer and removed an envelope. Out of it, he counted and removed money. Then he picked up the telephone on his desk and made a call. The conversation with the other party was brief. Gil didn't understand a syllable.

When the call ended, Myung-Dae took the gym bag and went into the backroom behind his desk. Five long minutes later, the old man returned—putting the bag on the desk and closing the backroom door before sitting down again.

"I have restocked your inventory and recorded it in the journal. You will do *exactly* what I've taught you from this day forward, and you will be on time for all future meetings. If I find I cannot trust you, or you don't learn, or are irresponsible beyond redemption, I will end our business association altogether. Do you understand?"

"Yeah, Myung-Dae. I fucked up. It won't happen again."

"I'm confident it won't," Myung-Dae said. He grinned, the gold incisor making an appearance. "What time next week?"

"Sometime between three and five in the afternoon."

"Three o'clock then."

"I'll be here, Myung-Dae."

"I don't enjoy sending Gunn on short notice. Now you may go. Please tell Gunn I want him on your way out."

Gil got to his feet, gym bag in hand. He never enjoyed coming here, even with Cam. But today's visit shook him to the core. Gayoon had a point; getting in deep with Myung-Dae brought headaches.

"Hey, Gump," Gil said with a smile as he walked into the foyer where Gunn waited, smoking a cigarette. "Myung-Dae wants you. He said to bring knee pads and a bottle of mouthwash."

Gunn grinned and exhaled smoke in Gil's face. "Soon for you, I think."

"Smash my door down again, and I'll blow your fucking head off," Gil said.

Gunn headed toward the study as Gil exited Myung-Dae's house. There was only one problem in making that threat. Gil didn't own a gun. As he trudged home through the snow, he realized he would need to buy one on the black market. It would be expensive and now necessary. *Unless I stop doing business with Myung-Dae.*

As Gil walked, snow fell harder. Because of the accumulation, some vehicles had difficulty getting through the mess, spinning their tires ferociously in search of dry pavement that didn't exist. In the distance, he could make out pulsing red lights. *Maybe someone slipped on ice.*

Getting closer, Gil's heart pounded harder with each passing step when he realized the vehicle parked in front of Gayoon's building. He went through the front door, down the hall, and up the narrow stairs. He would've taken the elevator, except it ran slow.

On the second floor platform, he opened the door and pivoted toward Gayoon's apartment. With the door still shattered, Gil saw a pair of EMTs standing alongside a gurney. On it laid Gayoon, an oxygen mask over her bloodied, swollen face. As Gil approached the gurney, an EMT grabbed and pulled him away.

She appeared dead, and Gil started crying. He wondered why Myung-Dae had been so condescendingly smug. Now he understood.

The EMT who pulled Gil away made eye contact. "Husband?" he asked Gil in English.

"Yes," Gil lied. "I'm going with you."

The EMT nodded as he took the front of the gurney, while another EMT manned the back, wheeling Gayoon toward the elevator while Gil held her hand.

"Where are you taking her?"

"Saint Mary's in Pyeongtaek."

In the elevator, Gil knew if he ever got his hands on a gun, he would take pleasure killing Myung-Dae and his goons.

****

The room was empty when Porter returned from his time with Ferguson. He enjoyed being outside with a rifle again. While the assignment still felt abstract, Porter wondered when the reality of it would kick in. They used ten-ring targets at a distance of two hundred yards. Porter routinely scored inside the two innermost yellow rings despite a strong headwind and falling

147

snow. Of course, things were different with a human target; even stationary, they were unpredictable.

Porter didn't figure to get more than two shots. One would have to be a headshot that Ferguson could easily confirm. Seconds after the gunshots would be chaos, with secret police getting the two presidents inside safely. It would take less than two minutes to find the expired assassin if Porter's aim was true. Regardless, some asshole medic would try to keep the assassin alive to find out who he or she worked for.

Meanwhile, Porter and Ferguson would run for their lives to the exfil site. Between cars, snowmobiles, and drones, Porter calculated the odds of making it to the exfil site at twenty percent. Or less. A far cry from the gaudy number Stillson bandied about as a pacifier. Porter grabbed his shaving kit and a fresh towel and hit the showers.

****

Porter met the taxi in front of the EM Club at two fifteen that afternoon. He jumped into the back seat and turned his GPS device on. The driver looked into the rearview mirror and made eye contact.

"Are you my Pyeongtaek fare?"

"Yeah. How long will it take to get there in this weather?"

"Today, it takes what it takes."

Porter cared little for the answer, but it didn't matter. He was going and could only hope Jeong would be there too. He didn't have her phone number to call and confirm.

Once the car drove beyond Anjeong-ri's commercial district, Porter realized what the driver meant. They passed two cars that had violently spun out, going down grill-first into a shallow ditch. Between the police, ambulances, tow trucks, flares, and rubberneckers, traffic crawled.

Now in Pyeongtaek, the driver pulled the taxi close to the curb in front of an octagon-shaped, single-story structure with white clapboards. The multicolored neon sign boasted Hangul characters. Zero Coffeehouse. The driver looked it up and down.

Porter looked at his watch and gave the man a ten-dollar bill for a five-dollar fare.

"If I'm not back in two minutes, keep it."

"Places like this, we get bonus not to tell CID. This place isn't for GIs."

"I don't give a damn who you tell," Porter said. "Will you wait or not?"

"Two minutes. Then I'm out of here."

Porter got out and entered the coffeehouse. There were but a handful of patrons, and Porter got the feeling coming here may have been a mistake. It was dimly lit, with booths along the walls and tables at the center of the long room. Like Duffy Club, it had more than enough secondhand smoke.

The place went quiet, with all eyes on Porter. His eyes found Jeong's as she stood and waved, her red ski jacket difficult to miss. When he reached the corner booth, she smiled and sat down. As good as she looked in the din of Duffy Club at night, in the light of day, she radiated beauty.

"You look nervous," she said.

"A little, maybe. This is the kind of place we're told to avoid. Should I worry about CID?"

She scoffed. "CID has enough to worry about in Anjeong-ri."

He gestured to her black eye. "I wanted to ask you in Duffy Club. What happened to your eye?"

Jeong didn't answer, and the server approached. They both ordered coffee and waited for full cups before speaking.

"Give me your hand," she said.

Porter leaned forward. "Didn't we do this already?"

"Yes. Did you not enjoy it?"

"Actually, I did." Porter extended his hand across the table, and Jeong took it. He felt her moist palm against his, and her dainty fingers twitched. Several seconds passed, and she released it.

"So what did you learn this time?"

Her expression turned serious, throwing him off.

"You got nothing?"

She leaned back. "Your wife and baby died not so very long ago, and you are still grieving. I'm so sorry."

Porter no longer doubted her gift, and his eyes stayed on hers as he nodded. "A car accident took them. I've been thinking about them a lot lately. When I'm not thinking about you, that is."

Jeong's stare lured him in, making him blind to all else. It was arousing and sensual in a place not conducive to it. Just beneath the surface, the dots aligned. That gaze reminded him of the way Felicity looked at him. With his mind on everything else, Porter just now realized it. Breaking her spell, he took this in a different direction.

"So now that I'm here, what am I here for?"

Jeong nodded. "To talk in Anjeong-ri is trouble for me."

"So you said. Because of the old man you work

for?"

"You know of Myung-Dae?"

"Only by reputation, which I'm sure you know isn't good. I hear he's very…protective of you." Porter pointed to the bruise on her face. "Is that his idea of a good-night kiss?"

"Myung-Dae had one of his men beat me."

"That doesn't sound like a healthy relationship."

"Relationship?" she whispered. "Myung-Dae and I have no relationship. I'm terrified of him."

Porter sipped his coffee. "The night we met, you looked up at a speaker when we walked to the table. What were you looking for?"

"Myung-Dae has cameras everywhere. They feed into his laptop. His men move them every so often."

Porter sat back, looking for signs of a lie. But the woman remained calm and resolute. "I'm still not sure why you asked me here."

"You're not like Gil and Cam. And certainly not like Alex," she said.

"Cam and Gil seem like nice enough guys. What do they have to do with this?"

"Yes, Cam and Gil are nice. They are sometimes silly and harmless men. But they work for Myung-Dae, and because of that, I cannot trust them. Or ask for their help."

"Gil and Cam work for Myung-Dae? Doing what?"

"Both sell black-market goods to him. Myung-Dae meets with them at his Anjeong-ri house on Saturdays."

"Do they do anything else for Myung-Dae?"

She shrugged. "I don't know. But the reason you're here with me today is because you *will* help me."

Porter again sipped the coffee. "How do you know

that?"

"You're angry I'm hurt. Your superiors will expect you to cast a blind eye to the evil that exists in Anjeong-ri."

Porter rubbed his chin. "What superiors are you talking about? I have many."

"Those who have the most power over you. I see two."

"This evil that you speak of. What is it?"

"Alex told me Myung-Dae pays GIs to marry working girls to send to America to be prostitutes there."

Porter took a moment. *Yeah, human trafficking qualifies as evil all right.* "Did Alex play a part?"

Jeong's eyes darted in both directions. "Yes. Same as Mr. Arthur."

"Mr. Arthur?"

"The man in charge."

Porter's eyes widened. "Arthur DiSilva? Major DiSilva?"

"Yes. Arthur DiSilva," she said. "That is his name."

"So Arthur DiSilva works with Myung-Dae?"

Jeong shook her head. "Not with. For."

"How does Arthur DiSilva even know Myung-Dae?"

"Mr. Arthur's wife is Myung-Dae's daughter, Chona."

Porter nearly dropped his coffee cup. "Mr. Arthur is Myung-Dae's son-in-law?"

Jeong nodded. "You didn't know that?"

"No. What happened to Alex, Jeong? Can you tell me?"

Her eyes dropped as she whispered, "Alex is dead. I was there. It was horrible."

"You saw Alex die, Jeong? Myung-Dae murdered him?"

She nodded. "Yes. Myung-Dae murdered Alex."

"How did Myung-Dae kill him, Jeong? Where did it happen?"

Jeong told Porter the entire story, including Doyoon's part in it.

"So Alex was still alive at that farm?"

She nodded. "Poison killed him. But with the pigs, Alex screamed forever. They buried him to here," she gestured to her shoulders. "I couldn't watch. But Myung-Dae made me listen."

The imagery grabbed Porter and refused to let go. *Mother of God, the old man is a savage.*

"Will the bartender back up what you say?"

"Myung-Dae killed him, too. I found him in my apartment, hanging from a beam. I took this before I called the KNPA." Jeong took out her phone and showed Porter the photo of a hanging Doyoon.

"KNPA is the police?"

Jeong nodded. "One of their men came into Duffy Club to question Myung-Dae. But he pays for protection and doesn't worry about them."

"How do you know Myung-Dae pays for protection?"

"Everyone in Anjeong-ri knows. I'm sure the KNPA agent that questioned Myung-Dae knows, too."

"That's interesting. But why did Myung-Dae kill Alex? It sounds like they were in business together with DiSilva, making money."

"Alex was selling something to Myung-Dae,"

Jeong said. "And Myung-Dae didn't like that Alex and I spent time together."

"Did Alex sell Myung-Dae a military ID card?" Porter took his ID out of his wallet to show her. "Like this?"

She shrugged. "Alex didn't say."

"Who else watched Alex die, other than you and Myung-Dae?"

"His men Gunn and Kiwoo. You will see them with Myung-Dae sometimes in Duffy Club."

"Was Mr. Arthur at that farm when Alex died?"

"No. Just Myung-Dae and his men. And me."

"So they just stood around and watched him die?"

Porter didn't want to scare Jeong even more than she already was, but she was a material witness to a homicide. And because of that, a threat to Myung-Dae Tang. Just as the departed Doyoon had been.

"Every day Myung-Dae grows bolder." Jeong extended her hand across the table and took Porter's. "So will you help me, Porter? Please? There is no one else to ask."

It was the look she gave him. One of humility, shame, and fear. He wanted to summon a good enough reason to back out gracefully. But looking into those eyes was like a drug. An addictive one at that. *I can't tell her how long I'll be here; I don't know myself. There's still the possibility she's an asset for the north or the Chinese. Even the KGB isn't out of the question. Except she hasn't asked about my clearance. Yet.*

"I'll try to help you," he said. "I can't promise much more than that."

She smiled. "I don't know how to thank you. What should I do first?"

"Do nothing for right now. As much as you can avoid Myung-Dae, stay clear. Working for him, I know that's impossible. But make no threats, don't purposely antagonize him."

She turned her head away. "He sickens me."

Porter nodded. Myung-Dae sickened him, too. "Tell me more about the working girls he sends to America. How does that work?"

"Myung-Dae pays men from your unit to marry working girls. They get citizenship and divorce a year later. Woman stays in America and pays Myung-Dae every month." Jeong explained the financial terms.

Porter remembered Claude's words on the trip to Humphreys from the airport. *Men marrying locals after getting separation orders.* Now that made sense.

"How is DiSilva involved?"

"He tells Myung-Dae who is leaving and arranges for visa at the American embassy." Jeong reached into her purse and pulled out her Duffy Club business card. She slid it across the table to Porter.

He looked at it and saw her cell phone number. He turned the card over. On the back, three names. Bingham, Searcy, and Miller.

"What's this?"

"Those men are the last three GIs from your unit that Myung-Dae set up with working girl wives. There are others. Miller is leaving soon. The others left soon after the New Year."

Porter recognized Miller's name. "How did you get these names?" he asked.

"I overhear working girls."

Porter nodded. "I want you to think about Myung-Dae's habits and weaknesses. Does he have a drug problem? A drinking problem? A gambling problem? Anything like that?"

"There is a rumor that Myung-Dae sells cocaine."

"Does Myung-Dae sell it himself?"

Jeong shook her head. "He hires others to sell for him."

"Have you seen evidence of this, Jeong? Seen payments made to others to do that work?"

She shook her head. "I see only club business."

"I need something on Myung-Dae that the KNPA can't ignore."

"It would have to be KNPA outside Anjeong-ri. Otherwise, you could end up in jail."

"A drug trafficking charge with the Far East DEA would keep him in prison for a long time. Think about how I can go about proving it."

"I prayed someone like you would come, Porter. Only that is not your real name."

That spooked him. He broke off eye contact because of it.

"You don't trust me, do you?" she asked.

"I *believe* you, Jeong. Trust comes over time. Believing is enough, at least for now."

"Well. I trust you."

"I need time to come up with a plan. Tell me, is Arthur DiSilva involved in Myung-Dae's cocaine trafficking?"

Jeong's brow furrowed before shaking her head. "I've not heard that."

Porter glanced out the window briefly. "A woman approached me last night in Duffy Club. Does she work for Myung-Dae?"

Jeong nodded. "Mina. She met with Myung-Dae

before she went to you."

Porter reestablished eye contact. "What did she want from me?"

"Myung-Dae sent her to keep you from me. My eye is black because we talked."

"What?"

"Myung-Dae had Alex killed because he feared Alex would take me to United States."

Porter took a sip of the coffee and looked again for signs of a lie. He saw none.

"Myung-Dae couldn't believe that you refused her," Jeong said. "And neither could Mina."

"Was Alex your boyfriend?"

Jeong considered the question before responding. "Alex was a friend. He wanted more, but I didn't feel the same way. Still, he wanted to take me and my family away from Myung-Dae. And that got him killed."

"You spoke of a house and a farm. Does Myung-Dae split time between them?"

"Yes. Most of the time, he stays on the farm. His wife lives at the Anjeong-ri house. He stays with her almost every weekend."

"Can you see the farm from the highway?" Porter asked.

"No. It's in a valley just outside of Anjeong-ri."

"Do you know how I can get a look without being seen?"

She took a sip of coffee. "Yes, from up on the mountain. It's the only safe place I could show you."

"Do you know how to get there?"

Jeong nodded.

"How long does it take to get there from this coffee

shop?"

"It depends. Most days, five minutes."

"Do you have any time off tomorrow?" he asked.

"I don't start work on weekends until six o'clock."

He didn't want to get into a discussion about DNA evidence that may still be in the pen. "I want to see where Alex died. Will you take me to the mountain?"

Jeong nodded. "Yes." She looked out the window. "But not today."

"No, not today. We'll meet here again tomorrow at noon. Will that give you enough time to get back into Anjeong-ri for work?"

"Plenty. Weather will be better tomorrow, too."

"Do you have clothes for the outdoors?" he asked.

Her eyebrows arched as she grinned. "Yes."

Porter chuckled. "Okay. I didn't think it was *that* stupid a question."

She giggled and looked at her watch. "Because the weather is bad, I should go."

Porter gestured for the server, and soon they were outside. He stood with her as she hailed a cab. She looked even more beautiful than she had inside. Jeong leaned in close and kissed him briefly. He couldn't remember a woman he'd been so smitten with so quickly. Not even Felicity. *Maybe she's right, and I'm still grieving. Or am I vulnerable?*

A cab pulled to the curb, and Jeong climbed inside. She waved goodbye.

Just don't let her take your eye off the ball.

Porter saw an unoccupied taxi slowly approach and flagged it down. And on the way back to Humphreys he realized that, vulnerable or not, he was sufficiently hooked.

Chapter Seventeen

The doorbell to the Tang's Anjeong-ri home rang.

"Moon-Kym, will you answer the door, please?" Myung-Dae bellowed from his study. That it was already three o'clock that Saturday afternoon surprised the old man, the day getting away from him. He knew Cameron had arrived. Soon he heard boots, with the soldier standing in the doorway.

"Ah, Cameron. Right on time. You should teach your friend Gilbert to tell time."

"Gil didn't show up on time this morning?"

"I don't wish to discuss Gilbert and his many problems. What do you have for me?"

They went through the ritual, the old man anxiously pawing every item from the bag. The receipt soon followed, as did the payment. They agreed to meet next Saturday at ten in the morning.

"I want to discuss your future," said Myung-Dae.

"What about it?"

"I'll be brief. If you marry Nari, I will pay you ten thousand dollars, American dollars. Right now."

"I can't do that."

"Just listen. She is a wife in name only. Where in America do you live, the nearest city?"

"Detroit, Michigan."

"She will move to the city, and you will live where you wish and divorce one year later. But if you take the money and don't marry—is a problem."

"I'll think about it," Cam said.

At that moment, Myung-Dae knew he'd been rejected.

"Don't think too long, Cameron. Spousal visas take time."

"I could use the money, sure. But I don't want to do that to Nari." Cam stood, but Myung-Dae gestured for him to remain seated.

"I understand you've made a new friend. Alex's replacement."

Cam nodded. "What about him?"

"What kind of man is he?"

"How do you mean? The guy just got here."

"Is he trustworthy, do you think?"

Cam fidgeted. "He seems okay."

Myung-Dae chuckled. "Cameron, I think you should study politics."

"Who knows? Maybe I will. I would like to leave; I promised Nari I'd go to the market with her."

"Yes, I understand. Enjoy your time."

Cam grabbed his empty gym bag.

Myung-Dae knew from last week that Cameron had no interest. Yet that didn't soften the blow. And like Mina before him, Myung-Dae didn't like the taste it left in his mouth. Not one bit.

****

Porter slogged through Anjeong-ri's thoroughfare on foot this dark Saturday night. This time of day and without a guide, he knew finding Cam's apartment would be challenging. *I should've set the GPS coordinates when I was there.* He doubled back, thinking it far easier to wait at Duffy Club.

A long line had already formed out front of Duffy's. Porter thought about trying Cam and Gil's method, but without Jeong's approval, it smacked of pretension. After all, Cam and Gil worked for Myung-Dae, thus earning preferential treatment. Porter got in line.

"Hello," a female voice said timidly from his blindside as he waited, tugging on the sleeve of Porter's jacket.

For a second, he thought Mina had returned. To turn and see Nari surprised him.

"Hi, Nari. Is Cam inside?"

"No. He is with Gil at Saint Mary's Hospital in Pyeongtaek. Gayoon is there, badly hurt. I have no money for a taxi."

"Let's go find one."

They walked briskly and silently to the thoroughfare, where Porter hailed a cab. They sat in the back and gave the driver their destination.

Snowplows had done their work, making the commute safe and fast.

"So what happened exactly?" Porter asked. "How did she get injured?"

Nari glanced at the driver's picture posted against the back seat. She looked at Porter and shook her head.

They said nothing until they were inside the hospital vestibule.

"Why couldn't we talk in the taxi?"

"That driver works for Myung-Dae. Not safe."

"Can you tell me what happened?"

"Myung-Dae's man Kiwoo beat Gayoon badly. Cam will tell you more."

"What room is she in?"

Nari shrugged, and together they walked to the lobby's information desk. From there, they went to the elevator, just off the desk. They exited on the third floor and entered room 311.

Gayoon lay asleep in the bed, with a string of IV bags and lines attached to her right hand. Under the oxygen mask, her face and eyes were so swollen Porter doubted she could see. Gil and Cam occupied the room's only two chairs. Porter glanced at Gil; the young man appeared twice his age. Cam jumped up from his chair, gesturing for Nari to sit before leading Porter into the hallway.

"Thanks for bringing her, Mike. Did she tell you what happened?"

"Something about one of Myung-Dae's guys working her over. But why?"

"Gil did something that pissed Myung-Dae off. He's a mess, brother."

Porter waited for the explanation, only Cam didn't volunteer it.

"Gayoon's gonna be okay, though, right?" Porter asked.

"Should be. Doctor said she's got a concussion and a fractured cheekbone. Maybe dinged a rib. It's bad but could've been worse."

"Why'd it happen, Cam?"

"Gil wouldn't say, but I have an idea. I'm sure you figured out that Gil deals blow for Myung-Dae."

Porter nodded. "He's not subtle about it, either."

"He snorts a lot of his own merchandise. I'm not sure how Gayoon comes into the picture, but instead of batting Gil around, Myung-Dae targeted Gayoon. They wanna keep her here for a couple of nights. I'm thinking it might be better if Gil stayed back at our old place for a while. I know I said you could stay whenever I was in Anjeong-ri, but this changes things."

Porter nodded. "No worries. I get it."

They went back into the room and stayed until eight o'clock when a nurse ushered them out as visiting hours ended. The party of four found a cab close to the hospital. Soon they were back in Anjeong-ri.

Along the way, Porter noticed that the contents of Gil's gym bag occasionally clanged. *Something metallic.*

Gil agreed to stay with Cam, and the group splintered off. Gil and Cam walked Nari to her parents' house while Porter hiked back to Camp Humphreys.

As Porter passed the front gate, he made the confession. Yes, he was leery of Myung-Dae Tang. Jeong's story made an impression. After everything he'd heard, Gil and Gayoon got off easy.

That Jeong never strayed too far out of his head had become worrisome. He couldn't even shake her in the hospital. Porter turned off the GPS device and made a decision.

It was time to call Stillson in Los Angeles.

Chapter Eighteen

Gunn and Kiwoo were waiting in the back of Duffy Club when Myung-Dae's car arrived Sunday morning. The old man cut the lights and engine and gingerly got out. Oddly enough, they locked Duffy Club only three hours earlier.

As usual, both Kiwoo and Gunn wore leather jackets with jeans and button-down shirts despite the meat-locker temperature. Myung-Dae harbored no such illusions of toughness and dressed accordingly.

Gunn turned on the small, thin flashlight he carried as they went up the short flight of stairs to the metal door. The doorknob turned easily, and they entered.

"Kid picked this lock easy enough," Gunn whispered. "Like cutting warm butter."

Quietly, the three walked down the hall to the office. Myung-Dae turned his office doorknob, unsurprised to find it unlocked as well. He turned on the light.

To the naked eye, the office looked untouched. At least until you examined the exposed safe, the cabinet door usually hiding it now wide open. It would take extraordinary vision to see the safe's small cavity, directly above the combination dial, from this distance. But that didn't mean it didn't exist.

For a man of Myung-Dae Tang's stature, his Duffy Club office wasn't much. Three-ringed notebooks and accordion folders littered the cheap wooden credenza behind a metal desk that belonged in a dumpster. On top of the desk were a pair of desktop computer monitors, reading lamp, telephone, keyboard, and a framed photograph. In the photo, Myung-Dae stood alongside his wife, unsmiling daughter, and newly minted American son-in-law. The daughter wore her elaborate wedding gown, the American in a U.S. Army dress uniform.

But nothing in this office intrigued visitors more than the glass bowl sitting on the far right end of the credenza behind Myung-Dae's tattered leather chair. The bowl contained rings of different sizes, shapes, and colors—the number difficult to estimate.

"I know you're in here," Myung-Dae said in a sing-song voice. "You can come out now, Namil. The game is up."

Gunn looked behind one of the file cabinets. "I've got him."

"Bring him out, Gunn."

Gunn loomed over Namil. "Lose the mask and goggles and sit against the front of the desk where Myung-Dae can see you. Bring your tools as well."

Namil removed the watch cap and safety goggles before getting to his feet and grabbing his bag. The young thief's eyes stayed on Gunn as he sat down on the concrete floor, placing the tool bag next to him.

"My, my, my," Myung-Dae said, smiling, his gold incisor winking. "The rats get bigger in this place every day."

Kiwoo chuckled while Gunn took his place alongside Myung-Dae.

Myung-Dae looked at Namil as a cat might a

mouse. "So, my young friend. It seems we must chat."

Sweat formed at Namil's temples, despite the cold. He looked at Myung-Dae. "There's a reason for this. I can explain."

Myung-Dae nodded. "Of course there is a reason. You want money. The safe has money. It's all very linear."

"It's not what you think. My mother, she's gravely ill."

Myung-Dae chuckled and looked at Gunn. "Did you hear that? His poor mother is ill. It's been some time since someone was so…creative."

"It's the truth."

Myung-Dae shook his head. "Uh-huh. You ask me for a job, and Kiwoo here tells me you're okay, so I hire you. And this is my thank you? Does that sound fair? What do you say, Gunn?"

"It's not fair," Gunn said.

"How about you, Kiwoo? You still think I should have hired this man?"

"I shouldn't have vouched for him."

Myung-Dae's grin went upside down, and he glared at the large man. "No, you should *not*. Nevertheless, you did."

The old man walked up to Namil's bag and looked carefully at the contents. "These are not the tools of an amateur. Do you have a prison record? Now is the time for truth."

"I did a five-year stretch at Pohang. Felony larceny and breaking-and-entering."

Myung-Dae shot another angry glance at Kiwoo and then looked back at Namil. "Who do you work for?"

"Up until now, I worked for you. I needed the money."

"Yeah, yeah, for the sick mother. I'll ask again. Who do you work for?"

"I'm alone in this, Myung-Dae. I swear it."

"Where did you say you're from again?"

"Daejeon."

"That's right, Daejeon. I suppose it's a coincidence that Ryung Dokgo lives in Daejeon. Did he pay you to rob me?"

"Who?" Namil asked.

"Call animal control, Gunn. We have an owl. Who? Who?" Myung-Dae cackled as he mocked Namil. "I'll ask but one more time. After this, it gets bloody. Who do you work for?"

"I work alone."

Myung-Dae nodded. "Very well. Now we'll go to *my* workshop. Pick up his gear and take him to the farm. I'll be there after I check everything and lock the place back up."

The blood drained from Namil's face. "Please, Myung-Dae, not the farm. I promise if you let me go, you'll never see me again."

"And I promise you that after today, you'll never want to see me again."

"How did you know I would be here this morning?"

"I've been watching you from the start. The next time you try robbing someone, you shouldn't make such an effort to count cash in the registers while you're working. You're not the first thief I've hired, and none of you have outsmarted me."

Namil hung his head. Gunn and Kiwoo put their

hands under Namil's armpits and lifted him up. The burglar eyed the ring bowl and the trophies inside as Gunn blindfolded him with a black bandana and applied zip-line handcuffs. Together, the thugs walked Namil to the truck.

****

By the time Myung-Dae arrived at the farm, Gunn and Kiwoo had already secured Namil inside the maintenance shed behind the barn. The lights were on, and the two thugs wore plastic smocks. Namil's terrified eyes darted about as he stood, his left forearm pinned by the vice grip bolted down at the end of the long bench.

Taking his time, Myung-Dae approached. He no longer tried to camouflage the joy this brought him. A foot away from Namil, the old man came to a halt.

"Please, Myung-Dae, I don't want to die." Namil whimpered.

"Shh, shh, shh." Myung-Dae reached over and patted a cheek. "You will not die today if we can help it. Consider this place a schoolhouse, and today you'll receive a valuable lesson. A painful lesson but one you'll never forget." He glanced at Gunn. "Hand me a smock. Let's begin."

Kiwoo moved in behind Namil, holding the thief in a bear hug. Namil's eyes bulged as Myung-Dae slid the plastic garment over his clothes.

"Tell me who you work for. I don't wish to disfigure you, young man," Myung-Dae said. "Appendages don't grow back once removed."

"I can't tell you, I can't," Namil shouted. "If I do, I'll die!"

"And if you don't, you'll be stealing with just your

left hand. Or maybe I'll take the entire arm. Once you're in shock, it won't much matter. Tell me, so I don't have to do this!"

"Okay, okay. The Dokgo brothers, okay? You were right, Mr. Tang. They sent me."

Myung-Dae took a step back, again giving Kiwoo a death-stare before refocusing. "Why did they send you? What are they looking for?"

"They wanted to know how much money your businesses brought in; they said you stopped paying tribute. But that's all I know. Please let me go; you'll never see me again."

"That's all? Nothing more?" Myung-Dae asked.

"I told you everything."

"Hold him tighter, Kiwoo."

Myung-Dae slid the topaz pinky ring Namil wore off the young man's finger and put it in his pocket. The elderly man then reached for a long, curved utility knife sitting on the bench. With pinpoint precision, Myung-Dae brought the blade across Namil's throat.

Blood sprayed in every direction as Namil gurgled, the thief drowning in his own blood, his eyes wide and panicked as he went into shock and began convulsing. Kiwoo, covered in blood, released his hold and backed away, as did Gunn and Myung-Dae. Kiwoo vomited at the sight, and Gunn looked away. Only Myung-Dae watched Namil die a slow and horrifying death.

"Why did you do that?" Kiwoo screamed. "The others you only took a hand. Why did you kill him? And what am I to tell his parents?"

"Tell his parents they failed him. Ryung Dokgo sent him; now let Ryung find him. Hand me a plastic bag."

Kiwoo reached over and removed a trash can liner from the box on the bench. Myung-Dae removed the smock and put it in.

"Make sure this mess gets cleaned up before you go anywhere. Don't forget to call the locksmith, Gunn."

"What of the body?" Gunn asked.

"I think you know what to do."

Myung-Dae took one last look at Namil's corpse. And walked out of the shed.

****

Porter unlocked the empty admin office and walked to DiSilva's desk. It was Saturday afternoon in Los Angeles.

The agent opened his cell phone, scrolled to Stillson's landline home phone number, and punched both his agency code and Stillson's number into DiSilva's landline. It took several minutes for someone to pick up.

"Hello," Stillson answered.

"Hi Walter, Mike Porter. I'm sorry to bother you over the weekend. Do you have a couple of minutes?"

"I'm glad you called. How are you settling in?"

"This is a strange place. Seems I stumbled onto some kind of sex trafficking ring with a narcotics component. And this unit commanding officer plays a big part."

"Human trafficking and narcotics?"

"South Korean women sent to the States to be prostitutes. I've got a local moving cocaine, and he's the CO's father-in-law. I'm sure this officer plays a part in the human trafficking. The cocaine element is iffy."

"How did you find out about them?"

"It fell into my lap, no pun intended. Soldiers

170

marry for money and look the other way when the wife sets up shop and gets citizenship. The couple divorces a year later. The CO may or may not be in on the cocaine."

Stillson said nothing for several seconds. "That's interesting but has nothing to do with why you're there. Those are criminal enterprises. Give it to CID."

"CID can't dig in the way I already have. I've got three names of guys who are out or getting out of the Army with Korean wives, neck deep in this. At the very least, ICE should be told."

"And they will be. Because CID will coordinate with them after you give them whatever you have."

"I'm a little disappointed to hear you say that. A soldier here got killed for being involved in the sex trafficking," Porter said.

"All the more reason to hand it over to CID. They work with the KNPA and have the resources to shut it down. You're spinning your wheels on something beyond our scope. If you're having trouble with a local, I can arrange contact with a KNPA subcontractor who's done some work for us in the past, assuming he's still active. If you meet with him, say *nothing* about why you're there. He's not cleared for it."

"I'd like to meet with him. Any headway into who we're looking for?"

"Not yet. The chatter's down to a trickle and oscillates between Anjeong-ri and Pyeongtaek. We haven't picked up on a pattern yet."

"Any mention of the Olympics? The opening ceremonies are less than two weeks away."

"Not a word," Stillson said.

"We haven't discussed the exfil."

"Flight ops will brief you pre-board; let me worry about the exfil. You've been training with your spotter?"

"Affirmative. We shot outside yesterday. On a technical level, he's the best spotter I've ever worked with. I'll admit, we're both getting antsy. Anything about the Osan drone?"

"Drone's flying out of Osan this afternoon, your time. But if it goes dark, I'll send everything we have on file because they won't send another."

"Yes, sir."

"So you'll hand those rings off to CID?" Stillson asked.

"I'm begging you to reconsider. I'm close to the local running this."

"Nothing to reconsider; it's beyond our scope. Is there anything else?"

"No, sir." *Jeong turned out to be right. Stillson wants me to turn a blind eye.*

"Hang in there just a bit longer. I need you to stay focused."

"Yes, sir."

The conversation over, Porter haphazardly put the phone's receiver in the cradle. It crashed to the floor.

He got out of the chair and picked the cordless handset up, putting it back in the cradle on the desk and berating himself for being so clumsy. Porter listened for a dial tone. And while it came up, the volume was choppy. Only that wasn't the problem. Porter also heard a rattle from inside the microphone end. He shook it.

Fuck me. I broke the damned thing. How the hell do I explain using and breaking DiSilva's phone?

Porter's belly burned with acid. He went to his

desk and grabbed a letter opener to pry the handset's bottom open. Inside, he discovered a thick dull-black button the diameter of a quarter.

He let it fall into his palm, sticky to the touch. With one side dimpled with many tiny holes, Porter recognized it from a textbook at Langley. *This thing is ancient. Who still uses them?* Porter stiffened. *Someone's listening to conversations. And just heard the one I had with Stillson.* Porter tried playing the conversation back in his head, wondering how much he'd given an unknown third party.

DiSilva wouldn't bug his own phone. That leaves Martz. Why would Martz be interested in DiSilva's phone conversations?

Using his cell phone, Porter tested DiSilva's phone. It proved capable of sending and receiving calls.

Porter checked his office phone. There was no listening device in it.

Walking down the hall and going into the utility room off the showers, Porter borrowed duct tape from the houseboys, taping the bug under the first basin.

Let's see how long it takes Martz to find it.

Before he reached his barracks room, Porter received a text from Stillson, telling him to check his agency email. Porter backtracked to the office and logged on to the agency email portal. The encrypted message gave Porter the name and mobile telephone number of the local KNPA subcontractor Stillson mentioned. His name was Jungho Bak.

Porter walked to his room. Simpson, engrossed in study, kept silent as Porter put on long underwear. Today's temperature was frigid, but with the sun shining, visibility was better than yesterday's. Porter said nothing as he left the room and walked to the bus stop.

Chapter Nineteen

Ferguson sat alone in the armory locker room when Porter arrived. Porter punched the combination to his locker and sat beside his spotter.

"The target stands in the ride?" he asked Ferguson.

"Yeah. Wind will be an issue today."

"That's why I'm counting on you, Fergie. I was on the phone with LA this morning. They're sending another drone north this afternoon."

"And if it goes down, what's next? Google maps?"

"They have intel on file."

"Yeah, but how old? It's been a long time since anyone from our side laid eyes on Panmunjom," Ferguson noted. "Any intel on the shooter?"

"I'll know soon enough about the drone. When I asked about the shooter, Stillson stonewalled."

Ferguson put his chest plate in the lightweight nylon duffle bag. "Ever take a bullet?"

"Nope. How about you?"

"No. What about shot at?"

"Twice in Iraq. What's eatin' you, Fergie?"

"I'm curious if getting hit in cold weather hurts more."

Porter scoffed. "Always the optimist."

"Do you know what North Korea does to political prisoners, Mike?"

Porter held up his hand. "No, but I'm sure it's

175

unpleasant. How about a little positive visualization for a change?"

"When do you think we're going?"

"Any day now."

A trio of MPs entered the locker room, having come from the indoor range. Porter was glad for it.

"I'm just as frustrated as you are, trust me," Porter whispered.

With body armor and weapons in the nylon bags, the pair left the armory's locker room for the vehicle Ferguson reserved for the weekend, sitting out front.

"You mind if I use the ride this afternoon, Fergie?"

"I don't care. Are you staying on the base?"

"No, I'm going to Pyeongtaek and back."

"Sure. Just make sure the motor pool gets it back before 1800." Ferguson turned the vehicle's key in the ignition. "Did the agency give you end-game pills?"

"Dude. I just got done asking for positivity." Porter glanced at Ferguson. "We prepare, we execute, and we bug out. I didn't come halfway around the world to commit suicide, and I hope you're not planning to."

"Is there anything else you can tell me?"

"Every day we get closer. So get your head right, and let's go to the pit."

****

Porter returned to the barracks two hours later. Simpson sat at the desk, reading.

"Top wants to see you, Mike. ASAP."

Good. He found the bug.

"Are his fingers busted, or did dementia finally kick in? He has my cell phone number."

"Save the arrows; I'm just the messenger."

"Uh-huh. If he comes back, teach that Neanderthal

how to text or make a phone call."

Simpson turned back to his study guide, and Porter undressed to shower. He waited until he was alone in the lavatory before checking under the first sink. He chuckled to see the duct tape no longer there.

When Porter returned to the room, Simpson had vanished. Porter strapped on the holstered pistol and walked out to the SUV he'd parked in the building courtyard. He turned on the GPS and headed for the main gate.

****

Jeong waited at the same booth they occupied yesterday when Porter entered the coffeehouse. Again, the place went into a hush after he entered, today's crowd larger than yesterday's.

Wearing jeans, hiking boots, and a sweater to compliment the parka, Jeong looked fashionably ready for their outing. She smiled as he sat down.

Binoculars hung from Porter's neck after he took off his jacket. He placed them on the booth's table before the server came to take their order.

"After we get a look at the farm, could you bring me to Myung-Dae's Anjeong-ri house?"

She shook her head. "Being seen together in Anjeong-ri is a death sentence for me and maybe you too. I'll show you the farm, but someone else will have to bring you to Myung-Dae's house in town. Cam or Gil could do that when they go to sell black-market goods."

Porter nodded. "That's a good idea."

The server set the coffee down and left.

"Is there any other place Myung-Dae would spend the night?"

She thought about that. "No."

"Tell me about your family, Jeong."

She leaned back. "Why are you asking?"

"You don't know that I'm interested in you?"

"In what way?"

You sure you want to take this chance? If she shuts you down, would you still help her? "Let's see…how should I put this? In a romantic sort of way."

Jeong flashed a smile, reached across the table, and took his hand. Porter's heart soared.

She began with Sejun's education. It was obvious she took pride in her younger sister's achievements. By the time she'd moved on to her father, the cups were empty. Porter shook the waitress off.

Jeong reached for her jacket. "Should we go now?"

Porter nodded. "I want to get you back home at a decent hour."

****

They were on the highway back to Anjeong-ri when Jeong told Porter to take a dirt road off to the left. The area was dense woodland, spruce pine, and birch trees mostly.

"Is the farm down this road?" he asked.

"No. Farther down is the road that leads to Myung-Dae's farm. This is his neighbor's."

Twenty-five yards in, Porter pulled the four-wheel-drive vehicle over. He held the door for Jeong and looked around before taking the GPS out of his pocket.

Jeong looked at the device. "What's that thing for?"

"GPS. It marks a spot, so I can find it again if I need to." Porter spotted a nearby deer path, and they began their ascent through thick pine trees. While not

Mount Kilimanjaro, in the snow and ice, it was a modest hike. They said little as they climbed, the wind varying in intensity as they wove between the trees.

Halfway up the range, they found a clearing with a dry, semi-flat ledge to sit on. There, in the valley, sat Myung-Dae's farm. Porter brought the binoculars up and ranged it, the barn three hundred yards away on a thirty-degree descent. In the snow, the farm appeared scenic, calm, and sedate.

Once again, Porter removed the GPS unit, marking and saving the coordinates.

"You're sure that's Myung-Dae's farm?"

"I'm sure, Porter."

He brought the binoculars up again and looked around. Aside from three calves wandering in the pasture just outside the barn, nothing else moved. Porter took several cell phone photos.

"The cars—who do they belong to?" Even at this distance, agency software could zoom in and display license plate numbers. Porter would then ask the KNPA contact to run the plates through the Korean DMV database.

"Myung-Dae's car isn't there, but that's his pickup truck. He has two men who work and live on the farm, so those cars may belong to them. His other men have rooms and stay there sometimes, too."

"How many men does Myung-Dae have altogether, including farm workers?"

She thought about that. "Four that I know of."

"The fenced area in front of the barn is where Alex died?"

"Yes."

"You've been inside the house?"

"Yes. Once."

"Have you ever seen or heard about Myung-Dae or his men using guns?"

"No."

"Not ever?"

"Not ever."

"I've seen enough. Let's get you down and back to Anjeong-ri." Porter got to his feet and helped her up.

"How about you tell me a little about yourself, Porter?"

"What would you like to know?"

As they descended, he fed her the agency-scripted biography he'd committed to memory.

Halfway through Porter's version, she stopped. "How about telling me the truth?"

Porter stopped as well, turning to look at her. "What makes you think it isn't the truth?"

"You still haven't told me your real name."

"And what do you think my real name is?"

"I don't know. But it's not Mike Porter. You only pretend to be in the army."

"Keep guessing." He was glad to be in front of her, where she couldn't get a look at his face. Her accuracy continued to trouble him. And he wondered if China or North Korea fed her intel. Yet that didn't make her any less attractive. He started walking again. She waited until they were in the SUV before asking questions again.

"How long were you married?"

Porter turned the key in the ignition. "Three years."

"Were you happy?"

He turned to look at her. With her complexion a rosy red from the cold, she was one of the most beautiful women he'd ever seen. "Yes, I was happy."

"You're not going to be on Camp Humphreys much longer, are you?"

Porter didn't answer and put the SUV in first gear. *Please don't ask about my clearance. Please, don't.*

"Are you coming into Anjeong-ri tonight?"

"I'm not sure yet." Porter didn't want to tell her he worried about Cam and Gil's drug use. He changed the subject. "I think about you. Sometimes too much."

"Yes. I think about you a lot too."

"I'd like for us to get to know each other better," he said. "Maybe more."

"I would like that too. Will you call me tomorrow?"

"Sure, if you like. I'll call your cell phone sometime around noon?"

"Yes. That is a good time," she said. "I have tomorrow night off. Can I see you then?" She told him of Kowloons, a Chinese restaurant she liked in Pyeongtaek.

"I would like that."

Porter took a secondary street to the right before they reached the Anjeong-ri commercial district. There, he stopped the SUV. She moved in close, leaned in, and kissed him passionately. At that moment, he felt like a teenager again, on cloud nine. Finally, they separated.

He opened the SUV door for her, kissing her once again before she walked away. He hadn't felt this way about a woman in some time.

Returning the car to the motor pool, Porter let his thoughts move on from Jeong to the listening device. He couldn't help but wonder how Martz would begin their awkward conversation about them later today or tomorrow morning.

Porter would be ready. He took the bus across camp to the barracks.

****

Gunn sat in the farmhouse kitchen with a cup of coffee when Myung-Dae returned from Anjeong-ri.

"Ah, Gunn. Can I assume the pigs enjoyed their meal?"

Gunn nodded. "The pigs haven't been well since Alex. I burned Namil's clothes and the smocks. Did you enjoy your family meal?"

Myung-Dae grimaced. "We may have to call the vet. And the locksmith?"

"Put a new lock in this afternoon. He made five keys." Gunn walked four shiny new keys over to his boss. "If you want more made, I'll run to the hardware store in the morning. Just give me a count."

Myung-Dae put the keys in his pocket and went to the stove to grab the kettle. He started filling it with water. "Do you think Kiwoo had a part in this morning's affair?"

Gunn put the coffee cup down slowly and cocked his head. "What?"

"The kid this morning. Do you think Kiwoo worked with him?"

Color drained from Gunn's face. "I hope you're joking."

"Do you see me laughing?"

Gunn shook his head and looked out the window. "Not a chance. Kiwoo didn't know the kid would pull that stunt."

Myung-Dae rubbed his goatee. "I want to believe that. I really do. Is Kiwoo here?"

"Upstairs."

"Would you ask him to come down, Gunn?"

"Wait a minute. You don't really believe Kiwoo had anything to do with that. What's this about?" *Is he losing his mind? First, the cruelty and killings, and now a sudden surge in paranoia?*

"I would like to ask Kiwoo a few questions, Gunn. Who are you to question my authority?"

Gunn grunted as he got to his feet and climbed the stairs. He knocked on Kiwoo's door. "Are you there, Kiwoo?"

Kiwoo opened the door. "Gunn. What is it?"

"Myung-Dae's in the kitchen asking for you. Listen, he's in a weird mood, so tread lightly."

Kiwoo nodded, and together, they went down the stairs into the kitchen. Myung-Dae still lingered at the stove as the men entered.

"You wanted to see me, Myung-Dae?" Kiwoo asked.

"We need to talk about what happened this morning."

"Good. It's been bothering me. What do I tell that boy's father? Put yourself in his parents' shoes for a minute. How would you feel if Chona had an employer who one day arbitrarily killed her?"

"Arbitrarily? How dare you. First, Chona wouldn't think to steal from an employer or anyone else! I don't care what you tell the parents. In my mind, they are just as much to blame."

"What you did was heartless and cruel. And not the first time you've reacted in such a way."

"Were you working with Namil?"

Kiwoo's face turned ash white. "After all these

years, how could you ask me that? I've never taken a thing that belonged to you. Never spoken ill of you."

Myung-Dae shook his head, grinning as he did. The gold tooth winked. "And I'm to take that at face value? After you tell me to hire that young man who wasted very little time robbing me? Shame on you."

"I had no way of knowing Namil would try to rob you. None. I didn't know about his criminal record. All I knew was that he tended bar in a social club in Daegu."

"This brings me to your judgment. You said I could trust him. Is that not correct?" Myung-Dae glanced down at Gunn, expecting reinforcement.

"There are limits on how much one man can know another," Gunn said.

Kiwoo took a step closer to Myung-Dae. "You were short a bartender. The kid tends bar; it's what he does." The pace of Kiwoo's speech quickened. "He came looking for a job. His father is my cousin. And now I have to tell him and his wife their only child is dead. For no good reason."

"No good reason? He had a mind to rob me from the start. And I suspect you were complicit."

Kiwoo's face turned from white to crimson. "What do you want from me, Myung-Dae? My resignation? Okay, fine. I resign. There's no future for me with you anyhow. I'll get my things and be out of this house in fifteen minutes."

Myung-Dae reached into a kitchen drawer below the countertop as the kettle on the stove came to a boil. He brought up the small .22 pistol the farmhands sometimes used to scare varmints bothering the livestock. Myung-Dae calmly disengaged the safety, aimed at Kiwoo's chest, and began firing as Gunn jumped out of his chair and out of the way.

The first round missed its mark, hitting Kiwoo in the shoulder. With a puzzled expression on his face, the much larger man lunged at Myung-Dae. Myung-Dae stepped back and kept firing until he emptied the magazine, all fifteen rounds, pumped into Kiwoo's chest and belly. After he finished, the old man dropped into a kitchen chair, physically spent, gently putting the empty pistol on the table.

Gunn walked over to his fallen friend and checked for a pulse that didn't exist. Kiwoo's eyes and mouth were still open; blood trickled from his nose and the corners of his mouth. Gunn went to the table, putting the pistol back in the drawer. "I can't believe you just did that. What do you want me to do with him? And don't even *think* about feeding him to your sick swine. This man served you well for over twenty years and deserves far better."

"You should know better than to preach to me, Gunn. But in the heat of the moment, it's forgivable. Bury him in the woods if you like."

"Bury him how? The ground's frozen solid, Myung-Dae."

"Figure it out for yourself, Gunn. Get rid of the body and clean this mess up. Ask the farmhands to help you; they'll finish milking soon. I'm going to bed."

Myung-Dae stepped over Kiwoo's body on his way to the stairs. Gunn went to the barn, not sure what he would say to either farmhand. Kiwoo was well-liked.

So tell them the truth, that they should buy pistols. Looks like I need to arm myself as well.

185

Chapter Twenty

Porter's alarm went off, and he slowly got to his feet. Getting Jeong out of his head took longer every day. He broke through as he showered, thoughts of Seoul finally taking shape. He looked forward to seeing something other than Camp Humphreys, Anjeong-ri, or Pyeongtaek, no matter how brief. There was something about a city skyline that upped his energy. After dressing, he went down the hall and reported for work.

Why he looked forward to a confrontation with Martz, not even Porter fully understood. After all, Martz held all the cards. The master sergeant could get a log of outgoing calls and speak directly with Stillson. *That'd be fun to explain.*

Porter took a deep breath and walked in. To his surprise, Gil and Cam stood by his desk in cammies, jackets on, hats in hand. The alarmed expressions on their faces told Porter nothing good was afoot.

"Don't get too comfy," Martz said from DiSilva's desk. Like the others, he had a jacket on.

"I haven't square-danced since the fifth grade," Porter said, walking toward his desk. "Even then, it sucked."

Martz chuckled. "Aw, Mike, always with the witty repartee. Go grab your hat and jacket while we wait; you're coming too."

"You mind telling me what this is about, Top?"

Porter looked at both Cam and Gil. Even on a winter morning, they appeared paler than usual. *They're scared shitless.*

"We're taking a little trip to the camp hospital. Random blood tests for you guys."

"Random? Sorry, Top, but this is the polar opposite of random. But I'm sure someone from JAG will give you a better working definition after we file the report."

"You'll be able to call a lawyer from the stockade, smartass. Hurry up; we don't have all day."

Porter glared at Martz. "Did you call for a cab, or are we taking the bus?"

"I've got a car in the courtyard. Nothing but the best for my little drug addicts."

"Prehistoric douchebag," Porter muttered under his breath as he pivoted for the door. He returned to the office two minutes later, hat in hand, jacket on.

"Okay, ladies. Follow me," Martz said.

Porter cut the office lights and locked the door while Martz led the others outside. They followed the master sergeant to an unmarked sedan. Porter felt embarrassed as he walked past a couple of the guys from the unit he'd recently met. Even the houseboys stopped their chores to stare. Porter imagined it was worse for Cam and Gil.

The very real probability that this might be the last time he saw these two guys hit home. Failing this test meant doing time in the stockade. And Porter calculated the odds that both men had traces of pot and cocaine in their bloodstream at one-hundred percent.

Cam and Gil climbed into the back seat while Porter got stuck riding shotgun. *Martz planned this since the Friday night run-in. Cam and Gil never expected being called out. Then again, who could've predicted Martz showing up in Duffy Club that night?*

Martz pulled into the hospital parking lot. He led them into the lobby, and once there, looked at the directory. Obviously, this was the first time Martz pulled this stunt. The lab was two doors down from the corridor to their right.

Martz escorted them to the lab and opened the door. A tech in a white lab coat sat behind the front desk of the small room.

"I put in an order for blood samples on these guys yesterday afternoon," Martz said.

The tech eyed Martz's name tag before turning his attention to the trio. He gave each a long, thin label and pen and a capped test tube. "Name and last four of your socials where it says. Then peel it off and put it on the tube, like this." The tech showed the men what it should look like. "Blood's drawn back there." The tech gestured to the door behind him. "Go in and take a seat. A medic is on the way."

"Can't we just do urine?" Porter asked. "I hate needles."

"Everybody hates needles, Sarge. Try to relax."

"It's okay if I wait back here?" Martz inquired.

"Sure, Top. Have a seat. This won't take long."

Cam opened the door and walked through first. Bathed in white paint, the room appeared sterile, with harsh fluorescent lights and four chairs with armrests. It smelled of rubbing alcohol.

"We are so fucked," Gil whispered to Cam after Porter closed the door. "And right after I reenlisted."

"Fuck you, Gil. They'll send me home with a dishonorable discharge. I've gotta live with that."

The medic entered from a different door, the man's face vaguely familiar to Porter.

"I must be dreaming," Cam said as he smiled. "Thank God."

"You guys piss someone off?" the medic asked.

"Please tell me you can get us out of this," Gil said.

"I've got clean samples. But let's not make a habit of this. You're lucky I'm on day shifts this week." The medic looked at Porter. "We haven't met. Mitch Carruthers."

"Mike Porter." Porter extended his hand, and Mitch shook it.

Mitch unlocked a cabinet drawer secured by a built-in combination lock. He poured clean blood into Gil and Cam's test tubes from a pair of unmarked test tubes in the drawer.

Mitch glanced at Porter. "You want in, Mike?"

"Sure. I hate needles."

Like the others, Mitch gave Porter a clean sample.

"Just out of curiosity, how fresh are these samples?" Porter asked, genuinely curious.

"Houseboys sold it yesterday. The samples are good. You guys understand you owe me and the wife a night out for this, right?"

"Oh, yeah," Gil said. "Where you been hiding, anyhow?"

"Areum wanted to take a break from Anjeong-ri nightlife. She wants to start a family."

Mitch removed three bandages and cotton balls from another cabinet. "Roll up those sleeves and let me put these on; give your dickhead master sergeant a show."

"Thank you, brother," Cam said.

When they finished, Mitch told the trio to go back to the tech out front and that he'd catch up with them in Anjeong-ri sometime soon. When Mitch walked out, Porter blocked the door leading to Martz before Gil could open it.

"Before you go back out, we have to look worried. Trust me; he thinks he's got us under his boot heel. Go out cocky, and you'll wind up back here in a couple of days."

Cam glanced at Gil and nodded. "No problem. We get it."

Gil walked through first, and Martz got to his feet.

"When will I have the results?" Martz queried the tech.

"Sometime this afternoon. I'll call when they come in, Top."

"Thank you." Martz's attention then turned to his men. "Okay, girls. Back to the car."

Driving back across camp, Martz appeared a little more relaxed. Cam and Gil kept their mouths shut and shoulders slumped.

"You're restricted to the barracks until further notice," Martz told Cam and Gil after parking the car. "Leave without authorization, and I'll have your worthless asses in the stockade that much sooner."

The pair said nothing, and the four split off when Cam and Gil went to their barracks room. Martz led Porter back into the admin office and closed the door, the master sergeant getting comfortable in DiSilva's chair. Porter wondered when Martz would ask about the listening device. Porter sat at his desk and started working.

"Your buddies are going down. You, I'm not so

sure about," Martz said. "Their pupils looked like Frisbees Friday night."

"You like to gamble, right Top?"

"Depends on what, and the odds, I suppose. What's on your mind?"

"You're in for a disappointment when those results come back."

"Bull-fucking-shit," Martz said with a gap-toothed grin. "Man, it's been cold the last few days. Is the weather warm in Los Angeles, Mike? That's where you placed the call."

Finally. Not even any foreplay.

"Let me guess. You're CID. You guys need better tech; that bug I found belongs in the Smithsonian."

Martz glared. "No point in being coy, now that we're both unzipped. Yeah, I'm CID. But let's talk about you. You smuggled a weapon into the barracks. On that alone, I could have your ass if I wanted it bad enough. That's a felony offense, carrying an unauthorized weapon on a military installation."

"What makes you think it's unauthorized? And how in the hell did you find out about it?"

"Ralph took a peek right after you got here. He knew the wardrobe's combination from his old roommate."

Porter shook his head and grinned. "I should've known. Speaking of Ralph, I want him off my ass. The guy's as subtle as a sledgehammer."

Martz nodded.

"Finding your bug tells me you're looking at DiSilva for something."

"And your chat with your boss in LA told me you know why. Only you're not here for DiSilva. So who do you work for, Mike? You're not FBI. That leaves ATF, NSA or CIA. Based on your conversation, I'll guess CIA or NSA."

Porter scoffed. "I can't tell you. But I'll share some things I've learned in the short time I've been here. Any soldier can score dope off-base faster than they could at a rock concert. Then there's the pesky human trafficking ring DiSilva is part of. You got any more bugs in this office I should know about?"

"Just what you found, which I put back, by the way. I didn't get authorization to bug the rest of the office."

"What did you hit?"

"I tapped DiSilva's car and house. His cell phone and security building office is off-limits. To read the transcripts, DiSilva's a choirboy. Which tells me he's discussing the marriage ring at some other prearranged site. Most likely Tang's house."

"Didn't Tomlinson's murder give you a reason to tag his cell phone?"

"Someone murdered Tomlinson? Now that's valuable information," Martz said. "Who did it? You have a body or witness? I'll settle for a murder weapon. Motive would come in handy too."

"Motive is that missing ID. And I have an eye witness."

"Willing to testify in open court?"

Porter shook his head. "No, probably not."

"Then you got squat."

"How familiar are you with Tang?"

"I know he's DiSilva's father-in-law and the money behind the ring. But when I requested help from the Anjeong-ri KNPA, they brushed me off. Told me

Tang didn't have a criminal record."

"That's because he pays them."

Martz snorted out a chuckle. "Ya think? Telling me Tang murdered Tomlinson doesn't help or impress me."

"Impressed or not, a woman who works in one of Tang's bars saw it. Only she's scared to come forward. Just like the rest of Anjeong-ri."

"My job is to nail DiSilva. Tang is a KNPA problem."

"Ask yourself how bad you want DiSilva," Porter said.

"I've been working this for eight months with nothing to show for it. So the answer to that is pretty damned bad. But because he's close to Tang and Tang runs a tight ship, I've made no progress. DiSilva's no dummy either."

"You're after DiSilva, and I need Tang. You agree to help me take Tang down, and I'll give you all the help I can to nail DiSilva for as long as I'm here. Which won't be for much longer. You have people listening in on the bugs?"

"Around-the-clock. Are you here for Tang?"

Porter cocked his head with an arched eyebrow. "Unless Tang has launch codes I don't know about, I can tell you he has *nothing* to do with why I'm here. And you already know that."

Martz nodded. "Okay. So what is your interest in Tang?"

Porter leaned in. "The woman I mentioned earlier who works for Tang? She lives in hell because of it. He needs to go down, and I'm past caring how I do it."

"What's she to you?"

"That's a little personal, don't you think?"

Martz grinned. "Maybe. But it's an honest question."

"I care about her."

"You've considered the possibility she works for the other side?"

Porter nodded. "Except she's never asked what I'm cleared for. If she belongs to China or the north, she needs better training."

Martz leaned back. "Maybe she's waiting for the right time to ask. What do you know about Tang for a fact?"

"For a fact? Nothing. Only what I've heard from others." Porter showed Martz the photo of Doyoon Chang that Jeong sent him. "This guy worked for Tang. She found him in her apartment one night after work. He unknowingly poisoned Tomlinson. You gonna work with me or not? Because if you are, I'll need bugs. Not phone bugs but something with decent range, say five miles out. Do you have access to anything like that?"

"Whoever you work for didn't give you any devices of your own?"

Porter shook his head. "Why would they? It's not part of my engagement."

"I can hook you up with something that fits your description. So I give you a few, and then what? Tang's going to invite you to dinner with DiSilva in his house?"

"I can think of a way to get into his house and maybe his Duffy Club office too."

"How you do it is how you do it. Okay. I'll work with you." Martz pointed a finger. "But if I get the sense you're holding out or grandstanding, this partnership is over."

"That's fine."

"The dynamic between us can't change. We stay antagonistic. Especially in front of DiSilva."

"That is *not* a problem."

"So according to your lady friend, Tang poisoned Tomlinson. Then what?"

"He took Tomlinson to his farm and fed him to his pigs, still breathing and in front of an audience. Only DiSilva wasn't there to see it."

Martz's left eyebrow raised as he leaned forward. "Tang did what?"

"You heard me."

Martz grimaced. "I've heard some gruesome shit in my lifetime, but that tops it all, hands down. Did Tomlinson die trying to sell an ID card?"

Porter shrugged. "That played a part. To hear Jeong's version, Tang started to get jealous of her relationship with Tomlinson."

"Jeong Guy? The good-lookin' woman who works in Duffy Club?"

Porter nodded. "You know her?"

"I've heard the name. Now you're involved with the same woman. What if Tang gets a hard-on for you?"

"That's why I never leave the barracks unarmed."

"What does she know about *why* you're here?"

"She knows I'm Tomlinson's replacement. Nothing more."

"And she asked you for help? Why you?"

Porter shrugged. "I've wondered that myself."

"Your buddy Shanahan, have you heard anything about him getting married? Because he's the next swinging dick out of here with separation orders."

"No. And I would have. Why?"

"I could trade out a dishonorable discharge. Have him approach DiSilva wearing a wire."

Porter chuckled. "Dishonorable discharge?"

"After they find eight kinds of dope swimming in his bloodstream, I'll have all the leverage I need to make that deal."

Porter shook his head. "Not happening. And maybe it should. Not for nothing, I worry about both of them. Gil in particular."

"You sound pretty confident those lab results come back clean. Are they magicians or something? Those two stunk of pot Friday night."

"If I tell you, I want your word that you'll pull strings to get Gil into some kind of rehab program and let Shanahan go home on time, no criminal charges filed against either man. Are you willing to do that?"

"Does Trotter have some kind of chemical dependency?"

Porter didn't answer.

"What about you, Mike?"

"Drug use? No, my employer frowns on dope, so I don't partake. And you know it. So you'll help Trotter and let Shanahan slide?"

"I'll do everything I can to get Trotter some help. Yeah, I'll let Shanahan go home on time. No charges filed."

"Okay. The medic that drew blood is a friend of theirs. He got them clean samples."

Porter watched Martz's face turn a bright crimson.

"I'll say this; they're lucky bastards. Getting back to DiSilva and Tang, so now I wait for you to drop the bugs I have to get you?"

Porter nodded. "Face it; you've got nothing else in play."

Martz took a deep breath and glanced at the clock. "You got everything ready for the embassy?"

"Yeah. You have a problem with me and Claude spending an hour checking out Seoul?"

"Drop the visa application off and come back. I already told Claude this isn't a joy ride."

"You're all heart."

"I still have trouble getting past you being a hotshot sniper."

"Who said I was?"

"C'mon. I read the transcript. You have a spotter. Only snipers work with spotters."

"The assignment's classified."

"I'm not a complete idiot; you've got something going on in Panmunjom. Something important enough to send a drone. There's only one reason for anything to happen in Panmunjom—a summit. That means you're there to assassinate someone or prevent one. Only you can know why you'd take on something so incredibly…risky."

He's baiting me, trying to confirm his guess.

Someone knocked on the door, and Porter was glad for it. Dunbarton entered, and Porter grabbed the visa application on his desk.

"No sightseeing, boys. I expect you both back here in two hours."

Porter smirked. He and Dunbarton left the room together.

****

Handing over Miller's spousal visa application took all of five minutes. Returning to Anjeong-ri,

Dunbarton unexpectedly pulled into a restaurant parking lot.

"What's wrong, Claude?"

"I gotta hit the head."

Porter nodded, and Dunbarton got out of the SUV. Porter used the time as an opportunity to call Jeong.

"Can you still make it out tonight?" she asked.

"You're kidding, right? What time?"

"Is eight o'clock good?"

"I'll see you then."

The couple said goodbye, and Porter called Jungho Bak, who agreed to meet with Porter tomorrow night. If Porter could find one honest Anjeong-ri KNPA agent, Myung-Dae Tang's days as a notorious crime lord were coming to an end.

****

After lunch, Porter sat alone in the office when the telephone rang. It was Martz, calling from the security building.

"Big surprise, the lab results came back clean," Martz said. "Tell your pals they're free to go."

Porter went down the hall to room sixteen and knocked on the door. Gil opened it.

"Martz just called. You guys are free."

Cam jumped up first, putting his jacket on. "Only wish I could've seen that asshat's face when the call came in. You going into town tonight?"

Porter could say nothing about seeing Jeong. Not to them. Not to anyone.

"I'm low on funds. But if I go, I'll see you in DC."

"I can spot you till tomorrow," Cam said.

"Thanks but money and friendship don't mix."

After Cam and Gil left, Porter returned to the

empty office. After a few minutes, he had a text message from Stillson.

"Check email."

Going to the agency website, Porter logged in and opened the encrypted email. Stillson attached a video file with topographical detail of Panmunjom from the drone. The quality of the video was sharp. He froze the video at various intervals, saving still photos of locations he'd shoot from if he were going to take out someone in front of Peace House.

Damn, but it's tight. Not much room to maneuver. Preventing the assassination was one thing. Getting out of such a compact area to the thick woodland a half-mile away on foot seemed all but impossible, even under cover of tear gas. *On a windy day, tear gas won't do shit.*

ATVs would overtake them quickly. The North Koreans' first instinct would be to take them prisoner. Then the torture. Making Ferguson's question about cyanide all the more relevant. Porter felt sick to his stomach.

All he could do was trust Stillson's exit strategy, which he wouldn't know until pre-flight. But the more Porter looked, the less he liked his odds.

Porter emailed Stillson a one-word question. "Who?" Until he had that, there'd be no shutting Ferguson up. Porter logged off the website. And cursed Luther for being such an idiot.

****

Later that afternoon, Porter and Ferguson finished running before hitting the weight room. They spoke sparingly, keeping conversation light and vague. And while Porter fully expected Ferguson to air his displeasure about the lack of a bona fide target, the spotter kept his mouth shut.

Back in the barracks, Porter showered and shaved before calling a cab. As was his habit, Porter wore the Glock and turned his GPS unit on before jogging across the street to catch his ride.

Porter arrived in Pyeongtaek to wait in Kowloon's bar ten minutes later. Like Zero Coffeehouse, a hush fell as he entered. Jeong appeared five minutes later. She wore a tight white sweater and faded jeans; every hetero man in the place put an eye on her.

The hostess soon seated them. He prompted her to carry the conversation, which consisted of amusing and sometimes bizarre Duffy Club events, done without mentioning Myung-Dae by name. Jeong laughed freely, and Porter realized just how keen a sense of humor she possessed.

After dinner, the talk turned darker. Jeong told Porter of yet another bartender's disappearance and the safe's strange divot, along with a new ring in the bowl.

"I need something from you," Porter said.

"What, Porter?"

"A meeting with Myung-Dae in his Duffy Club office."

Jeong nodded. "He'll ask why."

"Tell him it's about Cam's black-market business. I want it after Cam leaves."

"I'll ask. But he may say no. He's careful about who he does business with."

He considered asking if she'd plant the bug. Only he didn't want to involve her in that way. Betraying Tang could get her killed.

Several times during the meal, their eyes made

contact, and everything in Porter's world stopped. Twice he forced himself to stop staring.

He prayed she wouldn't ask about his clearance. That would end this, and fast. Jeong asked no questions, not about that anyhow. Her eyes were calm and stayed on him.

After coffee, they held hands while leaving the restaurant. And before she hailed a cab, they kissed. It was a brief but passionate kiss that left him wanting more. But out in public, in a culture that didn't appreciate spectacles of affection, they kept it in check. Porter made no move to sleep with her. This was the kind of woman you waited for. She would give the cue. And she didn't. Not yet, anyhow. Which was fine with him; his status only complicated things.

"So when can we do this again?" Jeong asked.

"The next time you're able."

Jeong smiled as a cab came to the curb. They kissed again briefly before she climbed in.

Porter waited five minutes for another taxi to appear. Getting in, he realized he was falling in love.

****

In the city of Gongju, Jungho Bak peered into the dumpster behind a strip mall in the north end of the city. One Gongju KNPA investigator took crime scene photos while another dusted for fingerprints. A supermarket manager found the dead man in the receptacle. They'd taped off the area to keep curious onlookers at bay. But beyond the tape, a crowd grew.

"This is outside my jurisdiction. So why am I here?" Bak asked the lead investigator.

"Victim's from Anjeong-ri, looks like. Thought you might know who he is."

With a gloved hand, the Gongju investigator displayed the name of an Anjeong-ri tailor inside the trouser's waistband. With the victim's face so bloody, it took an effort for Bak to recognize the man.

"He's with Myung-Dae Tang. Used to be anyhow." Bak rubbed his jaw. "It's strange; I just spoke with Tang last week about another murder I'm sure he played a part in."

"There's no evidence this happened here," the investigator said. "Maybe there's brass or the weapon in the dumpster. I'll know soon enough."

Bak nodded. "With no particular motive, this kind of thing puts everyone on edge."

"I'll tell the reporters it's a gangland thing. Why would Tang kill one of his own?"

Bak stepped away from the dumpster. "That's the question, isn't it? Send me a copy of the medical examiner's report when you have it."

"Think you can help me out with this?" the investigator asked. "We don't see a lot of homicides."

Bak nodded. Like it or not, returning to Duffy Club for yet another heart-to-heart chat with Myung-Dae Tang now loomed.

Chapter Twenty-One

In the admin office the next morning, Porter waded through the message traffic that came in from last night. And while the vast majority of it proved routine, there was one surprise.

Cameron Shanahan was flying out of Osan Air Base on February 26th. His enlistment would end a few days later at Travis Air Force Base in California. That wasn't the surprise.

Major Arthur DiSilva and his wife were to depart Osan two days later, scheduled to report to Blue Grass Army Depot Base in Richmond, Kentucky on March 16th.

"You get a look at this morning's unclassified traffic, Top?"

From DiSilva's desk, Martz brought the morning newspaper down from his face.

"Not yet. Why?"

"Something you should see. I'll forward a copy."

Martz turned DiSilva's desktop computer on and accessed his email from DiSilva's monitor, pecking away clumsily on the keyboard.

The senior NCO read only the first line before his head dropped. "I don't believe this shit. Could my luck get any worse?"

"Did you know he was this short?"

"Yes and no. He told me his extension was a lock. I

never gave it another thought."

"Seems he got a little ahead of himself. I've got Cam Shanahan's orders here too."

Porter reached for his cell phone, remembering he told Cam he'd text the news when the orders arrived. "I'd love to catch DiSilva's expression when you tell him."

"You may get the chance at Sean Miller's going-away party at 1600 in the EM Club. I'll hit him up with it then unless I run across him before that. Now we're really on the clock. Plus, I'm never sure when you'll dry up and blow away."

"Out of my control, Top."

"No shit. Hey, not a word of the major's orders to anyone."

"No problem. But what makes you think I'm going to Miller's going-away party?"

"You *will* be there, Mike. For the good of unit morale."

"My absence would make a difference? I met the guy once."

"You don't have to wear a lampshade, and it won't kill you to show up. You're not dragging me into an argument about it, either." Martz glimpsed at the clock. "I've got a meeting." He put on his jacket. "Hey, this is your first payday here, isn't it?"

"You know it is."

Martz chuckled as he walked toward the door. "You're gonna love it."

****

Porter crossed the street to the EM Club just after four o'clock. He was no stranger to these unit get-togethers and disliked them on principle.

Sean Miller looked uncomfortable making the rounds with his bride, a young skanky-looking prostitute named Pamela. *I wonder how many in this room were clients?*

Porter tried to ignore the financial aspects of this union—Jeong explaining the payoffs to him fully. Only after paying Myung-Dae thirty-five thousand dollars plus interest was the "bride" truly free. Jeong explained the housing conditions, work hours, and meals. There were no holidays or days off. No personal or sick days. No going-away parties.

And heaven help the woman if she somehow conceived.

Martz had a beer in his hand and held court with several other unit lifers in one corner of this function room. Gil lucked out. He worked a day shift and wouldn't be here, but Porter expected Cam to show, although he'd yet to arrive.

Porter bought a beer and sat alone at the bar, watching a basketball game. Because of his role, he had no shop talk to discuss with unit peers. His thoughts were with Jeong, with Panmunjom hovering in the background, never too far away. Within minutes, a hush fell on the crowd, prompting a curious Porter to turn his head to look.

Arthur DiSilva entered the room. Say what you would about his wishy-washy leadership and laissez-faire management style; the man remained popular with the soldiers who served under him. DiSilva worked the room like a life insurance salesman at a chamber of commerce event. He had a grin painted on as he cordially glad-handed one and all. Porter watched as DiSilva chatted with Miller and his wife.

There it is—the king and his loyal subjects. What they're doing is nothing new, I suppose. Porter never saw Martz creep in on his blind side.

"Careful, Mike," Martz said. "You look pissed for no reason."

"Oh, there's a reason. Remind me to break down the payouts later. Does DiSilva know?"

"Not yet. I'll let him wander over here before I hit him with it."

DiSilva, having schmoozed with everyone but Porter, Martz, and the lifers in the corner—approached the bar.

"Beefeater," DiSilva said to the bartender. His head turned to Porter and Martz. "You two appear to have found common ground."

Martz glanced at Porter with an arched eyebrow before facing DiSilva. "I wouldn't go that far. More like a truce. Have you seen today's unclassified message traffic, Major?"

"Not yet. I planned to swing by the admin office after this breaks up. Why?"

"Your orders came in."

The transformation made being here worth it. DiSilva's shoulders slumped as he eyed the liquor bottles stacked behind the bar. He stared blankly for several seconds. "My orders?"

"Yes, sir. Blue Grass Army Depot Base in Richmond, Kentucky. Out of here at the end of February to report mid-March. Congratulations."

DiSilva's head dropped as if examining his shoes. Slowly, it rose again.

"Desk jockey out of the DC told me the extension was certain. I can't believe it." DiSilva grabbed his drink and flopped onto the barstool next to Porter. His stare went from the liquor bottles to the televisions as he sipped his cocktail.

"I'm going to the security building," Martz said. "Unless you need me here for something."

DiSilva stared ahead. "That's fine, Ollie."

"Cam Shanahan's orders are on your desk for signature too, Major," Porter said. "You think it'd be okay if I bugged out a little early?"

"I'll take care of Shanahan's orders, Mike. Sure, you can take off a bit early."

Porter slid off the barstool and grabbed his jacket. He had a meeting with Bak and wanted to avoid the bottleneck leaving the base, if possible. He already scrubbed tonight's workout.

Porter didn't expect this party to be entertaining. And felt glad to be wrong.

****

Porter took a cab from Camp Humphreys into Pyeongtaek. Not yet 1700 hours, Anjeong-ri was already alive with activity as pockets of soldiers walked from bar to bar. It felt good to be out of the village.

Standing outside Zero Coffeehouse, Porter sent a text telling Jungho Bak he'd arrived. Porter only had an old, grainy CIA photo of the man to go by. While hating the attention, Porter reluctantly entered.

A man sitting alone several booths down from where Porter met with Jeong stood and gestured. The tall man with graying temples and a ready smile shook Porter's hand.

"Mr. Porter," he said in Korean. "It's a pleasure meeting you."

"I appreciate your willingness to meet," Porter

replied, also in Korean. Not even Jeong knew he spoke the language.

The waitress came and they ordered coffee, continuing when she departed.

"It's been ages since I last worked with Mr. Stillson. How can I be of service to you?" Bak asked.

"How long ago did you work with Mr. Stillson, if you don't mind me asking?"

Bak shook his head and grinned. "Before you were born, I believe. At the time, we had martial law. In the 1970s and 1980s, new tunnels materialized at the DMZ with alarming frequency; all initiated from the north. Many who made it through were the worst kind of criminals. Your agency proved to be an invaluable resource in getting that problem under control. I owe Walter Stillson my life."

"I need help with a local man you may know, Myung-Dae Tang."

Bak took a sip. "Strange you should mention him. I'm currently running two separate murder investigations that I believe involve Tang. He's an interesting and deadly fellow. What's your interest?"

Porter removed his cell phone and pulled up the picture of Doyoon hanging in Jeong's kitchen. "I'm guessing this is one of the investigations."

Bak looked the photo over. "Yes, it is. Tang also killed one of his own, dumping the body in the city of Gongju, shot multiple times. There's trouble within that organization. How did you come to be in possession of that photo?"

"A friend gave it to me."

Bak grinned. "Jeong Guy?"

Porter nodded. "She's afraid of the man and told

me of another murder. This one on Tang's farm. An American soldier named Tomlinson."

Bak shook his head. "I know nothing about that. As you probably guessed, Tang is well-protected. It embarrasses me to say that Tang pays the Anjeong-ri KNPA Commandant directly."

At least the guy is honest about it. "I made certain discoveries linking Tang to an American sex trafficking ring," Porter said.

"Please explain."

Porter described to Bak what Jeong told him of Myung-Dae and DiSilva's collaboration.

"I'd heard the rumor Tang did business with his American soldier son-in-law. There is another rumor circulating through the KNPA regarding Tang that may interest you, again involving his son-in-law."

"Oh?"

"I've heard Tang is moving cadavers from mainland China to Mokpo Port. Along with a substantial shipment of heroin hidden within each cadaver. I don't know more than that, I'm afraid."

Porter cocked his head. "How many cadavers?"

"Ten thousand."

Porter leaned back, his eyes wide. "Ten *thousand?* How sure are you about the American son-in-law being involved?"

Bak ran his hand through his hair. "My source is very reliable."

Wait until Martz hears this. Porter cleared his throat. "I'm sure Tang distributes cocaine. I know of a soldier who sells for him, seen it with my own eyes. I wouldn't have guessed he dealt heroin."

"Tang's drug trafficking goes back fifty years. In

that time, he's become very proficient."

"Never arrested?" Porter asked.

"Not once. We arrested a well-connected cocaine trafficker from South Chungcheong Province who bought from Tang in the early 2000s. He was willing to testify against Tang in exchange for immunity. We kept the man sequestered in a private cell and on suicide watch. Yet two days before the trial, we found him face down in the showers with multiple stab wounds, bled to death."

"That's convenient."

Bak took a sip of his coffee. "Tang's always been eccentric. But his newfound passion for death has my department's attention."

"The cadavers. What the hell does he plan on doing with so many dead bodies?"

"We've heard he's selling them to medical schools. Oddly enough, that's not contraband cargo. Unusual. But not illegal."

"You guys have nothing on DiSilva?"

Bak's fingers tapped the table. "Nothing beyond innuendo. He keeps a very low profile."

"I appreciate your candor. Is there anything else you can tell me?"

"Nothing I can readily confirm." Bak produced a business card, putting it on the table. "Where it comes to Tang, please understand I'm compromised. But if Tang were to die unexpectedly, his protection would cease to exist. Someone killing Tang, let's say in self-defense, would liberate Anjeong-ri."

Is he encouraging me to kill Tang? It sure sounded like it.

Bak slyly grinned. "Of course, that action would

incur the wrath of those who benefit from his assorted nefarious activities. By that, I mean his associates. Tang is currently down a man, but he will hire a replacement soon enough. So one should only take that action with eyes wide open."

Porter took a sip. "Let me try this on. If I'm detained or incarcerated as a result of tying Tang directly to a crime, would you be able to get me safely back on Camp Humphreys?"

"If detained by Anjeong-ri KNPA, yes. I owe Walter Stillson that much. But if you're in custody elsewhere, I'm powerless."

"The men living on Tang's farm, whatever information you have on file would be helpful," Porter added.

"Useless I'm afraid. Tang doesn't hire men with criminal records. That old buzzard is sharp. Have you ever met him?"

Porter shook his head. "No. Not yet."

Bak glanced out the window. "You have no idea what it feels like to watch Tang do whatever he wants, whenever he wants, to whoever he wants. I can't think of a single day when I haven't contemplated requesting a transfer. Not because of Tang, but the infestation of corruption."

"Forgive me for asking a personal question, but why haven't you?"

Bak grinned. "My wife cares for her failing mother."

Porter nodded. "Yes, I understand. And appreciate your help."

"A word of caution, young man. With men like Tang, things escalate quickly. They don't know when or how to quit. Avoid being alone with him if you can. Nothing good can come of it."

The pair finished their coffee. Then Porter shook Bak's hand and caught a cab back to Anjeong-ri.

****

The volume of GIs pouring into the small town was astounding. Porter exited the cab on the Anjeong-ri thoroughfare and walked toward Duffy Club.

Getting inside the club conventionally would take all night; Porter guessed the line ran fifty deep. He texted Jeong and waited for the reply. Once she agreed to let him in from out back, he went there and rang the bell by the metal door. It took a while. He thought about ringing it again when Jeong opened the door.

She kissed him and led him inside. "Avoid the bay. There are cameras there."

Porter nodded, staying close to her.

"You're sure asking Myung-Dae for Cameron's black-market business is a good idea?" she asked.

"I'm not sure of anything except I need to get inside that office and his house."

"He's going to tell you he doesn't want you anywhere near me. So expect it."

Porter nodded. "I'll agree to that for your safety. We can always talk on Skype or meet in Pyeongtaek."

"Good," she said, her hand clasping his. "Will you text me later tonight? I want to make sure you made it back to the base okay."

Porter nodded.

She leaned in, putting her arms around him. "I try not to think so much about you but can't help it."

What brought that on? He couldn't help but smile. "I do it too."

212

"Are you ready?"

Porter nodded. "Just don't forget what you need to do once I'm in there. Three minutes."

Jeong nodded and led the way to Myung-Dae's office. She knocked on the door with Porter standing alongside her.

"Come in."

She left Porter in the hallway and entered. "Porter asked for a minute of your time. He knows you're busy."

Myung-Dae's head shot up. "Porter? Do you know what he wants?"

"He told me Cameron is leaving soon and wishes to replace him."

Myung-Dae stroked his goatee. "Yes, that's true. Send him in."

Jeong kept the door open as she left. Porter entered.

He eyed the office, inventorying and cataloging, an old habit. If any one thing stood out, it was that nothing stood out, save a bowl of rings on the credenza. There was nothing to suggest that this man was evil personified. Porter wondered if those who visited Hitler's offices thought the same when they met him face-to-face for the first time.

The desk abutted a wall, leaving a narrow gap. *Couldn't ask for a better place to plant this thing.* That Myung-Dae was alone was surprising.

Bak's warning came to him. '*Avoid being alone with him if you can. Nothing good will come of it.*'

"Please sit down." Myung-Dae gestured. "And close the door behind you."

Porter closed the door and chose the cheap plastic chair nearest the wall.

"I often wondered if we would meet," Myung-Dae said.

Porter looked into Myung-Dae's eyes. They were cold and hard.

"Thank you for seeing me, Mr. Tang. I know you're busy, so I'll be direct. You know that Cam Shanahan is leaving, and I would like to replace him."

"You mean selling rationed goods from your base commissary to me?"

"Yes."

"You're aware that it's illegal?"

"I don't plan on getting caught."

Myung-Dae chuckled. "Nobody ever does." His eyes bored in harder. "Have you ever run afoul of MPs or CID?"

Porter shook his head. "No."

Myung-Dae leaned forward. "And what of Jeong?"

Porter did his best to appear puzzled. "Jeong? I'm not sure I understand."

"Come now, Porter. It's a mistake to think me naïve. I honestly thought that you and I would meet under a very different set of circumstances. Unpleasant ones at that. She is a valued…employee. And I've been told you are friendly with her."

"Are you telling me you resent my friendship with Jeong?"

"Please call me Myung-Dae." His gold tooth caught the light as he grinned. "And yes, now that you admit it. I resent your friendship with Jeong."

Porter rubbed his jaw and nodded. "I'm sure we could arrange a reasonable accommodation."

"You…are wiser than the man you replaced." Myung-Dae leaned back, his eyes softening as his fingers strummed the desktop. "So you would like Cameron's concession?"

"Yes."

"What I would like to see happen is you having no future contact with Jeong outside of this establishment. None. Is that unreasonable?"

Porter shrugged. "Not unreasonable. Anjeong-ri has many beautiful women." *I wonder if my nose just grew.*

Myung-Dae stared at Porter, his smallish fingers once again strumming the desk. "What to do, what to do?" he asked in a sing-song voice.

In Porter's left parka pocket, he carefully rubbed more of the sticky epoxy Martz gave him onto the bug. Porter's eyes never strayed from Myung-Dae's as Bak's advice thundered in his head.

Myung-Dae stopped strumming as he sat up and leaned in. "I could tell you to stay away from her without giving you a thing. You know that?"

"I know that, Myung-Dae. You have all the leverage." *Where the hell is Jeong? It's been too long.*

Myung-Dae grinned, appearing pleased with the response. Porter took a breath, trying to relax. There was a knock at the door, and Porter felt relieved.

"Yes?" Myung-Dae shouted.

Jeong opened the door and stuck her head in. Seeing Myung-Dae's attention on her, Porter casually stuck the bug in the gap between the desk and wall. Quickly pressing it down hard before removing his hand.

"Could you have one of your men bring up a full keg and dispose of the empty?" she asked. "It's a zoo out here."

"Let me finish with Mr. Porter, and I'll take care of it."

Jeong nodded and closed the door. Myung-Dae turned his attention back to Porter.

"Okay. So you will come to my Anjeong-ri home on Saturday with Cameron. We'll see if you learn. But I warn you, Jeong is off-limits from this moment on. If I see or hear of you with her, our next meeting will be a regrettable one. Do you agree to those terms?"

"Yes."

"Now, if you'll excuse me, this is a busy night."

"Thank you, Myung-Dae."

Getting to his feet, Porter nodded and walked out of the office. After washing his hands of the epoxy, Porter found Cam and Nari sitting at the bar.

"I've got a favor to ask," Porter said to Cam.

"Sure."

"I just met with Myung-Dae. I'm going with you to his house on Saturday if you're okay with it."

"Sure. What brought that on?"

"I agreed to leave Jeong alone in exchange for your black-market business."

Cam nodded. "I don't know why you want to work for him, but that's on you. Sure, you can come with me on Saturday. I'm meeting him at ten that morning."

"No Gil and Gayoon?" Porter asked. He remembered that Gayoon had returned home from the hospital today.

"She's not up to many people right now. We're not staying long; I hate payday nights."

Porter nodded. He would understand if Gil and Gayoon decided never to set foot in one of Myung-Dae's bars again for the rest of their lives.

Porter left with Cam and Nari. Duffy Club was wall-to-wall. He saw nothing good by staying here. Besides, the deal he made with the devil was giving him indigestion.

Back on the base, the GPS turned off, Porter texted Jeong as he walked to the barracks and thanked her for the help. He would call her tomorrow.

He thought of Stillson and Panmunjom. And knew his time left here was short.

****

Jungho Bak entered Duffy Club shortly after eleven o'clock that evening. The place was still going strong. He searched for Jeong or anyone else who could bring him to Tang. Because the bartenders were frantically busy, they would be a last resort. Then he saw her.

"How are you tonight, Ms. Guy?" Bak asked.

"Good to see you again. Can I get you something?"

"Thank you, no. I'm here to see Mr. Tang again."

Jeong grinned. "Come with me."

She lifted the bar section and led Bak down the hall to Myung-Dae's office, where she tapped on the door before entering.

Bak couldn't hear the exchange in the office. Not that it mattered. Soon Jeong emerged, leaving the door open. Bak stepped into the doorway.

"Inspector Bak. I'm beginning to think you'd like an office here."

"That's not a very warm welcome. May I enter?"

"Oh yes, please come in and sit down, make yourself comfortable. I have *nothing* better to do on a GI payday night than entertain you. Perhaps I could ask one of the bartenders to make you some tea? Or should

217

a waitress fetch you a blanket and pillow?"

Bak walked in and sat down in the chair Porter occupied earlier tonight. "Ms. Guy already asked if I wanted anything."

"She is far more cordial than I am. Why are you here now? Did someone slip on a banana peel and identify me as the culprit?"

"I found a man who works for you in a Gongju dumpster. Shot several times at close range with a .22 caliber handgun. Not a single bullet casing found at the scene. That tells me he didn't die in Gongju. His name is Kiwoo Jong." Bak brought up his phone and showed Myung-Dae one of the dozen crime scene pictures he took. "I'm sure he's looked better."

Myung-Dae scoffed. "Ugh. You and your gruesome photos. I wondered where my Kiwoo went."

"You don't sound surprised to learn he's dead. An otherwise healthy man, the coroner's report says."

"How would you expect me to sound? Kiwoo worked for me for many years. I'm sad to learn of his passing."

Bak chuckled. "Yes, I can see how choked up you are. I'm curious as to how he ended up in Gongju. Why didn't you just throw him in your dumpster out back?"

"How very droll. Are you implying that I had something to do with his death too?"

"Did you have something to do with his death?"

"Come spring, remind me to buy you a fishing rod. You waste my time with your speculative innuendo. You come here trying to intimidate and frighten me. Do I look frightened or intimidated?"

"No. You don't."

"There you have it. Next dead body you find,

please don't jump to the conclusion that I am responsible. Good night to you."

Bak rose from the chair. "You better pray that I don't find another dead body, Mr. Tang."

Myung-Dae stood, his eyes narrowing. "Be careful what you say to me, Bak. Count your blessings you're with the KNPA. Now leave me in peace."

Bak departed Myung-Dae's office, walking quickly past the soldiers and prostitutes as he exited this house of debauchery. He would take pleasure seeing that untouchable criminal in a cage.

Even if he wasn't entirely sure how to go about putting him there.

Chapter Twenty-Two

Myung-Dae strolled into the First Anjeong-ri Bank vestibule soon after it opened that morning. His slicked-back white hair topped an old suit, dated tie, and buckle dress shoes. The tellers—all women—giggled behind Myung-Dae's back as he wandered down the hall to manager Hajoon Lee's office.

Seeing the partially open door, Myung-Dae stuck his head in. "Hello?"

The young, chunky, and impeccably dressed Lee wore a tailored suit from an upscale Seoul clothier. He had never been seen with a woman. The rumor of Lee's homosexuality swept through Anjeong-ri like a sausage wrapper on payday night. He looked up from the monitors that had his attention. "May I help you?"

"It's Myung-Dae Tang, you idiot. I'm here to close on that loan."

"My apologies, Mr. Tang, I didn't recognize you." Lee scrambled to his feet. "I must say, you look very…polished."

"Can we start now, or shall you continue to kiss my ass? You're not the only thing on my to-do list today."

Lee removed the loan packet sitting on his desk and looked again at Myung-Dae. "No attorney?"

"I trust lawyers even less than you bankers. But I try not to worry. If you swindle me, I'll send my men to find you."

Oh my God, he just threatened me.

Myung-Dae grinned. "A joke."

A visibly shaken Lee forced an awkward grin. "We'll close in the conference room, gives us more space."

Lee led Myung-Dae to the conference room down the corridor. The bank manager flipped on the switch, the elaborate light fixtures giving the long mahogany conference table and leather chairs a graceful elegance. The men took seats on opposite sides at the head of the table near the door.

"Where do you want these funds disbursed?"

"Wuhan Bank and Trust in China. I have instructions." Myung-Dae handed Lee a neatly folded deposit ticket from the inside breast pocket of his jacket.

"If I may, Mr. Tang...permit me to say this. I'm a banker, not a financial advisor. But if I *were* a financial advisor, I would never recommend sending all of your cash to one bank. Especially one out of the country. You're painting yourself into a corner and leaving all of your personal assets vulnerable."

Myung-Dae grinned. "Thank you for your unsolicited advice. You are not me."

"Once that wire leaves the bank, we have no way of getting the cash back. If you have even a whisper of doubt about this transaction, please reconsider."

Myung-Dae's face reddened. "You think I wanted to collateralize my entire estate to do this? It was the only way I could get this loan, despite my net worth. You bankers are shameless vultures. So spare me your disingenuous concern and lectures about risk."

Lee felt his stomach knot. He only wanted for Tang

to leave. Like everyone else in Anjeong-ri, Lee heard too many stories about the man.

They went through the pages one by one, Lee showing Myung-Dae where to sign or initial. Myung-Dae skimmed hastily through the document, paragraph by paragraph, barely reading a word. By the time he left the bank, Myung-Dae had executed a promissory note collateralizing all of his assets—doing so without Moon-Kym's knowledge or consent. In exchange, he obtained cash proceeds for an estimated seventy-five percent of his estate's current market value, as quickly and conservatively appraised by the bank.

Myung-Dae rubbed his right palm. "I hope the carpal tunnel is free."

Lee again forced a grin. "Don't forget to sign and date the last page."

Myung-Dae did so and loudly sighed. "Please tell me we're finished."

"Yes, that was the last of it. May I ask one other thing, Mr. Tang?"

Myung-Dae sighed aloud. "If you must."

"Why?"

"This took a long time to put together. I don't imagine seeing an opportunity like it again."

The bank manager nodded. "Congratulations. I'm confident your import/export venture will succeed."

Myung-Dae reluctantly shook Lee's hand, the deal done. The manager would execute the wire transfer personally. He walked Myung-Dae to the bank's front door and just now felt the sweat that had built up at the back of his neck. He wiped it off, relieved Tang had departed the building.

Returning to his office, Lee picked up the

telephone. *Try to scare me? We'll just see about that.*
****

Martz was halfway through his inspection of the weekly stats in his intel building office. The office telephone rang.

"Martz."

"Hey Top, it's Booth." Craig Booth worked for Bayer as part of the team Martz assigned to his special op. "We've got audio from the Duffy Club bug you'll find interesting, a telephone call. I emailed the transcript and the audio."

"Give me the highlights."

"We're pretty sure it was Tang. He made a call discussing a loan with payment going to a Chinese bank. That loan must be for big money because Tang put up his entire estate to get it. A Chinese freighter coming into Mokpo Port. The cargo is unidentified with no mention of specific dates."

"Any mention of narcotics?"

"Nothing like that, Top. Sorry."

"I'll give it a listen and look. Thanks, Craig."

Martz hung up and locked the office door before going online to hear and read the attachments. They were exactly as Booth described. Tang drove the conversation, the other party unknown.

Martz forwarded both files to Porter.
****

Porter sat in the admin office requisitioning supplies when Martz walked in. After removing his hat and jacket, he walked up to DiSilva's desk and sat down.

"You read the transcript?" he asked Porter.

"Yeah. I'm a little surprised Tang went through a

conventional bank to finance the cadavers and heroin he's bringing in."

"How sure did that KNPA agent sound about DiSilva's involvement?"

Porter nodded. "Pretty sure. But not an absolute certainty."

"Did you feel like the guy's a straight shooter?" Martz asked.

"Bak? He's honest enough but doesn't carry much weight. I'm surprised Tang's importing heroin. If anything, I would've bet on cocaine. He said his source was sure DiSilva's part of that."

"Why would you bet on cocaine?" Martz asked.

"Things you hear in the bar."

"It sounds iffy. Iffy doesn't cut it for me."

"Why wouldn't Tang involve DiSilva? He's a family member who lost his moral compass some time ago."

"Wishful thinking, Mike."

"Don't give up on this, Top. I need to drop that bug in Tang's house on Saturday. They talk in that house."

"I'm not getting my hopes up, even if you drop the bug."

"You'll see. Now there's money on the line, and they're on the clock."

"And your status?" Martz asked.

Porter shrugged.

"Nobody's told you anything about when you expect to go?"

"Welcome to my world, Top."

Chapter Twenty Three

In the apartment he shared with Gayoon, Gil woke after four hours of sleep. She thrashed and groaned a great deal over the course of the night, but that played only a small part of it. The guilt he felt weighed heavy.

Gil fought through his fatigue and, knowing he was on midnight shifts starting tonight, should be sleeping. "Are you okay, Gayoon?" he put a hand on her shoulder as she laid flat on her back in their bed.

Gayoon stirred. "Why aren't you sleeping?"

Gil sat up. With his mind churning, he knew sleep wouldn't come. "Is that market down the street open?"

"If it's after eight o'clock, then yes. Why?"

"I'll run down and bring back some of those tangerines you like."

"Would you? That would be nice."

Gil picked up his clothes, thrown carelessly onto the floor, and dressed. Ordinarily, he'd have a cup of coffee. But not today. In the bathroom, he opened the medicine cabinet. There, a half-full bottle of oxycodone the doctor prescribed for Gayoon's pain sat on the shelf. Gil siphoned two pills and popped them in his mouth. He let the water run, cupping his left hand to wash the tablets down. He then looked in the mirror and told himself he'd pilfer no more of her painkillers.

Soon he'd be in Shangri-La, where guilt and remorse ceased to exist. The lone drawback was the

225

brevity of the visit. He walked down the stairs and out of the apartment building into the arctic Anjeong-ri air. The small fruit and fish market stood just off the street corner, and Gil slipped into a daydream, remembering the first time he saw Gayoon.

She was a sometimes server and occasional working girl at Rasputin's, a jazz bar *not* owned by Myung-Dae. She was short and pretty, with full lips, dimples, short black hair, and the darkest, prettiest eyes he'd ever seen. Gil never believed in love at first sight until he saw her.

There were scant few people in the market at this hour, and Gil could buy a half-pound of salmon and a small bag of tangerines without waiting in line.

Goods in hand, he returned to the apartment, bounding up the stairs as the oxycodone did its work. Walking down the carpeted hallway, he saw fresh wet boot treads that led to their door. He instinctively knew something was wrong.

Gil turned the unlocked doorknob. He and Gayoon had made a habit of keeping the apartment locked since Gunn's uninvited visit. Bag in hand, Gil opened the door.

"Hey, Gay—"

An arm swung violently around Gil's neck before he closed the door. A flash of light reflected off a knife's stainless steel blade now under his chin, and Gil became still. He dropped the grocery bag near his feet and listened to the door close.

Gil never saw a face but guessed his assailant was Korean, the unmistakable smell of kimchi clinging to the man's hands and clothes.

"Easy," Gil said, hoping this man understood

English. "My wallet's in the right front pocket. Take it and leave."

"Shh, shh, shh," the man behind him whispered.

"Gil?" Gayoon cried out from the bedroom.

The door was halfway open, but he couldn't see her.

Gil's assailant pulled the knife back just a little before elbowing him.

"Are you okay?" Gil called out.

Another man from inside the bedroom said something to Gayoon in Korean, his tone strangely calm.

"They will take the bag and the money in your wallet," Gayoon said. "Then they will leave, and no one gets hurt. Is the bag in the closet?"

A moment passed as Gil slowly processed the request. The man from behind elbowed him again, this time harder.

"Yes. Tell this guy my wallet is in my left front pocket." *That bag's worth six large to Myung-Dae. Where the hell will I find the cash to pay him back?*

Gayoon translated. Gil listened to the closet door slide open. The man from behind him reached into the soldier's left front pocket and brought the wallet up. After removing the cash, the thief lobbed the wallet onto the kitchen table before opening the apartment door.

The thief from the bedroom dashed out, carrying Gil's burgundy gym bag. He wore a woman's nude nylon over his head, making his facial features indistinguishable. A second later, the knife at Gil's throat disappeared, the intruder shoving him before sprinting down the hall for the stairwell.

Gil rushed into the bedroom. Gayoon sobbed, sitting cross-legged on the bed while holding a pillow against her chest and stomach. Gently, Gil removed the pillow and held her close as she cried.

"It's okay, baby. We're okay."

Only Gil knew the truth. He was the furthest thing from okay. He'd dug a hole, and dug it deep.

"What will you do, Gil? Everything in the bag belonged to Myung-Dae."

"Give me a minute. Let me think this through."

Cam was the only person Gil trusted on Camp Humphreys. Actually, Cam was the only person Gil trusted, period. And Cam was on a day shift. Gil held Gayoon, stroking her black hair and kissing her forehead as her sobbing slowed.

"Do you have Nari's telephone number? I want her to stay with you while I go on base."

"Go on base? On base for what, Gil?"

"I need to talk to Cam. He might help."

"How can Cam help, Gil?" Gingerly, she swung her legs over to climb out of the bed and moaned as she stood. He could see she was in agony.

She crept to the telephone in the kitchen and called Nari's cell phone.

****

Cam knew something was wrong the moment he saw Gil in the security building wearing civilian clothes. That was only the beginning. Gil's eyes were wild, his skin an unusual shade of pale.

"Gil, what are you doing here?"

"We've gotta talk."

"You look like shit. What's the matter?"

"I need your help."

Cam led Gil to the empty break room. They sat at a table, the lights from the vending machines giving this otherwise dim and bleak area an upbeat appearance.

"You gonna tell me now?" Cam asked.

"Me and Gayoon got robbed, dude. An hour ago. I went to the market, and when I got back, two guys were already in the apartment with knives. They took the bag with the blow and cash and took what I had on me."

"Everything in that bag belonged to Myung-Dae."

Gil nodded. "That's why I'm here. Gayoon called Nari, and I waited until she got there; I didn't wanna leave Gayoon alone after that."

"Did you see either guy?"

"They had nylons over their heads. They were Korean."

"If they had nylons over their heads, how did you know they're Korean?"

"Kimchi. They stunk of it. And they only spoke Korean."

Cam's head dropped. "Now do you understand why you don't sell out in public? Did you report it to the KNPA?"

"And tell them what? Excuse me, sir, a pair of thieves made off with cocaine I've been selling for Myung-Dae Tang? Yeah, that's brilliant. Somehow, I need to make this right with that old psycho. And it needs to happen *now*."

"What am I supposed to be able to do?"

Gil took a deep breath. "Come with me to talk to him. I've gotta straighten this shit out; otherwise, I'm dead. Remember what he did to Gayoon after I missed *a meeting*? What do you suppose happens when he finds out about the bag?"

"I'm not a magician, Gil."

"He won't do anything if you're there," Gil replied. "For whatever reason, Myung-Dae likes you. I really need your help, brother. And I have an idea."

"Yup, here it comes."

"Do the deal that Miller got. I'm sure Myung-Dae made you the offer. I heard Miller pulled down ten large. You can cover my losses with Myung-Dae, and I'll pay you back before you leave this base. I swear it."

Cam swallowed hard. "You think I should marry Nari to help you climb out of Myung-Dae's doghouse? And you'll pay me back before I leave in less than a month?"

"You know I'm good for it," Gil said.

"That's not the point. You're leaving me with a wife I don't want. Marriage isn't a currency, Gil. I have no intention of marrying Nari. None. She knows and accepts that. I thought you had money stashed away for the wedding?"

Gil frantically scratched his arm. "Not yet. I've been dipping into my supply."

"I thought you put your reenlistment bonus in the bank?"

Gil's sheepish grin said it all.

"I'm not getting married to save your ass. There's gotta be another way."

"Fine," Gil said, getting to his feet. "But my blood is on your hands."

"Oh no. Don't even *think* about putting this on me. I *begged* you not to sell for Myung-Dae."

"This is one time I don't need you to tell me I fucked up. Now I'm just trying to find a way out."

"Shut up and let me think a minute, Gil."

Gil lowered himself back into the chair.

"How much was that bag worth?"

Gil took a breath. "Fifty-five hundred dollars by my math. Closer to six large if you asked Myung-Dae."

"You could take out a personal loan with the credit union in Seoul for six thousand dollars," Cam said. "Problem solved."

Gil sat upright. "That's a great idea. How long before I can get the cash, you figure?"

"Two working days. Maybe three."

"Three days? I've got between now and two o'clock Saturday afternoon to find a six-thousand-dollar binky that fits in Myung-Dae's mouth. What else?"

"You could rob a bank," Cam said.

"Fuck you. Are you really gonna make me beg?"

Cam put his head down, wishing he were someone else. Anyone but Gil, anyhow. "You're really asking me to do this?"

"I'm in a full-beg mode. But what about this…you tell Myung-Dae you'll marry Nari. Then I take out a loan through the credit union. I pay you back next week, and you give Myung-Dae his money back. Tell him you got cold feet. Everybody wins."

"Everybody wins? How does Nari win? She's gonna tell her friends and family, only to have the rug pulled out from under her a few days later. Nobody with half a brain calls that a win."

"You could let Nari in on it before you tell Myung-Dae. That takes care of the damage control. You're literally saving my life, brother. Try looking at the upside for a second."

"I'll talk to Myung-Dae with you, Gil, try to smooth this over, buy you some time. Then you're

231

going online to fill out a loan application with the credit union. That's as far as I'm prepared to go."

"Any chance you can take the rest of the day off? Help me get out in front of this? If we can talk to Myung-Dae before he finds out from someone else, I might stand a chance."

"I'll try. In case you haven't noticed, Martz has been moodier than usual." Cam looked into Gil's eyes. They appeared wilder now than they had only minutes ago. "Yeah, okay, I'll ask for the afternoon." He glanced at the clock on the wall. "Meet me *inside* the Pyeongtaek Catholic church at one o'clock."

"I doubt Gayoon can make that trip."

"Why does she have to?"

"If Myung-Dae finds out first, he'll send a goon to the hooch. If I'm not there, he'll waste her and then look for me. She has to be with me, or this won't work."

"*You* figure out a way to get her there. I've gotta get back."

"Why the church, Cam?"

"It's the last place Myung-Dae and his goons will want to look."

****

Gunn was enjoying tea with his mistress in a Pyeongtaek restaurant when he overheard the story from another table. Two punks boasting they'd robbed a drug-dealing GI outside of Camp Humphreys, making off with cocaine and cash. When Gunn heard the GI lived with an Anjeong-ri prostitute, he *knew* they were talking about the one they called Gil.

"We're going to have to cut this short, my dear," Gunn told the woman. "Duty calls."

"But Gunn," she pouted, "I thought this was your day off?"

"Trust me. I'm going to get a phone call any second now."

"I think you have another woman waiting in the wings. That's what I think."

"Because I have to work?" Gunn scoffed. "We'll talk about this later."

To Gunn's surprise, his phone didn't ring. That meant nobody told the boss yet. Gunn dropped his mistress off at the Pyeongtaek apartment he kept for her and raced to Jumpin' Jack Flask. Given the time of day, this was where Myung-Dae would be.

Gunn parked his car out back of the bar, next to Myung-Dae's car. After letting himself in, Gunn walked down the hall. With the office door partially open, Gunn knocked to avoid startling Myung-Dae. Kiwoo's replacement, a large young man named Sang Doak, who most recently worked for the Dokgo brothers, stood off Myung-Dae's shoulder. Because Sang appeared arrogant and condescending, Gunn disliked him immediately.

Myung-Dae looked up. "Gunn. What are you doing here?"

"There's a story making the rounds that might interest you." Gunn repeated what he'd overheard. "I thought it sounded a lot like your friend Gil."

"My friend?" Myung-Dae fake-spat on the floor. "He's a moronic drug addict who can barely keep a thought in his head. And now of all times to do something reckless with money I can ill-afford to lose."

That Gunn reported this before the new hire or anyone else would help keep him in Myung-Dae's good

233

graces, however temporarily. Yet, there was a downside. Being a chronic herald of woe carried its own risk.

"I want that junkie and his whore girlfriend found," Myung-Dae said. "And I mean now. I should have done this after he missed our meeting. That's what you get for being soft. No good deed goes unpunished, you two, remember that. It's time to cut my losses."

"The woman had nothing to do with this. Besides, Kiwoo beat her badly," Gunn said.

"And so?"

"I don't understand why you want to include her."

"I'm not in a mood to explain it to you, Gunn. Take Sang and go find them."

"What do you want us to do when we do?"

"Find me and bring them to the farm."

"May I offer a suggestion?" Gunn asked.

"I'm sure you'll give me one whether I wish it or not."

"You're responding to this emotionally. Why not take a day, mull it over? The man got robbed, and as much as I dislike him, I'm sure he'll get your money back if you let him. Why should you do all the work after he makes the mistake?"

Myung-Dae cocked his head. "Anything else?"

"We've been spilling a lot of blood lately. That KNPA agent is ready to pitch a tent out front. We haven't seen that before."

"I pay the KNPA, just as I pay you. So are you going to do this, or should I send Sang alone?"

"And if the American holes up on the base?"

"Then we take the woman and flush him out. Collateral is useful in this business, Gunn."

"If he's smart, he'll hole up on the base."

"Find them, and then find me. I'm running a business. To let this slide invites others to take advantage. Besides, it gives you the opportunity to show Sang what is sometimes necessary."

Myung-Dae had the same look on his face now as he had when he gunned Kiwoo down. Under Gunn's leather jacket hid a shoulder holster carrying a .45 pistol. He watched Myung-Dae carefully, unsure if there was a weapon in one of the desk drawers. The old Myung-Dae listened to advice, even if he didn't always take it. This version of the man was coming undone, and fast.

"May we use your car? If the KNPA sees us in your car, that might be enough to keep them from interfering if it becomes a public tug-of-war."

"Fine." Myung-Dae handed Gunn the keys to his car. "But if you put a dent in her, I'll have your ass. Find them, both of you."

Gunn glanced at Sang. And together, they left the office.

****

Myung-Dae's German luxury car cruised the streets of Anjeong-ri, searching for the young couple. Gunn had no idea how he and Sang would coax them to the car without confrontation. Still, it was fish in a barrel. With an injured woman and a drug-addicted GI to track, this affair lacked dignity to Gunn's way of thinking. And with the KNPA boldly sniffing around and asking questions, this seemed a poor time for such nonsense.

Gunn had to admit, the KNPA worried him more every time he saw that agent lurking about. They'd always kept a respectful distance, at least until Myung-Dae's appetite for death spiked.

Gunn thought about Kiwoo and what his former partner said about the future. *Maybe the time has come for me to move on, too.*

****

It was ten minutes to one when Gunn saw Gil and Gayoon on the street, coming toward their position in the car, parked on the thoroughfare. The couple wore garden-variety winter clothes, with Gayoon's dark red parka difficult to miss. She walked with a limp, and Gunn could see that she was still hurting.

"That's them," Gunn said, lowering his head. "Get down, moron."

Sang lowered his head. "There's no need to insult me. One day, you may push me too far."

"Let's just get through today, huh?"

When the couple passed the vehicle, the thugs sat back up. Gunn let the pair continue as he watched from the rearview mirror. Gil and Gayoon were thirty yards down the thoroughfare when they crossed over and turned down a side street.

"Nice and easy, Sang. I don't want to spook them."

"You've got to be joking. The woman can barely stand upright, and what's the soldier going to do in a two-on-one situation?"

"You've got a lot to learn. We're out in public, so just do as I say."

Both men exited the vehicle, Gunn using the keyless remote to lock the car. Not wanting to attract attention, they maintained a casual pace as they crossed the thoroughfare.

"Where'd they go?" Sang queried.

A puzzled Gunn looked in every direction. "They couldn't have gone far. If they're not in that church, we'll have to go door-to-door."

They jogged to the church, going up the steps and walking into the vestibule.

The number of people sitting in the pews praying surprised Gunn. Had he or Sang bothered to examine the schedule, they would've known the parish priest was listening to confessions.

Gunn caught a flash of dark red exiting through a side door nearer the front of the church. *How did they figure out we were following?* "Side door to the left," he whispered, elbowing Sang. "You stay down the front steps, and I'll drive them to you."

With church parishioners now watching, Gunn trotted toward the side door while Sang went back outside.

From the church's side door, Gayoon had climbed onto Gil's back, and the soldier struggled as he lumbered down the street, carrying her piggyback. Gunn jogged to overtake the couple while Sang walked casually toward them.

Breathing hard, Gil stopped and bent, letting Gayoon climb down. She groaned in agony.

"Dude," Gil said to Gunn between gasps of air. "I can get Myung-Dae's money."

"It's not up to me," Gunn said in English.

"She had nothing to do with this. I'll see Myung-Dae alone."

"Myung-Dae ordered us to take you both to the farm."

"Cam will meet us here any minute now. Then we'll talk to Myung-Dae. We have a plan to get the man's money; isn't that what this is about?"

Gunn didn't acknowledge Gil's question. Instead, he lobbed the keys to Myung-Dae's auto to Sang.

"Bring the car around, so she doesn't have so far to walk," Gunn said.

"Why?"

"Because I said so. Can't you see she's in pain?"

Sang muttered under his breath while walking back to the thoroughfare. Gunn couldn't help but feel sorry for the woman. She did no more than fall in love with a drug addict. As he saw it, she'd suffered enough.

Soon the car arrived, and Gunn handcuffed the couple with zip-ties before easing them in the back seat. If any of the local KNPA had eyes on this, they did nothing.

With Gunn riding shotgun, Sang drove to Jumpin' Jack Flask.

"Take them to the farm," Gunn told Sang before climbing out. "I'll bring Myung-Dae in my car in a few minutes. Do nothing until we get there, understand?"

Sang nodded before turning the car around.

****

Gayoon's eyes met Gil's in the back of the car. Sang stopped the car as Anjeong-ri's only traffic light turned red. Gayoon sat behind Sang.

"Can't you let her go?" Gil asked. "She had nothing to do with this; it's my fault."

Only Sang neither spoke nor understood English. He asked Gayoon in Korean what the American GI wanted. She relayed the request.

Sang's eyes never left the road. "I'm only following orders. This isn't personal."

"Well?" Gil asked.

"He doesn't care."

From the moment the thieves broke in, Gayoon saw this scenario play out in her head. When she heard Myung-Dae would deal with them at the farm, she knew from rumors what lay ahead. Gayoon considered her options and quickly reached a decision. Handcuffed with arms out front, she planned her strategy.

It was no secret that Myung-Dae knew nothing of forgiveness or mercy. Whatever was about to happen on that farm would be terrible. Glancing at Gil, she could see he appeared oblivious to all of it. *Maybe that's for the best*.

The car moved from the pavement to an unmarked dirt road. While Gayoon didn't know precisely the farm's location, she guessed they were close. Gayoon was glad neither she nor Gil had a chance to buckle up—explaining her plan to him would take time, and time was not their friend.

She didn't want to go without a fight. As weak and in agony as she was, Gayoon rose from behind Sang in the back seat. With both hands clasped together—she brought her arms back as if swinging an imaginary baseball bat, her fists aimed at Sang's right temple.

Sang's eyes found her in the rearview mirror just before impact. Her hands found their mark, slamming against the goon's head. Sang lost control of the car. It veered left, slamming headfirst into a grove of large spruce pine trees.

The car's grill folded like an accordion, the windshield shattering into a million breakaway fragments. The front-seat airbags deployed, crushing against Sang. If this car had other airbags, they failed to engage.

Gayoon's world went white, the pain from her right arm intense as she heard a bone snap. She heard Sang groan, and glanced at a too-quiet Gil. His eyes were open wide, with blood running down the corners of his mouth. His complexion turned a fish-belly white.

"Gil?" she whispered hoarsely.

Her man didn't speak nor move. As sorrow overwhelmed her, Gayoon understood unless she crawled out from under the wreckage and made it to safety; she would soon join him. Gayoon weakly brought back the door release and opened it, falling out of the back seat and onto crusty snow. She inched forward two feet before stopping to catch her breath. She coughed, bright red blood spattering into the snow.

Despite the wind, she heard a car approach, the tires crunching against the frozen gravel driveway. Gunn's car came to rest when it was parallel with Myung-Dae's wrecked auto. She glanced behind her, Sang leaning against a tree as he moaned and vomited.

Myung-Dae exited Gunn's car first.

"Look what that idiot did to my beautiful car!" Myung-Dae screamed. "Check on Sang. Kill the others."

Gayoon wondered about the afterlife as Sang continued to wail in pain. She told herself she wasn't afraid to die. Only that wasn't the truth. She listened to Gunn's boots as they walked on through the crusty snow to Myung-Dae's ruined car.

"The American is dead," Gunn shouted.

"Be sure," Myung-Dae barked as he walked toward the farmhouse.

Gayoon involuntarily jumped when the gunshot rang out.

The approaching footsteps told her it was time to depart this world. She hoped the next one would be beautiful, the transition painless. She heard another gunshot before the pain abruptly ended.

****

Getting Martz to authorize the afternoon off proved easy, which came as a surprise to Cam. Many of the men discussed privately that Martz hadn't been himself lately. The popular theory attributed it to stress, the result of Tomlinson's disappearance coupled with DiSilva's unexpected transfer to Kentucky.

After showering, Cam changed into civilian clothes and jogged to the main gate, arriving at the church five minutes late. He went inside, panicked that neither Gil nor Gayoon were in the pews waiting. Cam phoned Gil's cell; it went quickly to voicemail.

With Gayoon hobbled, he hoped she and Gil were running late too. He backtracked to Gayoon's apartment. With no sign of the couple, Cam went into the building, took the stairs, and knocked on the door.

He could see an eye peek from the peephole and, for the briefest of moments, felt relieved. At least until Nari opened it. After that, Cam's anxiety clicked back in, hard and fast.

"Nari. What the hell? What happened to Gil and Gayoon?"

"They aren't with you?"

"Do you see them with me?"

"They left thirty minutes ago."

"Did they have to stop somewhere else?"

"I don't think so. They told me they were meeting you at the church at one o'clock."

"They weren't there," Cam replied. "I got there

late. I don't know where else to look."

"Do you think they got scared and left town for a little while?"

Cam shook his head. "They have no money and nowhere else to go. Plus Gil has a midnight shift."

Nari took her jacket hanging from the back of a kitchen chair. "Well…come on. We have to find them."

"Do you really think we will?" he asked.

"No. I do not."

Chapter Twenty-Four

Porter walked into the admin office just before 0800. Earlier this morning, he'd received a text from Cam, telling him Gil and Gayoon were missing, that Gil owed Myung-Dae money. And while Cam didn't say it, Porter considered the possibility the couple was dead.

Martz was sitting at DiSilva's desk, hanging up the phone as Porter entered. Looking over at the master sergeant, Porter saw an unfamiliar expression on Martz's face. It was the look of bewilderment.

"I've got some bad news, Top. I think something terrible happened to Gil Trotter."

"Yeah, I know. I got a call just after the midnight roll; Trotter didn't show for his shift. What do you know about it?"

Porter sat down. "Not much, just a text from Cam earlier this morning that Gil and his woman went missing yesterday."

Martz rubbed his temples. "What in the fuck is going on around here? Tell me the truth—do you think they're still alive?"

"The truth? No. I don't."

Martz leaned back. "Why do you think that?"

"Gil owed Tang money."

"And why would Trotter owe Tang money?"

Porter took a breath. "Trotter dealt cocaine for Tang. That's as much as I know."

Martz glared at Porter. "Are you kidding me?" He slammed his fist on the desk. "Why did you not *tell* me that? I would've put him in a clinic and saved that man's life. Is anyone else in this unit slinging dope?"

"I would've told you, except you were hell-bent on throwing those two in jail. No. Not that I'm aware of."

"I asked you point-blank if Trotter had a chemical dependency, so don't make me out to be the bad guy. What about Shanahan?"

"Cam Shanahan isn't selling dope, Top."

"How do you know that?"

"I would've seen it or heard about it."

Martz's eyes stayed on Porter's. "So how do I go about explaining this to DiSilva?"

"Tell DiSilva that Trotter's gone AWOL and hand it over to legal."

"That's two of my men in two weeks, Porter. Vanished without a trace. The Joint Chiefs will assign a task force to investigate this shithole and will leave no stone unturned by the time they're finished."

"If they pick up the scent on DiSilva, that solves your problem. Have the bugs picked up anything new?"

Martz ran a hand over his bald head. "Not in this office. But I've learned lots from the Duffy Club bug. A bartender is screwing a waitress, and the janitor is gay. This is a damned nightmare."

"Two guys who made poor decisions, Top. That's a lot of guilt to swallow, and yes, I should've told you about Trotter. Still, I expected nothing like that to happen. I hate to pile on, but unless we tie DiSilva in with Tang's unconfirmed heroin deal—we're baying at the moon."

"So DiSilva goes to Kentucky a rich man?" Martz

asked. "I wonder what happens to Tang's empire once his heir apparent is in America."

"I don't care, and I'm sure you don't either. The news about Gil could mess up my plan for getting in Tang's house on Saturday."

"How so?"

"I counted on Cam to take me. But if he's afraid enough of Tang, he might decide to sit this one out. And not for nothing, I wouldn't go anywhere near Tang unless I had to."

"Can you go to Tang's house alone?"

"Sure. But if you're calling off the dogs, what's the point?"

"You think there's still the chance DiSilva is helping Tang move dope?"

Porter nodded. "Yes, I do."

"What are the chances of you finding anything more sophisticated than a handgun?"

Porter leaned back. "I have access to an assault and sniper rifle. Plus a riot gun with tear gas. I can hook you up with full body armor—for a day or two anyhow. You're roughly the same dimensions as my spotter. What are you thinking?"

"Your spotter's okay letting me borrow his gear?"

"He'll never know it left the armory. What we'll need is more ammo for the M-4 and a half-dozen teargas canisters. Some flash-bangs might come in handy. I'm sure a guy with your influence could get those easy enough."

Martz nodded. "I can get respirators too."

"No need. Agency provided bulletproof night-vision capable helmets with built-in respirators. State-of-the-art. You still haven't told me what you're

245

thinking."

Martz grabbed his jacket to leave. "Not yet. I need to think about this. So you'll drop the bug in Tang's house tomorrow morning and see where that takes us." He started toward the door. "In the meantime, find out whatever you can about Trotter's disappearance. Please."

"When will you tell DiSilva about Gil?"

"I'll call from the security building."

Porter nodded.

****

Chona DiSilva woke when Arthur started twitching. She worried about him—her husband acquired two new bad habits: thrashing and talking in his sleep. Her father's name came up more than once, the context of which wasn't altogether warm and fuzzy.

She remembered the first time she heard someone tell her what her father *did*. It was in grammar school when she was nine or ten years old. She didn't believe it at first and asked her mother. Moon-Kym told her that villagers made up the stories, jealous of her father's success.

But the innuendo picked up steam throughout high school. Chona had been so peppered that gradually, she learned to accept her father's transgressions. As a father, he never laid a hand on her. Still, Myung-Dae's reputation frightened the boys; she didn't have a single date in those four years.

Going to university in Seoul changed everything. There, she lost the village and escaped her father's reputation for four glorious years.

Every now and again, Chona thought of Sung-ki. He was the handsomest man Chona had ever seen in real life. She gave him her virginity and was in love with the young man two years her senior. Seeing the photos they took together, Moon-Kym fell in love with him too. She told Chona she hoped they would marry and have beautiful children.

Unfortunately, Myung-Dae thought differently. He thought the young man privileged and doubted Sung-ki worked a day in his life. In the end, it didn't matter. She caught her lover in bed with one of her closest friends. The pain was indescribable, and she abstained from dating as a result.

Coming home that summer after graduation, she still remembered the smug look on her father's face. Then Myung-Dae forced DiSilva on her, describing the soldier as a "bird in hand." That Myung-Dae had so easily manipulated Arthur was unnerving. She found Arthur generous but cold. Forgiving Myung-Dae for the match had been difficult.

"Are you awake, Arthur?"

"I am now. You're not teaching this morning?"

"Students are taking standardized tests, and I'm not proctoring." She sat up. "I'll make coffee." She got to her feet and poured water into the coffee machine. The combination of short days, cold nights, and giggling, snot-nosed schoolchildren was changing her mind about starting a family of her own.

With a bathrobe on but untied, DiSilva staggered out of the bedroom to go to the bathroom. In Chona's eyes, her husband had it made. Unless there were exercises in-country his unit was part of, Arthur worked his own schedule. Sure, there was the occasional late night. But he didn't come home drunk or smelling of cheap perfume. And that was good enough—at least for now.

Soon Arthur opened the bathroom door and walked into the kitchen. Chona poured coffee and watched him slide into a chair at the table across from a stack of papers she needed to grade today.

"You're up late," she said. Chona put the carafe back on the heating plate and sat down alongside her stack. "That means something's wrong."

"You remember telling me you wanted to live someplace warm when we left Camp Humphreys?"

She stopped and leaned forward. "Yes. What about it?"

"I should've told you already but couldn't work up the nerve. I got orders to Kentucky yesterday. We're scheduled to leave February 28th and be in Richmond, Kentucky March 16th."

Chona's head dropped. That she wanted to live somewhere warm for a change was true. She envisioned Hawaii or Southern California. But Kentucky? She knew nothing of it. This wasn't welcome news.

"You told me staying was all but certain," she said.

"That's what the detailer in DC told me."

"Have you spoken to Father?"

"Of course not. You come first."

Chona reached across the table and took her husband's hand. "These things happen for a reason. We'll visit my parents a few times a year, and that will be more than enough."

He took a sip of coffee. "I only want you to be happy."

"You being separated from my father isn't a bad thing. I'm afraid he's been a bad influence."

"Might be the other way around, you know."

DiSilva grinned as he took another sip.

Just then, DiSilva's cell phone rang. She listened as he went into the bedroom and picked up.

"Is everything okay, Ollie?" she heard her husband ask.

There was a pause as DiSilva listened.

"For the love of God…this transfer I didn't want is looking good right about now. After he's been UA for twenty-four hours, I'll call legal. Until then, let's look around for ourselves; maybe he'll turn up," DiSilva said before hanging up.

He returned to the kitchen.

"You look frazzled, Arthur. Is something wrong?"

"Another of my men went missing."

"Are you serious?"

DiSilva nodded. "This is bad."

"When did you plan on telling my family about the move?"

"Sunday after dinner. I'll deal with your father. I'm counting on you to handle your mother."

"Yes." She nodded. "I should give the school my notice. That will be sad."

DiSilva said no more, and she was glad for it. She picked the first paper from the stack and uncapped the dread red pen.

****

At 1630 hours, Porter texted Ferguson, telling him he was taking the night off. He gave no reason or excuse. Gil's disappearance bothered him more than he cared to admit.

Jeong never strayed too far out of his head, with Panmunjom right behind her. They talked every night on a webcam app, but it proved a poor substitute for the real deal.

Thirty minutes later, Porter shut the office down, took a shower, and changed clothes. He went down to Cam's room and, seeing light under the door, knocked.

Cam opened the door looking disheveled, wearing an old, ratty-looking sweatshirt and jeans. His eyes were bloodshot.

"Hey, Mike. What's up?"

"Let's go grab a beer and something to eat across the street."

"I don't know, man. I'm not feeling so hot. It's best I keep a low profile."

"Getting out of this room will do you some good. And across the street is as low-profile as it gets."

"Yeah, okay."

Cam threw on a jacket, and the pair left the barracks. Looking toward the main gate, they observed the conga line of soldiers leaving camp.

"Are we still on for Saturday morning?" Porter asked as they sat at the bar and ordered beers and examined the menu.

With Cam's hands on the bar as the beer and menus came, Porter noticed they shook ever so slightly.

"I've been thinking about that. Seeing Myung-Dae again." Cam shook his head. "I've always been leery of him, but now I'm straight-up terrified."

Porter nodded. "I don't blame you one bit."

"You still want to go?"

"Yeah. I thought you said he makes an order every week?"

"He does. I'm sitting on a couple hundred dollars' worth of merchandise. But I'll eat it before I go to his house."

"If you want, I'll take your stuff, and you get paid."

Cam turned to look. "You're willing to do that? I'll give you half, no problem."

"Nah, I'll do it as a favor. Thing is, I don't know how to get there."

"I'll whip up a map. Finding his place is tricky, but once you spot the house, you'll know it belongs to Myung-Dae. You don't know how much I appreciate it."

"No problem."

They ordered food. Porter felt better seeing Cam's hands level out.

"You hook up with anyone since you stopped seeing Jeong?"

"I honestly haven't been looking. So you don't plan to go back into Anjeong-ri the rest of your time here?" Porter asked.

"You couldn't *drag* me into Anjeong-ri. Not anymore."

"Do you know what happened to Gil?"

"I haven't told anyone what I'm about to tell you." Cam told the story of Gil in the security building break room. "Gil begged me to help him. I keep thinking that if I'd done what he wanted, he'd still be alive."

"You're blaming yourself for Gil? You want my advice?"

"Sure."

"Let yourself off the hook. I know it's none of my business, but what are you gonna do about Nari?"

"I don't know what to tell her. The way I see it, it's easier to stay on the base and let her find another guy. If you see her and she asks, tell her the truth. That I'm afraid of Myung-Dae. And I'm sorry for not having the balls to tell her myself. The next time I'm out that gate, I'm on a bus headed for Osan."

Later that night, Porter and Jeong spoke on Skype from the admin office. He thought about Cam's decision regarding Nari. And wondered how he would tell Jeong before going north.

Chapter Twenty-Five

Porter turned on the cell phone he charged overnight before getting ready to shower. The phone chimed, and Porter read Stillson's text, telling him to check his agency email.

Martz wasn't already in the office when Porter opened it, a first since his arrival. The agency comm was brief, the meat in the attachments. There were several photographs and a bio for Taeho Eom—who defected from North to South Korea eight months ago after escaping a North Korean prison. A North Korean court found Eom guilty of treason and declared him a dissident. Lieutenant Eom had been a member of his country's special operation forces—an elite marksman. Then the North Korean dissident slipped away from South Korean surveillance.

The email went on to say someone allegedly spotted Eom in Pyeongtaek only days ago, corresponding with a spike in chatter. Eom possessed the skills and motive to assassinate the sitting North Korean president. That the Pyeongtaek sighting was unconfirmed mattered not at all.

Porter now had a name and face. *But does Eom work alone? Stillson said the consensus was the man worked without a spotter. But how does he know for sure? I suppose it doesn't much matter; I'd have to put both down and then bug out.* Ferguson was sure to weigh in. And every time his spotter did, Porter slept less than he had the night before.

Porter still needed the time and date. There was a time after Felicity and Sara when Porter welcomed death. Trading his life for Luther's freedom wasn't so tough a decision. Only that was no longer the case. He was in love.

Jeong changed everything.

****

Jaewon Dokgo was getting a massage in his Seosan office when his receptionist told him he had an urgent call from his brother.

"Why don't you take a break, sweetheart?" Jaewon instructed the masseuse as he got to his feet. "Just wait in the lobby; I need the room a few minutes." He waited for her to leave before picking up. "I was going to call you. I have some news. But what's so urgent?"

"Have you talked to Namil since we sent him to Anjeong-ri?"

"Now that you mention it, no. He didn't update you?"

"He doesn't answer his cell phone."

"Did you try calling that bar he worked in?"

"Duffy Club. I called; whoever answered said he missed a shift and never returned."

Jaewon rubbed his left temple. "So how do you want to handle it?"

"I'll have to send two of my men to Anjeong-ri to find out where he went. What's your news?"

"Do you remember a bank manager by the name of Hajoon Lee?" Jaewon asked.

"No. Should I?"

"When we bought that land in north Daejeon a

couple of years ago, he was at the closing. Lee manages a bank in Anjeong-ri and shared something interesting. Seems Myung-Dae Tang took out a huge loan and wired all the proceeds to a Chinese bank. He collateralized his entire estate."

"That is interesting, Jaewon. When did the loan close?"

"A few days ago."

"Why would Tang do that?"

"Lee said it was for an import-export startup. Except Lee doesn't believe that. Tang's obviously onto something big," Jaewon said.

"Do you think Gunn might know?"

"Who else?"

"Gunn may very well tell you to go fuck yourself," Ryung said. "Does he still work for Tang?"

"Last I heard. I'll have Whan track him down and call."

"Gunn can't stand Whan anymore than he can stand either of us," Ryung said.

"I heard Sang Doak just caught on with Tang. Maybe he knows."

"I'd rather deal with Gunn, Jaewon. Besides, I doubt Sang knows much if he's new. So tell Whan to find and call Gunn and set up a meeting for tomorrow morning in my Daejeon karaoke bar, eight o'clock."

"Why so early?" Jaewon inquired.

"I'm playing tennis later."

"I'll try. You don't suppose Namil decided to just leave town on his own?"

"If his woman and daughter are still here, I doubt it," Ryung said. "Do you think Myung-Dae is bringing in narcotics from China?"

"I can't think of anything else that would require so much cash. Something else. I heard the KNPA found Kiwoo Jong's body in a Gongju dumpster."

"That's interesting too," Ryung said. "Clearly there's trouble in paradise."

"I've never heard of him killing one of his own, so maybe you're right. One problem I have about meeting tomorrow morning, Whan's out on collections. Can you spare any of your men, Ryung?"

"I'll bring Sunsin."

"What do you think we should do with Gunn once he tells us what Tang is up to?" Jaewon asked.

"Nothing. I want Tang and his crew all in one place. Eliminate them in one fell swoop. If Tang's not there, we find him. I want them gone, bag and baggage."

"I'll take care of it, brother."

****

It was early afternoon when Gunn and Sang walked into the farmhouse, having returned from Mokpo Port.

"Gunn, Myung-Dae wants you to call him at Jumpin' Jack," the older of Myung-Dae's two farmhands said.

Gunn grabbed the kitchen phone and called while Byung returned to the barn and Sang went upstairs.

Myung-Dae picked up on the first ring. "Well? How did you fare?"

"The Chinese freighter docks February 5th, ETA noon."

"The forklift drivers you hired, you vetted each one?"

"Ten drivers. Done."

"That's good work, Gunn."

"I don't really see the need for your son-in-law, not if he can't operate a forklift. He'll only be in the way."

Myung-Dae took a deep breath. "I know. But let him think he's in charge. Once we're paid in full, and you're back in Anjeong-ri, you'll never have to see him again."

"Sang can't operate a forklift and will only be in the way too. He's a capable enough guy but doesn't seem to understand that actions have consequences. He sees only the action."

"Give him a chance, Gunn. I remember thinking the same thing about you when you first came to me from the Dokgos. He won't learn if we keep him tethered."

Gunn had no choice but to concede the point.

"Take tonight off, Gunn. You've earned it."

"Are you sure? It's a busy night, Myung-Dae."

"Send Sang. Tell him he needs to be here in an hour; he can drive the pickup truck."

"Thank you, Myung-Dae. I appreciate it. I'll tell Sang."

Gunn hung up and went up the stairs to give Sang the news. Then he went into his room and closed the door.

****

An hour later, the telephone in the farmhouse kitchen rang. Gunn, nursing a cup of coffee at the table, picked up.

"Is Gunn Lim there?" a man's voice on the other end asked.

The voice sounded familiar, but Gunn couldn't place it. "Who is this?"

257

"Whan Kym. How have you been, Gunn?"

Hearing the voice invoked the memory. Gunn worked with Whan twenty-five years ago, back when both were on the Dokgo brothers' payroll. When Gunn refused to set fire to one of Ryung's apartment buildings filled with women and children, his employment with them ended abruptly. While Whan had nothing to do with Gunn's dismissal, he never cared for the man.

"How did you get this number?" Gunn asked. *The Dokgo brothers are onto Myung-Dae's Wuhan deal. They want details before they kill every one of us because Myung-Dae's too blind and stubborn to pay tribute.*

Whan chuckled. "You were never the tracker that I am. Jaewon and Ryung are hoping you could spare a few minutes to talk, to get a better understanding of information they happened onto. Probably just rumors, but you remember how cautious they are."

Gunn remembered all too well. "What information are you referring to? I could clear it up for you right now and save everyone a lot of time. What's troubling them?"

"That I don't know. They wanted me to ask if you could spare a few minutes tomorrow morning. So that's what I'm doing."

That's a lie. They likely have eyes on this farm and Myung-Dae's Anjeong-ri house and the bars. And on my place in Anseong. There's only one way out of this, and undue protesting won't help.

"When and where?"

"Do you remember Ryung's karaoke bar in Daejeon?"

"I remember. What time?"

"Eight tomorrow morning."

"I'll be there."

"Thank you, Gunn."

Whan then gave Gunn instructions to follow once he arrived, designed to deter anyone stupid enough to wear a wire or carry a weapon.

"I'll see you then," Whan said.

Gunn hung up. He thought about calling Daeum to tell her to pack a few things—only she'd panic. He'd tell his wife after the Dokgo meeting.

If I told Myung-Dae about the Dokgos, how would he likely respond? Would he accuse me of being in league with them, and in a fit of rage, try to kill me as he did Kiwoo? No, that's not an option. There's another way.

Gunn needed to find a new place to live, out of the country, early tomorrow afternoon. And he would need to do it quickly and quietly, with a minimal paper trail. Because neither he nor his wife spoke any other languages except Korean and a barely passable English, that narrowed his choices considerably.

Stringent immigration policies narrowed them further still. Looking at all possibilities, he saw only one that checked all the boxes. The Philippines. Gunn read many Filipinos speak English, especially in and around Manila. That it was inexpensive with warm weather year round were delightful bonuses.

Gunn looked at a map on his laptop. And decided it would be best to take up residence in a Manila suburb, where he and Daeum could get lost in plain sight. They would rent a house and pay cash for everything.

Taking a deep breath, Gunn began consolidating

his various assets. He needed to get liquid, putting the cash into his Cayman Islands account that nobody knew anything about.

Over the years, Gunn had successfully taken on many challenges. But making this move under the radar would be among his greatest.

Chapter Twenty-Six

Gunn hated feeling anxious, considering it a sign of weakness. He willed his hands to remain steady at the wheel as his car entered Daejeon city limits. This time of day, traffic moved smoothly, and he parked directly in front of Ryung Dokgo's karaoke bar. Bordering the red-light district, this bar sat in one of the seedier neighborhoods in the city.

From his time working for the Dokgos, Gunn understood how the brothers operated. Ryung was the more cerebral in working through a problem, younger brother Jaewon the more emotional. One needed to be careful in dealing with them. To be condescending or patronizing, however unintentional, was tantamount to suicide.

Gunn considered this from every angle and concluded there was no silver lining. The only reason to comply was to buy time. The inherent risk was that if the brothers didn't like what they heard, they could murder him in this place this very morning. But that wasn't so much their style. Like Myung-Dae, they preferred style over substance when doling out punishment. They would wait until they had all the rotten eggs in one basket before reaching for the sledgehammer.

If the Dokgos didn't want to get their hands dirty murdering Gunn today, their other tactic was to spread innuendo. They might let Myung-Dae hear that Gunn sought the meeting, hoping to sell the brothers information. Either way, Gunn ended up on a slab.

Gunn got out of the car and walked to the bar's front door, striking it with an open palm three times. He listened as the deadbolt unlatched and the door swung open. It was dark inside.

"Take two steps in and halt," a man's voice said. It was deep and foreboding.

Gunn took two steps and stopped. He listened as the door closed and locked. Dim lights came up inside the dank, dreary saloon. Fifteen feet away, Ryung and Jaewon Dokgo sat at a small round table, an empty chair between them. Gunn heard footsteps come up from behind.

"Keep your eyes forward and take off your boots. Then stand and spread your arms and legs."

Gunn got down on one knee and began following the instructions. The man patting him down was husky and tall, with a shaved head that bore a deep scar over his left ear. Gunn had never seen him before.

Nothing had changed since Gunn last visited, a long time ago. The same layout, tables, chairs, and barstools. Even the DJ booth and equipment were the same.

The large man grinned and produced a wand, the type used by airport security. He checked Gunn before turning the device off.

"You can put your boots back on. Your feet smell, in case you were wondering. Baby powder might help."

Gunn put his boots on, eyeing the big man all the while. Why this oversized dolt wanted to pick a fight, Gunn didn't understand. But if the Dokgo brothers weren't here, he would gladly give this Neanderthal a lesson in humility.

"Please join us, Gunn," Jaewon said. "You'll have to excuse Sunsin. He doesn't get out much."

"I'm glad you're both looking well. And still cautious," Gunn said, forcing a grin as he walked to the table.

"Please sit down," Ryung said, gesturing to the empty chair.

Gunn sat down.

"What can we get you?" Jaewon asked. "Coffee or tea? Or a cocktail, perhaps?"

Drinking alcohol with these two men was unwise, regardless of the occasion or time of day. But coffee, knowing Sunsin would have to wait on him, Gunn couldn't resist.

"I'll take a cup of coffee, black. Please," Gunn said.

Jaewon gestured to Sunsin, who started filling the coffee machine with water.

Ryung's eyes locked onto Gunn's. "You're probably wondering what this is about."

"I'm naturally curious. Whan offered little information."

"We have a great deal of respect for you," Ryung continued. "An acquaintance tells us your boss recently took out a large loan and sent the proceeds to a Chinese bank, Wuhan I believe. We know nothing beyond that, which is why we've asked you here. Perhaps you can elaborate."

Gunn felt his heart pound. "It's always been important to me to have your respect. However, I know nothing about a loan or Myung-Dae's dealings with the

Chinese. Like you, he is cautious and discusses business more with his son-in-law than his associates."

Ryung glanced at his younger brother. "My concern here is Myung-Dae, who is in arrears concerning tribute. Has he been well? Thinking lucidly?"

"I've noticed no decline in Myung-Dae's motor or cognitive skills. He's still prone to unprovoked ramblings and colorful observations, but that's nothing new. He plays his cards closer to the vest these days."

Sunsin approached and put a mug of coffee on the table in front of Gunn, who grinned but offered no thanks. Sunsin lumbered back to his spot behind the bar.

"We understand that you're loyal to Tang, a commendable trait," Ryung said. "But if you're withholding information about an activity where large sums are changing hands, you're doing everyone a disservice. Including yourself."

A not-so-veiled threat. Watch yourself. Sweat rolled down Gunn's armpits and beaded on his temples.

"I didn't want to bring this up but feel I must. It embarrasses me to say that I no longer have Myung-Dae's full confidence."

"Now there's a surprise," Sunsin muttered aloud.

Ryung pointed an index finger at Sunsin. "You, shut up. Please, Gunn, continue."

"I'm afraid there's nothing more I know. Myung-Dae is incrementally phasing me out."

"Has he added more men?" Jaewon asked. "Increased the volume of his drug trade?"

Gunn fidgeted. "In a fit of rage, Myung-Dae killed Kiwoo Jong only last week. He hired a man you both know as a replacement, Sang Doak. I'm not aware of any uptick in his narcotics trade."

Ryung nodded. "We know about Kiwoo and Sang."

"It's clear Sang is to be my replacement."

"Is it possible Sang knows more about this transaction than you do?"

"It's possible but unlikely. Myung-Dae has been spending a great deal of time with his American son-in-law lately. But if I hear of anything regarding the purchase or sale of a large quantity of narcotics, I will contact you immediately."

"You've always been a trusted friend," Ryung said. "We thank you for your time."

"As always, I'm honored." *Keep your mouth shut and just keep moving.*

"One more thing," Ryung said. "Recently, Myung-Dae hired a young man we both know. A bartender named Namil Seu. Do you know him?"

Damn. So Ryung really did hire that little weasel. Gunn took a breath. "A bartender, you say? I have little to do with Myung-Dae's bar operations other than serve as an occasional bouncer. Do you have a photo of the man?"

Ryung looked at his brother, who only shrugged. "No, not offhand."

"Without one, I won't be of much help. I remember faces but names, not so much. Between Myung-Dae's bars, there's a great deal of attrition. What was his name again?"

"Never mind, Gunn. It's not important," Ryung said. "I'm sure he'll turn up."

Want to bet? "I'm sorry I couldn't be of more

help."

Both Dokgo brothers stood, signaling the end of the meeting. Gunn rose and shook hands with both men before Sunsin opened the bar's front door. Gunn wasted no time getting back into his car. He turned the key in the ignition and realized that from this moment on, he would sweat with fear every time he did this. No matter where he was or how much time had passed.

They know I was lying; I'm sure of it. Gunn waited until Ryung's bar disappeared from his rearview mirror. Then he pulled the car over and called his wife.

"Where are you, Daeum?"

"I'm home. Where are you?"

"Listen to me carefully. I need you to do something for the both of us."

"What is it, Gunn?"

"Grab our passports and book a flight from Seoul to Manila. First one out, first class, one-way. Pack everything you *need* that fits in four suitcases. Don't pack a lot of clothes; we can buy them there. Anything left behind stays behind. You'll need to book a hotel for two weeks, someplace decent. And for God's sake, woman, not a word of this to *anyone*, and I mean anyone. That includes your family. Do you understand?"

"Manila? What will we do in Manila? Have you lost your mind, Gunn?"

"I don't have time to argue." He repeated the instructions. "Don't linger; every second counts. Now tell me you understand!"

"Are we in danger?"

"Listen to me," he yelled. "That's what I'm trying to avoid. Can I count on you to do what I just instructed?"

"What about my family, Gunn?"

"What did I just say? We won't be back, and you'll say nothing to anyone about where we're going. We'll talk about your family at the airport. Right now, I need you to book the flight and hotel. Then text the information, and I'll meet you at the airport."

"Why Manila?"

"We'll talk about that in the airport, too."

"I would prefer Thailand, Gunn."

"Do you speak Thai?"

"No," Daeum said.

"Wherever we go, we'll be residents, not tourists. Got it?"

"It has to be today? We'll pay a fortune to leave on such short notice."

He imagined reaching into the phone and wringing her neck.

"Book the very first flight out after twelve noon. You'll have to take a cab to the airport."

"What have you gotten us into, Gunn?"

"Just do as I say and text the information. I'm losing cell reception," he lied.

Gunn hung up before she could think to ask another question or say anything else that raised his blood pressure. The last fifteen hours had been stressful enough.

****

"What do you want to do?" Jaewon asked his brother after Gunn left. "Any fool can see the man was lying."

Ryung nodded. "But let's not throw the baby out with the bathwater. Gunn may yet prove useful. Does he still live in Anseong with his wife?"

"Maybe. I'm sure Whan can find out where Gunn and his wife live."

"I want eyes on Tang's house and bars. If Gunn still has the place in Anseong, I want eyes on it as well. I believe Tang is doing something big. I want to surprise him when he shows up to take it."

****

Gunn read Daeum's text as he watched the Anseong apartment building they lived in from farther down the street. That Gunn used her as bait in case the Dokgos sent someone would emotionally crush the woman if she found out. Still, it was necessary. Gunn knew it was a matter of time until the brothers sent people to watch his place if they hadn't done so already.

Her text message was brief. Gunn needed to be at Gimpo Airport for Korean Air flight 315 from Seoul to Manila, scheduled to depart at one o'clock that afternoon from gate fifteen. She emailed the e-ticket and would be at the gate waiting, bags checked.

He sent a text asking if she'd vacated the apartment yet. He wasn't in the habit of testing her, but today he'd take no chances. She replied she would be out in ten minutes. Gunn would follow the cab to the airport as discreetly as possible.

Once in Manila, they would spend two weeks looking at rental houses. With the equivalent of two million U.S. dollars stashed in his Cayman Islands account, they could rent a mansion if they wanted. Only he wanted nothing extravagant or flashy, no matter how much Daeum protested.

Gunn never cared about living somewhere warm,

as Chona DiSilva did. But he certainly wanted to die somewhere warm. He watched his wife climb into a taxi, the driver hoisting her oversized bags in the trunk.

He followed the cab all the way to the airport. And for the briefest of moments, Gunn felt safe as he parked his car in the airport's long-term parking garage and trotted into the terminal.

One o'clock couldn't come fast enough.

****

On the Anjeong-ri sidewalk, Porter shifted the weight of Cam's gym bag as he glanced at the map once more. The part of Anjeong-ri he suddenly found himself in was a toilet, and Porter considered the possibility that a guilt-ridden, frightened, and sorrowful Cam drew him a map of Middle Earth.

Finally, Porter found the Georgian-styled brick house with four white columns out front. He walked to the front door and rang the bell.

It took several seconds before an older woman appeared. She smiled and bowed and gestured for Porter to enter. She led him down a long, wide hallway with every door closed. Porter felt no joy in this place. It was like walking into a dentist's office. *Or a morgue.*

The last door down was partially open, and she nudged it gently, letting Porter in before scurrying away.

"Right on time; we're off to a good start." Myung-Dae looked over Porter's shoulders. "Where is Cameron?"

"He's not feeling well, so he asked me to act on his behalf."

Myung-Dae nodded. "Very well. I see you met my wife, Moon-Kym."

"She didn't introduce herself. This is a beautiful home you have, Myung-Dae."

"Thank you. Yes, my wife is shy. Until you get to know her, that is."

Porter's eyes took in the room, aware Myung-Dae watched his every move. With bamboo hardwood flooring, stained baseboards, and wainscoting of the highest quality, Myung-Dae spared no expense. The liquor display, elaborate chess boards, figurines, and brass-armored knight made an impression.

Myung-Dae's desk here was as messy as his Duffy Club counterpart. That the desk was out in the open was disappointing, but Porter came prepared. He removed a stick of chewing gum and popped it in his mouth.

Myung-Dae went behind his messy desk and moved a stack of hardcover ledgers off the top, putting them on the floor behind him. He then motioned for Porter to put the bag up on the desk, which he did.

"Let's see what Cameron bought for me," Myung-Dae said. "Please sit down. This takes some time, I'm afraid."

Porter sat down, and Myung-Dae unzipped the bag and brought the first item up with animated glee. It was a carton of cigarettes. Myung-Dae placed the box on the floor behind him, wrote in his journal, and reached back into the bag for the next item.

As Myung-Dae removed a bottle of gin, Porter fake-sneezed, the masticated gum now in his palm. He waited until Myung-Dae reached into the bag again before taking action. It took no effort to plant the bug on the bottom of his chair, the gum serving as an adhesive.

One by one, Myung-Dae examined the items,

checking the brand before recording it in his journal and putting it on the floor behind him.

As Myung-Dae warned, the process took time. Finally, when the last six-pack of beer was on the floor, Myung-Dae re-zipped the empty bag, handing it back to Porter, who then removed the envelope of receipts.

The abacus appeared, and Porter, like Cam and Gil before him, marveled at Myung-Dae's dexterity as he tallied up the transaction.

When he finished, Myung-Dae sighed. "I will miss Cameron. He was my favorite buyer." He handed Porter a sheet of paper. "This is my list for next week."

Porter folded and pocketed the list. Myung-Dae removed a metal box out from a desk drawer and counted out thousand-won bills.

"Cam's not coming back into Anjeong-ri, Myung-Dae. He asked for payment in American dollars this one time, as a favor."

"I'm sorry, but no. The reason I'm so generous is knowing my Anjeong-ri business partners will spend their money in the community, hopefully in my establishments. You're Cameron's friend—I'm sure you could see your way clear to exchange won to dollars for him."

Porter nodded. He would agree to anything that got him out of this house faster.

"What time shall we meet next Saturday?" Myung-Dae asked.

Porter came to this meeting expecting to tell Myung-Dae he no longer wanted Cam's concession. But his instincts screamed otherwise.

"Is noon good?"

Myung-Dae nodded. "Noon it is then. I will show

you out."

He led Porter back to the front door. When he heard the door close, he jogged to the thoroughfare, thankful he'd never have to return.

Chapter Twenty-Seven

The doorbell rang thirty minutes after Porter left Myung-Dae's Anjeong-ri house Saturday morning. With the German luxury car still in the shop for repairs, Gunn was to have brought Myung-Dae to Jumpin' Jack ten minutes ago in the truck.

It's about time he showed up.

"I'll return tomorrow morning, Moon-Kym," Myung-Dae yelled from the bottom of the stairs. He put his parka on and opened the door, surprised to see Sang. "Where's Gunn?"

"Gunn's not at the farm, Myung-Dae. Byung told me he left early this morning but didn't say where he was going. I'm here because he didn't return."

They walked to the truck, Sang holding the door and helping the old man get in before climbing up behind the wheel.

"Nobody knows where Gunn is? He simply took off saying nothing?" Myung-Dae asked. "Gunn's never done that before. Hand me your cellular phone."

Sang gave his phone over to Myung-Dae.

Myung-Dae fumbled through the keypad until, at last, the call went through. It went straight to Gunn's voicemail.

"Do you know Gunn's Anseong phone number?" Myung-Dae asked.

"The man can't stand the sight of me. So the

273

answer to that is no."

"I'll call it from Jumpin' Jacks. Let's go."

****

Myung-Dae sat alone in his Jumpin' Jack office as he dialed Gunn's home phone in Anseong. An answering machine picked up. Myung-Dae felt his blood pressure rise.

"Sang," Myung-Dae bellowed from behind the closed office door.

Slowly, Sang poked his head in from behind the door. "Yes, Myung-Dae?"

"Get in here and close the door behind you."

Sang entered the office and closed the door.

"Gunn said *nothing* to you about where he would be?"

"If I knew where he was, don't you think I'd tell you?"

"Grab your jacket. It looks like we're going to Anseong."

****

The drive to Anseong took thirty minutes. For most of it, Myung-Dae muttered and stewed. *Just before the biggest deal of my life, everything is falling apart. Why is this happening? Am I now cursed?*

Inside Anseong city limits, Myung-Dae pointed to a five-story apartment building with a polished black granite facade that came into view. "That's the building. Park as close as you can to the front doors and let me do the talking."

Sang parked the truck on the street just down from the building's front entrance. Myung-Dae waited as Sang opened the door for him, and together they trudged down the sidewalk. As they approached the entrance, the doorman intercepted the pair.

"Excuse me, may I help you, gentlemen?"

"We're looking for a man who lives here," Myung-Dae replied. "Gunn Lim."

"I'm sorry, sir, but I haven't seen Mr. Lim for several days."

"And what of Mrs. Lim?"

The doorman grinned and shook his head. "I'm sorry, but what business is that of yours?"

Myung-Dae took Sang by the elbow, positioning him in front of the doorman. "See my large friend here?"

"He's difficult to miss."

Myung-Dae looked at Sang and pointed. "Please stand over there for a minute."

Sang complied. Myung-Dae once again faced the doorman.

"That man is a dear friend of the Lims but mentally unstable. I'm afraid he can become quite violent when a panic attack comes on. If he thinks the Lims are in danger, it will take more than the two of us to subdue him. We're here because he's worried about them. So I'll ask again, where is Mr. Lim? Otherwise, my large friend may feel inclined to run your head through that plate-glass door, for example."

The doorman's thin grin went upside down. "I don't know where Mr. Lim is. And I don't appreciate being threatened."

"What about Mrs. Lim?"

"She left two hours ago in a taxi. Alone and carrying luggage."

"Did she say *where* she went off to?"

The doorman glanced over at Sang. "I didn't ask,

and she didn't say. But I'd assume she's going to the airport or train station."

"Who could let us in the apartment to have a look around and make sure everything is as it should be?"

"That would be the building superintendent."

"Would you be so kind as to show us where to find him?"

The doorman once again glanced at Sang, making brief eye contact. "Let me get the door."

With everyone in the lobby, the doorman pointed to a corridor. "Super's office is down that hall. Two doors past the elevator on the left."

"See? That wasn't so hard." Myung-Dae put five crumpled one-thousand won bills in the top pocket of the man's uniform and patted it.

The doorman stayed in the lobby as Myung-Dae and Sang went down the hall. With the super's door partially open, Sang peered in. The man sat in a recliner watching a variety show on a small television, drinking coffee from an oversized thermos.

"He's in there alone, Myung-Dae."

"Stay out here until I call for you. If I call, come in with an attitude."

Sang nodded, and Myung-Dae walked into the super's office.

"Excuse me; can you help me, please? I need to get into the Lim's apartment, and I'm told you're the man I need to talk to."

The superintendent glanced briefly at Myung-Dae before refocusing on the TV. "And I need a tuggy from the massage parlor down the street. Now fuck off, old timer. Can't you see I'm busy?"

"Ah, I see we're off to a poor start. I came here

with a friend of Mr. Lim. I don't relish the idea of telling him you not only refuse to help but are ill-tempered as well."

The superintendent looked back up, his eyes locked onto Myung-Dae's. "You're still here? What did I just tell you?"

"Let's try this one last time. I need to access Mr. Lim's apartment. Your massage parlors and deviant sexual behavior are of no interest to me or my friend waiting in the hall. He wants to have a look inside the Lim apartment to make sure it's clean and tidy, with nothing missing or stolen."

"Okay…let me try *this* one last time. Go away before I call the cops."

"Sang, would you come in here, please?" Myung-Dae called out.

Sang stormed into the room, making a beeline for the superintendent and leering down into the much smaller man's face. The superintendent took one look and jumped out of the recliner.

"What's your problem?" Sang asked. He reached over and grabbed the man by the front of his shirt. "He asked for the key to the Lim's apartment, and you insult him? I'll give you five seconds to find the key and take us there or so help me; I'll break your fingers one at a time."

"Whoa…easy, friend. I didn't mean to offend anyone." The super's eyes darted from Sang to Myung-Dae. "I'll let you in, but I need to go with you."

Sang released his grip, letting the super smooth out his shirt and regain his composure.

"That would be fine," Myung-Dae said, patting Sang on the shoulder. "Now we all understand one another."

The super opened the master key box and led the way to the elevator, pushing the button for the fourth floor once they were inside.

Myung-Dae watched the super's hands shake as he turned the key and opened the apartment door.

"Please sit down and stay quiet," Myung-Dae told the super, pointing to a kitchen chair.

Sang and Myung-Dae began a room-by-room search. Myung-Dae went into the bathroom, leaving the bedroom to Sang.

"No shaving gear, toothbrushes, combs, or brushes. No women's makeup and incidentals. This doesn't look good, Sang."

Sang didn't reply as he rifled through the closet and dresser drawers. Seeing the laptop at a desk in the room, he brought it out to the kitchen table and turned it on. He then began going through the machine's history, looking for anything that might help him find Gunn or Gunn's wife.

Myung-Dae saw Sang and took a seat next to his associate.

"She was on the Korean Air website, interested in a flight from Seoul to Manila this afternoon at one o'clock," Sang said. "She booked two seats, first class, one way."

Myung-Dae looked at his watch. It was almost one o'clock. "What else is in there?"

"She searched for a hotel in Manila. First one on the list is the Rizal." Sang checked the recent activity and discovered the hotel booking. "Yeah, she reserved a room at the Rizal until February 14th."

"Can you find anything else?" Myung-Dae asked.

Sang shook his head.

"Shut that thing off. We'll take it to Anjeong-ri," Myung-Dae said.

"I can't let you do that," the building super protested.

"Make no mistake, mister. We *are* taking it," Sang said. He hurriedly shut the machine down and unplugged it. The super said nothing more as he got to his feet.

With the laptop and cord underneath his left arm, Sang turned out the lights, and the super re-locked the apartment.

"What are you thinking, Myung-Dae?" Sang asked once they were back outside.

Myung-Dae stroked his goatee. "The same thing you are. Gunn's not coming back."

Chapter Twenty-Eight

"Please, Daewon, sit down," Myung-Dae said from behind his desk in Jumpin' Jack's office.

The medium height, thick man with a full head of jet black hair and goatee slid into the chair to interview for Myung-Dae's unexpected vacancy. Sang stood directly behind Myung-Dae.

Anger or hurt, Myung-Dae wasn't sure which emotion was stronger thinking about Gunn's betrayal. Interviewing this man out of desperation wasn't Myung-Dae's style. But Daewon Cheom found his way onto Myung-Dae's short list when he hired Sang, and he'd vetted the man, saving time. And time, particularly now, was a valuable commodity.

"I'm not a violent man, Mr. Tang," Daewon said. "I imagine a man like you needs violent men."

"Do you know how to defend yourself?"

"Yes, but that's not what—"

Myung-Dae watched a big bead of sweat gallop down the side of the large man's face. "Can you follow orders?"

"Yes, Mr. Tang."

"Are you honest?"

"I try to be, always."

"Do you have a cellular phone?"

Daewon looked down at his shoes. "Sure I do."

"A car?"

"I have a car, Mr. Tang. But I walked here today."

"Are you a responsible man?"

Daewon's eyes met Myung-Dae's, and the big man nodded. "Yes."

"You have experience operating a forklift?"

"Yes, sir."

"Then I foresee no problem hiring you. You're obviously interested in working for me; otherwise, you wouldn't be here." Myung-Dae understood Daewon had a young wife and infant daughter to support. Like the Dokgos, Myung-Dae appreciated collateral, a principle learned from the Sicilian Cosa Nostra.

Daewon was Myung-Dae's last and only option of replacing Gunn quickly. Nobody else had come forward after the old man made it known he had a vacancy. Not even from outside Anjeong-ri.

Myung-Dae gave Daewon the same terms he gave Sang. Daewon appeared humble, an attribute Myung-Dae never fully understood.

"Welcome aboard," Myung-Dae said. He grinned and shook Daewon's hand. Sang did likewise. They led Myung-Dae's newest hire out of the nightclub from the back entrance. "Be here at noon tomorrow; we'll go through everything then."

"I'll be here." Daewon walked away.

"First impressions?" Myung-Dae asked Sang.

"Honestly? He seems thick in the head."

"That's more your problem than mine. You're the new number one. So be patient breaking him in."

Sang grinned.

"Thick or not, at least the man can operate a forklift, which is more than I can say for you. Bring me to my house, Sang."

Myung-Dae locked the back door, and Sang helped him into the truck. He would drop Myung-Dae off at his Anjeong-ri house before returning to the farm.

****

When DiSilva handed Myung-Dae a bottle of expensive bourbon as the newlyweds entered the Tang house, Myung-Dae knew more bad news was on the horizon.

Just what I need, Arthur has a problem. It probably has to do with that idiot Gilbert. "Such an extravagant gift. We'll discuss your problem after dinner."

At the table, Myung-Dae could see whatever Arthur had to say affected Chona. She had always been an upbeat, positive child, a joy, really. Except today she seemed as morose as her husband. *This isn't about Gilbert. Don't tell me the marriage is already failing.*

After the meal, the men retreated to Myung-Dae's study. DiSilva carried the bottle, leaving the glassware to Myung-Dae. The old man took his usual seat behind the desk. DiSilva sat in the chair Porter occupied only yesterday. The American Army officer poured them both a drink from the bottle, neat. Myung-Dae brought out the cigars from a desk drawer.

"Whatever it is, Arthur, just spit it out."

"You remember when I told you staying here another year shouldn't be a problem?"

A jolt ripped through Myung-Dae. This caught him completely off guard. "You lied to me?"

DiSilva leaned back, his eyes wide. "Lied? That's uncharitable. At no point did I say staying here was an absolute certainty. We're leaving Camp Humphreys at the end of February."

"You certainly led me down a primrose path. Don't

deny it."

DiSilva nodded. "Yes, you're right. I didn't want to concern you with it."

Myung-Dae's head dropped. "Give me a moment, Arthur." The host rose, choking up. He went into the hallway, quickly closing the door before the tears fell. He couldn't recall the last time he cried. Thirty seconds later, he blew his nose and regrouped. After all, with his biggest deal ever around the corner, he had an image to uphold. He went back into the study and sat down, his eyes hard on his son-in-law.

"You're seeing this in the wrong light," DiSilva said. "We'll be here as often as you like. It's not like I'm locking Chona up and throwing away the key. And of course, you and Moon-Kym are always welcome to visit."

"So where are you taking my little girl?"

"Kentucky."

"Kentucky? Where they hold the big horse race?"

DiSilva nodded. "Kentucky is halfway around the world, Myung-Dae."

"I suppose you're right about not seeing the positives. If nothing else, it will give me and Moon-Kym a chance to see America. Do you know we've never been? Chona is telling her mother this afternoon, yes?"

DiSilva nodded. "Should be any second now."

"Just so long as I don't have to tell her," Myung-Dae said, a slight grin forming.

"I'm glad you're taking it well."

"Believe me; alone, I will grieve."

"Did you talk to Cameron Shanahan?"

"As I've known from the start, he's not interested.

He didn't have the guts to come to me yesterday; instead, he sent your new man, Porter."

"Porter came here? He's very new to Humphreys." DiSilva sipped his bourbon. "I'm reluctant to bring this up, but I had another man turn up missing."

"Gilbert."

DiSilva sat up straight. "Yes, Gilbert Trotter."

"Gilbert and his whore girlfriend are no longer among us."

DiSilva's face turned crimson. "What?"

"Did you not hear me?"

"I heard you. What's gotten into you lately? That's two of my men."

"You're leaving for Kentucky, remember? What's that American expression? Out of sight, out of mind?"

"Washington will send a task force to investigate. Not that you'll care," DiSilva said. "What's the word from Wuhan?"

Myung-Dae took a breath. "Everything is on schedule. Gunn's been ill. It's doubtful he'll be able to join us Tuesday. I told him to sit this one out."

"Gunn is ill?"

"A respiratory illness and quite contagious, I'm told. Even if he's feeling better, I won't risk infecting everyone involved."

"At least Kiwoo is available."

Myung-Dae shook his head. "I'm afraid not. He hired someone who tried breaking into the Duffy Club safe, so he's no longer with me."

"What does that mean?"

Myung-Dae took a sip and glared at DiSilva. "What do you think it means?"

DiSilva took a hit off the cigar. "I counted on at

least one of them to help get an accurate count with those forklifts on the move. You still have the team of forklift operators showing up, yes?"

"I spoke with the foreman earlier this morning. Ten of them. And I hired two new associates, one of which knows how to operate that machinery. We'll leave for Mokpo Port early Monday morning. The Chinese freighter's ETA is noon, dock seventy-eight. It will be you and I with my new men, who you've not met. The contractors will be waiting. You're taking a week's leave?"

DiSilva nodded.

"We'll stay at a nearby hotel Monday night. I expect to return Wednesday morning if everything goes well. Then I can focus on my Anjeong-ri investments, and you can focus on going to Kentucky," Myung-Dae said.

"You're traveling to Mokpo, too?"

"Without Gunn or Kiwoo, I need to go. I've got everything riding on this. At the very least, I can weigh the heroin."

"You don't think I can't get this done?"

"It's not a matter of trust, competency, or leadership, Arthur. But now, with new men, I feel the need to oversee this."

"Just so long as we don't run into trouble with the Dokgo brothers. Have you reconsidered giving them something that will prevent a war?"

"There you go with the Dokgo brothers again. I think you must be on their payroll." Myung-Dae's face reddened. "I will give them a taste of my hard work on *my* timeline—not theirs and not yours. Because the heroin and cadaver buyers are separate, I have to wait on both payments before we're finished. Then I'll think about how much I wish to give those vultures."

"It's your money, Myung-Dae."

Myung-Dae clapped and nodded. "I'm glad you finally understand."

Upstairs, the women began wailing.

Myung-Dae's eyes glanced skyward as he grinned. "I'm glad Chona didn't back out."

While Myung-Dae tried to hide it, today's news upset him. After the men finished their drinks, as the women upstairs howled in despair, DiSilva asked Myung-Dae if he objected to cutting the visit short.

With Myung-Dae's and Moon-Kym's blessing, DiSilva escorted Chona to the car and drove his wife home.

****

Whan called Jaewon's cell phone. The younger Dokgo brother picked up on the first ring.

"Please tell me you found Gunn," Jaewon said.

"I know where he and his wife went. My friend at Gimpo checked all the manifests. Gunn and his wife Daeum left yesterday, one in the afternoon on Korean Air flight 315 from Seoul to Manila."

"That snake left right after our meeting. Do you know where they're staying?"

"The Rizal. At least until February 14th."

Jaewon rubbed his temples. "Do you know that for sure, or is it your best guess?"

"I'm certain. The superintendent overheard the name and lingered in the room when Tang and one of his men came around and searched Gunn's apartment."

"I'll tell Ryung," Jaewon said. "After he gives the okay, how do you feel about going to Manila to handle this?"

"Would it be just Gunn or his wife as well?"

"Both. The wife still has local ties and could hire someone for vengeance."

"Wouldn't it be cheaper to hire a Filipino contractor? Besides, I don't speak Tagalog, and my English isn't the greatest."

"Your English is fine. But I can't trust an outsider to do this. They could photo a staged execution and tell me it's done. No, I need someone I can trust handling this. Once Ryung gives the word, take the first flight out and book a room anywhere you want. I know someone there that will fix you up with a weapon and ammunition."

"Make sure whatever he brings has a silencer," Whan said.

"Okay. I don't care where you do it, just so long as it's done. Then take some time for yourself, enjoy the warm weather for a few days."

"Thank you, Jaewon. I appreciate that."

"But do nothing until after I talk to Ryung," Jaewon said.

The conversation over, Whan walked into his bedroom. Contrary to popular belief, the big man didn't enjoy taking lives, especially when he knew the victim. Reluctantly, he began packing for a vacation he never wanted to take.

Chapter Twenty-Nine

Arthur DiSilva peeked at his wife as she lay beside him in bed, finally asleep. She'd been crying intermittently since returning from her parents' house yesterday afternoon.

It was almost three that morning, and he hadn't slept a wink. His chat with Myung-Dae left a nasty aftertaste and no small degree of worry. Myung-Dae's excuse for Gunn's absence made no sense. Myung-Dae would *never* put the welfare of another ahead of his own interests. Kiwoo's murder didn't pass the sniff test either. Why not punish the thief and let it end there, especially with so much on the line?

DiSilva's mind came back to Gunn. Unless Gunn was dead or fled the country, DiSilva couldn't see any scenario where Myung-Dae permitted his most trusted and capable man to sit this one out. As much as DiSilva disliked Gunn, he respected the man. That the Dokgo brothers got to Gunn one way or another made the most sense. And if it was enough to scare Gunn, it had to be frightening.

The Dokgos are onto Myung-Dae's shipment. I knew this bullshit would start a war. DiSilva imagined the Dokgos and their small army sitting on dock seventy-eight, waiting to take possession of Myung-Dae's heroin and add to the number of corpses to be sold to area medical schools.

To die was one thing. To die badly and publicly was another matter entirely.

Would Myung-Dae kill me if I found an excuse to bail? Don't be stupid; even married to Chona, you know the answer.

DiSilva knew he wouldn't sleep, not now. He considered his position and options. There was a solution to his problem, as he saw it.

But only one.

****

Across town in his Anjeong-ri house, Myung-Dae lay awake too, his sleeplessness also on Gunn's account. Finally, Moon-Kym stopped crying. She now snored gently by his side.

That Gunn fled infuriated Myung-Dae. That his little girl was moving to Kentucky yet another thing Myung-Dae had no control over. And he was angry with Arthur for letting him believe they all had another year together.

Myung-Dae truly didn't want to be in this house tonight. He slept so much better at the farm. But Moon-Kym begged him to stay, so Myung-Dae grudgingly obliged her. The couple spoke little and had a light supper before turning in.

Myung-Dae swung his legs out and sat upright on the edge of the bed. He wanted to sleep. But the hurt and anxiety said no. Moon-Kym stirred.

"What are you doing awake, Myung-Dae?"

"I can't sleep. I'll go to the study—I haven't touched the real estate binders for almost two months."

"Would you like me to put on some tea?"

"No. I want you to rest."

Moon-Kym nodded, and Myung-Dae stood and

dressed. She fell asleep again before he left the bedroom. While tea was part of his morning ritual, today he wasn't in the mood, at least not yet. He turned on the lights and descended the stairs to his study.

Myung-Dae put the abacus on the desk and reached down for the first real estate binder near his feet. Only he lost his grip, and the contents slid onto the floor.

Myung-Dae stood, walking around to collect the papers on the floor. As he bent down, he spotted something dark and oval clinging to the bottom of the chair nearest the wall.

What the hell is that? Chewing gum? Forgetting the binder and papers, Myung-Dae fingered the object in the middle of the gum. *Sticky, with tiny holes.* With a box cutter, he pried the object loose and held it to the light. *Hard plastic, maybe even rubber.*

Slowly, the true purpose of this object came to him. He was sure it was a device used to listen to conversations. Myung-Dae shifted gears, focusing on who and how recently which guests occupied that chair.

Arthur had nothing to gain and everything to lose; he was out. Who else? The list was few. *Cameron? The dearly departed Gil? Mitchell? All were possible. Porter? Yes, he was here only Saturday morning and was in the Duffy Club office too.*

What did he hope to hear? A confession that I rid this world of his friend, Gilbert? Details of my heroin purchase and sale? Yes. Nothing else makes sense. Then he knows about the Chinese freighter and the shipment details. And he knows about Gilbert and the whore.

I'd better have Duffy Club swept for these little listening cockroaches. Let me think this through. If

Porter is CID, all they can do is hand it over to the KNPA, who will do nothing. Or would they? Jungho Bak is rattling sabers long dormant. If Porter isn't CID, who would he work for? Perhaps an agency I'm not aware of. He must hope to make a name for himself by destroying my drug trade. Myung-Dae thought about Porter's weaknesses, the only one he knew of, anyhow.

Porter works for Arthur. Would they be working together? It's entirely possible. I knew Porter spelled trouble from the start. If I find Arthur is playing both sides, Chona would need a new husband. For her, that wouldn't be terrible news.

Calmly, Myung-Dae tried crushing the device under his boot. Only the hard synthetic shell prevented it. Myung-Dae disabled the home's alarm, put on his jacket, and walked outside. He side-armed the device as if skipping a stone, throwing it as hard as his frail frame allowed. Now he would have tea before calling Sang and taking care of what needed his attention.

****

DiSilva watched Chona back the car out of the driveway from the kitchen window.

With day-old stubble on his face, the man looked several years older than his actual age. He went up the stairs to their bedroom and removed the nickel-plated nine-millimeter pistol hidden in his sock drawer, along with a full magazine. This was a gift from Myung-Dae last year, who wanted DiSilva and Chona able to defend themselves if someone broke in.

He thought of various ways to kill himself, and none of them were appealing. Hanging was no sure thing; he couldn't imagine dangling from a rope trying to breathe. A codeine overdose from cough medicine sold in an off-base pharmacy wasn't certain either. The idea of hugging a toilet bowl until the bitter end seemed worse than hanging. No, this pistol would be the least painful, surest, and fastest way out.

DiSilva had never been a spiritual man, never thought much about death until now. But being tortured by the Dokgos until death overtook him scared DiSilva more than anything he could think of at this moment. If that was his destiny, he would take his life in a manner of *his* choosing without being tortured or ending up at the bottom of the ocean.

He thought briefly about calling his mother. *Now that's a great idea, you selfish bastard. Let the poor woman believe she's the reason for this.*

He fired up the laptop and began collecting his thoughts. Two letters were necessary, one for his wife, another for his mother. When he finished, DiSilva signed and left them on the kitchen table, where he sat with the pistol.

DiSilva checked the safety and put the gun under his chin. The gun vibrated in his shaking hand. Arthur DiSilva prayed God was a merciful God.

Then he pulled the trigger.

Chapter Thirty

Porter was alone in the office when he re-read Martz's email and the complete transcript from late yesterday afternoon again. If Panmunjom wasn't on the horizon, he'd be on cloud nine. He wanted to see Myung-Dae in handcuffs. Only then would Jeong be free.

Martz had to be excited. To nail DiSilva to the heroin trumped the human trafficking ring. But only Bak had the authority to arrest them. Whether the KNPA agent could find a local prosecutor with the balls to take it to trial was another matter entirely. Still, it offered hope for Jeong.

Porter had no way of knowing if he would still be on Humphreys February 5th. He sent Jeong a text, asking what time they could talk on Skype tonight. He never had to wait longer than an hour for her response. After putting the cell phone on the desk, Porter went about his work.

Five minutes later, he heard a text notification chime, surprised that Jeong responded so quickly. Only the text didn't come from Jeong. It came from Stillson.

"Check email ASAP."

A feeling of dread came over Porter. *Can only mean one thing.*

Porter logged on to the agency site and opened the encrypted email. He and Ferguson were to be at the

Flight Operations building on the Humphreys flight line at 0400 Thursday morning, February 1st. Once there, he and Ferguson would meet the pilot, co-pilot, and gunner prior to departure at 0415. Now it was real.

Within minutes, Ferguson texted Porter, asking if he'd heard.

Martz came into the office at 0845. While his uniform was as polished as ever, there were dark circles under his eyes.

"Surprised to see you rolling in so late, Top."

Martz walked slower than usual to the desk. "The bugs went dark. Tang's house went first, at four this morning. Duffy Club cut out just before seven."

"He found both?"

Martz nodded. "Looks like." He took off his hat and jacket before sitting in DiSilva's chair. "I still can't believe DiSilva let himself get involved with Tang's drug trade."

"You're not happy?"

"With the result, sure. Still, the man had to work his ass off to get this command. I don't expect you to understand."

"You're conflicted," Porter said.

"Something like that."

"I've got some news."

Martz leaned back, twisting his neck right and left until he heard a snap. "Let me guess. You're out of here."

"Early Thursday morning."

Martz looked out the window. "Well, we knew that was coming. I'll bet you're relieved."

"Relieved?" Porter grimaced. "No. That is definitely *not* the right word."

The master sergeant took a breath. "Let me ask you this; is there any reason for me to continue investigating DiSilva's involvement in the human trafficking ring?"

"You're asking me? I'd imagine your CID CO has a few thoughts on the matter."

"We can only hope Bak arrests them when they meet that freighter. If he doesn't, and DiSilva goes back to the States…I still haven't tied him to the human trafficking ring. My last hope was Shanahan, and he didn't take the bait."

"They've squeezed their last drop out of that ring, and there's not a shred of evidence implicating DiSilva at this point in time. Now, all we can do is hope for Bak to come through and bust up that heroin buy. If he does, it's doubtful the Korean courts would hand DiSilva over to the provost marshal. Both he and Tang would be looking at life sentences. It all comes down to Bak."

Martz leaned forward. "Can I ask a personal question?"

"What?"

"Your woman. What happens if Bak can't or won't make a case against Tang?"

Porter looked down. "Nothing would give me more satisfaction than putting a bullet in Tang's head before I go on that flight line."

"You don't mean that."

Porter looked across the room, his eyes finding Martz's. "Try me."

"Maybe you do. But don't do it."

"Give me *one* good reason."

"Let those Dokgo brothers they're so terrified of do the dirty work."

"That doesn't help Jeong much in the short-term if

Bak shits the bed. Besides, I'd like to see Tang dead with my own two eyes."

Martz shook his head. "About camp business, anything new?"

"Orders came in for DiSilva and Shanahan's replacements."

"Any other day that passes for news," Martz said. "But not today."

The pair went about their morning. Porter had a tough time shaking thoughts of Panmunjom. And wondered why Jeong hadn't yet returned his text message.

****

A panicked Jeong searched her apartment. Unable to find her cell phone, the frazzled young woman looked everywhere. It turned up under her bed, having fallen off the nightstand and taking a weird hop during the night. And she'd forgotten to charge the battery, the device now operating at three percent.

She read Porter's text from earlier. He sent them every morning, reminding her to be careful and how much he missed talking to her in person. Jeong missed him more than she cared to admit.

Today she took the plunge, her text asking if he could meet her somewhere farther than Pyeongtaek Thursday night, which she had off. A place where they could spend the night. It was a big step for her, and she hoped this fledgling relationship could bear the weight. Porter had more than proven himself. He was handsome, intelligent, and responsible; she couldn't ask for more.

Yet, so much about the man remained a mystery. She could feel his time on Camp Humphreys would soon end. She didn't want to get hurt. To become so hopelessly attached only to see him disappear, it happened every day in this place. *Yeah, but that happens to working girls. I've never let anyone else get this close.*

Her phone's battery died before she could send the text. She plugged the device's charger into an electrical outlet and went about her chores; she would send it before leaving for work.

****

At noon in the Jumpin' Jack office, Sang knocked on Myung-Dae's door.

"Come," Myung-Dae shouted.

Sang opened it and stuck his head in. "Sorry to interrupt, but your new man is in the bar wanting to know what you want him to do."

Myung-Dae looked at the clock. "I almost forgot about him. Take him to the farm in the truck, Sang. He'll drop you off and return here. Take the afternoon off; let's see what he can do."

Sang grinned. "Really?"

"Sure. We've got a big day coming up, and you're due some downtime."

"Thanks, Myung-Dae."

"Just tell Daewon to park out back and come in through the back way. Make sure he has a key to the building."

Sang nodded and disappeared.

****

Fifteen minutes later, Myung-Dae heard the truck return to the back of Jumpin' Jack Flash. He listened as Daewon walked down the hall and knocked at the door.

Myung-Dae locked his office, and together they

went out to the truck. He waited for Daewon to open the truck door and help him up before backing out to go to the thoroughfare.

"Wherever it is, we're going…you'll give me directions, won't you, Mr. Tang?"

"Please call me Myung-Dae. When you get to the thoroughfare, take a left."

"I doubt I'll spend many nights on your farm, Mr. Tang. My wife, she won't like it."

Myung-Dae nodded.

"Sang told me about the man I replaced. I know I told you before, I'm not a violent man."

"Please call me Myung-Dae. I don't expect you to be Gunn. Just follow directions, and we'll have no problem."

"My wife. She begged me not to work for you. Oh, I probably shouldn't have said that, huh, Mr. Tang?"

Myung-Dae didn't reply. He'd been alone with this man for all of two minutes and was already considering taking the gun from the glove box and shooting either himself or Daewon. *Sang is right; this man is a simpleton.*

"Can you tell me where I make the turn, Mr. Tang?"

Myung-Dae summoned every ounce of willpower he had to keep from exploding. After next week's delivery, he would happily send Daewon back to the wife he couldn't shut up about. "Take a right at the next street up and park anywhere on that corner."

Slowly, Daewon nestled the truck in a parking space near the stairs leading to Jeong's apartment across this street.

Myung-Dae popped the glove box open and

removed a small canvas bag.

"What's in the bag, Mr. Tang?"

Myung-Dae didn't bother asking Daewon to call him by his first name yet again. It was hopeless. "Listen to me carefully, Daewon. I have a loaded firearm and handcuffs in here. We're going up those stairs to a young woman's apartment." Myung-Dae pointed at the door to the stairs. "She will go to the farm with us, but not willingly, I'm afraid. So you will need to subdue her while I put the handcuffs on. You won't have to touch the handcuffs or the gun, and there is no need for violence, although I expect her to give us trouble before the handcuffs go on. I only need you to hold her arms out in front of her body, and I'll take care of the rest. Can you do that? Because if you can't, I'll need to find Sang and prematurely end your employment."

"I need this job, Mr. Tang. I can do it."

Myung-Dae grinned, his gold tooth winking as he patted Daewon's forearm.

Daewon got out and opened the truck's door for Myung-Dae. The boss stepped out onto the sidewalk in the frosty Anjeong-ri air.

"Should I lock the truck?"

"No, Daewon. We won't be long."

Myung-Dae led the way, Daewon following the old man across the street and up the stairs as a puppy would his master. Myung-Dae could only hope that his new man had the constitution for this.

So few did.

****

Jeong dressed in the bedroom after her shower. She checked her cell phone's progress, the battery now seventy-six percent. She would text Porter before leaving for work.

Heavy footsteps climbed the stairs. *Oh dear God. It's Myung-Dae and Gunn.* She knew better than to wonder what Myung-Dae wanted. And this time, she couldn't use her menstrual cycle as an excuse.

"Jeong?" Myung-Dae called out as he knocked on the door. "I know you're here. Open the door."

She walked to the door. "What do you want, Myung-Dae?"

"I'd like to introduce my newest associate."

"You know I'm scheduled to be in at two o'clock. I'm sure it can wait."

"May we come in?"

"I'll meet him at Duffy Club, Myung-Dae. Please let me finish getting ready."

"I don't want my new man to destroy your door. Please let us in."

She knew Myung-Dae wouldn't hesitate to order his newest toy to do it. Jeong unlatched the deadbolt and opened the door.

Jeong knew Sang served as Kiwoo's replacement. Who this new man replaced was a riddle. One she had no interest in solving. All she wanted was for Myung-Dae and his new goon to leave.

Myung-Dae walked in with the man on his heels. While Myung-Dae's men had an air of entitlement, this man appeared…meek. At face value, anyhow.

"How is this so urgent?" She pivoted toward the stranger. "Hello, I'm Jeong."

"Daewon. Pleased to meet you."

Jeong pivoted back to Myung-Dae. "There, okay? We've met. Now, will you please leave so I can get ready for work?"

"I'm here to invite you to the farm as my guest."

"The farm? This again? No, I have no interest in going to your farm. And you of all people should know it." *Could Myung-Dae have Porter? No. He hasn't left the base since his agreement with Myung-Dae. Besides, we haven't been together.*

Myung-Dae lowered his head. "And you of all people should know to watch what you say to me. Perhaps that sounded like a request. I'm not asking. Pack whatever you need to spend a few days on the farm. Don't worry if you forget something—ask, and I will make sure it's provided for. I've taken care of your Duffy Club schedule for the next week; your salary paid as if you'd worked. I apologize that we'll all have to squeeze into the truck, but it's a short drive, and I'm confident we'll manage."

"A few days? Have you gone insane? Why on Earth would I spend a week on your farm? It's out of the question."

A thin grin formed on Myung-Dae's face. "You know how I hate repeating myself. Please pack now."

"Let me guess. I leave with you peacefully, or Daewon drags me out kicking and screaming?"

"Why must you kick and scream? No harm will come to you; I won't lay a hand on you. That I can promise."

"I know all about your promises, and I'm not going to your farm, Myung-Dae. Now I want you and Daewon out of here."

Myung-Dae nodded. "That sounded like an ultimatum. I didn't want it to be this way." Myung-Dae unzipped his canvas bag, removing the metal handcuffs before turning to Daewon. "Pin her wrists together so I

301

can slip these on."

Jeong's eyes locked onto Daewon's. She could see his dread.

"Please, Miss. Don't make me do this," Daewon pleaded. "I don't want to hurt you."

Without thinking, she pivoted and bolted for the living room. She heard Myung-Dae's voice behind her.

"Well, idiot? Bring her here."

Jeong heard heavy steps get louder. Frightened, she unsheathed the sword from the display mounted on the wall as Daewon blindly turned the corner.

She screamed as she ran the sword through Daewon's thoracic aorta with a sickening, squelching sound. The large man's eyes rolled in his head as he stumbled backward and hit the floor with a resounding thud, his face a deathly white, the blade killing him instantly. Daewon lay on his back, the sword sticking up like a toothpick in a finger sandwich. Blood poured from the wound and the corners of his mouth and was already pooling on the hardwood floor.

Myung-Dae crept toward the living room.

Jeong's mind snapped. "I only wanted to scare him. I never meant for that—"

"To happen," Myung-Dae said, finishing her thought as he entered the room. In the old man's right hand, a pistol. He grinned. "Never bring a knife to a gunfight, dear. Kindly pack a bag."

"I can't just walk out. He's bleeding everywhere, Myung-Dae."

"Do you have a shower curtain?"

"Yes," she replied, her eyes still on Daewon.

"Take it down and wrap him in it. I'll send two of my men to retrieve the body later."

Jeong went into the bathroom, with Myung-Dae still holding the pistol. She tugged at the vinyl shower curtain, tearing it down and spreading it on the living room floor. Putting her foot down on Daewon's shoulder, Jeong yanked the sword free before rolling him onto the shower curtain. She felt lightheaded and ill at the sight of so much blood. She ran back into the bathroom and purged.

After vomiting, she put the blade in the bathtub, cleaning the blood off first. It took three beach towels to sop up the mess in the living room. Under Myung-Dae's watchful eye, she quietly packed a bag.

"Would you please put that gun away?" she asked. "I don't want to get shot."

"After you put the handcuffs on."

"What's this about? What do you hope to accomplish by taking me to your farm against my will for an entire week?"

"Your friend Porter has become a problem. I believe he works undercover for some American agency or other that coordinates with the KNPA. Did you know that?"

"No. And I don't believe it."

"I don't think he's CID. I know most of the Anjeong-ri CID. You'll keep me company a short while, and I'll return you intact once I flush Porter out and rid myself of him."

"I don't understand; I have nothing more to do with that man."

Myung-Dae slapped her face. "I don't believe that. You know I hate being lied to."

She put the handcuffs on, letting Myung-Dae hear the click before checking the tension. For the briefest of moments, she thought about testing Myung-Dae's resolve. But his eyes had grown hard, even with her.

Myung-Dae led her to the truck, turning the key Daewon left in the ignition. Jeong feared for her life as the old man drove them to the farm. Once inside the farmhouse, she listened as Myung-Dae ordered Sang and his younger farmhand to go to her apartment to retrieve Daewon's body and mop the place down.

"What do you want us to do with him?" Sang asked.

"Find a dumpster outside Anjeong-ri, Sang. I don't care where."

Some people worked longer for Myung-Dae than others. That Jeong understood all too well. Daewon's tenure set a new low.

Chapter Thirty-One

Porter kept his cell phone on the bar as he ate a late lunch alone at the EM Club. He worried about Jeong. She still hadn't replied to his last text. And that was odd. He tried calling her again. Only it went right to voicemail.

Taking a bite of the Rueben sandwich he was halfway through, his cell phone chimed. When he saw the text was from Jeong, he relaxed and opened it quickly.

"Watch," the text read. There was a video file attached. *This email didn't come from Jeong.* Porter opened it as his heart rate climbed.

Jeong sat on a sofa, bound and gagged. Her face was an unhealthy red, with both eyes as swollen and puffy as Gayoon's had been. She shouted incoherently through a coiled bandana wrapped around, covering her mouth. Porter didn't recognize the room—a fire roared in the fireplace behind her, and the sofa looked new. The camera panned left, and Myung-Dae entered the frame.

Gotta be the farm, right?

"Your meddling made this necessary," Myung-Dae said. "I found your little disks. If I see you off that base again, she will die, right along with you."

The video ended.

Stay calm. She's still alive, but would he kill her? If

305

he felt threatened enough, yeah, I think he would. And I know where that farm is, thank God for that. He's forced my hand and knows I'll go get her. How many men are really on that farm? Would Bak have an accurate count? Can't hurt to ask.

Porter quickly fired off a text to Bak, asking for a headcount and biographies if he had them. Then Porter texted Martz, attaching the video, telling the master sergeant he needed to see him, *now*, in the admin office. Then he left the rest of his meal on the bar and jogged back across the street.

****

Chona parked the car in the condo's driveway and got out. After unlocking the front door, she entered, removing her jacket and putting it in the closet. The place was eerily quiet, not that Arthur was prone to making much noise anyway. The television was off, same as the radio.

"Arthur?" *Maybe he's taking a nap.*

She entered the kitchen. There, sitting at the table, was her late husband. What remained of his head drooped down, the pistol on the floor in the pool of blood as his arms hung lifelessly at his sides. Gore splattered against the window, curtains, cabinets, sink, appliances, and ceiling. On the table, two blood-splattered envelopes, one addressed to her. After checking her clothes for blood, she went into the living room and read it.

How could you do this to me, Arthur? What seemed so terrible you had to do this?

Tears ran down her face, and her mind raced, unsure what to do. *Do I call the base? Who on the base? The hospital? The MPs?*

She found Arthur's cell phone in his blood-drenched shirt pocket. He never turned the phone off, and she scrolled down his contact list. Having met Oliver Martz and Captain Jeffrey Lambert at the unit Christmas party only last month, Chona found Martz the more personable and approachable of the two. She pressed down on Martz's phone number and placed the call.

****

"So Tang's holding your woman hostage on his farm, huh?" Martz asked, removing his hat and jacket as he walked into the admin office. "Should you have expected that?"

Porter nodded. "Yes. Mentally, I'm not firing on all cylinders right now."

"What do you want to do?"

"I think you know. I'm done playing games. And I'm not asking your permission."

Martz sat down and looked at the video Porter sent on his phone once more. "I think if he wanted to kill her, she'd be dead."

A text came back from Bak, and Porter looked over at Martz. "A text from the KNPA agent. I asked how many guys are on that farm and their bios. He says four, including two hired hands. Five if you count Tang."

Porter's gaze moved from Martz to DiSilva's credenza. DiSilva recently placed a new framed picture of himself with Chona on it. They stood in the snow, with DiSilva smiling while Chona looked in need of a stool softener.

"DiSilva and his wife live off base, yes?" Porter asked.

"Yes." Martz followed Porter's eyes, turning to

look at the credenza. "What's on your mind?"

"Tang's daughter would hold some value, I'd think."

Martz recoiled. "You want to hold DiSilva's wife hostage?"

"Straight-up trade works for me." Porter glanced at his watch. "Or is there some kind of etiquette I need to follow?"

"You're serious?"

"Tang just crossed the line. All I need is a car and a few things from the armory."

"You're talking about kidnapping an officer's wife. You'll spend the next thirty years in a federal prison."

Porter chuckled. "Compared to where I'm going, that's a bargain. I don't expect you to come along. Just pull some strings and get me a car from the motor pool while I look up DiSilva's address from his service record."

"But kidnapping? What if DiSilva's there?"

"One more bargaining chip."

Martz heard and felt the cell phone in his pocket buzz. His office phone in the security building forwarded all calls and messages. He looked at the caller ID.

"Speak of the devil. It's DiSilva," Martz muttered. He pressed the talk button. "Martz here."

"Oh, thank God. Oliver, it's Chona DiSilva, Arthur's wife."

"Yes, Mrs. DiSilva." Martz snapped his fingers, looking over and making eye contact with Porter. "What can I do for you?"

"I came home early from work, and...there's no easy way to say this. I found Arthur dead in our kitchen. He shot himself. There's blood everywhere; I don't know what to do!"

"First, calm down a bit. Are you absolutely sure he's dead?"

"Half his head is against a kitchen cabinet, and he's not breathing. Yes, I'm sure."

"I'll be there in a half-hour. Just take it easy. I'll help you sort it out, okay? But please do nothing rash, and for the time being, let's keep that information between us."

"I should tell my family," Chona said.

"Please don't do that *yet*, Mrs. DiSilva, they'll only be in the way, and I'm sure you don't wish to traumatize them. I'll call the base medical examiner, and after they're finished, *then* you can tell your family. I'm on my way now."

"Thank you, Oliver. Yes, I won't do anything until you get here."

She hung up.

"Did I hear that right? DiSilva's dead?" Porter asked.

"She found him in their kitchen. Shot himself."

"I won't ever get this lucky again. I'll hit the armory and then grab her."

Martz appeared stricken. "Jeez, Mike...the woman's husband just committed suicide. Where's the compassion?"

"Compassion? You're kidding, right? Wanna see that video of Jeong again? And that's not the first time he's done that. Think about what he did to Tomlinson and in all probability, Gil Trotter."

"I don't have the time to argue. But think about what you're going to do."

"I'm going to get Jeong. With or without you."

"I've spent twenty-seven years of my life in the army, three more to full retirement and a pension. You're asking me to give it all up to help rescue your girlfriend."

Porter took a deep breath. "I'm not asking you to give up anything."

"Do you have some kind of plan?"

Porter nodded.

"I won't take a life unless it's in self-defense."

"That's reasonable, Top. Nobody expects you to go full savage. I'll take Tang and his muscle out, we'll grab Jeong, and I'll figure out a way to get her the hell out of Anjeong-ri. I need you to keep DiSilva's wife out of my line of fire once it begins. It's bad enough I'll have to work around you and Jeong."

Martz rubbed his temples. "You make it sound easy."

"Trust me; it isn't. Especially without a spotter. Maybe five men, all armed. All in motion and scrambling for cover."

Martz held up a hand. "I'm already nervous. So just stop." The master sergeant picked up the phone to reserve a car from the motor pool while Porter went to his room to grab his hat and jacket.

Leaving Martz in the admin office, Porter took a bus across camp to the motor pool.

****

After a brief stop at the armory, Porter waited in the car while Martz entered the DiSilva condo. Porter stayed low and watched everything that came and went from the neighborhood. MPs were here, their car parked on the street. Soon an ambulance appeared with red lights on as the gurney went inside.

Neighbors began congregating on the street to see what all the fuss was about. Soon the gurney exited the residence, DiSilva's corpse hidden in a black body bag as they loaded it in the ambulance for the trip to the morgue. Next, a pair of MPs exited the condo, getting in their sedan and driving away.

Porter texted Martz, reminding him that Chona needed to dress for the weather.

Then the condo door opened, with Martz escorting her to the car. She dressed accordingly, and Porter was thankful for it. Martz held the back-seat passenger-side door open for her before sliding in alongside her.

A puzzled Chona looked at Porter. "Who are you?"

"Sergeant Porter. My condolences, Mrs. DiSilva. I'll be your driver. Everyone ready?"

Chona looked quizzically at Martz as Porter turned the car around in a vacant driveway.

Chapter Thirty-Two

Byung entered the farmhouse from the barn to warm his aching hands, the older farmhand's arthritis flaring in the cold and damp. Jeong sat upright on the sofa, handcuffed, as he approached the hissing fire. If her eyes were open, he couldn't tell. On the coffee table laid a tightly rolled bandana, parts still wet from spittle.

His hands now warm, Byung went into the kitchen. Sang sat at the table, watching videos on a tablet device. He didn't care for Sang, thinking him too cocky. Sure, Gunn and Kiwoo could be cocky too, but they'd earned it.

"Why is she here?" Byung asked Sang.

"Boss brought her."

"Did you do that to her?"

Sang's head dropped as he refocused on the video.

Byung smirked and shook his head. "You should be ashamed of yourself. Where is Myung-Dae?"

"In the dining room, I think. He got a phone call a few minutes ago that pissed him off. Hasn't said a word since."

Byung walked into the living room, passing Jeong on the sofa, and opened the door to the adjacent dining room. Sitting at the oversized table, Myung-Dae sat staring out of a window.

The elderly farmhand took the chair alongside his oldest friend. They had grown up together in Anjeong-ri.

"What's wrong, Myung-Dae? Sang tells me you got a phone call that angered you."

Myung-Dae's eyes stayed on the window. "Chona called. My son-in-law is dead."

"Arthur is dead? That was sudden; he was a relatively young man. Was it his heart?"

"His balls. The coward committed suicide. Shot himself in the head."

It took a moment as Byung let that sink in. True, he'd only met Arthur twice. But Myung-Dae spoke of the American in glowing terms.

"I'm sorry for your loss, Myung-Dae. I thought Arthur was helping with your deal at Mokpo?"

Slowly, Myung-Dae's head turned, making eye contact as he took a deep breath. "Not anymore."

"Will this impact your transaction?"

Myung-Dae nodded. "I was counting on Arthur tomorrow. First Gunn. Then Daewon. Now Arthur. A GI refused to take my offer to marry. And Mina, a popular prostitute, wasn't able to seduce a man I needed to control. I don't understand this run of bad luck."

"Tell me, was what you had your new hooligan do to Jeong necessary?"

Myung-Dae's eyes hardened. "And now you question me?"

Byung nodded. "I lost myself. Please forgive me." He quickly got to his feet and left the room.

Old friend or not, he knew better than to stay in this room with Myung-Dae. In his present frame of mind, the boss was a wounded bear. A dangerous one at that.

****

Dusk descended as Porter checked into the spacious two-bed Pyeongtaek hotel room. The room was on the first floor, just feet from the door to the back parking lot. He and Martz quickly escorted Chona into the room before removing the blindfold, gag, and zip-line handcuffs she wore.

"I'm only going to say this once, lady. You yell or scream, and I'll keep you cuffed and gagged until you go back to daddy. Got it?"

Chona nodded. After Porter took off the gag, she unwrapped the complimentary hotel cup and went to the sink, pouring tap water. She guzzled it down and had another before sitting down at the small table.

She glared at Martz, who sat on the edge of a bed. "Are you going to tell me what this is about? I still can't believe you lied to me, Oliver."

Porter took a seat at the table opposite her. "Forget about that. Who knows about your husband?"

"Why should I tell you?"

"I could keep you bound and gagged, for starters. You're not in a position of strength here, lady."

Chona looked down. "Just my father. I'm sure he told my mother."

"Show her the video," Martz said.

"What video?"

Porter brought out his cell phone and played the video clip of Jeong. "This will help explain why we're here. Your father sent me this. You recognize this place, Mrs. DiSilva?"

When the background came up, Porter froze the screen, letting Chona look.

"Yes. That's my father's farm."

Porter let the rest of the video play. Chona gasped

when she saw Jeong.

"Do you know her?" Porter queried.

"She works for my father."

Porter nodded. "Care to guess who supervised that beating?"

"Are you implying my father had something to do with that?"

"He had everything to do with that. And you know it."

Chona looked at Martz. "There's no proof of that. Oliver. What you're doing is illegal. If this goes no further and you take me home right now, I'll forget this happened."

Martz cleared his throat. "Do you know anything about the women your father and husband sent to the United States to be prostitutes there?"

Chona scoffed and shook her head. "What will you think of next? My father isn't a monster. I don't expect you to believe me, but I know nothing of any business Arthur or my father engaged in."

Porter's eyes met hers. "Sorry, lady. All of Anjeong-ri knows your father murders men and women he feels threatened by. The way he killed them will keep you up at night. So don't sit there and insult my intelligence."

"What are you going to do with me?"

"We'll get to that. Right now, you need to call your mother and tell her about Arthur if she hasn't already heard. Convince her you want to be alone tonight and you will visit her first thing tomorrow."

Chona scoffed. "And why would I do that?"

"If she goes to an empty condo, her first instinct will be to go to that farm. Then she becomes part of this, and we don't want that. And neither do you. So call her and insist she stay put until tomorrow. This is for your mom's safety. Another hostage would give me more bargaining power, and I'm sure you don't want that either."

Chona nodded and removed the cell phone from her parka pocket.

"Put her on speaker," Porter said.

He and Martz watched and listened as Chona called. Moon-Kym explained she knew about Arthur from Myung-Dae. Worried sick, Moon-Kym had already been to the condo and found it empty. Unsure what next to do, the older woman returned home and waited for this phone call.

Chona explained she went to a hotel, wanting to be alone for the night and out of the condo. Slowly and steadily, Chona persuaded her mother to stay home, telling Moon-Kym that she was okay, promising to visit tomorrow. After that, Porter brought his cell phone camera up, aiming it at Chona.

"Smile."

She looked at him, and he clicked a photo.

"What's the purpose of that?" she asked

"What's your father's cell phone number?"

"He doesn't have a cell phone."

"I don't believe that."

"It's the truth."

Porter shrugged. "Then let's call that farm. See if he's there."

"What are you going to do with me?"

"The woman in the video is very dear to me, Mrs. DiSilva. And I worry your father may kill her. So let's get Daddy on the phone before he does something regrettable."

Again Chona scoffed. "You're all talk, mister."

She called the farm from her cell phone and asked for Myung-Dae. Porter took the phone from her and again put the call on speakerphone.

"Hello?" It was Myung-Dae's voice. "Chona, are you there?"

Porter nodded for Chona to speak.

"Daddy? Oliver Martz and a man called Porter have me. But I don't know where."

Porter covered Chona's mouth. "Hello, Myung-Dae," Porter said in Korean. "Remember me?"

"You have my daughter?"

"I'm sure by now you know we're not in the condo. All I want is Jeong back, so I'm proposing a simple exchange. Your daughter for Jeong. I'm not interested in your heroin or cadavers from China. Then you're never to see or talk to Jeong or her family again."

"How dare you presume to give me terms," Myung-Dae said. "You're a dead man."

"I need to speak with Jeong. Put her on the phone."

"I will not," Myung-Dae said.

Porter took his hand away from Chona's mouth. He then calmly brought the pistol up from his ankle holster, putting the barrel to her forehead and pulling the striker back. His eyes found hers, and for the first time since meeting, Porter saw genuine fear in her eyes.

"Daddy, he has a gun pressed to my head."

"Don't be frightened, Chona. It's merely a bluff."

Porter's eyes bored into Chona's.

"I don't think he's bluffing."

"Put Jeong on the phone, Myung-Dae. I won't ask

again."

Porter listened to the muffled screams and movement away from the phone. He removed the pistol from Chona's forehead.

"Porter?" Jeong's voice was raspy, and he heard her breathing hard.

"I'm going to get you out of this. I promise."

Again, the muffled sounds of a struggle away from the phone.

"There. You've heard her voice. She is fine. My Chona is okay?"

"Tell him," Porter told Jeong.

"I'm okay, Daddy."

"We make the exchange," Porter said. "But I'm warning you, after tonight, if Jeong tells me you've threatened or hurt her or her family, I'll find your daughter *and* your wife. Then I'll find you."

"Idle threats. Very well. Eight o'clock tomorrow morning."

"Tomorrow morning? Why not now?" Porter looked out the window. Dusk had given way to darkness.

"Eight o'clock tomorrow *morning*, when I can see your face. That isn't negotiable. You'll wait up the driveway after the farmhouse comes into view. Stay there, and we will come to you. And if you've harmed my little girl, I will kill you and Jeong where you stand."

Porter heard the phone cut out, followed by a dial tone. He gave Chona's phone back to her.

"Why does my father want to wait until tomorrow morning?"

Porter glanced at Martz. He could think of only one

reason. Porter pushed the sickening imagery aside and looked at his wristwatch.

"Looks like you're going to keep us company for the next fifteen hours, Mrs. DiSilva. You can thank your father for that when you see him."

"You said something about China, heroin, and cadavers. That involves my father?"

"Ask him tomorrow morning. I need to go on base to pick up a few things and then think I'll make a Chinese takeout run. Anyone else hungry?"

"I didn't know you spoke Korean," Martz said.

"Yeah. I'm full of surprises, Top."

****

Porter returned ninety minutes later, a large paper bag in one hand and two plastic PX bags in the other. He made a separate trip to the car for the armory's green nylon bags after dinner.

The three ate in an uneasy silence. After dinner, Chona watched a Korean movie on television, while the men worked on the bag's contents.

After Chona's movie ended, she took one bed and Martz the other. Sitting at the small table, Porter would stand the first watch.

Then, in the words of the late Tom Petty, came the hardest part.

Chapter Thirty-Three

Porter woke to the smell of coffee. Chona had brewed some in the hotel coffee maker and sat at the room's small table with a Styrofoam cup. Martz sat at the desk with a cup, wearing earbuds and watching the news on his cell phone. Porter went into the bathroom and soon returned.

"Would you like coffee?" she asked Porter.

"Yes, thank you."

Chona got to her feet and prepared a cup with Porter's eyes on her. Granted, he'd never seen a young widow hours removed from her husband's death. He expected her to be morose and sullen. Angry even. Only Chona DiSilva displayed none of that. If anything, Porter thought she appeared…relieved.

Realizing Porter was awake, Martz took the earbuds out. "You still wanna leave at the time we talked about?"

Porter nodded as he eyed the green nylon bags. He would finish the coffee. Then came the time to prepare.

He put the helmets on the bed. Chona gazed at the black visors and the rest of the body armor. "What's that supposed to be?"

Porter took a sip of the coffee. "Body armor."

"Bulletproof?" she asked.

"That's what it's designed for."

"Does it work?"

Porter grinned. "I don't know. Would you like to try it on, so I can test it?"

Chona smirked. "You think wearing that is necessary?"

"You *really* don't know much about your father, do you?"

Porter and Martz checked their gear one last time. Satisfied, Martz looked at his watch and nodded. It was time.

Martz advised Chona to do whatever she needed to before they left. The sun would be up in fifteen minutes, and it was already getting light. The weather called for a cold and clear day, with excellent visibility.

"I'll run out and let the car warm," Martz said. He picked up his long nylon bag.

Chona returned from the bathroom, and Martz soon returned.

"Okay, Mrs. DiSilva, it's time," Porter said. He held both the handcuffs and bandana.

Chona's eyes hardened. "Are those necessary?"

Porter returned the glare. *Yup, the return of the bitch.* "I don't wanna hear it; we're talking about a very finite length of time, maybe fifteen minutes, tops. Hold your wrists out for me, please."

She did, however reluctantly, and he put the zip-tie handcuffs on.

"That's not too tight, right?"

"It's okay, I guess."

Porter held up the bandana. She looked at him and glared.

"Have I given you any reason to use that?" she asked.

"Not yet. Look, in ten minutes, you'll be with your

father, God willing." Porter gently applied the bandana. "Can you breathe okay?"

Chona nodded.

Porter looked at Martz. "Can we get her out of here without being seen?"

"It's pretty quiet; let me check first."

Martz stepped out of the room, leaving the door partially open. He returned seconds later.

"It's clear."

They rushed Chona through the hotel's back entrance and slid her into the back seat, the car idling only feet from the door. With Martz behind the wheel, Porter returned to the room, making sure they had everything and grabbing his nylon weapons bag. After checking out at the kiosk, he went to the car.

Martz popped the trunk using the cab's floor lever at his feet. Porter placed his bag in with Martz's and got into the front passenger seat.

It sure got tense in a hurry.

They drove to Anjeong-ri in silence.

****

Myung-Dae's driveway alarm sounded ten minutes to eight o'clock. He glanced at the kitchen clock and looked out of the window facing the driveway. Two minutes later, at the top of the knoll stood two figures. He walked into the living room, where a fire smoldered in the fireplace. There, in a comfy leather recliner, Sang sipped tea. Jeong lay on the sofa in the fetal position.

"It's time," Myung-Dae said. "They're here."

Sang looked up. "Already?"

"They're here early. Let's get her ready."

Sang glanced at Jeong before eyeing Myung-Dae. "I may have to carry her. I doubt she can make it on her own."

"Idiot. I think you broke her ankle."

"Don't blame me. You were standing right there."

"Shut up and get her ready to go outside," Myung-Dae ordered.

Sang got to his feet and went into the kitchen as Jeong stirred.

Myung-Dae leered down at her. "We're going to get you ready; it's time for you to go to Porter, dear. Can you stand?"

She struggled to sit upright and then attempted to push herself off the sofa. Only she could not stand on her own. Sang came out from the kitchen dressed in a parka, ski hat, and gloves.

"Help her to her feet," Myung-Dae said. "I need to get ready."

Sang held her arms as she groaned loudly, struggling to rise. Like a newborn calf trying to stand for the first time, her legs shook before she lost balance and landed back on the sofa.

They tried once again, only to get the same result.

Myung-Dae came out of the kitchen with his brown parka and gloves. "Well?"

"She can't do it alone. We'll need the ATV."

"Okay. Use the back entry and load her from it. Before you do, come out to the kitchen. I want you to look at them with the binoculars." Myung-Dae led Sang to the kitchen and handed over the binoculars. "Tell me what you see."

Sang brought the binoculars to his eyes and looked. "Your daughter and a guy wearing a ski helmet and cheap body armor he probably bought online."

"He's using my daughter as a human shield, the

spineless coward. Whatever else happens, after we make the exchange, I want you to kill him. Understand?" Myung-Dae handed Sang the pistol that once belonged to Alex Tomlinson not so long ago.

"You got it."

"Let's get her dressed," Myung-Dae said.

Together, they got Jeong ready for the outdoors.

Sang exited the farmhouse from out the back, needing to go to the maintenance shed for the ATV. He returned soon thereafter, carrying Jeong to the seat. He would get behind her to steer while Myung-Dae trekked up the driveway alone.

****

Porter saw the farmhouse door swing open and Myung-Dae emerge. The ATV with Tang's goon and Jeong were next. "Here they come, Top," he said over the helmet's microphone. "Oh my God, one of Myung-Dae's goons has to drive her."

"Copy that, Mike. Stay focused."

"Easier said than done, and you know it."

With a hand on her forearm, Chona repeatedly tried to break away and lose the bandana while Myung-Dae slowly ascended the driveway's pitch, alongside the slow-moving ATV.

Myung-Dae's group stopped abruptly, the parties fifteen feet apart. Sang helped Jeong get to her feet, where they stood next to Myung-Dae.

"Are you ready to make the exchange?" Myung-Dae stared at the helmet's visor behind Chona. "What's that taped to your sleeve? Some kind of camera? And take that ridiculous helmet off. I told you I want to see your face."

The camera Myung-Dae noticed fed directly into

Porter's cell phone.

Over the microphone in Martz's helmet, Porter spoke from a two-way radio. "Grab Chona and move a yard to your left, Top. It's time for Tang to say good night."

Martz grabbed the handcuffed Chona tightly, pulling her off to the left from the trio in front of them. A gunshot from high up the range farther down the valley rang out. A tenth of a second later, Myung-Dae looked quizzically down at the exit wound through his chest. Touching the bright red blood, he looked surprised before dropping to the frozen, brittle gravel. Chona screamed.

Sang dropped Jeong. She fell to the gravel with an audible thud, yelping in pain as she did. His eyes wide and wild, Sang slid his right hand in the parka's pocket, removing the pistol. Another shot rang out, and Sang's torso spasmed as the spent bullet exited his chest, landing harmlessly farther up the road. Sang fell face down into the gravel, the pistol bouncing off the driveway's frozen gravel.

Martz let go of Chona, who dropped to her knees beside her father, still screaming uncontrollably into the bandana. Martz pocketed the gun before snipping her handcuffs. Chona quickly untied the bandana and shouted obscenities, calling Martz and Porter cold-blooded murderers.

Martz lifted the visor and got into a crouch, looking at Jeong. "Are you okay?"

She nodded.

"How's Jeong doing, Top?" Porter asked. He collected the casings from the sniper rifle up on the ridge overlooking the farm; the GPS bringing him back here. It felt like only yesterday he was here with Jeong.

"She's okay, Mike."

"Copy that. I'll call for the ambulance and the KNPA. Give me a few minutes to make it down to you."

****

Porter was halfway to the farm when he heard the first of the sirens. He'd put the helmet in the weapons bag and now spoke with Martz from his cell phone.

"I sure hope one of those sirens is an ambulance," Porter said.

"It's a pair of ambulances and a pair of KNPA cars. EMT says they're taking your woman to Saint Mary's in Pyeongtaek. Do you know where that is?"

"Yeah, I do. I'll be there in ten minutes. When the cops start asking questions, ask for Inspector Bak and tell him I'll be there directly but nothing more."

"Copy that."

****

Porter and Martz sat in the farmhouse kitchen while Bak took the farmhand's and Chona's statements in the living room. Both soldiers had changed out of the body armor and wore the uniforms they had on when first going to the DiSilva condo.

Outside, other KNPA detectives photographed the victims, took measurements and gathered samples. Soon EMTs loaded the bodies of Myung-Dae and Sang into an ambulance.

Porter could hear Chona angrily accuse him of murdering her father in cold blood before alleging that he and Martz raped her all night in a Pyeongtaek hotel room.

When told she needed tests done at the hospital to

validate the rape charges, she withdrew the accusation.

Byung also identified Porter as Myung-Dae's killer, although he and a younger farmhand were in the barn the entire time. Whether or not they saw anything was inconclusive. And with Myung-Dae and Sang Doak dead, it mattered little.

Bak then took Porter and Martz into custody, slapping on handcuffs in the kitchen, reading them their rights, and leading them out to his car, where he lowered each man's head before putting them in the back seat of his sedan. Another KNPA agent placed both duffle bags in the trunk of Bak's car.

"Is that your car farther up the driveway?" Bak asked Porter in Korean.

"Yes."

Bak drove up the driveway. Reaching the clearly marked Camp Humphreys sedan, beyond the farmhouse's sight, the KNPA agent stopped the car and got out. He helped both Americans out of the back seat and removed the handcuffs before opening the trunk.

"So what happens now?" Porter inquired.

"Now you get in your car and return to Camp Humphreys. You won't get any awards, but you liberated Anjeong-ri."

"Chona DiSilva will come at you hard. She'll demand to press charges," Porter said. "That older farmhand too."

"They can want. Another of her father's victims turned up in a Yongin dumpster yesterday, run through with a sword. A man named Daewon Cheom."

"That won't dissuade his daughter."

Bak grinned. "My biggest obstacle is explaining how you two overwhelmed me on the way back to

Anjeong-ri. But it's a small price to pay for a problem that festered and boiled for far too long. Go back to Humphreys and stay there for a while—let the dust settle."

"How can you get around the ambulances?" Porter asked.

"What ambulances?" Bak looked around and grinned. "Now that Tang's gone, the commandant will do everything he can to distance himself from the man. Our Coast Guard will intercept the Chinese freighter you emailed me about, and that ends it. Do you have everything?"

"Yes. Thanks again. I owe you."

Bak nodded. "Good luck."

"If you ever get bored, that pigpen is crawling with DNA."

"Now that the farm is a crime scene, we can finally go through it."

Porter and Martz followed Bak back into Anjeong-ri. Once inside Camp Humphreys, Porter dropped Martz off at the senior enlisted barracks, with the understanding he'd return the car to the motor pool tomorrow. Porter's first stop was the armory, where he cleaned and stowed the weapons and body armor.

Porter's next stop was Saint Mary's. He asked to see Jeong, but the desk nurse turned him away. She was noncommittal when asked if he could see her tomorrow. Porter called Ferguson, telling him he was taking the night off. The spotter's protests fell on deaf ears.

If not for Jeong and the flight line Thursday morning, Porter would've wanted to celebrate. Instead, he battled depression, and felt miserably alone.

Porter returned to camp. And with Simpson gone, let himself fall into a fitful, uneasy sleep.

Chapter Thirty-Four

Porter woke at 0600 to the sound of Ralph snoring lightly. His thoughts turned to Jeong. Being unable to see her in Saint Mary's yesterday still stung.

After showering, Porter went to the mess hall. He couldn't remember the last time he was this hungry. Yet, his heart was heavy. Both Jeong and Panmunjom worked on him from different angles. And while playing clerk with the 501st Intel Battalion was priority none, he went into the office anyhow.

Seeing Martz sitting at DiSilva's desk, feet up, reading the paper comforted Porter in a strange way.

"I feel like I'm in a time warp," Porter said.

The paper came down. "What the hell are you doing here? You didn't need to come in."

"I slept for shit and didn't wanna hang around the room for too much."

Martz leaned in. "The orders for your replacement came in yesterday; he'll be here next Wednesday."

"I'm sure you'll manage. Does Lambert realize he's the interim commanding officer?"

Martz nodded. "Thank God it's only temporary."

"I feel guilty leaving you to clean up the shitstorm on the horizon."

Martz grinned a gap-toothed grin. "You didn't make the mess. This place will survive. Who knows, but maybe some good comes of it. Did you turn the car in yet?"

Porter shook his head. "Not yet. Saint Mary's wouldn't let me see Jeong yesterday, so I'll try again this morning. Occurred to me I never thanked you for the help. I couldn't have done it without you."

"I'm thankful nobody got hurt except Tang and his goon. That KNPA agent came up big when he had to, too."

Porter nodded and approached Martz. He extended his hand, and Martz shook it. "So what's next for you?"

"I don't know yet. After the change-of-command wraps up and whatever investigations have ended; I'll request a reassignment. It'll be my twilight tour. I'm thinking either Germany or Italy."

Porter handed Martz two sealed envelopes. One stamped with a mailing address, the other only a name.

"What are these?"

"If you haven't heard from me by eight o'clock tomorrow night, you'll make sure these go out?"

Martz nodded. "Good luck to you, Mike. And Godspeed."

****

Porter parked in the Saint Mary Hospital parking lot and walked into the pristine lobby he now knew only too well. He carried a dozen red roses, a card, and a box of chocolates.

The young woman at the help desk gave him Jeong's room number and didn't run him off. He went to the elevators but didn't feel like waiting. Bounding up the stairs three at a time, he entered room 421.

Jeong was alone. Her face was so swollen it was difficult to believe that underneath the mass of purple skin was a beautiful woman. Porter followed the IV from her hand, the pair of hoses running up the stand where two clear plastic bags hung in place. Oxygen ran from a tank to her nostrils. Standing by the side of the bed, Porter felt the weight of his anguish, invoking memories of 9-11.

"Who's there?" she asked. Her weak voice cracked.

"Porter."

She tried to grin but only winced. Porter moved in closer, bent down, and kissed her forehead while she groped for his hand. He put the roses, card, and candy on the tray beside the bed.

"Don't talk, just listen," Porter said. "I'm leaving Camp Humphreys early tomorrow morning. I'm sorry I couldn't tell you sooner. Myung-Dae took you before I had the chance. I hoped for more time together."

"Will…you…be…back?"

"Yes."

Jeong squeezed his hand for several seconds. "You don't think so," she whispered.

A nurse came in. "Sir, she's due to go to radiology. Today's not a good day for a visit."

Porter nodded. He kissed Jeong once more on the forehead before turning toward the nurse. "Put those in water for her, yes?" Then he turned back to Jeong. "I *will* be back. You'll see."

The nurse wheeled in the tools of her trade, and Porter left the room.

In the stairwell, he sat and let the tears fall before collecting himself. He would return the motor pool car and try to get some sleep.

But doubted he'd be able to.

****

Whan Kym held on tight as the plane taxied down the Manila Airport runway. While darkness had descended, this proved to be the first flight out of Seoul bound for Manila today.

Sweat poured from the large Korean man as he waited in line to pass through customs, an overnight bag in one hand and a garment bag slung over his shoulder. He'd never been here before; going from below-zero temperatures to jungle heat would take getting used to. And Whan imagined the converse would be just as problematic.

His feelings about being sent hadn't changed. A few days off after this wrapped was nothing more than window dressing on Jaewon's part.

Passing through customs, Whan spotted the ground transportation exit and walked outside; a whoosh of hot and sticky air slamming against him. Soon he was wiping down his temples and neck with the handkerchief he had the foresight to carry. He watched as a trio of porters rushed toward him.

"I only need one of you," Whan said in English, displaying an index finger. He pointed at the chunky man to his right. "You."

The porter grinned as the others looked for another passenger to descend upon. After flagging a cab, the man threw Whan's bags in the trunk when the taxi pulled to the curb. Whan tipped the porter, and the driver pulled out into traffic.

"Where to?" the driver inquired.

"Imperial of Makati."

At the hotel, Whan checked in and texted the phone number Jaewon gave him, telling the arms contractor he'd be in the lobby. Thirty minutes later, a slender, suave-looking Filipino in a suit and tie walked in, his head on a swivel.

Whan approached. "Are you with Jaewon Dokgo?"

The Filipino nodded and led Whan to a light-colored luxury car parked under one of the hotel's back parking lot lights.

"Get in," the Filipino said. They didn't travel far. Just down the street, the car pulled into a busy fast-food parking lot. The Filipino reached into the back seat behind Whan, bringing out a stiff cardboard shoebox.

Whan opened it. Inside was a compact H&K.45 pistol and two full magazines carrying ten rounds each, along with a silencer and leather gloves.

"Such an expensive weapon for a single use," Whan said.

"It's what Mr. Dokgo ordered and paid for. It will definitely do the job. I was told to remind you to wipe down and discard everything in separate locations upon completion."

Whan nodded. "What's the best casino in Manila and number for the best call girls?"

The Filipino grinned. He had that information, too.

****

The cab from the Imperial dropped Whan off under the carport at the Rizal Hotel. He was happy that the lobby was empty. Walking up to the pretty Filipina at the front desk, Whan wore sunglasses, a loud oversized Hawaiian shirt and baggy shorts. While he felt stupid wearing sunglasses at night, he knew it was necessary. He counted three security cameras.

"Excuse me, miss. A friend of mine is staying here, Gunn Lim. Could you tell me what room he's in?"

The Filipina looked up at Whan's sunglasses and

stifled a giggle. "I'm sorry, sir, but I'm not permitted to disclose that information."

Whan thought about bribing her. Only that would bring unwanted attention. "I understand. Is it okay if I wait in the lobby for him?"

The Filipina's expression changed from amused to concerned. "Who knows when he'll be through here? You might wait a long time."

"I'll sit right over there." Whan pointed to a sofa partially hidden behind artificial ferns. While he saw no camera pointed in that direction, that didn't mean there wasn't one. Or more.

The pretty girl nodded. "I guess that would be okay."

Whan thanked her and moved to the sofa. He tried finding something interesting to watch from his cell phone, but the sunglasses taxed his eyes. Whan knew the young woman was right—the Lims might very well be in their room now, not coming through this lobby until sometime tomorrow morning.

He could do nothing but wait.

****

Two hours later, Whan heard a woman speaking Korean enter the empty lobby. He put his phone down and slowly turned his head. Gunn and Daeum Lim walked from the front doors to the pair of elevators fifteen feet away from the front desk.

"I'm sick of looking at houses, Gunn," Daeum said. "I only want to go up to the pool and drink piña coladas until I get sleepy."

The elevator to the right opened, and the couple got on, the door closing.

The desk clerk wasn't standing behind the counter,

and Whan casually strolled to the elevators. Down the corridor, he observed a chambermaid examining a form, her cart full of mops and assorted cleaning equipment and spray bottles. He approached.

"Pardon me, ma'am, but where is the pool?"

The chambermaid looked up, puzzled. "Rooftop on the sixth floor, sir. Just follow the signs."

Whan thanked her and returned to the elevator, pressing the button to go up.

As the chambermaid said, on the sixth floor, there were signs leading to the rooftop pool. Whan walked up a long ascending concrete ramp and could smell the chlorine halfway up. The area surrounding the pool was pleasantly lit, with multicolor Christmas tree lights draping a tall, chain-link fence. Tiki torches from poolside stands gave it a Polynesian ambiance. There were no small children at this time of night. One young couple looked cozy at the far end of the pool, and another couple laughed and drank highballs in the adjacent hot tub.

Whan's eyes darted in all directions under the sunglasses. There was no sign of the Lims.

I hope they didn't change their minds.

To blend in, Whan went to the bar and ordered a whiskey sour.

"Sunglasses at night?" the young bartender chuckled as he mixed the drink.

"Retina surgery."

The bartender nodded, and money changed hands.

Drink in hand, Whan occupied a poolside chair with a clear line of sight to the top of the ramp. He took a long pull from the cocktail and tried to relax. *What would've happened if I'd kept my mouth shut about*

Gunn's location? I doubt it would matter much. Jaewon isn't one to quit the moment he hits a roadblock. I only wish they'd chosen someone else to do this.

Twice it was necessary to wipe down the perspiration as he polished off the drink, ice cubes and all. He thought to get another when he heard Daeum coming up the ramp with Gunn, complaining about the heat. Then he saw them at the top of the ramp. She looked as miserable as she sounded. And poor Gunn appeared exasperated. *Right about now, I'm doing him a favor.*

The Lims wore swimwear with towels over their shoulders as they made their way to the far end of the pool near the hot tub. There, they claimed two cushy deck chairs and sat as the only server hustled to take their order.

Whan casually went back to the bar. "I'll take another whiskey sour and need a favor. Could you call a cab for me?"

"Do you have a destination?"

"Cityscape Five."

"No problem."

Again, Whan paid cash for the drink and tipped the man generously before returning to the chair. After sitting down, he took a sip of the drink, putting it down on a nearby table. Whan then casually walked to pick up a slightly used, unoccupied towel three chairs over. He put on the leather gloves from his pocket and removed the pistol and silencer, separately tucked in his cargo shorts pocket. Under the towel, he screwed the silencer on.

Whan rose and started walking toward the couple, holding the pistol and silencer under the towel. All he could hope for now was that the Lims stayed put, and that Gunn didn't recognize him. To kill Gunn and have to chase Daeum in this hot, unfamiliar place would be disastrous.

Moving closer, Whan brought the camouflaged gun up as Gunn lit a cigar. By the time Gunn figured out that it was Whan Kym behind the sunglasses, three bullets hissed in the thick Manila night air. Gunn slumped forward, each round hitting his chest dead center.

Daeum, still complaining as she lay on her stomach facing the opposite direction, didn't know what was about to happen. She never saw a thing as Whan took her life with a trio of bullets artfully placed in the center of her back. Walking away, he heard no screams. Nobody poolside realized what had happened until he was at the bottom of the ramp.

Towel still in hand, Whan wiped down the gun, mags, and silencer while walking toward the stairwell. He threw the gun in a hallway trash receptacle. The towel and gloves found a receptacle close to the stairs, which Whan used to descend to the lobby.

By the time he reached the lobby, the first of the sirens hummed from several blocks away. The cab waited under the carport, and Whan slipped into the back seat.

"You're going to the Cityscape Five?" the driver asked.

"Yes."

At the Cityscape Five, Whan took another cab back to the Imperial. Returning to the room, he ditched the sunglasses. After showering and changing into fresh clothes, he was ready to hit the casino.

Chapter Thirty-Five

Porter's alarm clock went off at 0250. Knowing Simpson worked a mid-shift, Porter turned on the light and unlocked his wardrobe.

His thoughts turned to Jeong. Nothing unusual about that. But soon enough, Panmunjom and the reality of today's business pushed her aside. Sadly, there was nothing unusual about that either.

Porter fought a bout of light-headedness and nausea as he showered. He wondered if death row inmates felt like this before their execution.

Porter was glad it was too early for the houseboys. Watching them scurry about sometimes upped his anxiety, and today that was the last thing he needed. The worst part about this time of day was the mess hall—it wouldn't open for another two hours. Not because Porter was hungry. He doubted he could eat a bite. But he craved caffeine. So he went to the upstairs vending machines for a can of cola and returned to the room.

Earlier, Stillson sent a text message wishing him luck. While Porter appreciated the sentiment, that message coupled with Jeong's comment about not coming back did little for his confidence. Without news to the contrary, Eom was still the agency's man. Porter only hoped that he and Ferguson could find him in Panmunjom before he pulled the trigger.

Porter put his toiletries back in the locker and sat on his bunk, sipping the soda. *If Eom succeeds, would anything change?* Porter supposed he had to believe it would and change for the worse. Otherwise, what would be the point? He finished the soda and, after securing the nine-millimeter pistol, closed the wardrobe door. Porter left the barracks wondering if he'd ever see it again. Porter turned his cell phone off.

Acid churned in his stomach, and Porter bent and vomited on the sidewalk on the way to the empty bus stop and the 0330 bus across camp.

Now he was ready.

****

Ferguson was already in the armory locker room when Porter arrived. Porter checked the room, making sure they were alone before sitting down. The spotter put the last of his body armor on.

"Where the hell have you been?" Ferguson asked. "We haven't done squat in days."

"I know. Unavoidable."

Ferguson began his weapons check as Porter opened his locker. He'd never seen Ferguson so wound.

"You seen the weather, Fergie?"

"High in the mid-thirties and clear with a ten-mile visibility, couldn't ask for better. Too bad the ground is like brick." Ferguson slid the M-4 next to the shotgun and boxes of ammo in the nylon bag before re-zipping it. "I'm ready."

Porter put the body armor on quickly. He had the benefit of a little more practice. He then checked the time: 0347 hours. Because he'd inspected his weapons and ammo after returning from Tang's farm, he only needed to spot check. Porter zipped his weapons bag a minute later. "Let's roll."

Bags in hand, the pair stood and started for the armory doors. In the vestibule cage, Porter glanced at the clerk before stepping out the door.

It felt colder now than it had twenty minutes earlier. They loaded the nylon bags into the back of the four-wheel-drive vehicle Ferguson reserved and were soon northbound to the flight line.

****

Just outside the Camp Humphreys Flight Operations building, the AH-64 Apache helicopter sat idle on the well-lit tarmac, rotors down, thirty yards from the building's front doors. There, Porter noticed three men huddled up under the front door lights as Ferguson parked alongside the cinder block building. He and Ferguson grabbed their gear from the back of the SUV and walked toward them.

All three men wore drab olive green flight suits. The tallest of the three eyed Porter.

"Ground ops?" the tall man asked. "I need the call sign."

Porter nodded. "Call sign Oscar, Sierra, Romeo, Delta 628. I'm Porter, and this is Ferguson."

"Ellsworth," the tall man said. "This is my co-pilot, Pendleton, and our gunner, Coolidge."

"We still green?" Porter asked.

"I'm going in now to confirm, so you guys chill. I'll be back in five."

Ellsworth walked into the building while the four men stood in a semi-circle. Porter realized the others were as pent up and tense as he and Ferguson were.

Porter eyed Pendleton, the co-pilot. "You guys do a pre-flight check already?"

Pendleton nodded. "Fifteen minutes ago."

"Is there an exfil plan? I keep asking my SAIC but haven't gotten a firm answer."

"The only one authorized to disclose specifics is Ellsworth. He'll brief you pre-board," Pendleton said. "I can tell you there *is* a plan."

The two minutes of silence that followed were the most awkward Porter had ever known. Finally, the door swung open, and Ellsworth appeared. Porter couldn't get a read on the pilot's face as he approached.

"We're standing down," Ellsworth said. "Officially scrubbed."

A wave of relief swept over Porter. He could scarcely believe it. His thoughts then turned to Jeong.

"Did they say why?" Coolidge asked.

"Need to know. Run that question by your home office SAIC, who I'm told will be in touch with each of you before noon today, our time, so check your comms."

Porter reached for his bag as he turned. "Well, Fergie, we might as well—"

In Ferguson's right hand, a .45 pistol with silencer attached. "Ellsworth, you're over here with me and stay there. Mike, put all the weapons in one bag. Starting with that nine-millimeter on your ankle, nice and slow."

Ellsworth moved to within a yard of Ferguson. Slowly, and with his eyes on Ferguson, Porter removed the pistol in his ankle holster and, after unzipping Ferguson's weapons bag, put it in. He then put the contents of his bag into Ferguson's.

"Put the bags in the cockpit," Ferguson instructed.

Porter lifted and carried the bag to the Apache while the others watched. He placed the bags on the floor behind the pilot's seat.

"Back there with the others, Mike. Move it."

Porter joined the co-pilot and gunner.

"You three are going to that hangar up ahead," Ferguson said. "Keep those hands where I can see them." He turned back to Ellsworth. "You, stay close."

He's gonna clip us in the hangar. None of us will make it to a phone to call Osan if we're all dead, Porter reasoned.

"I don't know where you think you're going," Pendleton said, walking. "Osan will scramble F-22s the second they get the call. They'll be on you inside of five minutes."

"You think I don't know that?"

The first hangar was bomber capable, almost twice the size of a conventional hangar. It took the group a full minute to reach the left corner of the entrance.

"You three get in there," Ferguson said, gesturing with the pistol as he kept Ellsworth close. "You almost had me a couple of weeks back at The Blue Turtle bar, Mike."

Porter remembered that snowy Saturday morning like it was yesterday. "That was you?"

Without another word, Ferguson aimed the pistol at Coolidge and pulled the trigger. The bullet entered the gunner's forehead, killing him instantly. Porter watched Ferguson's eyes move in slow motion as he brought the .45's barrel around to aim at him.

All this time, I thought I'd buy it running for my life in North Korea or on Tang's farm. Porter clenched his teeth, and his body tensed as he braced for impact. He closed his eyes and heard a gunshot. There was no pain, only the murmurs of background noise. Porter's eyes opened.

Up ahead, Ferguson lay down on the tarmac. Pendleton looked around as if in a trance. Ellsworth stood over Ferguson's body, one hand over his eyes to cut the glare of the tarmac's floodlights as he faced north, coming from one of the other hangars on the tarmac.

Porter sprinted toward Ferguson's body, unsure if he was dead or merely wounded. But getting closer, he saw Ferguson wasn't getting up—the spotter's eyes open in a pool of blood.

As Porter bent to check for a pulse, he heard boots on the tarmac's asphalt and understood now why Ellsworth looked in that direction. A man's silhouette emerged from the glare of the flatline lights, and soon Porter made out the facial features. *McFarland?* The armory sentry had an M-4 rifle slung over his shoulder.

"Who did that asshole hit?" McFarland asked the group.

"The gunner, Coolidge," Porter said.

"Will one of you confirm that he's expired?"

Pendleton jogged over and checked Coolidge for a pulse. "He's gone."

McFarland took a breath. "I'm an agency pull out of San Diego. You can confirm it with your home office SAIC when you're debriefed. Here's what happens now. I'll call this in to the MPs while you guys disperse. Until you're debriefed, you're not authorized to discuss this with anyone *except* your SAICs. So grab your gear and bug out before this place is crawling with MPs and EMTs."

Porter sprinted for the SUV, thankful Ferguson left the keys in the ignition. He drove it to the Apache and grabbed the weapons bags. He was about to ask if any of the others needed a ride, but he was alone. Porter punched the gas for the armory, due south.

On his way there, sirens screamed as a pair of cars with blue lights raced by in the opposite direction. Two ambulances and a fire engine followed. Within a minute, the flight ops building and the hangar beyond it was lit up in a sea of red and blue light.

Porter checked his text messages before entering the armory. He saw Stillson's text, time-stamped at 0357. After reading it, he put the nine-millimeter back in the ankle holster before rearranging the weapons bags. He brought them inside after being buzzed in.

"How you doing this morning, Sarge?" the young, pimply-faced PFC asked from inside the cage. "What the hell's going on out there? Did somebody rob the bank?"

"I need someone to inventory these bags." Porter patted the bag on the left. "This bag belongs to a guy named Brock Ferguson. A nine-millimeter, ankle holster, and full mag are missing from mine."

"Why isn't Ferguson here to give me this?"

"You'll have to ask Corporal McFarland."

The private sighed. "Aw, shit. I'll be straight-up; you're gonna be here all day filling out paperwork."

Porter shrugged. "Then I guess I'm here all day filling out paperwork."

The PFC shook his head. "Bring the bags to your locker and sit tight. Someone will be out to take a count and check 'em back in."

It didn't take all day. But it wasn't until mid-morning until Porter was free to go. Maybe Porter didn't need the pistol. After all, Myung-Dae and his men were no longer a threat. But then again, why take the chance?

The MP station house was eerily quiet as Porter entered.

"I need a secure line," he told the MP Officer-of-the-Day. He displayed his agency ID.

"We were wondering what happened to you," a short, beefy first lieutenant said. "We haven't seen you since you checked in."

Porter cocked his head. "I've had a rough couple of days. You gonna fix me up with a phone or not, Lieutenant?"

"Yeah, sure." The OOD escorted Porter to an office, and Porter called Los Angeles.

"Stillson, here."

"It's Porter, sir."

"I was starting to worry. I know about Ferguson and heard what happened."

"And McFarland?"

"Is the reason I know. He's out of San Diego, GS-8. I sent a comm at 0357, but you were in transit or already on the flight line and didn't see it. How are you holding up?"

"I read the comm before returning our weapons at the armory. I'm okay. Can you tell me what happened?"

Stillson told the story. The Honolulu office intercepted a comm from an Anjeong-ri cafe to the leader of a Chinese cell out of Wuhan at 0331 this morning. It referenced the assassin flying north and setting down a hundred klicks from the DMZ.

"They must've arranged ground transportation at a prearranged site for Ferguson to take a tunnel across the

DMZ," Stillson continued. "After decoding and translating their comm, we put McFarland in motion."

"So Ellsworth knew when he came out of the flight ops building?"

"Ellsworth didn't know who the assassin was until Ferguson made his move. All Ellsworth knew was that McFarland was approaching from the north. I heard Ferguson killed the gunner."

Porter shifted in his chair. "I should've guessed it myself. I thought it was weird Ferguson never asked about the exfil."

"You're on a flight out of Seoul Saturday morning. Take a couple of days and be in my office on Wednesday at 0900. I'll email the itinerary."

"I'd like to request two weeks of downtime. Call it a vacation, personal time, or you can dock me if you like."

"You've earned some time. But you're not to discuss any aspect of this until we meet and you're debriefed. Is your cover still good?"

"Yes."

"I want you off Humphreys ASAP. There's a guest hotel on Osan Air Base, Turumi Lodge. I'll have my assistant reserve a room for a couple of weeks."

"That's okay, Walter; there's a hotel I'll stay at in Pyeongtaek."

"Okay. After we meet, you'll go to Kadena to interview for that deputy job we discussed."

"I'll be ready for it."

"We'll send a new itinerary and see you here in two weeks. Go to Pyeongtaek, rest up. But stay the hell out of Anjeong-ri."

"Yes, sir."

****

Porter took the bus across Camp Humphreys and walked into these barracks for the last time. He heard Simpson stir as he entered.

The CIA agent unlocked his wardrobe. It took all of thirty seconds for Simpson to rise and find his way to the desk.

"What's going on, Mike?"

"Sorry to wake you, but I'm outta here. Time to say goodbye."

"Goodbye? What are you talking about? You just got here."

"I have to go back to the States. Family matter."

"Are you coming back?"

Porter shook his head. Simpson approached, a baffled look on his face as he extended his hand. Porter shook it.

"Take care of yourself, Mike."

"You too, Ralph. Ace that sergeant's exam. And one last thing. Tell Martz to shitcan the letters I gave him."

"Huh?"

"He'll understand."

Simpson nodded and disappeared behind the wardrobe on the way back to his bed. Soon he would snore lightly again. Porter finished packing before calling a cab.

****

It was oddly coincidental that the taxi followed a KNPA cruiser as it left Anjeong-ri, blue and red lights on, siren screaming. It took the dirt road leading to the Tang farm. Porter didn't want to guess. He felt not a shred of regret or remorse pulling the trigger that ended

Myung-Dae's life. No more than he did in Iraq. The way he saw it, they were both threats. Tang got off easy.

Soon the cab pulled into Saint Mary's Hospital. He asked to speak to Jeong Guy's doctor and, twenty minutes later, took the elevator to the fourth floor. He entered room 421.

Jeong was alone in the small and dreary hospital room. He noticed only one IV bag hanging on the stand today. The swelling in her face had gone down some, but her eye sockets appeared soot black. Yet she looked better than she had only yesterday.

He kissed her forehead and watched her eyes pry open ever so slightly. Jeong grabbed Porter's arm and began to cry. Porter stayed in that position until she released her grip, holding back tears of his own.

"See? I told you I'd be back," he whispered, sitting down.

"I didn't expect to see you again. So where do you go next?"

"I'm staying at a hotel down the street until you're out of here. After that, what would you say about spending a few days with me in Seoul? Your doctor told me you should be up and around in a couple of days, after the swelling goes down. Start a new chapter."

"You mean it?"

"Yes."

"I can finally work where I want and know my family is safe, maybe in Seoul. Thank you."

"Do you have a passport?"

"Yes, Porter. Why?"

"I want you in my life, Jeong." He took her hand.

"I have to go to Los Angeles for a few days and would like it if you came with me. After that, I'm going to Okinawa. Air Force flies from Kadena to Osan and back all the time. I'd like for us to continue."

"Yes. I want that too."

He'd tell her his real name when the time was right. Porter held her hand and stayed by her side until the hospital nurses asked him to leave. He would be back first thing tomorrow morning.

And the day after that.

A word about the author...

OPERATION STORMWATCHER represents my second finished manuscript. I am a member of the Burlington Writers Workshop as well as groups on Facebook. I'm a professional business consultant, entrepreneur, and U.S. Armed Forces veteran.

Thank you for purchasing
this publication of The Wild Rose Press, Inc.

For questions or more information
contact us at
info@thewildrosepress.com.

The Wild Rose Press, Inc.
www.thewildrosepress.com

www.ingramcontent.com/pod-product-compliance
Lightning Source LLC
Chambersburg PA
CBHW051132030726
47504CB00004B/822